BELIEVING THE I

FAVORED

TERI LYN TOBEY

Favored

Trilogy Christian Publishers

A Wholly Owned Subsidiary of Trinity Broadcasting Network

2442 Michelle Drive

Tustin, CA 92780

Copyright © 2024 by Teri Lyn Tobey

Scripture quotations marked NASB are taken from the New American Standard Bible® (NASB), Copyright © 1960, 1962, 1963, 1968, 1971, 1972, 1973, 1975, 1977, 1995 by The Lockman Foundation. Used by permission. www.Lockman.org. Scripture quotations marked NIV are taken from the Holy Bible, New International Version®, NIV®. Copyright © 1973, 1978, 1984, 2011 by Biblica, Inc.TM Used by permission of Zondervan. All rights reserved worldwide. www.zondervan.com. The "NIV" and "New International Version" are trademarks registered in the United States Patent and Trademark Office by Biblica, Inc.TM

All rights reserved, including the right to reproduce this book or portions thereof in any form whatsoever.

For information, address Trilogy Christian Publishing

Rights Department, 2442 Michelle Drive, Tustin, Ca 92780.

Trilogy Christian Publishing/ TBN and colophon are trademarks of Trinity Broadcasting Network.

For information about special discounts for bulk purchases, please contact Trilogy Christian Publishing.

Trilogy Disclaimer: The views and content expressed in this book are those of the author and may not necessarily reflect the views and doctrine of Trilogy Christian Publishing or the Trinity Broadcasting Network.

10 9 8 7 6 5 4 3 2 1

Library of Congress Cataloging-in-Publication Data is available.

ISBN 979-8-89333-815-7

ISBN 979-8-89333-816-4 (ebook)

Disclaimer

The voice of God is inspired by Scripture.

This novel is a work of fiction. Though some characters reflect actual historical figures, their situations and dialogue in this novel are fictitious and the work of the author's imagination. Any resemblance to persons living or deceased is entirely coincidental and beyond the intent of the author or publisher.

Dedication

To all who long to be favored by God.
Dear brothers and sisters, may you know you already are!

Acknowledgments

I would be remiss if I did not acknowledge the love and encouragement of my family. David, Victoria, and Andrew: God has truly blessed me through you.

To my personal assistant, writing confidante, sounding board, typist, editor, and critic, Sam Davis. May you be blessed as you continue to bless me.

Table of Contents

Foreword 13

Preface.. 15

Prologue 17

Chapter One 21

Chapter Two 29

Chapter Three.. 37

Chapter Four 47

Chapter Five.. 57

Chapter Six.. 63

Chapter Seven 75

Chapter Eight 85

Chapter Nine 95

Chapter Ten 107

Chapter Eleven... 113

Chapter Twelve 123

Chapter Thirteen 133

Chapter Fourteen.. 141

Chapter Fifteen 149

Chapter Sixteen 157

Chapter Seventeen 165

Chapter Eighteen.. 175

Chapter Nineteen 181

Chapter Twenty 189

Chapter Twenty-One 195

FAVORED

Chapter Twenty-Two 205

Chapter Twenty-Three 213

Chapter Twenty-Four 227

Chapter Twenty-Five 233

Chapter Twenty-Six 243

Chapter Twenty-Seven 255

Chapter Twenty-Eight 261

Chapter Twenty-Nine 269

Chapter Thirty 281

Chapter Thirty-One 299

Chapter Thirty-Two 319

Chapter Thirty-Three 343

Chapter Thirty-Four 363

Chapter Thirty-Five 375

Chapter Thirty-Six 391

Chapter Thirty-Seven 417

Chapter Thirty-Eight 427

Chapter Thirty-Nine 435

Chapter Forty 445

Chapter Forty-One 459

Epilogue 471

Glossary of Terms 479

Discussion Guide 483

About the Author 493

Coming in 2025: Fragile 495

Foreword

I am honored to write the foreword for Teri Tobey's work of historical fiction, *Favored*. It is a work that awakens our imaginations and brings the past into our present with vividness and impact.

To paint, think, and write about Mary, the mother of Jesus, is nothing new. Artists across time have attempted to "explain" her to us through word and image. According to Timothy Verdin in his book *Mary in Western Art*, the earliest depictions of Mary date to early Christian art of the second to third centuries found in the Catacombs of Rome. Many Orthodox traditions, still strong around the world today, have created and honored the iconography of images of Mary since the eighth century. In the Western tradition, depictions of the Madonna were greatly diversified by Renaissance masters such as Leonardo da Vinci, Michelangelo, Raphael, Bellini, and Caravaggio. We have always been curious about this young woman who bore the Christ child. Who was she? Why was she chosen? How did she do it?

This Jewish woman from Nazareth, who lived in ancient times, teaches us something about how we might live our lives today. She had courage. She took risks. She made mistakes. But God, in His infinite mercy, uses her to bring forth the gospel—to bring forth the Savior of the world.

Like Mary and the fictional counterparts in the narrative so creatively spun by Teri, we live in what can feel like desperate times. Many seek answers to the complex questions of our humanity. The lessons we can learn from this woman are applicable for us today. This work of historical fiction enlarges our hearts and reminds us of the hope, faith, and love required of those who surrender their full lives to Jesus. It is through the world of imagination which takes us beyond the restriction of provable fact, that we touch the hem of truth.

FAVORED

While there is much of the story of Mary that has been imagined here, we do well to remember that she was a woman who really lived. Teri has based this narrative on the biblical account. The outline of the story is provided in Scripture, and this foundation is where Teri began. Building on that, she has created action, dialogue, internal motivation, and additional characters that are consistent with the biblical and historical record. It is obvious that Teri's desire is to invite us all into Mary's journey so that we, too, might see the Christ child in the manger and recognize the Savior of the world at the foot of the cross.

Stories invite us into the imagined circumstances of another. In his book *The Christian Imagination*, Leland Ryken says:

> *Literature enlarges our world of experience to include both more of the physical world and things not yet imagined, giving the actual world a new dimension of depth. This makes it possible for literature to strip Christian doctrines of their stained-glass associations and make them appear in their real potency.*

Favored does that for us. It strips away the "stained-glass" view of the Madonna and child and brings Mary into our hearts. We see her in all her humanity, and our hearts get bigger so that there might be more room for the love and grace of her son to occupy.

—Tracy Manning

Artistic Director and Professor
of Theatre at Taylor University

KCACTF Indiana State Chair

Executive Director of Hoosier Festival Shakespeare

Preface

I was a psychology major at Taylor University. I had written a paper for one of my psychology classes. The professor came to me to discuss my paper and said, "Teri, it's clear you have an innate grasp of human nature. However, I believe you should be a writing major and not a psychology major." I laughed and thanked him, then scoffed at the idea. Now I'm sure he's the one laughing.

After doing theater for thirty years, I retired. Like most of us who have been working in a certain field for as long as I had, you wonder what the next phase in life will hold. While doing Beth Moore's study "Believing God," I felt the Lord leading me to write a novel. I had written monologues, short stories, and narratives, but not a book. I halfway surrendered to what God was laying on my heart.

I said, "Okay, Lord, I'll give You one day. If nothing happens, if nothing comes to mind to write, I'm done." Talk about throwing out a fleece. I can still see God laughing. I do believe He takes joy in His creation.

I'll never forget that day. Laundry got done, dinner was on the table by the time all my family was home, and three chapters had been written. I read them to my husband after putting the littles to bed. He said, "That's good. It's really good." Thus, *Favored* was born.

I felt very inadequate as a writer, but God continued to encourage and push me forward. He constantly reminded me that He doesn't call the equipped; He equips the called. I can't remember when I first heard that, but I just love it. Don't you?

When my daddy died in 2012, I stopped everything—including writing. I put myself in the grave with my daddy. I stayed there for years.

I've mourned the years lost in grief. God raised me back from the dead. He healed the broken and hurt places in me. I eventually was able to pick the book back up.

When I began talks with Trilogy Publishing, Mark told me that TBN started Trilogy just eight years ago. Even though I felt dead, God continued to work on my behalf to bring about His blessing to me, and I pray, in reading this novel, you will be blessed as well. No time is wasted when it comes to God.

I like to think of people in the Bible as being just like us. It is even said of Jesus that He was tempted in all ways as we are. As God began to direct me as to what to write, I landed on Mary and Joseph.

Specifically, why was Mary favored by God above all others? What made her so special? How does God favor me and you? How is that different from the way the world sees being favored?

I pray favor blesses you, beloved. I pray it encourages your faith in a mighty, working God who has not forgotten you. I pray you enjoy it. I pray you know that His still, small voice is still speaking to us today.

Thank you from the bottom of my heart for spending time with me reading *Favored.* I thank my heavenly Father for this indescribable gift.

All to His glory.

Teri Lyn Tobey

Prologue

The sliver of light that broke through the seams around the window looked like a strand a spider might weave. Had it been hours, and if so, how many? Or had it been days? God forbid—not days. Anna shook her head as another stab of pain rushed through her body, starting in her lower back and working its way to her stomach, causing her swollen belly to become hard.

"Breathe."

Who said that? Who is with me? Where is Joachim? He had promised that when her time came, he would stay close.

The pain began to diminish. The familiar hand wiping the sweat from her forehead and face belonged to her aunt. *Dear Miriam, how many babies have you helped bring into this world?* There were streaks of silver in her hair, but her face was lit by an inner joy that kept her age a mystery.

Pain gripped Anna. "How…?"

"Soon, precious, soon," Miriam said.

Was this how it was for her mother? Endless hours of sweat and pain, only to die before ever suckling her babe to her breast?

Please, God, no. I cannot die giving birth to this child. Joachim needed her to rear their babe. God would not answer their prayers by blessing their union only to take her life in the process of delivery.

"Anna, God has blessed you with a strong body for such a time as this. The child will be delivered into your waiting arms. You will laugh like Sarah. Your husband will rejoice in God as Abraham did. You both have waited patiently for God to answer your prayers. The time is soon."

"You always did know how to comfort me. I want to be a gentle mother as you have been."

FAVORED

How many times in the past nine months had Anna spoken that wish? Now the time was upon her, and Anna did not feel prepared in the least for motherhood. Of course, the house was in order; Anna and Miriam had spent countless hours preparing it. The cradle Joachim had carved out of the "finest wood in Galilee" seemed to rock in anticipation of the tiny bundle it would hold. Swaddling clothes were cleaned and neatly folded. But a house was not a home without a mother.

The pain seemed to be washing over her in waves, one right after the other. What was Miriam saying? *Breathe? What is she saying?*

"Push."

God, please let the baby be strong.

"Push, Anna. It's time."

God, Joachim said he'd be happy with a boy or girl. God, please let it be...

"One last push, Anna. You will be a mother."

The cry of the baby broke the pain and heaviness that had filled the small room.

Anna closed her eyes and slowly lowered her head. *Is it really over?* She could hear Miriam's quiet movements—washing, wrapping, and singing to the babe.

"Anna, your daughter is here. You did well, precious, very well."

"Joachim?"

"He is not far. He stayed outside the house during your time. I will go to him."

Anna looked at her daughter, the answer to their prayers and the blessing that came from the love that she and Joachim had for each other. *Would Joachim be pleased with a girl? How could he not be?* She was perfect. Anna touched the top of her head. The dark brown tendrils were soft. Her eyes, barely opened, were as black as onyx. Anna slowly unwrapped the cloth. The baby had all ten fingers and toes.

"You'd better wrap her back up before Miriam catches you allowing the cold to seep into our babe's body."

Anna did as instructed. "You are pleased? With a girl?"

The question seemed silly when Anna looked into her husband's eyes. His smile warmed her soul. How handsome he was. How well they fit together as a couple. When Anna was worried, Joachim was at peace. When she would doubt, he would encourage. When she would pull away, he would pull her close. When she became frustrated with the waiting, he was patient.

Joachim reached for their child. Anna watched her husband's strong arms cradle their infant tenderly. "She's…" Anna waited for him to find the right words. "Beautiful." This tall, strong man was virtually brought to his knees by the sight of a wee babe. His wee babe.

Anna watched a tear slip down her husband's cheek. He was speaking in a very soft voice to the baby. No, he was praying, giving thanks to God.

Miriam gently touched Joachim's back. Neither of them had heard her reenter the room. "Your wife needs rest, and your child needs to suckle. Have you considered a name?"

Joachim handed Anna their child. "Mary."

Chapter One

Shielding her eyes, Anna stepped out into the late afternoon sun. *Where could that girl have gone?* Sometime between noon and evening, under Anna's watchful eye—*not too watchful, huh, God?*—Mary had slipped away, leaving her household duties partially done.

"Am I once again going to have to call after her like a ewe calls her lamb?"

"Call who?"

Reluctantly, Anna turned to see her friend and neighbor eyeing her from behind her broom.

"Excuse me, Rachel," Anna stammered. "I thought I was alone."

"So I can assume you were talking to yourself. Does this mean you've lost your mind as well as your daughter?"

At times, Rachel could be sweet, helpful, and kind, exuding all the qualities one would want in a friend. Other times, it took all the patience God gave man or woman to be around the busybody. Now, news would spread through Nazareth that Anna had lost Mary again.

"I've not lost my daughter," Anna said with more confidence than she felt.

"Of course. But, in case you were wondering, I saw Mary happily skipping toward the well not more than an hour or so ago."

"Good. I had asked her to fetch some more water before dark."

"Funny. I didn't see her with a pitcher."

Anna flushed with anger. Turning so Rachel would not see her red face, Anna entered her home, slamming the door behind her. *How am I going to get out of this one?* She caught sight of the pitcher on the corner of the table. In case Rachel was still outside, Anna decided to leave quickly with pitcher in hand, allowing Rachel to think whatever she liked. Hopefully, she would assume Anna was taking the pitcher to Mary, allowing her to maintain some level of dignity.

Without thinking, she rushed out with the pitcher, tipping it in the process and spilling what water remained down the front of her tunic. What little dignity she had felt just moments ago vanished with the water. Now, Rachel would know the truth, and so would all of Nazareth.

Pulling herself together, pitcher in hand, Anna left the house, heading in the opposite direction of the well. At least this way she would not have to confront Rachel directly.

"Anna!" Rachel called. "Dear, the well is…."

Though she could hear Rachel laughing, she kept walking. Each step was more like a stomp, causing those she passed to be covered in the dust she left in her wake. The harder she walked, the angrier and more humiliated she felt. *Children are a blessing from God—how could one child be such a source of frustration? Why can't Mary understand her place?* The tongues would be wagging once again about Anna's inability to keep a tight rein on her daughter. *Why is it that I've become the source of entertainment for everyone in this town? People should learn to mind their own business.*

Anna came to an abrupt stop as the memory of Miriam on her deathbed came flooding back to her. Anna reached her hand out in hopes of feeling her aunt's soft skin one more time. Unaware of the tears streaming down her dust-streaked face, Anna recalled the final words her aunt had spoken: "Mary is favored. Love her unconditionally, no matter the cost." In Miriam's final moments, her thoughts were for Anna's daughter. Anna hung her head in shame. Pride: that's all it had been. Pride blinded her from seeing Mary for the gift she was and the gifts with which God blessed her.

The sound of pottery shattering brought Anna back. Through tears, she gazed into the faces of those glaring at her.

"You, woman, is there a problem?"

Anna wiped her face with her hands before turning to face the man who had spoken. Deliberately averting eye contact, she shook her head.

"Clean up this mess you have made and be on your way." The soldier towered over her, blocking the rays of the sun. His shadow fell over her.

Bending down to pick up the shards of broken pottery, Anna wanted to become the dirt beneath her feet. She was nothing like the mother Miriam had been to her. All she did was remind Mary of all the things she did wrong.

"Anna, I saw Mary earlier today. Her smile makes others smile with her. Do you need help?" Anna silently welcomed the unintentional hint of her daughter's whereabouts.

"Oh, no. I mean, I'm fine, Martha. Just clumsy. You saw Mary?"

"She passed me a few hours ago with Lydia. Those two are inseparable."

"Yes, I suppose so. Which way were they headed?"

"I'm not sure, but I wouldn't be concerned. Mary is a good girl. Those hooligans knocked over Silas' cart, and there was Mary, helping him pick things back up. She is a kind girl."

"Rachel says I should rein her in. She's too 'flighty,' according to Rachel, that is."

Martha spat onto the ground. "That's what I think of Rachel's opinion." She shifted her basket to the other hip. "You've reared her well. Don't let anyone tell you differently. She's beautiful

FAVORED

inside and out. Since you don't need my help, though, I should be on my way."

Martha's words renewed Anna's confidence. Standing, she took in her surroundings. The sun was going down. Joachim would be wondering where she was. Anna headed straight for home with pieces of broken pottering in her hands.

The worried look on Joachim's face confirmed her greatest fears: Mary wasn't home. As soon as he caught sight of Anna, a smile spread across his face. *Could it be that he was actually worried about me?* She smiled.

Joachim hurried to meet her. He embraced her with such a force that her feet left the ground. She giggled as he spun her around and around. Anna, caught up in the love she had for her husband, allowed the day's events to slip away. It wasn't until the shards of pottery poked her skin that Anna remembered her daughter.

Between the kisses Joachim planted on her forehead and cheeks, Anna whispered, "Mary. Do you know where she is?"

Joachim gently released her. Anna laughed at the quizzical look on his face.

"Mary is in the house, preparing the evening meal. It is you, dear wife, who had me worried. Where were you? Your poor hands are cut and bleeding! What has happened to the water pitcher?"

"If you only knew."

With Joachim leading her into the house, Anna caught sight of their daughter. Her dark, wavy hair hung loosely down her back. Mary was humming to herself as she stirred something over the fire.

Why did I worry so?

Mary turned at the sound of her parents' footsteps. "Oh, Mother, we were so worried about you." She reached for her mother, then gasped at the sight of blood on Anna's hands and tunic. "What happened?"

"It's nothing, my daughter. I left to go to the well for water, and in my clumsiness, I dropped the pitcher on the way. I didn't realize until I got home that the shards had cut my hands."

"But, Mother, I went to the well this morning so you wouldn't have to. Why did you need to go again?"

Sensing Anna's weariness, Joachim suggested she wash and dress her wounds before supper, gently guiding her away from Mary's unanswered question. Anna was grateful for his discernment. He stayed by her side, helping replace the broken pottery with tenderness as she cleaned and dressed her wounds. *Wounds on the outside are easily cleaned, but what of the wounds on the inside?* The thought was fleeting but left Anna feeling empty.

Seeing the concern on her husband's face, she smiled up at him. "You must be famished. I've kept you from your evening meal. Please forgive me, Husband."

"There is nothing to forgive. I am thankful you arrived home safely, with only minor scratches. Tell me, Wife, why did you leave today?"

"I… We needed water."

"You and I know that is not the reason. Come. A wife shouldn't keep secrets from her husband."

"No, but shouldn't some things be between oneself and God?"

"As you wish." Joachim pulled Anna close. In her presence, he felt years younger.

"What kept you busy today?"

"I spoke with Joseph. You remember Jacob's younger boy. It seems he's doing quite well as a carpenter. He told me that there have been more and more skirmishes between our people and the Roman soldiers. Even here in Nazareth, more Hebrews were rounded up to be taken to Rome for auction. The oppression we face saddens me."

"I sometimes wonder if God has forsaken us altogether," Anna admitted.

Joachim chilled at the thought. He had considered the very words Anna had spoken aloud but dared not speak them himself. "God will bring salvation from the Romans. He will keep the covenant He has made with His people."

"Are you trying to convince me or yourself?"

"Dinner is served," Mary called.

Joachim cleared his throat. "We will be out shortly," he called back. "We must not give Mary any reason to worry. We will not speak of this anymore while we have dinner," he said quietly to Anna.

Anna started to rebuke his admonishment, but she was silenced by Joachim holding a finger to her lips. He bent down and kissed her on the forehead. "Not a word more," he whispered. The two left the small room to join Mary.

Mary talked of her day. Once again, she mentioned that she had drawn the water from the well so her mother wouldn't have to. While she was hanging up the clothes to dry, Lydia had stopped by to see if she could go for a walk. She was sorry if her absence had caused her mother to worry. The girls hadn't realized how warm a day it was until they had reached the outskirts of the city, so they decided to rest beneath a grove of trees. She had hurried home to finish her duties only to find her mother had gone. Taking it upon herself, she had decided to cook dinner.

"Is the meal to your liking?" Mary asked her parents.

Anna listened to her daughter, not so much hearing the words she spoke as seeing, for the first time, the woman Mary had become. No longer did a child of thirteen sit at their table. The girl facing her, with long, dark hair soft as silk, onyx eyes that danced beneath long lashes, cheeks flushed with joyful youth, and a laugh as sweet as David's psalms, had become a young woman overnight. The light touch of her husband's hand on hers drew her thoughts back to the conversation.

"You've barely touched your food. Is it not to your liking?" Mary posed the question to her mother with a gentleness that reminded Anna of Miriam.

"It's wonderful, precious. I'm just not hungry tonight."

"I think worship will be brief for your sake, Wife. You look as if rest would do you a heap of good."

Anna had to admit she was tired. She was not as young as she used to be. After a short time of prayer and devotion, the family of three said goodnight.

In the quiet darkness, Joachim softly spoke to his wife, "I think it is time to consider Mary's future. It is obvious she is no longer a child but a young woman. She will be fourteen in a month's time. We will talk tomorrow after you have rested. I have much more to discuss with you. Joseph is quite a capable man. He has a good head on his shoulders, and he would make a fine husband for a girl like Mary. I'm considering broaching the subject with the man to see where his feelings lie." With that, Joachim fell fast asleep.

Anna lay next to her husband, allowing the darkness to hide the tears that fell on her pillow.

Chapter Two

Mary lay on her mat, not a stone's throw from her parent's room. Their home was modest, like most of the homes in Nazareth. In the main room of the house, there was a small area designated for cooking meals, and a long table used to prepare meals sat along the outside wall. Just above the table was a small window for light and an occasional breeze. The table for eating, fellowship, and worship sat in the center of the room with four chairs around it. Mary's mother could not bring herself to remove the fourth chair, even though Miriam had died more than a year ago. "Besides, what if we have company?" her mother would often say. "Where would they sit?" No one ever came. The fireplace was near the work area, and on the inside wall was a flight of stairs that led to the rooftop. The roof could be used as an extra room if needed. Her father went there to pray every morning and evening. Her parents' room was just to the right of the stairs. Miriam had told Mary that was where she had been born. It was in that room that Miriam had died. It was now the room where Mary could hear her father making mention of her future.

A knot began to grow in the pit of Mary's stomach. It was obvious she was coming of age. Her body was maturing into a woman's body. She had started her courses, as many of her friends had. She thought back over the conversation she had shared with her mother the day her courses began to flow. Her mother had found her sobbing into her mat.

"What, Mary, child, what's wrong?"

"Nothing."

"Oh, well, if you want to talk about it, I'm willing to listen."

FAVORED

Her mother turned from her and began to sweep the dirt out the door. Mary enjoyed hearing the swish of the broom.

"Mother, why do you clean the dirt from a dirt floor?"

"Because the dirt of my floor is packed and clean. The dirt that comes in from the street is dirty. It has no place in my home."

"Lydia said it would be wonderful."

"What would be wonderful?"

"Becoming a woman. That I would feel graceful and beautiful. But I don't feel any of those things."

"How do you feel?"

"Like skipping through the brush and feeling the wet of dew on my feet or standing in the middle of the street to hear the potter's wheel as it turns. I might even hide behind a crate and watch the boys knock over Silas' cart. That always makes me laugh."

"Sounds fun. May I join you?"

"What? You would do those things with me?"

"Why not?"

"Because you're…"

"Old? A woman? Mary, becoming a woman doesn't mean you give up the things you enjoy. Womanhood just adds a dimension to the enjoyment of it."

"I don't know. Right now I feel miserable."

"This, too, shall pass. Listen…I just love tapping my foot to the rhythm of a carpenter's hammer."

Joseph: was that the name she had heard her father mention? He was at least ten years older than her. Maybe more. Granted, he was quite handsome. All the girls thought so. She giggled again at the conversation she and her friends had only a few days before. Each one dreamed about what young man her parents would match her with. If her mother knew of their conversation—if any of the mothers knew—all the girls would have been severely disciplined. Mary laughed out loud, clamping her hand over her mouth to stifle the sound. Joseph seemed very quiet and reserved. How had Lydia described him? "Handsome but stoic." That was it. Mary could not recall a time she had seen Joseph smile.

Of course, many of the men his age had not smiled for a long time. They had seen too much, endured too much, and labored under a heavy yoke. Maybe that's why Joseph didn't smile. He was simply too old to do so.

Mary laughed to herself. If Miriam were still alive, she would be laughing with her. Mary could always share her innermost thoughts with her grandmother. That's how she thought of Miriam: as her grandmother. Every girl needed a grandmother to confide in, to laugh and sing with, and to learn from.

She sighed and rolled over on her mat. Mary could see through the small window on the opposite wall; the night sky was clear and full of bright stars. She thought the stars probably looked like crystals in the black sky, but she had never seen a crystal in person before. Lydia had, though, and she could describe them in great detail. Her family went to Jerusalem each year for Passover and always returned with extraordinary tales of her adventure. Mary had never left Nazareth.

If her father was planning on making a match between her and Joseph, Mary was certain she would never leave Nazareth. Joseph wasn't the type. He was content to stay in his carpentry shop and let life pass him by. Mary groaned.

She caught sight of one star that seemed to twinkle brighter than the others. "Miriam," she whispered, "if only you were here. You would know just the right words to say to put my mind at ease so I could sleep." Often Mary had heard her grandmother praying in the dead of night. When Miriam prayed, peace would wash over Mary like water from the well. It made her feel clean.

She remembered waking one night when she was about five to the sound of her grandmother praying.

FAVORED

"Grandmother? What are you doing?" Mary had asked.

"Praying to God, precious, seeking His wisdom and mercy."

"Can I pray to God too?"

"Of course you can."

Miriam had listened patiently as Mary prayed for every animal and friend she could think of. Her grandmother had taught her about faith. Believing in what you cannot see; weren't those the words Miriam had used to describe faith? Mary thought for a moment, then looked up at the window. The star was shining just as before. "Morning will come all too early for a girl without sleep," her mother would say, "and it will show on one's face."

Mother was always worrying about one trifle or the other. Mary knew she was the cause of most of her mother's anxiety. She turned her back to the window and faced the wall. She really was trying to be the girl her mother wanted her to be. There were just too many distractions.

Mary stood and stretched, giving up on sleeping for the time being. She walked to the table downstairs, poured herself some water, and sat down.

"I thought I heard movement in here."

"Sorry, Papa. I didn't mean to wake you."

"You didn't. Mind if I join you?" Joachim sat across from his daughter. "Why can't my beautiful girl sleep?"

"You know Mother didn't go to the well for more water. She came looking for me."

"Now, Mary, your mother worries about you because she loves you. That's all."

"If Miriam were here, she would have talked some sense into Mother."

"Perhaps."

The two sat in silence, each sipping water in an attempt to find comfort from its coolness.

32

TERI LYN TOBEY

"You overheard your mother and me?"

Mary nodded.

"Miriam used to say that God knit you together in your mother's womb, creating you to be all He desires. She would tell us that God has a plan for you. I believe He does, Mary. I have watched a beautiful woman develop from a child."

A tear ran down Mary's cheek.

"Pray for peace, child. Perhaps then you can rest." Joachim kissed his daughter's forehead and padded off to bed. Mary returned to her room after he left her.

Turning back to look at the night sky, Mary bowed her head. "Please, God, hear the prayer of a young girl. Open my parents' eyes to see who I truly am and want to be. Help them know Joseph is not the man for me."

What of My plans for you?

Mary opened her eyes and quickly scanned the room. She was alone. She kept very still as she listened to the sound of slumber coming from her parents' room.

Was that a voice, or a thought she had just heard or sensed or... *What was that?* There was no mistaking what she had heard: "What of My plans for you?" Needing some sort of cover, she ran to her mat. Sitting, she brought her knees to her chest and crossed her arms around her legs, tightly clinging to herself. She had heard her parents speak of people who heard voices in their heads. These voices would tell the one afflicted to do all sorts of crazy things. "Possessed by the devil" was the diagnosis her mother had given. Surely that was not happening to her. Mary shivered. However, she could not deny the words spoken so lovingly into her mind.

Silently, she gazed out of the tiny window, only to find the twinkling stars being replaced by slivers of orange and gold. It would soon be morning. Her mother would see the dark circles under Mary's eyes and assume she was coming down with some

FAVORED

sort of ailment. She would force Mary to stay indoors the whole day and drink an awful concoction thought to be a remedy for whatever might be ailing her young daughter.

"Oh, Grandmother, if only you were here."

Behold, I am with you always.

There was no mistaking the words that came to her mind. Her grandmother had spoken those exact words concerning God's promise to be with their people. Was God speaking to her now? Was it possible God would comfort a girl from Nazareth? She had always assumed God only spoke to the high priest or the elderly who had lived a righteous life, like her grandmother.

Oh, why am I even thinking this way? This type of thinking got a person nowhere. Maybe she had misunderstood her father's words. No, she had heard him correctly. Grandma Miriam would tell her, "Let tomorrow worry about itself. There is too much to do today." Mary lay back on her mat and closed her eyes. Joseph might not even desire a wife. After all, most men his age were already married with children, but he had remained single. Not by choice, some said, but still, he had been of age for quite some time and could have taken a wife of his choosing if he'd so desired. Obviously he didn't, so maybe he wouldn't desire her as well. One could only hope and pray.

Trust Me, beloved. The words were clear as the fresh water she pulled from the well.

"God?" Mary whispered. *Do I dare talk to the Most High?* She waited, hoping for a response. *What if the voice in my head is that of evil?* If it were from the evil one, would she have this feeling of protection and comfort? She spoke to God what was on her heart, "I want to trust—honestly, I do—but I feel like such a failure at times. Could You truly care for one like me? I can't even keep up with my daily duties, let alone mind the commandments."

Trust in My promises.

The words spoken by her grandmother more times than Mary

could count came to her lips. "In You will I put my trust." A peace beyond understanding washed over Mary in the same way it had when she prayed with Miriam. In that moment the room seemed to come alive with the sun sending brilliant beams of gold through the small window.

Mary sighed with contentment. God knew her heart, her innermost thoughts. He would protect her from a *betrothal* to a man she did not love. *Trust Me.* Those were the words spoken to her heart from her God. Mary felt her eyes become heavy with sleep. As she yawned she felt her body relax, and she allowed sleep to take hold as the early light of dawn blanketed her with its warmth.

would sound if it echoed off the walls, or how the air had
been a undefinable scent and character. Who knows what had
when she prayed. She wanted to understand why she seemed
to come alive in the silence of little light that spilled through
the small windows.

I Mary sighed with the intangible of love. Her hand, her
important thought. If I would not of being. Who knows what
had she did but most of all. She then and the understood into
that heart from her room felt not far in the of the heavy who
sleep. As she sunk into the silk of the moon that she talk the
sleep to that held to the the light of and it looked for with
its warmth.

Chapter Three

Joseph woke, startled. The knock at the door was not a knock at all but a bang. One came right after the other. He shot out of bed, his feet barely hitting the ground before he threw open the front door. He found himself staring into the eyes of a Roman soldier.

"Are you the carpenter they call Joseph?'

Joseph felt that even if he wasn't, he'd better find a way to be.

"I am he."

"Your skills are needed by Rome. Gather your tools and come along with us. Be quick about it. However, you may want to dress first."

The rousing laughter behind the man made Joseph realize two things: first, the soldier had brought three others with him, and second, in his haste, he had answered the door in only his undergarment. Joseph started to close the door, but the Roman put his foot in the jam.

"Leave the door open," the soldier demanded. Joseph shrugged and stepped back into the darkness of his home.

He could feel the eyes of the soldiers on him as he went to the wash basin to splash water on his face. From the peg on the wall, he grabbed his tunic and pulled it over his head, then tied his sash around his waist. He attempted to step beyond the threshold, only to have the soldier block his way.

"What of your tools?"

"I have them next door in my shop. If you allow me to pass, I can retrieve them, and we can be on our way."

FAVORED

The Roman stepped ever so slightly to the side, allowing Joseph just enough room to exit. As they walked the short distance to the shop, Joseph found himself surrounded by the four men, two in the front and two behind. *What was so important that they felt the need to send four soldiers to fetch one carpenter?* He had been summoned before by one Roman or the other to fix any number of items that needed repair, but never four. These men were acting as if he might attack them at any moment.

"What needs to be fixed?"

"You'll find out soon enough."

"But I need to know the job that is to be done so I can bring the proper tools."

"Bring them all."

Joseph looked around the shop. Picking up his hammer, he thought of how many times he'd heard his father admonishing him to "treat a tool like you would a woman. Be gentle and soft with your touch, and she will do whatever you ask." As he gathered what items he might need, Joseph laughed to himself. With age, he'd come to realize his father knew very little about women but everything about tools and carpentry.

He arranged his tools in his satchel and returned to the soldier. "I have all I need."

"Good. Then we will be on our way."

"How far are we going?" It was not uncommon for Romans to round up Hebrews in order to sell them to the highest bidder. Joseph's people had been sold through the whole of the Roman Empire, from Galilee to Ephesus, Corinth, and even Rome. Word had spread from those who had escaped that many of those sold into slavery were required to do horrible and humiliating things, unspeakable things.

Are my brothers…? Joseph couldn't finish his thought.

Joseph prayed every night that God had been merciful to his

two older brothers by allowing them to die with dignity. They had been taken when Joseph was about ten. At the time, a ten-year-old was not needed by Rome. Joseph had been spared the humiliation of being sold into slavery, but not Matthan, named after his father's father, and not Josiah. Joseph firmly believed that the loss of her two older sons was what killed his mother. Though her death was eight years after her sons had been taken, Joseph knew his mother's soul had died that day. Her body just took longer to decay. He blamed Rome for her death and for his father's. Jacob lived two more years after Joseph's mother died, but his life had been taken with hers. Rome may not have killed them by sword, but Rome had killed them nonetheless.

They had stopped walking, and the Roman was eyeing him suspiciously. Joseph looked down to see that both of his hands were drawn into tight fists. His fingers were numb. He released his hands and flexed his fingers. The stab of pins and needles coursed through his hands. He looked straight into the Roman's eyes.

"We seem to have walked for some time," Joseph said. He briefly took in his surroundings and then returned his gaze to the Roman's face. "How far did you say we were going?"

"I didn't say. But I'd watch my step if I were you." With that, they resumed their pace.

Obviously, the Roman was not one for small talk. The other thing that was becoming clear to Joseph was that the Roman trusted him no more than he trusted the Roman. Joseph looked around. He knew this area well. He had played in the surrounding hills of Nazareth as a boy. For now, the entourage was sticking to the main road. They were heading south, which might mean that a camp had been set up between Nain and Nazareth. Romans were known to patrol the areas in Galilee on a regular basis, squashing the skirmishes that might arise. As of late, there had been more uprisings than Joseph desired.

He could not deny that in his younger years he had considered

FAVORED

being part of some sort of revolt. He hated Rome as much as the next man. But, fortunately, with age comes wisdom. Sometimes he would attend the secret meetings in the darkness of night, always standing in the shadows so as not to be noticed but intently listening to their talk of rebellion. It would start with the taking of just a few Roman lives, but by the end of the evening, and with too much to drink, the young men would be so wound up that they believed they could take on an entire *legion*. Inevitably, their senses would return, leaving all present feeling defeated. A few would take up the cause and strike out against a Roman traveler, leaving the road stained with blood. Yet, for every Roman killed, whether it be a citizen or soldier, at least one hundred Hebrews would be slaughtered or enslaved. The knowledge of this kept revolts to a minimum. Hebrews had learned to live under Roman oppression and would continue to do so until God saw fit to redeem them.

Joseph wiped the sweat from his brow. It would be a warm day. As they topped the hill, he was relieved to see what appeared to be a small camp a hundred yards or so from the road in a clump of trees. He followed the two men in front of him, feeling as if the two behind him practically pushed him on as they left the road in the direction of the camp.

Many of the men in the camp were eating some sort of stew, the smell of which roused hunger in Joseph, reminding him that he had not had anything to eat. Some were stretched out, resting beneath the trees. Others were casting lots, hoping to win some sort of treasure. Whereas some gave him no more than a glance, others seemed very curious about the Hebrew in their midst.

They came to an abrupt stop in front of a tent much larger than the others and situated in such a way that it was protected on all sides.

"Wait here." The only soldier in their group who had spoken to Joseph disappeared inside the tent. Within a few moments, a very robust man stood in the opening of the tent. He wore a white robe with gold embellishments around the collar and sleeves. In his hand was a goblet which, from the smell of it and the man, was filled with wine.

"So this is the Nazarene carpenter you've brought to bring my darling's dressing table?"

"He comes highly recommended," the soldier replied.

"Good. He's quite handsome. I suppose my darling will enjoy watching him work. Thank you for your kind and timely attention to the matter, Theo. Now, let us step aside so the man can come in and do what is expected of him. You may go."

"Sir, I think it best if I stay and make sure all goes well. Don't you?"

"As you wish."

Joseph quietly gasped. Beneath his feet were plush green rugs woven in rich hues of scarlet, blue, and purple. In the center of the tent was a round table, intricately carved and made of the finest wood Joseph had seen. All sorts of delicacies to tempt the palate were on the table. Joseph's mouth watered at the sight of grapes, raisins, dates, and many other foods displayed before him. With the heads of each touching the other were two long couches covered in white. One sat empty. On the other lay a woman. Her head rested on a round pillow, her hair piled high on her head and adorned with flowers. Her eyes were closed, but her mouth looked like she was kissing the air. Her body was draped in pale green fabric so sheer it left nothing to one's imagination as to what lay beneath. She was beautiful.

"My darling wife, so sorry to disturb your rest, but the carpenter has arrived."

The woman slowly opened her eyes. Turning her head to greet them, she came up on one elbow, eyeing Joseph mischievously. Her eyes shone like emeralds, accentuated by the color of her dress. Something in her eyes told Joseph she was not to be messed with. Taking in the full scene that confronted him turned Joseph's stomach sour. This was the type of woman he had been taught to

FAVORED

avoid. Joseph turned away and looked at the small dressing table to the right. The leg had been broken in half, so the table lay on its side.

In one quick stride, Joseph was bending over the table and picking up the broken leg. "Is this what you have summoned me to fix?"

Her voice as soft as a rose's petal, Dalena purred, "Yes."

It was one word, but the sound of her voice sent chills up Joseph's spine. He had to be careful, or he could end up like his namesake, caught in a spider's deceptive web. She was very attractive, and her presence stirred a desire in Joseph that he had not felt for quite some time. He stood and turned to the soldier. "I need to search for a proper piece of wood to replace the broken leg."

Standing in order for Joseph to take in the full view of her, Dalena asked, "Can it be repaired?" She looked like a child about to cry. It was a look she had perfected to get everything she wanted and from whomever she wanted it.

"It won't look as it did, but it will be usable," Joseph replied, averting his eyes.

"Oh, darling." Dalena turned to her husband. "But I do want it to look the same."

Joseph watched as she pressed her body ever so lightly against her husband's. It was just enough to cause the man to sweat. Before he spoke, Quirinius licked his lips with desire. Just the scent of her aroused him, let alone her touch. "I'm sure the man will do the best he can. If it is not to your liking, we will buy a new one as soon as we reach Pella."

Those words seemed to appease the woman, for she gave the portly man a light kiss on his cheek and then turned to face Joseph. She tilted her head ever so slightly to the side. There was a look of arousal in her eyes that seemed to turn them black. She glided across the room as if on air, making sure that each movement drew every man's eyes right to where she wanted them. She reached out and touched Joseph on his arm. The softness of her hand sent a rush of heat through his entire body.

"I'm sure you will do the best you can."

Theo cleared his throat. "Carpenter, you can follow me into the wooded area to look for the piece of wood you need." He took hold of Joseph's arm and led him out of the tent.

Like a man who had been saved from drowning, Joseph sucked in the fresh air.

Theo laughed. "That was your first time in the presence of a woman like Dalena, wasn't it? Don't worry. Do your job, and I'll make sure she doesn't bother you. Unless you would like some sort of payment for your services." Seeing Joseph's ashen face made Theo roar with laughter.

Joseph, jaw firmly set, went about looking for a piece of wood that would suffice for a leg to hold up the dressing table. *Why me, God? Why our people? Haven't we suffered enough to have to continue to deal with such degradation?*

"You don't like Romans very much, do you, carpenter? I can see it in your eyes. You're built well—tall, strong arms and legs. You'd make a fine man to have around in battle."

He picked up a piece of sturdy wood, then turned to look back at Theo. "This should work." Joseph returned to the tent with the soldier close at his heels.

He was pleased to see that the woman was busy entertaining her husband with some delectable sweets. Appearing as the protector of the privileged class, Theo positioned himself between the couple and Joseph, who got the sense that Theo was protecting him, especially when he caught a glimpse of Dalena watching him. For the first time since the Roman had banged on his door, Joseph was grateful for his presence.

Joseph noticed how the woman's scent floated through the room. She would laugh just loud enough to distract him. To

Joseph, this lady, if one could call her that, knew every move to make a man fall at her feet. *Are all Roman women trained in such ways?* For all the power Roman men seemed to possess, they were foolish when it came to their women.

He allowed his thoughts to turn to the girls in Nazareth. How different they were from the woman only a few feet away from him. Most were young, not much older than fifteen. Many were coming of age to marry. Joseph had considered marriage a time or two in the past ten years, but he couldn't bring himself to do it. He had chosen to love once. At eighteen, that love was taken from him. Joseph shook his head as if doing so would shake the memory of Hannah from his mind. If he was honest with himself, he was still a boy trying to be a man.

Joseph swore as the hammer hit his thumb. Shaking it off, he chided himself for allowing his mind to wander while working. "That's how men die," his father would say, "by not paying attention to the task at hand. Keep your mind focused on what you're doing."

He ran his hand over the leg of the table. It would hold. He stood and stretched, then turned to Theo. "The job is done. I trust it will be satisfactory. Not beautiful, as I said, but it will hold until you are able to replace it."

Drawn from their entanglement by Joseph's announcement, Dalena all too willingly released her hold on her husband, allowing Quirinius to stand. "Theo, give this to the man for his trouble and send him on his way. My wife and I would like some time alone." Theo nodded and motioned toward the opening to the tent.

Joseph noticed how eager the man was to perform his husbandly duties, but from the expression on the woman's face, she was not looking forward to being left alone with him. Perhaps she was being forced to be the man's wife. The thought sickened him. *No, she knew exactly what she was doing marrying him. They deserve each other.* As they left, Joseph could hear the woman laughing. It disgusted him.

Theo walked Joseph all the way back to the top of the hill. "For your trouble." He tossed Joseph a pouch. From the rattling of the coins, he knew it was not a small sum: fair pay for a day's work. He had not been cheated.

He began to leave, but his curiosity got the best of him. "Who are they?"

Theo laughed at the man's ignorance. "You were just in the presence of the new governor of Syria. Take care, carpenter." Theo headed back across the field.

Joseph began his walk back to Nazareth. It would be time for the evening meal before he reached home. As if on cue, his stomach growled in anticipation. *If only there was someone waiting for me at home.* He didn't allow the thought to linger. He had been down that road before, and all it brought was heartache.

He knew what the people in town said about him, still a bachelor at twenty-five. Some would shake their heads in pity as if he couldn't find a wife if he wanted to. Others would question his character. He learned to let wagging tongues fend for themselves. He was not about to do what he didn't want to do just out of fear of what people would think. That was not the type of man he was. He was a man of integrity. He dealt fairly with his neighbors. He worshiped on the Sabbath and kept the commandments. That should be enough for any man to maintain respect without having to take a wife.

He caught sight of Nazareth just ahead. One thought that had troubled him of late was the idea that he might be the last of his family. He had no idea whether his brothers were even alive, let alone if they had sired offspring. If he didn't take a wife, the family tree could end with him.

The staff etched with his family history stood against the far wall of his home. He had not touched it since the day his father died. Joseph recalled how weak his father had been as he motioned for Joseph to bring him the rod. When he returned to his father's bedside, his father gently placed his hand on the staff. With pleading eyes his father had begged Joseph to not let the family line die.

His father knew him too well. Hannah was gone, and Joseph's heart was in pieces. There was no way he would allow himself to love again. Joseph closed his eyes at the memory. Before he knew it, he was opening his front door. He placed the pouch of coins on the table, dropped his tools to the floor, and untied his belt. After splashing water on his face and head, he broke off some bread and devoured it. That was enough to settle his stomach. Pouring himself some watered wine, Joseph positioned himself at the table. He opened up the pouch the Roman had given him and counted out his wage: four *sesterces*. It was enough to equal one denarius. It appeared the Romans were as free with their money as they were with their affection.

He sat for a long time. The only sound came from him twirling the coins, one right after the other, on the table. The house felt strangely quiet. Usually he enjoyed his solitude, but after all he had heard and seen today, it would be nice to share the happenings with someone. He glanced over and saw the staff against the wall.

As he stretched out onto his bed, he thought of the only girl in Nazareth who had caught his eye. She was young. She seemed strong enough to handle the daily duties of a wife; maybe young was okay. Since he knew he was older, her youth might inspire him. He smiled to himself. Still, he knew in his heart that he could not love another, save for Hannah.

Joseph yawned. He had much to think about. The memory of the Roman couple sickened him; they were too brazen in their affection. However, seeing them together had stirred a passion in Joseph he thought had died long ago. Perhaps it was not too late. As his eyes grew heavy with sleep, a thought crossed his mind: *It is time, beloved.*

Chapter Four

Dalena watched as the handsome Hebrew left the tent. She was not accustomed to a man who wouldn't give her the time of day. Still, she had sensed the heat pulse through his body when she touched him. She smiled. She could not help but notice the broadness of his shoulders and the definition of his arms, even through his tunic. He had dark brown eyes and tanned skin. Though his beard covered most of his face, she could tell he had a strong jaw. She wondered what it would feel like to be kissed by a man with a beard. She didn't think she would like it, but that was nothing that couldn't be dealt with. What was not so easy to deal with was that he had not paid any attention to her at all. Plus, Theo had remained in the tent, as well as Quirinius. This forced her to pay attention to the man who was her husband.

Now he stood before her, panting like a dog for scraps of food. True enough, he was wealthy and had secured for himself the appointment of the *proconsul* of Syria. However, she couldn't help but feel she had not quite been able to fulfill her dream. She had wanted to move among the upper crust of Roman society. Instead, she had to settle for a man who was dragging her off to Syria.

Quirinius bent down and whispered in her ear, "You liked the Hebrew, didn't you, darling?" She felt the heat of his breath on her neck and shivered. He drew her to himself and kissed her so hard and long that she thought she might faint. His touch on her body held no love but pure desire. Her mind began to dream that the man touching her was not her husband but the handsome carpenter.

As if sensing she was slipping away from him once more,

FAVORED

Quirinus jerked her face toward his, forcing her to look directly in his eyes. "Pay attention, darling," he hissed. "I want you to know it is me who is having you and no other." He loosened the belt from around her waist, allowing her dress to fall to the floor.

Dalena stayed very still as she lay next to her husband. He had fallen asleep, and she did not want to disturb him. Not out of courtesy—she simply did not want to have to endure another minute of his passion. It seemed she could never quench his thirst for her.

Making sure Quirinius was sound asleep, she slowly slid from the couch. Dalena went to the washbasin and began trying to scrub the feel of this touch from her body. She had not felt clean in a long time. As she stood in the dark, she realized she was shaking. Dalena grabbed the goblet left on the table and gulped the remainder of the wine. She felt its warmth go through her body, steadying her nerves. She donned the robe carelessly tossed over the chair by her dressing table. Tying the sash around her waist, she caught a glimpse of the unstained piece of wood the Hebrew had fashioned into a leg. She wondered what it would be like to be loved by such a man.

Dalena could not remember a time she ever felt loved. Growing up, her mother had taught her all she knew concerning the ways of men. Dalena had not realized it at the time, but it was how her mother made a living for herself and her illegitimate daughter. Her mother was a kept woman, a delicate, the mistress of one man. At an early age, Dalena became aware of her station in life. Once or twice a week, a *litter* would deliver the man to their door. She would be sent outside to entertain herself. She always played alone. The local children knew what she was, even if she didn't.

Her fondest memories were of sitting in the coolness of the *atrium* at her mother's feet. There they waited for him. The conversation was always the same.

"Will he bring me a toy this time, Mommy?"

"I don't know."

"Will he take me for a ride in his litter?"

"If there is time."

"He lives in a big house, doesn't he, Mommy?"

"Yes."

"He's a very important man."

"Very important."

"Father will be here soon?"

Her mother never corrected her. "Soon" was all she would say.

She had wondered why the man never greeted her as she had seen other fathers do with their children. He would simply dismiss her upon his arrival. She told herself that his time was precious, for he had important matters, more important than her, to oversee. She would tell herself that he loved her and her mother very much.

The truth became all too real one late afternoon when, upon his arrival, Dalena had made the mistake of taking his hand and saying, "Father, won't you play with me today?"

Immediately, Dalena knew she had done something terribly wrong. Her mother's face turned ghostly white. Pushing Dalena away so hard that she fell to the floor, he screamed at her mother, "What have you told her?"

"Nothing! I swear by the gods!" was her mother's reply. "She simply makes things up. You know how children are."

The man stormed out and never returned. Dalena knew him to be her father, for every month money was provided for her and her mother to live. No man would do such a thing unless he was obligated in some way to do so. That was what she was: an obligation.

Dalena felt like she was suffocating in the tent. As she stepped

FAVORED

out into the cool evening air, a deep loneliness surrounded her. She tiptoed into the covering of the trees. She had thought she would be quite content being married to Quirinius. He had all the wealth and power she longed for. She had convinced herself that the combination of money, power, and men would fill the void in her life. Yet, the void was now a chasm, and no matter who or what she held in her arms, the emptiness continued to engulf her.

The sound of a twig snapping brought Dalena to her feet. "Who's there?"

"I'm sorry to have startled you. I've warned you about wandering out at night alone. It's dangerous!"

Dalena recognized the voice and relaxed. Theo's face was outlined in the paleness of the moonlight.

"Oh, it's only you." With a deep sigh, she allowed the tension to leave her body. It was replaced with a very tantalizing thought. She needed something or someone to numb the feelings that had started to surface only moments ago. It was too irresistible.

Stepping toward her, Theo asked, "Are you all right?"

Taking full advantage of the opportunity, Dalena allowed her robe to slip slightly from her shoulder, barring just enough to arouse but not enough for suspicion. She lowered her gaze and gave a soft whimper, causing Theo to come closer, playing right into her hand. She looked up at him. Batting her eyelashes, she lifted her delicate hand to her cheek as if wiping a tear. "I'm sorry if I've troubled you. It's just…"

Theo had not stayed alive for the past seven years in service to Caesar to be so easily deceived. However, she made a fetching picture. The next few moments could make or break any man. "Let me escort you back to your husband. I'm sure the warmth of his bed and perhaps some wine are all you need."

Dalena could not endure another man turning down her affection. She needed her confidence restored and was sure Theo had been sent by the gods to do just that. Stepping closer to him so he could see what was beneath her robe, she pleaded, "Please, don't send me back to him tonight."

"Dalena, the last time I found you wandering alone, things happened between us that I swore would not happen again. It's best for both of us if I see you back to your tent."

"It was just a kiss."

"A kiss that should not have happened. I want to get you safely back before Quirinius notices you are gone." Theo turned to go.

"Theo, please don't send me back there tonight." Dalena grabbed his arm and pulled him toward her. "You don't know what he's capable of." She pressed her body against his and let out a soft sob.

The softness of her body and the engulfing smell of lilac caused Theo to pulse with desire. It had been some time since he had been with a woman. Taking a deep breath and a step back, he looked deep into Dalena's eyes. "Has he hurt you?"

With one step, Dalena closed the distance Theo had tried to create between them. "I've been hurting since the day I was forced to marry him. But that is a story for another time. A story that, for tonight, I want to forget ever happened. Help me forget, Theo." Her breath was warm against his neck. "Please, help me forget."

She ran her hands down his chiseled chest. Sensing his willingness, Dalena tilted her head up in order to meet his gaze. The moonlight filtering through the trees caused the green of her eyes to shine. She lightly brushed her lips against his.

Theo allowed himself to be caught up in her seduction. He pressed his mouth to hers while allowing his hands to run the course of her body. He had never known a more beautiful woman.

Being taken into his arms gave Dalena the power she had lost with her husband. There was not man who could not be had, given the right motivation. Dalena allowed herself to believe that this was all she needed to feel loved. For the moment, wrapped in the arms of another man, she felt the deep chasm in her heart

FAVORED

close.

They lay wrapped together until the streaks of dawn began to break through the trees that had been their blanket. With the dawn, Theo came to his senses. He cursed as he untangled himself from Dalena. "Wake up," he demanded. He chided himself for the sternness in his voice. He had just been with this woman, and now he was casting her out. But she would understand. That was the type of woman she was.

Dalen stirred at the sound of his voice. She looked up at him, not even noticing the tone he had taken with her. "Is it morning already, my love?"

"I am not your love. Get up and put your robe on before we are found."

Dalena was finally taken aback by his tone. Then the realization struck her: he was not her conquest; she had been his. He was no different than the other countless others she had been with. Still, she sensed his dear and knew she held some power. Slowly rising from the ground that had been their bed, she saw that his back was to her while he dressed. This brought Dalena's anger to a boiling point. She had to maintain composure if she was going to maintain control over him.

"What's wrong? Did you not enjoy yourself? Have I disappointed you?" Her voice was soft and childlike.

It had the effect she desired. Theo turned to look at her, only to find she had not put her robe back on yet. Taking hold of the wave of desire that swept over him, he reached down and grabbed her robe off the ground. "Cover yourself; then we'll talk."

Smiling, she did as he commanded. They would set up another time to meet, and the weeks ahead would be filled with pure pleasure despite being in the company of her husband. As always, she had gotten what she wanted.

Laughing, she asked, "Same time, same place, tonight?"

Theo could not believe what he was hearing. Didn't she

understand the danger that could come from this? The glint of fire in her eyes told him that she did understand, but she didn't care. The realization angered him. He had been a pawn in her silly game. Grabbing both her shoulders, he shook her as if doing so might make her come to her senses.

"We both know what happened here last night. It cannot happen again. We will not speak of it. What is done is done."

Dalena became like stone, and her voice took on an icy tone. "You chose to be with me last night. No one forced you. My preference would have been to enjoy the company of the Hebrew carpenter, but as it was, you sufficed. If I may speak so boldly, I dare say you enjoyed yourself quite a bit. For me, it was simply a more desirable way to pass the time than lying next to my husband. As I see it, you have one of two choices: you can have the pleasure of my company as we travel this wasteland, or you can ignore my advances, forcing me to make life very uncomfortable for you. I suggest you choose the first option. It would be quite a bit of fun for the both of us."

Stunned, Theo released his hold on her. For the first time, he knew how defeat felt. He stayed very quiet while contemplating the choices he had. She would never confess to Quirinius where she had been and with whom. There was danger in it for her as well. Quirinius might very well kill her, but Theo had seen how the man looked at Dalena. Quirinius lusted after her every minute of the day. He might not be able to stomach killing what he desired most. It was becoming clear that she knew her husband better than Theo gave her credit for. However, was she willing to endure his wrath? This was quite unlikely. This could be to his advantage.

Dalena impatiently asked, "Well, do we have an agreement?"

"No, we do not. Somehow, I cannot see you being willing to subject yourself to public humiliation just to have me punished for having my fill of you. Quirinius might take great pleasure in having you stripped naked and flogged before a throng of people

FAVORED

for degrading your marriage bed. I think it unlikely that you would live through such a punishment. Besides, do you really want those in your social circle to know you lowered yourself to sleep with a simple soldier? For that matter, would you want your friends to know you for the vamp you are?"

Words she had heard before slapped against her like a whip, tearing away at her very flesh. She would not appear weak, even though she felt like her legs could buckle at any moment, causing her to crumble to the ground in a heap. Why had she allowed herself to be fooled into thinking what had happened between the two of them could become something more? Where in the recesses of her mind had the lines between love and desire crossed? The deep chasm that had seemed to disappear in the dark hours before dawn slashed through her, leaving a gaping hole in her heart. From deep within her rose the anger that had sustained her through similar situations. The power had been hers, and it would be hers again.

Her eyes seemed to turn black and then flashed red with anger. Theo saw deeper, though, past the recesses of color, into her soul. His words had wounded her. For a moment, he felt sorry for her and what he had done. She had given him no choice.

Turning to leave, she hissed, "You will be sorry you ever tangled with me."

"I already am." As he watched her leave, a sense of doom came upon Theo that he could not shake. He was sure she would not confess their indiscretion. However, he was equally aware that things done in secret have a way of being discovered. Once they reached Pella, he would request a transfer.

Dalena fumed all the way back to the camp. *Men! Stupid creatures.* However, she was the stupid one. *Why, why?* Why did she always feel the need to be in a man's arms? She always left a night of passion feeling used and abandoned. There was no one to blame for this but herself. Her thoughts came to a halt when she entered the tent and found Quirinius pacing back and forth. She was counting on him to be asleep when she returned. He drank so much wine that night, she was sure he would sleep for hours. Now his face was ablaze with anger. In his eyes, she could tell he already knew the truth.

"Where have you been, and who have you been with?" he shouted as he took hold of her.

Fear coursed through Dalena like never before. *He is capable of killing me.* She cried, "You're hurting me!"

"That should be the least of your worries, darling. I could have you killed for what you've done!"

Frantically, Dalena tried to think of some explanation. She silently thanked the gods as a thought took shape in her mind. Glancing down at herself, she realized how believable her story would be. Her robe was covered with dirt and leaves. Her hair was hung in a tangled mess, with grass caught amongst some of the strands. In her haste, she had forgotten the sash to her robe, and it hung open, exposing her body.

Immediately she collapsed in her husband's arms. Wailing, as if struck, she cried, "Oh, darling, I didn't want you to know! It was stupid to leave our bed, but I was so hot. It was dark and quiet outside. I thought I would be safe if I stayed near the camp." Her sobs grew louder with each false confession.

Quirinius was suspicious of his wife's reaction. He figured she had been with another man and that, when questioned, she would simply try to weasel her way out of it. He had even gone so far as to dream of the punishment he would bestow, taking great pleasure in the many ways he could hurt her. This was an unexpected turn of events. "What do you mean 'be safe'?"

Dalena could hear the suspicion in his voice. She had to be believable if she was to have her way. She lifted her tear-streaked face and met his gaze without flinching. "All I wanted was to get some fresh air, but when I walked into the thick of the trees, he, he…." She let her voice trail off as a cry escaped her mouth. "Don't you see? I thought I was safe. I thought I was safe!" She

FAVORED

crumpled to the floor.

He felt his blood grow hot. Someone had deliberately hurt his wife, or so he wanted to believe, and he was determined to find the man and have him crucified. Sensing his wife needed gentleness, he knelt beside her and began to coax the truth from her trembling lips.

"Darling, I'm sorry I thought the worst of you. Forgive me. I should trust in our union. Now you must trust me. Tell me the whole of it."

Power. She had it. It was hers. *Men! Stupid, foolish creatures!* Even now she loathed his touch, but she had to accept his kindness in order to be believed. Sheepishly, she said, "If…if I tell you, you won't think less of me? You will…still desire me?"

Quirinius lifted her face to his so that she could see the love he had for her. *It is love, isn't it? Desiring someone this much?* "I could never not want you."

Knowing that she had him right where she wanted, Dalena spun her web of deceit. "He was in the trees, waiting." She began to shake with anticipation at the outcome of her tale.

Quirinius thought she was shaking with fear. "Who was in the trees?"

"He approached me. I should have run, but he seemed harmless. He asked if I needed help, if he could help me. He came closer…" She broke into another sob. "Don't you see? I was foolish. Before I knew what was happening, he had torn the sash from my robe and… Oh, please! Please don't make me say what happened!" Crying, she fell prostrate to the floor.

Quirinius stroked her hair as he whispered, "But, darling, you must tell me who did this unspeakable thing."

She turned and looked up at him, attempting to keep a smile from her curling her lips. "The carpenter. It was the carpenter." Her cries were heard throughout the camp.

Chapter Five

Theo took his time returning to camp after Dalena stormed off. It wouldn't look good for both to return at the same time. He was sure she wouldn't give a second thought to parading through camp and waking Quirinius. It was the consequence of such an act with which she would have trouble dealing. He had to think for both of them. He needed a plausible reason for not being in his tent for most of the night. There was no way he could come clean with the truth.

Theo thought back to the grand city of Rome. Augustus had made sure that reform took place. The city was starting to thrive. Theo had enjoyed a brief reprieve from active combat while stationed there. Most of the men under him had teased him about his new position in service to Augustus. They joked that he would become soft—feasting on the food, wine, and women that would be at his beck and call in Rome. Even with all the luxuries, he had found himself tormented night after night. The countless faces of men he had met on the battlefield came back to him. Soldiers were taught to deal with the deaths of others as well as their own. Many of his friends had lost their lives in valiant efforts of bravery and sacrifice. His dreams seemed to rob the glory rightfully due to his fallen comrades.

It wasn't so much the number of men he had killed that bothered Theo. He was trained to kill men. It was the women and children. Wet with sweat, he would wake to the sounds of their cries seared in his mind. He couldn't dwell on that. It was his duty to help maintain civil obedience in Rome's provinces. Why couldn't those conquered see the benefits Rome brought to them? Rebellious people forced a soldier to have to do things no man should ever have to do.

Theo kicked a rock from his path and watched it roll away out of sight. It was as if he was watching his life roll away from him. He often wondered if other men suffered with the same affliction night after night. There was no way to find out. It would be considered a weakness; he might be stripped of the status he had worked hard to obtain in the Roman Army. Of course, after last night, preserving his life seemed more important than status.

If he was honest with himself, the dreams did make him weak. How else could he have been so vulnerable to the seductions of a woman? He unsheathed his sword and slashed out in frustration at a branch that had snagged his cloak. It was beyond him why he had been sent to protect the new proconsul of Syria. This was a wasteland, nothing but dirt, rocky hills, a few trees from which to find shade, and stiff-necked people. Quirinius had paid for the best of the Roman legion to accompany him to his new home and see to his protection. Evidently, Theo was one of the best.

The moment he had seen Dalena and the way she treated Quirinius (all the while watching every man to guarantee she had his attention) made Theo aware she might be trouble for him and his men. Dalena was the only woman in their entourage. He had given them all a stern warning to keep their eyes to themselves, as well as their hands. It would be a long while before they could partake in the sweetness of a woman's touch. Until such a time, they were to keep to the duty at hand. In a moment's time, he had succumbed. Now, he would have to live with the consequences. Even if no one ever learned the truth about the night before, he would know—another guilt to add to the already long list that plagued him.

Even though he was still a good distance away from camp, he could hear Dalena's cries. He wanted to run, not away but to her. He was just as much at fault as she had been. Granted, she had been very persuasive, but he had willingly partaken of the fruit she had so generously offered. His training as a soldier had taught him to be patient and survey the situation before making a decision. If only he had been prudent last night. He forced himself to continue at the same pace into camp.

He joined some of his comrades huddled in a circle and listened in on their conversation to see if he could find out what was happening. None knew the reason for the woman's cries, just that she had awakened the whole camp with them. Many fumed and vowed that, even when they had completed their service, they would never take a wife. Women were too much trouble. Theo grew impatient. He had to discover if Quirinius knew of their indiscretion and was hurting Dalena. Just as he was about to march into their tent, the cries hushed.

Theo waited. Perhaps it wasn't what he had thought. Maybe all would be fine. Dalena had a way with Quirinius and with him, too, evidently. However, he had to be sure. Theo realized that for the remainder of their journey, he would be nagged by the fear that Quirinius would find out the truth. Dalena had taken hold of him and was not about to let go. He waited to hear or see anything coming from the tent. After a few moments, Theo went back to his own shelter to rest. If no one came for him, if he heard nothing, all would be fine.

Quirinius held his wife while she wept, but he was getting annoyed. He wanted the carpenter killed, and the sooner, the better. He could not allow such an act of treason. It was an insult. He looked down at Dalena crumpled on the floor. Her words came back to him: "Will you still desire me?" *Would I?* Seeing her in this shape made him wonder. He knew when he married her that she had been with other men. He was no fool. Most modern women were exploring all their options when it came to love. He couldn't fault her for that. What stabbed at his pride was her ability, even desire, to attract all manner of men to her. She wasn't content with just his affection; she wanted to feel the touch of every man in the room. Not wanting to be near her, he released his hold on his wife and motioned for her maid to come.

FAVORED

Leaning over Dalena so only she could hear, he gave her strict orders, "You need to see to your appearance. When I send for the Hebrew, I don't want the men to see you in such a state." He reached for her white *sola* with the blue *palos*. "Wear this. It might actually make you appear decent. Do something with your complexion as well. You look haggard." He turned to the maid. "Put her hair up, but don't make it look too ornate, no matter what she says." With that, he left the tent.

Dalena pulled herself up off the floor. A small part of her was hurt by Quirinius' strict instructions concerning her toilette. The man cared little for her. His words gave away his true feelings. She was just one of the many things he needed to maintain his position with Rome. Any husband would have stayed with his wife if she had been traumatized as Dalena said she had been. But she wasn't truly traumatized. Quirinius didn't know that. *Does he know it's a lie?* It was obvious he cared more about retribution than her needs.

She watched as her maid braided and then began to pin her hair up. "Put pearls in as well."

"But, my lady, your husband—"

"My husband knows nothing. Do as I say, or I'll have you beaten."

Dalena noticed how her maid's hands trembled as she wound the pearls into her braids. She could not allow Quirinius to think he could control her. She even momentarily debated wearing a different outfit than the one he had instructed her to wear. Yet some of what he had said made sense. She did need to maintain, for a time, an aura of having been abused. However, she wanted to look her best when Theo returned. She took some lilac oil and rubbed it onto her skin. She wanted to entice all of Theo's senses. She hoped that when he recognized the control she had over her husband, he would be willing to continue their affair. She took one last look at herself. *Perfect.* Dalena went to the table and poured herself some wine. All she had to do was wait for Theo to return with the carpenter, and the plan would be complete. She giggled in anticipation.

Quirinius walked in on Theo as he rested. "I should have you beaten."

His heart pounding in his chest, Theo brought himself to a standing position before the governor. He would not show fear or any sign of knowledge as to why Quirinius would say such a thing. "I apologize if I have done something to offend you." He bowed in respect.

"You've done more than offend. You have neglected your duties to me and my wife."

Theo was stunned.

"Seeing how you have pleased me in service thus far, I will not report any of this to your superiors. For now, you will return to Nazareth and bring the carpenter back to me." Quirinius departed after delivering his orders.

Theo couldn't believe what he had just heard. Could Dalena's tears and Quirinius' anger simply be about something the carpenter did or did not do correctly? Theo thought through the whole conversation as he attached his *cingulum* and *brassards*. He made sure he had his short sword in its sheath before stepping out.

He could not help but be proud of all he had accomplished in the last seven years in service to Rome. Perhaps secrets could be kept between two people. Taking three other men with him, Theo headed north toward Nazareth. He looked up at the sun. It had already crossed the sky, meaning it was past the noon hour. It would be dark before they returned to camp with the carpenter.

Chapter Six

In the early morning light of dawn, Joachim reached over and tenderly kissed Anna on her cheek. She stirred at his affection. Opening her eyes to meet his, she smiled at him and touched his face. Joachim silently prayed as he took his wife in his arms. *I love her endlessly, God.*

They lay in silence for a time. Then, Joachim spoke, "I have business to attend with Joseph, Jacob's son. You know who I speak of?" Anna nodded. "You realize we have a responsibility to Mary, to see to her future. I know you are afraid, but you must trust me. You do trust me, don't you, Anna?" He asked the question with such gentleness that Anna could not help but nod in affirmation.

Joachim slipped from their bed and donned his tunic. He placed the *tallis* on his head and went to the roof for morning prayers. After some time, he came back down to the kitchen and kissed his wife goodbye. As he opened the front door to leave, he glanced over at Mary, still sleeping. She was precious to him. *Will another find her just as special?* He did not linger on the thought. He had to do what God was calling him to do. He felt the touch of his wife and paused.

"I'm letting her sleep," she said, tilting her head toward Mary. "She seemed to not have rested well last night."

Joachim nodded and quietly closed the door behind him. She would need her rest to receive the news he hoped to bring her.

He walked toward the carpenter's shop. Joachim was already beginning to perspire from the heat, and it was still early. He paused for a moment. As of late, he had difficulty walking distances without having to stop and catch his breath. He was

FAVORED

getting old. He rubbed at the soreness in his arm. As he continued on, his mind turned to all the friends he had lost to death or captivity in recent years. He often wondered why he had been spared. Miriam had said, "God has a plan for all His children. Captivity or death was not part of His plan for you, Joachim."

He sighed as he reached the threshold of Joseph's shop. He could hear the steady rhythm of the hammer. *Has Joseph even noticed my daughter? He seems to live in his own world. Are You sure, God?* Joachim threw the prayer up to God one last time. Peace came over him like a flood. He knew the answer. Thinking, he stroked his gray beard—he wasn't sure how to approach the man. *Should I just make small talk as we have before, or should I get right to the point?* Not sure how to get Joseph's attention, he coughed.

Joseph jumped at the sound. Looking up, he was surprised to see Joachim at his door. "Can I be of service to you, sir?" He extended his arm in a friendly greeting.

"I wondered if you could spare a moment for an old man."

"Of course. Any friend of my father is welcome. You look as if you could use a drink. I have some watered wine."

Joseph was courteous, and there was kindness in his warm, brown eyes. Joachim felt encouraged. "Sounds fine." He followed Joseph into his home. It took a minute for Joachim's eyes to adjust to the dimly lit room. It was neat and well-kept. He watched as Joseph poured two cups and motioned for Joachim to sit. He sat in the nearest chair, and Joseph took the opposite seat. Joachim noticed the family rod in the corner behind Joseph. *Has he given any thought to marriage since Hannah?* Joachim couldn't help but wonder. No one in the small town had ever been told what happened between the two of them. Joachim figured it was none of his business, so he had never attempted to find out. He lifted the drink to his lips. It was cool and refreshing.

Take courage in God.

Joseph watched as Joachim nodded as if talking to someone. He wondered what the old man might want. Typically, if people needed a job done, they just said so. Many of his father's friends came by to chat about one thing or another, but this seemed much more important than a job or chat. Joseph waited respectfully for Joachim to speak.

Finally, the older man cleared his throat and began. "I'm not sure if you are aware that my wife and I have a daughter." Joachim watched as a shadow fell across Joseph's face. He silently prayed as he took another sip. *Am I making a fool of myself here, God? Did I hear You correctly?* Joseph did not respond, so Joachim continued, "I'm not sure if you've noticed Mary around town." He waited for a response. None came. "She is coming of age for marriage, and seeing how you must know several families, I thought you might advise me." Relief seemed to flood over Joseph's face, but then it was replaced by something else. Joachim wasn't sure what emotion it was.

Joseph didn't understand what the man wanted from him. First, he had thought Joachim was going to offer the hand of his daughter. Then, Joachim had totally caught him off-guard with his last inquiry. *How am I to answer this?* He certainly could not tell Joachim that he had noticed Mary. He might consider it an insult. But he had noticed her. She was the only girl who had caught his eye in a long time. The memory of yesterday came back to him. Seeing the Roman woman who had aroused a feeling in Joseph he had thought died. *Are You trying to tell me something, God?* Joseph prayed while he waited to see if the older man would say anything else. The silence was making him uncomfortable.

Joachim waited. *I have to know if he is ready, God.* Finally, he stood and walked behind where Joseph sat. He picked up the rod and ran his hands over its etched surface. "Your father spoke often of your lineage, son. He was very proud of you and the way you were following in his footsteps. He had hoped to see you wed and with children before he passed."

FAVORED

Joseph could not remember the last time someone had called him son. He felt comfort in that word. However, as Joachim continued, Joseph felt pangs of guilt. He knew where Joachim was heading with this topic. He gulped the remainder of his wine. He did not want to be rude to his father's old friend, but he would not listen to much more should the conversation stay on its current course.

Joachim sensed the young man's tension. *I must know.* He pressed further, "Have you given thought to the idea? I would hate for the last name on the staff to be yours." He laid the staff on the table in front of Joseph. "There is no greater joy in this world than holding one's own offspring." Joachim returned to his seat.

Joseph sat in silence. He had heard his father say similar things. Sadness seemed to engulf him. He knew Joachim spoke the truth. *How can I make him understand?* The wounds from Hannah were still too fresh. Or were they? It had been over ten years.

"I do not know what happened between you and Hannah. Your father never spoke of it. I do know that many men have been hurt by love. I've been fortunate. Anna and I are very much in love. I can see pain in your eyes, Joseph. God has been good to you, no matter what may have happened. He has protected you in ways you probably don't even realize." Joseph's mind flashed back to yesterday, and he nodded. "Good," Joachim said. "Then you must know God causes nothing to happen that is not for our good."

"How can being left alone with no family be for my good?" The bitter tone in Joseph's voice was not lost on Joachim.

"You are not the boy you were ten years ago. You are a man. I've watched how you handle yourself. You are honest and fair in your business practices. You deal kindly with your neighbors, and you are not given over to rage or hasty decisions. Can you say that is who you were when you were betrothed to Hannah?"

The question stunned Joseph. He had not thought of those

things before. Of course, he would have to answer no. He had been young and immature when he found his life turned upside down so long ago. Was immaturity causing him to hold onto the past like a shield, guarding him from his future?

Joachim did not wait for him to answer but continued probing. "You are a better man for all that you have been through. You have matured. There is a lot you could offer a young woman." He watched the young man take in all he was saying.

Joseph wondered how this man could know his thoughts. *Did I hear from You last night, God? Is it time?* Joseph prayed fervently for God to answer.

Instead, he heard Joachim say, "Don't you think it's time?"

The words rushed over Joseph. *It is time.* He nodded as he looked into the eyes of the man in front of him. What he saw was a fatherly concern. Joachim held no hidden motives. The man had simply spoken the truth. The truth seemed to pull down the very walls Joseph had built around himself.

He glanced down at the staff in front of him. In that moment he knew what was required of him. He also knew that if Joachim were to offer his daughter, he would accept. However, he would not allow Joachim to leave without knowing the reason for his agreeing to such a proposal.

Joachim watched the tension leave Joseph. *He is ready.* He cleared his throat. "May I have some more wine?" He watched Joseph replenish his cup. The man was built strong. He had the same ruddy complexion that ran through his family line for many generations. He would make a good provider and protector. After Joseph filled his one cup and seated himself, Joachim asked again, "Have you noticed my daughter, Mary?"

It was a simple question. Joseph knew he had to be honest. "I have."

"Good." Joachim seemed pleased. "Then you have seen what a beautiful woman she has become."

FAVORED

"I have."

"I can assure you she is beautiful on the inside too. There is a gentleness about her that I have not seen in most her age. She completes her duties with confidence and is not given to fancy. She would make a very good wife."

Joseph wasn't sure what his response should be. He had noticed the girl. He had caught a glimpse into her dark eyes one afternoon after several of the boys had turned over Silas' cart for the hundredth time. At first, Mary laughed. Then, seeing the man's desperation, she knelt down to help pick up his wares. Joseph joined in the act of kindness, and when they both reached for the same piece of fruit, their eyes locked. She had the warmest complexion that seemed to glow from something deep within her. Even after she had left, he had remained in the street, breathing the scent of her that lingered on the breeze. Reason began to take hold of Joseph. "She is very young. Thirteen? Maybe fourteen?"

"That is why she needs someone to depend on. I'm not going to sit here and try to fool you, son. Mary is a wonderful girl. But there are times she is just that—a girl. She needs a man's direction and guidance, a man who will see potential in her. A man who will protect and provide for her."

Joseph noted that he did not mention the word love.

"I can tell you that she is ready to fulfill her wifely duties. She can cook and sew. She has been taught the ways of gardening in harsh soil. She also has great faith in God. She has not given her mother or I any cause for shame. The moment Mary was born, Anna and I felt favored by God. I guarantee that any man who would have her for his wife would feel favored as well."

Joachim has said all he was going to say. It was now Joseph's turn to speak, and he was hesitant. How could he tell a father, who obviously loved his daughter very much, that he didn't know if he was capable of loving? Joseph looked intently in the old man's eyes. "From all you have said, I hear the love you feel for your daughter. I've not taken a wife these past ten years because I do not feel I could love someone again." Joachim nodded in understanding. "I must confess to you that lately, I have considered the same things you spoke of earlier. Recently, I made the decision to take a wife." *If Joachim only knew how recently.* Joseph smiled at the thought. "You need to know that I'm only taking a wife with the intention to keep my family line flowing for generations to come. I would protect and provide for a wife and family until breath leaves my body. But that is all I can promise at this time."

Joachim nodded, a grin spreading across his face. "Then you would consider my daughter, Mary, to be your wife?"

"I have already considered her and find her most likely to be the one."

"We have an agreement then? Can the betrothal be announced next week?"

"We do."

Joachim stood as Joseph made his way to stand in front of the man. Joseph saw peace in the old man's eyes. To Joseph's surprise, Joachim reached out and hugged him. "Don't look shocked. You are about to be family," Joachim said with a laugh.

Joseph led the old man to the door. "I will inform my family of what all transpired here today. I know God has His hand on both you and my daughter." He watched as Joachim, humming, headed up the street.

He couldn't help but smile as he turned toward his shop. For the first time in a long time, Joseph felt at peace. He had made the right decision. Joachim accepted all he said. There would be no expectations of love. Mary would know what she was getting in the way of a husband: a provider and protector. Nothing more.

Joseph returned to his work. *Will taking her as a wife ease the guilt and pain?* "I can't expect that of her," he said out loud, answering himself.

"Can't expect what of whom?"

He had not realized he wasn't alone until the Roman soldier repeated his sentiment to him. "What do you want?" Joseph demanded, turning to fully face the Roman.

"Now, now, carpenter. There is no reason to get testy. The governor is requesting that you join him this evening."

"For what purpose?" Joseph felt an uneasiness come upon him.

"I'm not quite sure. He didn't say. All he said was to bring you to him, and that's what I intend to do." Theo liked the man. Joseph had willingly gone with him the first time, and there had not been problems. He had spoken honestly with Quirinius and Dalena concerning his ability to fix the table. He had not led them to believe that he could do the impossible, and he had done the work without asking for payment of any kind. Additionally, he had withstood the advances of a seductress. That was more than Theo could say for himself.

"Look, carpenter, I'm not sure why you have been summoned. Knowing Dalena, she probably misunderstood your ability to fix the table back to its original state. I'm sure you will just need to explain again what you did, after which you can be on your way."

Joseph wasn't so sure. He knew, however, he didn't have a choice. He grabbed the tools he thought he might need and followed Theo out of the shop. Glancing at the sky, he knew the day would be over soon. The walk might do him good. He could use the time to think on all that had transpired.

One thought that had begun to nag at Joseph concerned Mary. Did she know what her father was up to? Or would this announcement shock her? Had she even noticed him?

The *sicarii* waited patiently for his prey to return. Earlier that afternoon, he had spotted the four Roman guards as they marched toward Nazareth. He had hidden himself behind the largest boulder that lay nearest the road. The wait gave him time to perfect his plan and think.

The sun beat down on the young man. As the afternoon waned on, beads of sweat began to trickle down his forehead. The combination of heat and sorrow caused a mirage of images to appear before him.

He reflected on the image of his father rocking his baby brother while his mother taught his sister how to bake the bread for Sabbath. He listened as his mind brought back the sound of his father's voice, instructing him on how to manage the flock so not one lamb would be lost.

He recalled the family trek to Jerusalem for Passover. What a time the five of them had in Jerusalem! The city swelled with throngs of people that entered her gates. The pleasant images were cut short as, once again, the young man relived the horror of their first night after Passover.

His father had chosen a secluded area for the family to rest, a place that provided shelter from the approaching storm. However, nothing could protect them from the storm of the Roman Army that overran their camp.

When the soldiers came upon them, he had fled and hidden in the rocks above. His father was stabbed numerous times. His brother was taken from his mother's arms and smashed against the rocks. As he had done that night, he covered his ears trying to muffle the sound of his sister's screams as the men raped and tortured her. Upon seeing the death of her husband and children, his mother had thrown herself upon the fire, which earlier had been a source of comfort. The stench of burning flesh was forever seared into his nostrils.

In the past five years, guilt from being the sole survivor crippled him and drove him to kill. He waited. From his rocky vantage point, he could see the men approach. Now there were five men. A Hebrew walked in the center, flanked on all sides by

FAVORED

the four Romans.

He figured he only had a few more moments left on this earth, but he also knew that he could kill at least one, maybe two, Romans before they killed him. Perhaps he would be the salvation his Hebrew brother needed. The young man's heart beat in time with each step that brought the men closer to him. He got down on his belly and inched his way closer to the road. He was taking aim at the *centurion* in the front. One, two, three more steps—his heart pounded out the count.

He jumped from his hiding place. Raising the knife, he ran toward the blond Roman. The sun's rays bounced off the blade of his knife, streaking the area with reflective light. To him, it was as if the glory of Jehovah had come upon him, blessing his deadly action.

Out of the corner of his eye, Joseph saw something silver glisten in the sun—moving rapidly toward them.

"Look out!" He pushed Theo out of the way of the blade that came within inches of stabbing him. Joseph grabbed the man's arm, trying to free the knife from his hand. Before Joseph realized what was happening, the man slumped in his arms. Blood began to ooze from the stranger's side and onto Joseph. In shock, Joseph released his hold on him and dropped the blood-soaked knife from his hand. Now, he knew what it felt like to kill a man. Joseph looked up to see three swords pointing directly at him.

"Relax. The carpenter was not involved. If he was, he would have not saved my life," Theo said, standing. "Thank you."

Joseph didn't know what to say. He looked back at the man on the ground. He was a Hebrew. Joseph had just saved a Roman rather than one of his own people. Guilt crept into his soul.

"We need to keep moving," Theo said.

Joseph couldn't bring himself to leave the man alone on the road. "We can't just leave him there."

Theo looked at Joseph. He saw the same guilt he had felt

many times. He took pity on the Hebrew. "Because you saved my life…" He motioned for two of the men to drag the man off the road. "Bury him, then catch up with us." The two nodded and began the task.

"Will that suffice?" Theo started walking without even waiting for a response. He knew he could not take away the guilt Joseph felt, but perhaps he could help ease it.

Joseph followed without saying a word. *God, God, what have I done?* He could never tell anyone of the incident on the road. No one would understand that he had acted instinctively. They would scorn him and Mary. *Mary. What would she think?* Joseph wasn't used to caring about what others thought of him. Now, not only did he have to consider his own reputation but that of his wife-to-be and her thoughts of him. Consumed in his own thoughts, Joseph did not realize that the other two soldiers had rejoined the group and they were nearing the camp. It wasn't until Theo told them to wait that Joseph focused his mind on the task at hand.

Just like before, Theo disappeared inside the tent only to reappear in a matter of moments. It disturbed Theo to find Quirinius still upset. Dalena seemed to not even notice her husband's sour disposition. She really didn't even seem to notice him. She had briefly glanced up and smiled. Nothing unusual about it. Theo led Joseph inside.

"Here is the man you requested, Governor."

Theo watched as Quirinius walked up to Joseph. He stared at him for a moment, his eyes becoming little slits in his head. Without a word, Quirinius hit Joseph so hard that he made him fall.

"How dare you rape my wife!"

Theo, stunned at what had just happened, didn't move. Out of the corner of his eye, he saw Dalena smile.

Chapter Seven

Mary woke to the sounds of her mother kneading bread. First, she would hear the pound of her mother's fist flattening out the dough on the sideboard. Then her mother would pick up the dough and toss it into the air, letting it land upside down in front of her. She'd roll one side against the other, and the whole process would start all over again. The light coming through the window above gave a halo effect around her mother's head. She looked beautiful. There were streaks of gray around her temples, and Mary had noticed small lines around the corners of her mother's mouth and eyes. In small ways, her parents' age was surfacing. It frightened Mary. They had been older when she was born; consequently, Mary was an only child. The thoughts of losing one or both of her parents scared her. She didn't want to be alone.

Her thoughts turned to the front door as Joachim entered the home, humming and clapping. Mary sat up and laughed as he scooped her mother up in his arms and danced her around the table. There was love in their eyes when they looked at each other. Mary wondered if they had always felt that way for one another.

After one last twirl around the room, Joachim plopped a breathless Anna into the nearest chair. Anna tried to resist being forced to sit, but Joachim held up his hand for silence. This meant he was about to make an announcement.

Whatever he was up to had certainly brought great joy for him to enter the house in such a manner. Mary didn't know if she should stay put on her mat or join them around the family table, so she waited until her father spoke. He always cleared his throat twice before speaking as if doing so made him appear more authoritarian.

FAVORED

"Mary, child, come sit with us, for the matter we are to discuss will be of some importance to you."

Her father had clasped both hands behind his back and was rocking on his heels with excitement. Mary was so caught up by his enthusiasm that she had not noticed the look on her mother's face. If she had seen this sullen expression, she would have known what her father was about to say. Instead, her mind was a blur of all the possibilities. *Maybe someone is coming to visit! Or, perhaps, do I dare hope Papa is planning to travel to Jerusalem for Passover, bringing Mother and me along?*

He was so thrilled at the thought of what he was about to share that it seemed he would bust out of his tunic. Mary laughed as she took her place at the table. "Papa, I believe your excitement is contagious! I can't wait to hear this news!"

"Now, now, there is time for that. I've prepared a speech for such a monumental moment as this, and I would like to complete it without interruption if you ladies do not mind." He winked at Mary.

Anna knew what was coming. She had realized that one day their beloved daughter would leave their home to start a family of her own. It's what she had been preparing Mary for, teaching her how to cook and sew and perform many other duties that would make her a suitable helpmate. Yet, she was still young. *Why does Joachim feel the need to push her out the door at such a tender age?* She thought she might choke on the resentment she was starting to feel toward her husband. Not even two years had passed since Miriam's death, and now he was planning to take Mary away from her as well. *Why?*

Anna had realized some time ago that she did not share the same faith that Miriam had. She believed in the God of her forefathers: the God of Abraham, Isaac, and Jacob. She did her best to follow the letter of the law. She was a good woman. However, Miriam had inner peace and joy that Anna had not grasped. She assumed those came with age and wisdom. Now, though, she was older and only felt more anxious and fearful. She had come to realize faith did not develop with age.

Anna recalled the many nights she had lain awake, listening to Miriam discuss things of God with Mary. They would talk and pray together. There was a special bond between the two of them that caused Anna to feel pangs of jealousy in her heart. Miriam had said the same words to her when she was a child. With Anna, the words were just that: words. Anna had faith and trusted in Miriam. Joachim was her provider and protector, and Mary, her constant companion. Those were the people whose touch she could feel. She could speak to them, and they would answer her. She believed in what she could see. "People will fail you, Anna, but God is ever constant," Miriam had said to her long ago when Anna had questioned why God had taken her mother from this earth before Anna even knew what a mother was—leaving a hole in Anna's heart.

Miriam had encouraged her to pray and ask God to "give her a child or change the desires of her heart." She needed only to trust in His perfect will for her. With each passing month that her courses continued to flow, bitterness had grown. Watching the women around her deliver child after child had only strengthened the pain of being barren. Then, it happened. God answered her prayers. She was with child, but He had waited too long. She'd known Mary would be her firstborn and her last. Mary had become her life. She knew it was wrong to heave her emotional needs upon a child, but Anna couldn't help it. She hated the thought of losing the people around her and being left alone. It terrified her.

God had not saved her mother. God had not answered her prayers in a timely fashion. Now God was allowing Joachim, her husband, to strip her only child from her arms. It was more than she could bear. She had to fight the tears that were welling up in her eyes and force the sorrow deep into the recesses of her soul. She wanted to scream that this was not what she wanted, but the words seemed stuck in her throat.

She had to think of Mary and what was best for her. Anna and Joachim would not live forever. Mary needed to be taken care of, provided for. Joachim was right in what he was doing for their daughter. It just seemed to be happening too quickly. It took all her will to force herself to focus on what Joachim was saying. She realized he was kneeling in front of Mary, clasping her hands in his.

"With that being said…" Anna realized she had missed the majority of her husband's speech. She would never know the beautiful admonitions and praises Joachim had spoken to their precious daughter.

As Joachim began his announcement, Mary eagerly anticipated what her father might say, but with each word he spoke, a sickening dread rose up in her. She did not want to hear this announcement after all. Even before he drew breath to continue, she knew what path her father was going to take. It was not a path she wanted to walk, at least not yet. *Didn't you hear my prayers, God? I had faith. Faith to believe You would answer. You told me to trust You. Please, please don't let this be happening.*

My will or yours, beloved?

The question, like a runaway cart, slammed into Mary. She recalled the many times Miriam had prayed, saying, "It must be done Your way, not mine." The words began to take shape in her head. She had considered the prayer to be one of an old woman who did not know exactly what she wanted and, therefore, left all in the hands of the Almighty. The thought had crossed Mary's mind that Miriam prayed such a prayer because she did not want to be disappointed.

In some ways this was true, but not in the way Mary had thought. The mystery behind Miriam's prayer seemed to unravel itself as Mary sat before her father. Praying "Your will" and not her own was an act of surrender. Her mind flashed back to a time when she and Miriam had been planting seeds in their little garden.

"Grandma, will these seeds grow into plants soon?"

"It will take time, but everything grows, and when the time is right, these seeds will grow into beautiful plants."

"Just like me. You tell me every day that I'm growing."

Miriam reached out and patted Mary's head. "Indeed, you are. I think you are taller today than yesterday."

"Grandma, you look hot. Can I get you some water?"

"Yes, child. Bring water for the seeds too."

Mary hurried back with the water.

"You see, child, we nourish the seeds with water, and God feeds them with the sun. That is how they grow. God does the same with us."

"He uses water and the sun to help me grow?"

Miriam laughed. "Not exactly. You grow on the outside from the food you eat and the rest you get. But God wants us to grow on the inside too. He nourishes our souls through the words of the prophets and by teaching us to trust in Him. He wants us to be dependent on Him, totally surrendered to Him. Like these seeds are surrendered to the task of becoming plants, we need to be surrendered to what God wants for us."

"Is that why you pray 'Your way and not mine'?"

"Exactly. God does not want us just to go through the rituals of repentance. He wants our whole bodies—heart and soul. That is why King David was blessed by God. He gave all his desires, hopes, and dreams to God. Even when he knew he was Israel's rightful king, he waited upon God. When Saul tried to take his life more times than he could count, he trusted God. Yes, David disobeyed several of God's commandments: deceit, lust, adultery, even murder. But God said David was a man after His own heart because he sought repentance and salvation from Him. Despite reaping the consequences of his sin, David took refuge in God. During his life, he allowed God to nurture and grow him, like these seeds allow us to nurture them."

"I don't know that I understand, Grandma, but I want to."

"I know, little one. In time it will all be revealed to you."

Praying, "Not my will, but Yours," was not an act of cowardice; it was the most compelling statement of bravery. In that simple statement, Miriam, like many before her, was surrendering her life—what she did not know, what she could not see—into the hands of the Almighty. She trusted, even knew, that God had only His best in store for her and those she loved. This was surrender. This was faith. This was the cause of Miriam's peace, her joy, the reason she loved without expecting anything in return. She was receiving all this from her heavenly Father.

Mary felt a tear fall onto her hand. She had not even realized she was crying. It was as if her thoughts had taken away her sense of feeling. She didn't have any recollection of her father kneeling before her and taking her hands in his. Her thoughts must have numbed her mind as well.

"With that being said…." Mary had missed most of what her father had said to her. She chided herself for not paying attention. This was the most important moment in her life thus far, and it eluded her. She could never ask her father to repeat what he had said, for it would hurt his feelings to know she had not paid attention. Plus, her mother would scold her for not being as attentive as she had been. The moment was gone, lost in the sea of countless other moments. She forced herself to listen despite the torrent of emotion that swirled inside her.

Joachim didn't know why he always felt the need to clear his throat before he began an announcement. It made him nervous to stand in front of the two most important people in his life. He was so nervous that he found himself rocking back and forth on his heels. The decisions he made concerning family affairs, at times, affected them in monumental ways. This was one such time. He had come into his marriage feeling the heavy weight of responsibility on his shoulders. For the first time, he had another person to take care of. He and Anna had been very young when they married. Just when he thought he had managed to become a good husband to Anna, Mary had been born. Then he had to learn to be a father as well. It wasn't hard. Whatever part of his heart that did not belong to Anna Mary had stolen the moment he laid eyes on her. Now, he was calling her over to tell her he was relinquishing the responsibility of taking care of her to another man. He felt the sting of a tear, but he pushed the emotion down. He had to be strong. Two women, dearer to him than his own life, were depending on him.

He knew Anna would feel he was ripping apart her very soul, and Mary would assume he didn't understand her feelings. What he said in the next few moments would bring peace and contentment or cause a rift in their family. Life was too short and precious to allow that to happen. How could he help them understand and trust that he sensed God speaking to his heart, telling him it was time? He had to choose his words carefully. He felt his throat go dry. He needed water, but the eyes of both women were upon him, so, clearing his throat one more time, he began the speech he had been diving in his head since his meeting with Joseph. *Help me, God.*

"Mary, child, come sit with us, for the matter we are to discuss will be of some importance to you." Hearing her laugh as she crossed the short distance between her sleeping mat and the table made him painfully aware that she had no idea what he was going to say. Fearing his emotions would get away from him, he simply winked at her.

FAVORED

"It has not been lost on your mother and me how much you have grown in the last year. You have taken it upon yourself to do many of the household duties, performing them with an attitude of submission, grace, and love. You have proven your maturity. Your outward beauty is only surpassed by the joy and peace that radiate from your face. Watching you grow into a lovely young woman has been a joy for me. No father could ever feel as much pride for his own daughter as I have for you. You were a gift from God to us, and you continue to be a blessing to all who know you. On the day of your birth, Miriam admonished me to not betroth you as an infant as it is customary. She gave me several logical reasons for such a decision. Times were hard. Rome was stripping away our people, forcing many families to wait to pick marriage partners for their children. It would be prudent to wait and see who survived and proved himself worthy of such a prize as our daughter. Later, Miriam admitted that she had heard from God that waiting is what God would have me do. 'God has a plan for Mary. Mary is going to need someone very special. Allow God to choose the man. Wait on His timing.' Thus, I waited. Today, I kneel before you to tell you that I, too, have heard from God. I have seen your faith, Mary. You and your mother must trust that the same God who speaks to your heart has spoken to mine."

Seeing Mary's tears, Joachim took both her hands in his. He knew what he was saying was hard to hear. It was a life-changing event for all of them. Taking a moment to catch his breath, Joachim continued.

"With that being said, I've spent several months praying to the Almighty to give me wisdom. I wanted God to show me the man He had chosen for you as Miriam had said God would do. I was just as shocked, as I'm sure you will be, at whose name God impressed upon me. I questioned and debated with God. But, in the end, I knew I heard Him correctly. So I sought out the man, and only minutes ago, we made an agreement.

"My heart delights to know that when your mother and I leave this earth, you will be well taken care of. This man is honest and full of integrity. He has proven himself wise and prudent, not hasty, in dealing with affairs. He will respect, honor, and protect you all the days of your lives together. He has given his word on that. In a week's time, your betrothal to Joseph, Jacob's—God rest his soul—youngest son, will be announced."

With that, he lightly kissed Mary on her cheek. Releasing her hands, he stood and went to her mother, kissing her as well. Then he quietly opened the front door and slipped out of the house, leaving the two women in a heavy silence.

Mary didn't know what to think. Her mind seemed to be spinning. She had missed most of what her father had said during his speech, but she had heard every word regarding her betrothal. The words hammered into her head as a carpenter drives a nail. A carpenter. She was to be the wife of a carpenter. And not just any carpenter but Joseph—a man as old as Methuselah! Joachim said Miriam had told him that God would pick her husband. He said he had prayed for God's insight and wisdom. Well, she had prayed too. *Didn't God hear my prayers?*

Mary hid her face in her hands. She knew her father was doing what he thought best for her. The love in his eyes was evident. He wasn't being mean or spiteful or doing this to help himself. That wasn't who her papa was. Everything Joachim did, he did out of love for his family. *Why, God? Why?* It was all she could think to pray.

Anna, numbed by her own emotional turmoil, watched her daughter's body sag in despair. She knew Mary needed her comfort. Mary needed her mother to say that all would be well, that marriage was wonderful. It had been for her and Joachim, but some couples were not as lucky as they had been. *Will Mary find happiness with Joseph?* Her husband certainly thought so. Mary needed Anna to tell her that she thought so too. But Anna couldn't move. Her world was falling apart around her, and there was not one thing she could do to stop it.

FAVORED

They sat in silence, neither of them moving.

After what seemed like hours, Anna's maternal instinct moved her, as well as the crutch she used for self-preservation: bitterness. Joachim may have made the arrangement, but God had caused him to do it. Joachim even said so. Once again, God was stealing what rightfully belonged to her. However, Mary needed her assurance. It was time she taught Mary how to be a wife, what it meant to love. They only had a year.

Sadness engulfed Anna as she went to her daughter. Wrapping both arms around her beloved child, Anna gently stroked her hair while whispering, over and over into Mary's ear, "It will be all right. You will see. All will be well." She wasn't sure if she was trying to convince herself or her daughter. She just knew it was what Mary needed to hear.

Mary buried her face in her mother's tunic. Her body heaved with every sob.

Chapter Eight

Dalena watched the scene unfolding before her. She tried, to no avail, to keep the smile from her lips. Watching Quirinius hit the carpenter and seeing the look on Theo's face was more than she had hoped for. The action reminded her of a tragedy performed by a group of *hypocrites* she had seen in Rome. Now she had her own tragedy, one of her own making. She had not written a single line, yet the players were playing their part superbly. Little did the men know they were playing parts she had orchestrated. She wanted to clap, as she had done at the play whenever something wonderful happened. However, today she was a performer as well. She had to play her part with dignity.

Quirinius did not allow Joseph time to speak. He hit him hard in his side and stomach. The rage that had built up in him while waiting for Dalena to return unleashed itself on Joseph. He didn't care whether the man was innocent or guilty. He wanted his pride restored. Joseph was simply a means to an end.

Theo was unable to speak or move. Had he heard Quirinius correctly? When did this alleged assault happen? He had been with Dalena most of the night. He escorted the Hebrew a portion of the way home. Had the man turned back? Had he watched Theo and Dalena give into their lust? Theo found the carpenter in his shop, so there would have been no time. *No time.* The questions came one right after the other like waves crashing against the shore. Theo looked at Dalena. She was too calm. That was what finally drove him to action.

He tried verbally to halt Quirinius. Then he reached for the other man's arm, but Quirinius pulled away. Quirinius wasn't strong, but he was big. Theo finally had to step in front of him,

FAVORED

but Quirinius was like a madman. He continued to throw punches, hitting Theo in the jaw. In one swift move, Theo managed to outmaneuver the other man, rendering him helpless. Theo held Quirinius in a choke hold until he felt the portly man relax and his hostility begin to subside.

"Governor, give me your word that you will remain civilized so we can get to the bottom of this. Then I can release you." Theo relaxed his hold, allowing Quirinius to give a nod of affirmation. Only after he was sure Quirinius meant to keep the agreement did he release the man entirely.

Joseph lay perfectly still. Theo could see his chest heaving in and out, so he knew the carpenter was still alive. Theo bent down over Joseph, making sure he kept a close eye on Quirinius and Dalena. He had been taught how to assess a person's injuries, so he quickly checked Joseph's bones and abdomen.

It was painful to take a breath. Joseph felt as if all the air had been sucked out of him. Searing pain shot through his right shoulder, and the taste of blood was on his tongue. Quirinius' first blow was so hard that Joseph had missed what the man had said. "What is happening?" he struggled to ask. Even saying those two words brought excruciating pain.

"Try to stay still. I believe you have a couple of broken ribs, and your shoulder is dislocated. I'll try to get to the bottom of this." In the past two days, Theo's respect for the carpenter had turned to admiration. Joseph had risked his life to save Theo's just an hour ago. Theo felt obligated to do the same, at least to the point of discovering the truth. Theo was sure Joseph had not raped Dalena. The timing was off. Plus, Theo had watched as Joseph maintained distance and composure, steering clear of Dalena's flirtations while he worked on repairing the dressing table. Joseph could not have done such a deed.

Turning to Quirinius, Theo commanded, "Explain to me what this is all about."

In the time it had taken for Theo to check Joseph, Quirinius had poured himself some wine in order to steady his nerves. "I do not need to explain my actions to you."

"I think you do. On the way here, this man saved my life at the risk of his own. Before I watch you take his, I would like to know the reason."

"Very well. But I tell you this only so you will see that I have every right to kill this man. I was awake when my darling returned home this morning. Her robe was undone, and she was covered in leaves and grass. She was a mess. She told me that she had awakened in the middle of the night and needed some fresh air. She walked alone, thinking it safe, only to find this man waiting for her. He forced himself upon her."

Dalena enjoyed watching Theo. He had overpowered her husband and shown compassion to the Hebrew. Now he was realizing just how much power she possessed. He couldn't tell Quirinius the truth, for by doing so he could condemn himself. Yet, he obviously had grown fond of the carpenter. Theo was trapped. The look on his face was priceless to her. She was pleased with herself. As long as she maintained control, her life might very well be perfect. Theo was not as easily manipulated as Quirinius, but that was what made him more exciting. The hunt was what thrilled her, not the kill.

At Quirinius' words, Theo's blood ran cold. He turned to look at Dalena. She was deriving pure pleasure from all that she had seen and heard. She had set the action in motion. She didn't care who she hurt or even killed as long as it benefited her. The thought sickened him. He could not allow this to continue. Dalena needed to be thwarted, but how could he help the carpenter without crucifying himself? He might not be able to come clean with the whole truth, but perhaps he could show the impossibility of Joseph's committing such an act.

No one had noticed that Joseph, head held high, jaw set, was standing until he spoke, "I have done no wrong by you or your wife." The pain coursed through Joseph's body, making it difficult to breathe, let alone talk, but he would not lie down and take a false accusation.

Anger welled up in Quirinius at Joseph's words. "I am not opposed to having you killed or killing you myself." He lunged at Joseph only to be halted by Theo. Regaining some composure, he gave Joseph an order, "Only speak when spoken to."

Theo fixed his gaze on Quirinius. "Why don't we allow the man to speak? What harm will it do? If we cannot logically find the truth, then it is in your authority to have the man killed."

"Are you saying my wife is lying?" Quirinius' tone was more threatening than questioning.

"I'm not saying she is lying—perhaps just mistaken on who the man was. Just yesterday, upon completing his work, I personally escorted him to the far hill. I watched as he headed toward Nazareth. Then today, upon your orders, I walked with three other men back to Nazareth to bring the carpenter back here. We found him working in his shop. He did not question our arrival or presence. There was nothing suspicious about him. Both days, he came willingly. Today, he had the opportunity to escape when my men and I were attacked. Instead, he saved my life. I do not think a man summoned by the husband of the woman he is guilty of raping would act in such ways. It doesn't logically fit. The timeline is off, and his actions speak louder than his accuser's words." With that, he shot a look at Dalena that only she would be able to decipher.

For the first time since the whole scenario had begun, Dalena was taken aback. Theo was not going to allow her to punish the Hebrew for ignoring her yesterday. She was beginning to sense that her scheme might backfire. She was confident that Theo would not speak the truth; however, he didn't seem at all impressed with how she had manipulated her husband. The look he gave her spoke volumes. He despised her. *If he doesn't play the game according to my rules, then he won't be allowed to play.* Still, she could tell Quirinius was being swayed by Theo's argument. She had to do or say something before everything fell apart.

"Perhaps Theo has grown so fond of the carpenter that he cannot bear to see him put to the sword. His affection might be clouding his judgment."

Her accusation was like a blade that cut Theo to the bone. The woman was pure evil. He could not—would not—let her win. It seemed that Quirinius was all too willing to believe the lies that came from her mouth.

"Is this true, Theo? Have you lost reason concerning the Hebrew?"

Joseph couldn't believe what the woman had just accused the soldier of. He had never been so blatantly confronted with immorality.

"Your wife's accusation is absurd. I'm only trying to discover the truth. I've seen too much death to watch the innocent slain."

Joseph was impressed with Theo's stance and remark. The Roman held up well under pressure.

Dalena kept her voice calm and catlike, "If it's the truth you are after, dear Theo, why don't you explain your whereabouts last night? Someone should have been protecting my husband and I. Were you slack in your duties?"

Theo's face flushed hot with anger. She was taking this too far. "The tent was being well watched. Perhaps if you had not ventured out alone, none of this would be happening right now." He knew he had not kept the contempt from his voice, but the woman drove him mad.

"Enough!" Quirinius yelled. He would not be played the fool. He took hold of Dalena. "You have one chance and one chance only to tell the truth. Did the Hebrew rape you last night? Are you sure it was the carpenter?"

Dalena saw in her husband's eyes that he knew the truth. Theo had made too much sense. Quirinius might not know the

FAVORED

man she had been with, but he knew it was of her own choosing. She only had one recourse. Quirinius did not want to appear weak in front of the men. His pride was at stake. If she held to her original story, then Quirinius would know that he had killed an innocent man for her, and Theo would know that he had allowed the carpenter to die. She would be the victor.

"Darling, I have spoken the truth. It was the carpenter."

Quirinius released his hold. He knew she was lying. She had been with someone, not by force but of her own will. He did not know with whom, and in truth, he did not care. He just wanted the whole matter over with. "Kill him."

"I will not allow an innocent man to die for something I did." Theo's statement silenced the room.

Joseph couldn't believe that Theo was capable of such an act. He realized that he had come to respect the man. Dalena sunk to the couch. Quirinius could only glare at Theo, then back at Dalena. The truth was evident on both their faces.

"It is true that Dalena left your tent seeking air. The rest of what she told you is a lie."

"Please, Theo, you don't know what you're saying!" Dalena stood from the couch.

"Let the man speak." Quirinius took a sip of wine. Dalena fell back onto the couch.

"I found her crying in the trees. I wasn't sure what the trouble was. My first mistake was in trying to console your wife. She used my comfort against me. She is a very persuasive woman. I am not putting the sole blame on her, for I chose my own actions. I willingly accepted her touch and she mine. No one was forced to do anything they did not already want to do. Dalena was with me last night, in my arms, until dawn."

Now that the truth was out, Joseph sagged under the weight of his pain. Theo went to his side. "I'm sorry for the pain I have caused you. If I had known this morning why Quirinius summoned you, I would have spoken sooner." Joseph could barely nod in response. It had taken all his strength to remain standing for as long as he had. Weak and exhausted, he blacked out.

"A fine mess we have found ourselves in. What do I do with my unfaithful wife and her soldier?"

Theo winced at Quirinius' words. Never again did he want to be linked with that woman.

"I could kill you both right now and be blameless." Quirinius pulled Dalena to her feet. She was trembling. "What a waste." He clamped his mouth hard to hers.

Theo was sure the man had gone mad. Yet, there was one thing he had to do. "Governor, if I may be so bold as to make one request before I die, I would like to see the carpenter safely home and taken care of. Strip me of my rank and sword, put chains on me if you desire, send my own men to keep watch over me. Just allow me to see to this man's care."

Quirinius paused for a moment to consider Theo's request. "I'm not going to kill you. I have great respect for a man who would speak the truth with such boldness. I may even feel some gratitude, for you have shown me what kind of wife I truly have. I know what a temptation she can be." He released his hold on Dalena and pushed her toward the couch. She fell in a heap of fear and guilt to the floor. "I'm not even going to report you or strip you of your rank and sword. I have no fear anything else will happen between the two of you." His venomous words were sent to warn.

Quirinius slowly walked toward Theo. "I do have to punish you in some way, though." He paused as if debating his next course of action. Neither Dalena nor Theo had seen the small knife Quirinius had picked up off the table and now clutched in his hand. "A transfer would probably be in order, but I have enjoyed your company, and, minus this one indiscretion, you have proven yourself trustworthy. I'd like to keep you around. So what is to be done?" With those words he was right in Theo's face. Before

FAVORED

Theo could speak, Quirinius had lifted the knife to Theo's throat.

"No!" Dalena screamed and buried her face in the couch.

"It seems my wife still has an attraction to you. Maybe with this"—Quirinius dragged the knife across Theo's right and left cheeks—"she will not find you so appealing, nor will any other woman. When asked about your scars, if they were received on the battlefield, may you remember this moment, knowing that it was a woman who brought this upon you. You may do as you have requested unless you desire to tend to your own needs first." Quirinius then turned his attention to his wife.

Theo could feel the blood dripping down his face. There would be no way to ascertain the damage to his face until he had seen Joseph safely home. Knowing what Quirinius had done to him made him concerned for Dalena. The man was out for more than blood; he was out for revenge. However, Joseph could die if he was not aided soon. He knew the men would question his injuries, but he needed help for the carpenter. Theo walked out of the tent and enlisted the help of his two most trusted guards. He could feel blood starting to dry on his face. This assured him that the wounds were not deep. Theo knew the guards had noticed the cuts on his face, but they made no mention of them.

Upon returning to pick up Joseph, Theo spied Dalena still lying crumpled, crying, on the couch while Qurinius calmly drank a cup of wine. With the help of his men, he laid Joseph in a wagon and began the journey back to Nazareth.

Quirinius waited until Theo had removed the Hebrew before unleashing his full vengeance on his wife. "Your reprieve is over, darling. Time to accept your punishment like a big girl."

He pulled Dalena upright. Fear had so overtaken her that she could not stand on her own strength. She had seen what her husband had done to Theo. He was marked for life. Would he scar her in a similar way? Dalena's identity lay in her beauty. Her mother said she was favored by the gods with beauty. Would Quirinius take the one attribute the gods had gifted her?

"Now, darling, this is not the brazen woman I saw only moments ago. Have you come to realize what a powerful man your husband is? If not, I have ways to show you." Anger flooded Quirinius; his own power blinded him. He stripped Dalena of her clothes, knocking her to the ground. "Get up. I intend for you to know how a real man treats a woman."

Dalena thought she had experienced all the ways of men. She had not. Her father had left her feeling betrayed. Quirinius left her broken. Even when he was through with his lust of her, he was not through punishing her. Outwardly, he did not leave marks on her that would not heal. He wanted her to retain her beauty for only him. Quirinius used every opportunity to remind her of that fact.

Chapter Nine

Joachim could hear Mary sobbing on the other side of the door. He wanted to go to her but knew it would not be wise. He was afraid he would succumb to her tears and call the whole thing off. He had done what he believed was God's will. He had to stand firm in that. Leaning against the frame of the door, he wired and watched as the sun began to dip to the west, casting yellow-pink rays across the sky. It would be dark soon.

Joachim listened intently, trying to hear what was happening inside his home. The sound of movement reached his ears, but he heard no sounds of sadness. Joachim heaved a sigh of relief. He would need to set up a time for Mary and Joseph to get to know one another. Both were hurting, and whether they realized it or not, they were hurting for the same reason.

It would be hard to go through life without love. Joachim couldn't imagine what his life would have been like without Anna's love. Mary was young and had little understanding of the word. Joseph had been hurt and wanted to protect himself. Joachim felt that it was his responsibility to teach them how to love. He did not want them going into their marriage simply out of a sense of duty. He wanted more for his daughter. He wanted more for Joseph. *Give me time to help them, God*, he silently prayed.

The smell of bread made Joachim's stomach growl. He cracked the door open and peeked into the house. Anna was placing some cups on the table while Mary fixed a plate of fruit. They were acting as if nothing had happened. Joachim slipped in and took his seat at the table. Neither Mary nor Anna acknowledged him. Perhaps he had been too optimistic. Mother and child took their

FAVORED

places at the table. Joachim prayed for God's blessing. They ate in silence.

The silence was oppressive. After he finished his meal, he dismissed himself from the table and went up to the room. He paced back and forth while he prayed. Joachim didn't like knowing that he had hurt both his wife and daughter. "I was only doing what I felt You had called me to do, God. Will they understand? How can I feel excitement for what is to come when my wife and daughter are burdened so?"

The sky had gone from pink to deep blue, fading to black. Joachim felt tired, and his body ached from the day's activities. Looking at the night sky, Joachim began to understand Mary's feelings. "She must sense that her life is like this sky, vast and dark—the future bleak and unknown to her. She has great faith in You, God. Speak to her heart. Give her the peace she needs."

He wasn't sure how to pray for Anna. He knew she felt that God had robbed her of those she held most dear. "Help my wife to know, God, that You are eternal. Wrap Your loving arms around her and give her the security I cannot give." With those two prayers on his lips, Joachim headed back down into the house.

Mother and daughter had slipped into the other room. They sat on the bed, Anna cradling Mary in her arms. Mary's back was to Joachim, but it heaved in and out with every sob. Though she remained silent, he could see that tears were in Anna's eyes as well. He thought it best that he give them space. Though he was tired, Joachim decided it was a nice night for a walk. He picked up his walking stick and left the house quietly.

As he passed familiar homes of friends and neighbors, Joachim realized he was heading in the direction of Joseph's home. Perhaps he could rest there for a bit. Maybe Joseph should be told of Mary and Anna's reactions so he would not be surprised. He pondered the thought but wasn't sure he would actually tell the other man the truth. Ignorance could be to one's advantage. When he rounded the corner he caught sight of three soldiers opening the door to Joseph's home. Joachim quickened his pace just as the men began reaching into the wagon they had with them.

"What is going on here?" Joachim posed the question with great authority.

Theo did not look up before responding. "This man has seriously been hurt and needs attention. Quickly."

Joachim felt his heart drop. "Is it Joseph?"

"Yes. Do you know him? Are you family?"

Joachim leaned over to the wagon to see how serious the situation really was. Joseph's face was covered in blood. His shoulder was misshapen, and it was obvious he was having trouble breathing. "What happened? He was fine this morning." Joachim looked into Theo's eyes to discern the truth.

"I can explain later. Right now, we need to get him inside." Theo tried to lift Joseph without hurting him, but he groaned in pain, causing Theo to rethink his next step.

"Joseph has no one to take care of him here. Follow me. We'll take him to my house, where my wife and daughter can help tend his wounds." Joachim didn't wait for a response. He immediately headed back up the street from whence he had come. Theo had no choice but to follow him.

With every jostle, Joseph felt pain renew itself. He knew he was slipping in and out of consciousness. He didn't know where they were taking him. He had a vague recollection of all that had happened but couldn't put the pieces together. Somehow he felt indebted to Theo. He knew that they had stopped moving, but the reprieve was brief. He thought he heard a familiar voice, but only for a moment. Now they were moving faster, causing the pain in his chest and shoulder to mount to excruciating heights. He wanted to scream but had no voice, so he allowed himself to sleep once again into oblivion.

Joachim did not even feel the pain and breathlessness in his

FAVORED

own body as he hurried through the streets of Nazareth. He knew Anna would know what to do. *Let me help, God. Please, God, let the boy live. He's the one. I know he is the one for Mary.* Joachim burst through the front door of his home. Anna and Mary were still where he had left them.

Anna jumped at the sound of the front door slamming against the wall. Joachim motioned for her to join him. Anna had never seen her husband so out of breath. She waited for Joachim to tell her what he needed. The sound of wheels scraping cobblestone made her peer into the darkness to see a wagon and three Roman guards stopping in front of her house.

Fear gripped Anna. She wasn't sure what she should do. She looked to her husband for an answer, and Joachim waved her on out the door. She hesitated. Urgently, Joachim pounded his fist on the table, moving Anna to action. She stepped out timidly just as Theo and the other two men were lifting Joseph out of the wagon. Anna could hear the cries of pain from the victim but had no idea who he was or why Joachim had brought these men to their home.

"Where shall we lay him?" Theo asked as he passed her and stepped into the house.

Anna looked down at the man they were carrying. It was Joseph. "Through here" was all she managed to say as realization took hold of her. She led the men into the small room. "Try to settle him while I prepare some warm water and bandages." She turned from the room to see Mary kneeling before her father, offering him a cup of water. *Mary.* In a matter of seconds, she had forgotten all about her daughter. *What will Mary think of all this?* There was no time to think about that.

Joseph's moans were heard throughout the house. Anna quickly got to work. She overheard Joachim breathlessly tell Mary how he had come upon the scene. He attempted to explain his decision to bring the men to their home. Anna could barely make out most of what he said, save that he felt there was no other option. "Joseph doesn't have a family. None but us—that is it."

Like a bolt of lightning, the magnitude of the situation struck Anna. She knew she had a responsibility to help the man who would be her daughter's husband.

She entered the room and found Theo standing over Joseph. The other two guards stood against the far wall. Though she was intimidated by their presence, Anna bravely asked, "Did he do something wrong to deserve this beating?" She needed to know if Joseph was bringing trouble into their home.

"No. He took the beating in place of another." It was the only explanation Theo gave.

It wasn't until Theo looked up at Anna that she noticed the two wounds on either side of his face, now caked with blood and dust. "You need attention yourself."

"I'll be fine. I think he has a dislocated shoulder. See how misshapen his right arm is? We need to pop the shoulder back in. He'll rest more comfortably if we can do that. The problem is he's having a hard time breathing. He took a good beating on his chest and stomach. I'm guessing he has some cracked bones. I don't want to pull on the shoulder and put him in more distress. I'm not sure what we should do." Theo was almost pleading with the woman for an answer. The longer he spent time watching Joseph suffer, the more guilty he felt.

Anna heard the deep concern in the Roman's voice. She didn't understand its origin. Most Romans would have left an injured Jew on the side of the road. There was more to the story than Theo was willing to share. She was impressed with his knowledge concerning Joseph's injuries, though. It was obvious to her that he had experience in this area.

She began to clean the wounds on Joseph's face while checking the shoulder and his chest. "Well, the good news is we can help him. He has a gash on his forehead, minor cuts around his mouth, and a broken nose." Anna continued to wash and clean Joseph's face, making sure she rubbed salve to help with the healing on the deeper cuts. "The arm does need to be adjusted if it is to heal properly. We'll just have to take the chance. He uses his arms and hands to make a living." Anna looked to Theo. "Have you done this before?"

"Yes, once. On the battlefield. What about yourself?"

"No, but I watched my aunt help a boy with the same problem. He fell from a tree. Once we have repositioned the shoulder, we can use these linens to keep it immobile. You pull; I'll try to keep him still."

Theo took note of how frail Anna appeared and motioned for the other two men to come and hold Joseph's legs. It was going to take all of them to hold Joseph down when Theo yanked on his arm.

Anna leaned her full body weight into Joseph's left side. "Make it quick. The faster you do this, the better. I'm ready."

Theo nodded, and with one quick move, the bone was back in its socket.

Joseph screamed in agony as pain shot through his right arm and down his back. The blackness engulfed him.

Anna glanced up to find her daughter, ghostly white, standing in the doorway. She quickly went to Mary. "Why don't you stay with your father in the other room? I'll tend to Joseph."

Mary shook her head. She slowly walked to the bed. She knelt down next to Joseph. "I'll stay with him. He is my future husband. He will need my prayers." She bowed her head, and her long, dark hair hid her face.

Anna thought she had never seen her daughter look more beautiful than in that moment. She knew that with Mary's actions came her acceptance of what was to be. Anna quickly applied the sling to Joseph's arm. She motioned to the Roman. "Help me sit him up. We will tightly wrap these swaths of linen around his chest.

With care and skill, Anna worked diligently to ensure Joseph would heal properly. Then she turned her attention to Theo. "Come. I'll see to the wounds on your face and prepare food for you and your men."

"We will not impose ourselves upon you any more than we already have."

"Nonsense," Anna replied. "You're already here. You brought my daughter's betrothed home. It is the least we could do to show our gratitude." She briskly departed the room, giving Theo no time to respond. She prepared a washbasin and tore some cloth for the soldier to use on his face. She then went to work preparing food and drink for the men.

Joachim had seated himself at the head of the table and was making small talk with the two other soldiers. It confounded Anna how he could make himself so at ease with the very people who oppressed them. She was only repaying their kindness by offering food and drink. She didn't expect them to stay and make themselves at home, nor did she feel compelled to associate with them beyond basic hospitality. Romans defiled everything around them. The sooner they left, the more comfortable Anna would feel. For all she knew, these men might have been the very ones who'd given Joseph his injuries. True, they seemed to have rushed him home, but that seemed to be more out of guilt than necessity. Joseph's wounds were serious but not life-threatening.

Theo paused for a moment before leaving the room. He looked over at the young woman kneeling beside Joseph. The light from the candle fell across Mary, casting her in a warm glow. It was obvious she was young, but her actions hid her age. She wiped Joseph's brow with tenderness. Theo could see that her touch was gentle, for Joseph did not stir. Theo realized that despite the plainness of her dress, she was beautiful. *Joseph is a lucky man*, he thought to himself.

He left the room and found his guards feasting on bread, fruit, and wine. He took the seat Joachim offered him. Anna poured

FAVORED

him some wine and placed a plate filled with meat in front of him. It was then that Theo realized he had not stopped to eat all day. The meat was moist and tender, while the bread seemed to melt in his mouth. The fruit was the sweetest he had ever tasted.

Theo took his time eating. He surveyed his surroundings. The home was a modest one with no luxuries. The man of the house seemed comfortable with their presence. His wife, however, made it a point to not come too close to any of them.

He didn't relish in the thought of explaining the reason for Joseph's condition, but as soon as he finished earring he broached the subject. "I should explain why our paths have crossed." Joachim and Anna nodded in earnest. Theo realized how anxious they were to know all that had happened, and he was thankful that they had not pressed him for information while he and his men ate.

Theo escorted his men outside. There was no sense in the whole camp knowing of his weakness. Anna, in her anxious state, had begun to pace back and forth behind her husband. Joachim gently encouraged his wife to take a seat while they waited for Theo to return.

Making sure the men were out of earshot, Theo returned to his seat at the table. He didn't know where he should begin his tale. He had always thought it best to share only the necessary details to get by. Somehow, this was different. He wasn't sure what possessed him to do so, but he told every detail, from going after Joseph the day before to sleeping with the governor's wife. He even talked about how desperate he felt trying to bring Joseph home safely. The truth flowed from his lips, and with every word, a sense of release swept over him.

Joachim listened to the Roman's sordid story. He was not easily provoked to anger, but his whole body shook from the tension building in him with every word. The anger began to subside as Joachim heard genuine sorrow in the Roman's voice. Joachim couldn't blame Theo. He felt sorry for him. Theo had been caught in a trap, just like Joseph. Granted, most of what had happened was his doing, but he didn't have to speak the truth to Quirinius, nor did he have to bring Joseph home. Theo had chosen to do both. *Thank You, God*, Joachim silently prayed.

Anna blushed crimson with every word the Roman said. She had never heard anyone speak that boldly of such things done between two people. She wondered why this Roman would take such a stand and save Joseph, a Hebrew, instead of himself. The thought that kept forcing its way to the forefront of Anna's mind was, *How can God let something like this happen to a decent man like Joseph?* It didn't matter that earlier in the day Anna had wished Joseph had never been born. Now he was to be family. There was nothing more important to her than family. Silently, she prayed, *Why didn't You do something?*

I did, beloved. Anna shoved the words from her mind.

When Theo finished his story, he looked up, half-expecting Joachim to hit him or at least cast him out of his home. Theo only saw love and gratitude from the man sitting across the table from him. The woman's expression was a different story.

Joachim extended his hand across the table. "I think it is only proper that I know the name of the man who saved my son-in-law."

"Theo."

"Theo, I am Joachim. This is my wife, Anna. How can we thank you?"

Theo was so taken aback by the old man's kindness that he couldn't speak. For the first time in his life, he felt like crying tears of relief. This man had shown him forgiveness. He didn't expect anything more from him. He had confessed, and they had forgiven. Choking on the words, Theo shook his head and replied, "You have done more to thank me than I deserve. It is time we take our leave." Theo stood to go, but Joachim stopped him.

"I am concerned for your safety. If this Quirinius is as angry

FAVORED

as you say—and from the look of your face and of Joseph, I have no reason to doubt you—then is it wise for you to return to his service? Can you not stay here for a few days and request a transfer?"

Anna gasped at her husband's suggestion. With her lips pinched together, she whispered, "Are you sure you know what you are doing?"

Joachim lovingly reached his hand out and patted his wife's arm. That was her cue to be quiet. Anna pulled her arm away from him and crossed both arms in front of her. He may not have wanted her to speak, but he couldn't keep her from showing her displeasure.

Joachim continued, "Maybe your men can be sent on with the explanation that you are receiving treatment for your injuries and will rejoin the party as soon as you're healed. By then, you could be well on your way to another post. Anna, why don't you take a look at our young centurion's wounds?"

Anna understood what her husband was asking of her. She didn't want to help the man standing across from her, but she would do what her husband wished. She motioned for Theo to sit. She prepared some salve and got to work washing and dressing his face. Theo felt her anger as she tended to him. She wasn't as gentle as she had been with Joseph. When she was finished, she giggled quietly to herself. She had wrapped Theo up in such a way he could barely see out from under the bandages that covered the upper portion of his face.

Joachim went to the door and motioned for the guards to come in. Even if they had an inkling as to what was afoot, they made no mention of it. They listened as Joachim explained Theo's perceived predicament. They agreed that Theo should remain in Anna's care until such a time that he could travel and rejoin their group. They were willing to apprise Quirinius of all that had happened and how badly Theo was injured. Joachim gave the men some wine and bread to take with them.

Theo thanked the men for their help. They assured him that he looked worse than they ever would. Laughing, they departed for camp. Theo watched them until they had disappeared into the darkness of the night. Only then did he become aware of the pain in his face. Theo entered the tiny house that would be his refuge for the next few days. Joachim and Anna were nowhere in sight, so he slipped into the bedroom to check on Joseph.

He knew he had startled Mary when he entered the room. She jumped. "I'm sorry. Were you resting?" Theo asked.

"No, praying."

"I see. How is he?"

"He is in a lot of pain. I've never seen someone hurt this badly."

"Will you stay with him all night?" Theo thought he noticed Mary's cheeks blush with the question. He wasn't sure why. Roman women always stayed with the men they loved. However, she was not a Roman woman. Theo realized he had embarrassed the girl and, consequently, himself. "I only mean…"

"I know what you meant. Yes, if my mother allows it. I will attend to his wounds until dawn."

"It will be dawn soon enough. The night has gotten away from us all."

"Yes, I suppose so. Mother and Papa are preparing a place for you upstairs. It's probably not what you're used to, but it should be comfortable and clean."

"I am grateful for your family's hospitality. It is more than I deserve." Theo still felt ashamed for his actions leading to Joseph's injuries. He looked at the young girl; her dark brown eyes held no condemnation. "I'm Theo, by the way."

"My name is Mary."

Theo watched as Mary turned her attention back to Joseph. The conversation had lasted less than a minute, but Theo had

FAVORED

heard more gentleness in that time than he had heard in his whole life. As he turned to go, he heard Mary softly say, "Thank you."

Chapter Ten

Mary shifted her weight from one knee to the other. She looked down at the man lying in her parents' bed. He was handsome despite the cuts and bruises beginning to show around his eyes. Seeing the shape of his body had been in when he arrived had almost sent her running for cover. She watched as his chest moved up and down with every difficult breath. The pain seemed to overwhelm him as his body used all its energy to keep the air flowing in and out of his lungs. Every so often he would groan or try to move, only to end up as he was now—perfectly still.

She had hoped her mother would join her in the vigil. She felt uncomfortable being left alone with him. She wasn't ready for that. A year would pass quickly enough without hurrying time. She still was having trouble believing it had only been a few short hours since her father had told her of the arrangement agreed upon between Joseph and himself. She had cried tears that came from deep within her soul for the better part of the day. Not one tear had been shed since Joseph had entered their home. Guilt came over her as she realized that while she had been feeling sorry for herself, Joseph was being brutally beaten for some unknown reason. She had heard murmurings between Theo and her parents but could not make out the details of the conversation.

Mary rose and stretched her legs before quietly moving to the door. She looked out into the small living area. Her mat lay empty on the floor. The candle that sat in the middle of the table was still lit, casting light on the remnants of the men's dinner. She glanced at Joseph, who was sleeping fitfully. She was comfortable leaving him alone. Yet, she felt alone. She was trying to be patient as she waited for her mother to join her. She listened for any sound that

FAVORED

would enlighten her as to what was going on between her parents and Theo. She could hear movement on the roof, confirming they were still helping the Roman settle in. There was really nothing she could do until her parents returned but continue praying for Joseph. Ignoring the protest made by her knees, she returned to her kneeling position.

It was difficult to pray. Her mind wandered from one thought to the next. She didn't even know this man. Why would he want to marry her? Why now? She was so consumed with the thoughts that she did not hear her father slip into the room.

Joachim lightly touched Mary's shoulder. "I brought a stool for you to sit on...thought you might be more comfortable." Mary nodded. She thought if she spoke, she might accidentally verbalize all the questions that kept echoing in her mind.

Joachim stroked his daughter's hair. "I can only imagine how difficult the day has been for you. Now, to have to tend to the man who is to be your husband..." Joachim didn't finish the sentence.

Mary looked up into her father's eyes. The words flowed from her mouth before she realized what she was saying. "Father, I have never questioned your motives. I've abided by all you have taught me. But this..." She pointed to Joseph. "I do not understand. Why him? Why now? I still feel like a child most of the time. I'm trying to accept it, trying to understand, but the longer I dwell on it, the more confusing things seem to be."

Joachim drew her close to him, wrapping her in a fatherly embrace. *How do I answer her, God, when I have asked the same questions of You and still have no answer?*

Share your heart.

The words entered Joachim's mind, and suddenly he knew how to begin. "I have asked God those same questions, Daughter. I have not been privy to the answer. I can tell you that I have sought God's guidance concerning your future. I did not enter into the arrangement with Joseph under false pretenses. I knew it would be a shock to you and your mother. In truth, it surprised me that Joseph agreed. So I don't have answers for you. What I can tell you is this: God has His hand on you, Mary. For whatever reason, God wants Joseph to be your husband. Trust Him. I could praise Joseph, telling you of his many admirable qualities, but that would not bring peace to your heart. Only faith in God can do that."

Mary pulled away from her father's embrace. "I do have faith in God. I'm just not sure you heard Him correctly."

Joachim smiled. "Mary, God doesn't always do what we think He ought to do. I am sure it was not Joseph's plan to end the day beaten and bruised, taking shelter here. Nor am I saying that God caused him pain, and I am not just talking about the physical pain he is enduring at this time. Joseph seems old to you because he has lived through so much. He has scars on the inside that are not visible to our eyes. It is not only you, dear daughter, for whom God has a plan but Joseph as well. You feel young because you are young. Why God wants Joseph for you, and you for him, I cannot say, but I knew beyond a shadow of a doubt that it is His will that you will be his wife."

Mary thought on her father's words and asked, "Why would God have a plan for me? I'm a simple girl from Nazareth."

"Because God loves you. He loves us all. God doesn't ask that we understand why He does things. He doesn't even expect us to be happy about all the things He does. He wants our faith and obedience. The understanding, the happiness, all those things will come if we choose to believe and obey."

Mary was silent. She reflected on the thoughts that had swirled through her mind during her father's announcement of her betrothal to Joseph. God had spoken deep truths to her heart about the meaning of submission to Him. At that moment, it dawned on Mary that the cost of submitting to God might be more than she was willing to pay. She couldn't remember a time when she had deliberately disobeyed her father. Now her father and her God were asking her to give her life to a man she didn't know or love.

Joachim watched his daughter. He could see her turmoil. "Mary, remember when Miriam would pray that God would open her heart to accept His desire for her? I've thought often about that prayer the last few months. I think the meaning of Miriam's prayer was that her desires would be changed to match God's desires. I'm not sure I understand how it all works, but I know Miriam did not live the life she wanted. She lived the life God had chosen for her. In doing so, Miriam found contentment, peace, and joy."

Mary replied, "Once, when I was a child, Miriam told me that she had surrendered her whole being to God…that God wanted her whole heart, not just part. I must confess I didn't hear all you said today, Papa. I was thinking about what God wanted of me. Not just part of me but all of me. I want to have my desires match God's desires for me. Truly, I do. There are just so many things I want for myself."

Despite the protest his body made, for it was becoming a very long day, Joachim knelt down in front of his daughter. Even as a child, Mary had been able to astound him with all she thought about. She dug deeper into the meaning of things than most her age. Whether or not she knew it, even now, she had insights into the ways of God that were beyond her years. "Tell me, Daughter, what things do you want?"

"Papa, you will think it sounds silly." Mary blushed.

"No. A father always wants to hear his child's desires."

"Well, I'd like to visit some of the places Lydia has been."

"Where would that be?"

"Caesarea, for one. Lydia says the sea is truly something to behold. Jerusalem is another—for Passover, of course. Mother never allowed us to travel with you for Passover because of her own fears."

"Of course." Joachim found himself taking pleasure in the hopes of his daughter. "Anything else?"

"I want someone to look at me the way you look at Mother. You love each other so much. I want to feel that way about someone. I want to be a good wife like Mother has been to you." By this point the dreams of a young girl flowed from her lips. "I want to be the kind of mother Miriam was to all of us. I want children, many of them, so none will feel lonely, as I have felt. I long to fill my home with laughter. I always want to find happiness in the things around me. To be content with all God has given me and will give me."

As she spoke, Mary kept her gaze on her hands, which were folded in her lap. Only when she looked up did she see the tears that glistened in her father's eyes. "Papa, I'm sorry. I shouldn't have said all those things. I shouldn't have disappointed you."

Joachim could hardly speak. He knew it was wrong to be proud of what one had, but he was very proud of the young woman who was his daughter. He wiped the tears from his eyes and took his daughter's hands in his. "I could never be disappointed in you. Don't you see I am very proud of you? Mary, my child, please understand the things you want, the desires of your heart, are pure and natural for any girl your age. Just as I have listened to you speak of your wants, God will listen to your desires. He will answer as He wills. He wants the very best for you, as do I."

"And you believe Joseph is the very best husband for me?"

"I do. I know he is the man God has chosen for you."

"I just feel that the two of us are strangers to each other."

"You are. But don't fret over that. You will have a lifetime to learn about each other. I learn something new about your mother every day. I have yet to be disappointed." Joachim stood and helped his daughter to her feet. Pulling her close, he added, "God always has a plan, Mary. He will take care of the details. Rest in Him."

"You're not...disappointed...that I questioned you?"

Joachim chuckled. "No. I would have been surprised if you had not."

"Mother..."

"I'll take care of your mother. You tend to Joseph. All things happen for a reason, Mary. Whether you realize it or not, Joseph needs you, and you need him."

Mary nodded slowly and turned her attention back to Joseph. He seemed to be resting more contentedly than he had been before. She didn't even notice that her father had slipped out of the room. She closed her eyes and began to pray—not for Joseph's healing, not for God to work a miracle and save her from a marriage to a man she didn't love, but that her desire would be transformed to match God's plan for her. She didn't know how long she prayed before her eyelids grew heavy, and she fell fast asleep, her head resting on her arms, which lay folded beside Joseph.

Chapter Eleven

The next few days went by quickly. Mary was either helping her mother with Joseph's care or with household duties. Joachim worked in Joseph's shop as well as seeing to the needs of his family. Theo helped out wherever he could. By the time evening rolled around, everyone was so exhausted that sleep came quickly.

Joseph slept most of the time. His jaw was sore and slightly swollen, which made eating difficult. Anna made sure the food she served him was soft and easily swallowed. He made no mention of what had happened to him or questioned why he was staying in their home. Mary didn't know if the reason behind Joseph's silence was because his body hurt him or simply that he didn't want to speak. She was pretty sure the latter was the reason for his continued reticence.

Theo had sent a request for transfer. Mary overheard him discussing with her father what his next move might be if the transfer was denied. Quirinius had every right to block the transfer and keep Theo in his service. Theo had many more years to serve in the Roman Army before he was released from duty and given a parcel of land to farm. Until then, his life belonged to Rome. He would do what he was told, even unto death.

Mary watched as her mother prepared a tray of food for Joseph. Her mother had taken to having more people in the house. She seemed to thrive on the extra mouths to feed, though she said very little to Theo and maintained a distance from him. She made sure Theo had plenty to eat and fresh linens, but nothing beyond that.

Joseph was another story. Any doubt Mary had concerning her mother's support of the marriage to Joseph had subsided. Anna

FAVORED

doted on Joseph. Overall, her mother seemed to have regained the contentment she had had before Miriam's death.

Mary continued to pray, as she had heard Miriam do countless times before her, that her heart would be changed. Even though marriage to Joseph still frightened her, she found peace in the midst of fear.

She was about to take a tray into Joseph when there was a knock at the door. Mary waited as her mother answered. "Come in." Lydia poked her head from around the door. Mary smiled at the sight of the other girl. She sat the tray down and greeted her with a hug.

Lydia was dressed in her best tunic. Her family had more money than Mary's, and Lydia made it a point to parade her wealth. Mary didn't mind. It was one of the things she had come to accept about her friend. They were two different people, destined to live in two different worlds. Mary knew that was what bonded them. She loved to hear Lydia's stories about the places she had traveled and the people she had seen.

When she looked at her friend, Lydia thought Mary seemed very grown up. It had been less than a week since the two had seen each other, yet there was something in the way Mary carried herself that made her appear older. "Mary, I thought some time in the sun might do you good. From what I hear, you've been cooped up in this house for the better part of a week. Some of us are meeting on the hill for a picnic. I thought you might want to come."

Mary's face fell. "I'd love to come, but Mother needs my help. I couldn't possibly leave today."

Anna couldn't bear to see her daughter disappointed. "Mary, you go out with your friends. I can manage here until you return. Besides, your father should be back any time, and he is planning on helping me around here today."

"Are you sure?" Mary didn't want to leave her mother, but

she longed to spend time with Lydia and the other girls.

"Quite sure." Anna pulled a basket down from the shelf and began to pack Mary a light lunch. "Just be back by dinnertime."

Anna kissed her daughter's cheek, and she ushered the girls out the door. She watched as Mary and Lydia took off toward the outer hills of Nazareth.

Mary looked around to make sure no one was watching. Girls were supposed to leave their heads covered for modesty's sake, but she wanted to feel the breeze blow through her hair. She removed her shawl from around her head, giving her hair a shake. She sucked in the fresh air and began to run as fast as she could through the grass. She couldn't believe it had been less than a week since she had been outdoors. It felt like much longer. Lydia laughed at her friend's enthusiasm. She fancied Mary's fun-loving way of enjoying life. Mary found pleasure in the smallest of things.

When they were out of earshot, Lydia took Mary's arm to slow her pace down. "So what's it like?"

"What's what like?"

"Don't you play that game with me, Mary. I'm your best friend, remember? You can tell me."

Mary looked at her quizzically. "Honestly, Lydia, I have no idea what you're talking about."

The blank look on Mary's face told Lydia that she was telling the truth. Lydia wondered if the gossip she had heard had been founded. It had to be true because even her father had seen the Roman at Joseph's shop, talking to Joachim. "You mean to tell me that you have nothing to say about the Roman staying at your home and working as a carpenter in Joseph's shop?"

FAVORED

"Oh, that."

"Yes, that." Lydia couldn't stand the suspense. She wanted to know all the details before they joined the other girls on the hill.

"There really isn't much to tell. Joseph was hurt, so the Roman brought him home. Papa just happened to suggest they bring him to our house…"

Lydia interrupted. "They?"

"Yes, there were two others with Theo."

"Theo. Is that his name?" Lydia tingled with excitement. This was better than she had thought.

Mary wondered how much she should tell. Knowing Lydia, she would want all the details. Mary was sure her father wouldn't approve of that, so she proceeded very cautiously.

"Joseph is pretty banged up. It will be some time before he returns to work. Theo wanted to help with his care and the shop. I don't imagine he'll be with us long. He has responsibilities with the Roman Army."

"What's it like?"

"I'm not sure I understand your question." Mary was relieved to see they were nearing the other girls.

Lydia stopped walking. "Honestly, Mary! Are you really that naive? Most of us have never been within two feet of a Roman centurion. We've been taught to keep our distance, let alone have one live under our very roof!"

"He's no different than any other man. He eats and sleeps like everybody else."

"Mary, you can be so exhausting." Lydia stomped off toward the other girls.

Mary just laughed. She followed behind Lydia, enjoying the fresh air. She purposely had not mentioned her betrothal to Joseph. Lydia didn't even seem interested in him anyway. No one had mentioned whether the announcement would still take place at the end of the week or not. Mary was stunned to realize that the end of the week was just two days away. Lydia would be hurt that Mary had not confided in her. Still, she wasn't comfortable telling her everything—at least, not yet.

She sat in the shade with Lydia. Mary listened as the girls talked of their week and all they had been doing. No one ever had a different story to tell; they all did the same things. Each of their days was filled with going to the well, sewing, tending to the needs of younger siblings, or cooking. Each did whatever was necessary in order to help with her family's needs. Once in a while, one would have a story concerning her family or a tidbit of gossip she had heard. Mary lay down on the blanket Lydia had brought and looked up at the sky. The clouds were fluffy white and floated past on a light breeze. It was a beautiful day.

Lydia tapped on Mary's leg. "Mary, everyone wants to hear about the Roman."

Mary sat up to find all eyes on her. "There really isn't much to tell."

"She's being modest. His name is Theo. Isn't that a very Roman name? It must be divine to have such a man living in one's home."

"Lydia, he's a Roman! Mary is probably afraid of him. Aren't you, Mary?" Sarah waited for an answer.

Before Mary could respond, Micah piped up, "I heard he has no beard to cover his face and he has two cuts on both his cheeks. How did he get hurt? Was he in some battle?"

"My father says it defiles your home to have a Roman staying with you. He doesn't want me to enter your home until that Roman is gone." Deborah quickly averted her eyes, and Lydia gave her a look of disgust.

One right after the other, Lydia, Sarah, Micah, and Deborah fired questions at her. Finally, all fell quiet while they waited for

FAVORED

Mary to respond. She looked from one set of eyes to the next. They seemed to be staring right through her. Mary found herself feeling upset that none of them had asked about Joseph.

"I'm not sure what you want me to say. He was kind enough to bring Joseph to us safely, so Father has offered him shelter until his wounds heal. He has agreed to help with Joseph's care until such a time that Joseph can return to his own home and work."

"You mean Joseph is staying with you too?" Lydia asked, surprised.

"Well, yes. He has no family to take care of him, so…"

"But why your family?" Sarah asked.

"I…well…" Mary didn't want to tell them the reason. "He needed care, and Mother has herbs and such things to help with healing."

In unison they responded, "Oh."

Mary was grateful to see the sun had started to disappear behind the clouds. "I had better head home. Mother asked that I not be out too long."

She stooped, straightened her tunic, and picked up her basket. "Thanks for coming to get me, Lydia. I had a nice time."

Mary began to walk down the hill toward home, and she could hear the others whispering behind her. She increased her pace as tears began to pool in her eyes. She had known most of them since childhood and considered each one of them to be her friend. Now, for whatever reason, their questions and accusations caused her pain.

"Mary, Mary! Wait up." Lydia was hurrying to catch up. Out of breath, she pulled Mary to a stop. "You're not mad, are you? Why, you're crying. Everyone is just curious—that's all." Lydia wiped a tear from Mary's cheek.

"I know. It's just they didn't ask one thing about Joseph and how he was doing."

"Mary, most of us didn't even know he was staying with your family. All we knew is that he had been hurt. Besides, it's not every day that a Roman lives in our midst. Don't mind Deborah and what her father said. You know how pompous he can be about things. Most of us find it exciting that someone of ill repute is living in your home."

Mary hugged her friend. "I understand."

Lydia held her friend at arm's length. "Mary, there is something you're not telling me. I can see it all over your face. What is it?"

Mary eyed her. *Should I tell her, God?* Mary knew Lydia would not let her go until she gave her the answer she was looking for. "As far as I know, it is going to be announced at the end of the week, so I might as well tell you. I am betrothed to Joseph or will be as soon as all the arrangements are made."

Lydia's face turned white. "Oh, Mary."

"I am at peace with it. At first I wasn't, but I've come to accept it. I guess that is why I was hurt that no one seemed interested in Joseph."

Lydia tucked her arm in the crook of her friend's, and they slowly walked back into town. She didn't know what to say to Mary. Lydia had wanted more for her. In every way, Mary was beautiful. Lydia knew her father would match her with someone who had the means to provide a lavish life for her. She wanted that for Mary too. Now she would live the rest of her life married to a carpenter, living in Nazareth.

They were walking past the carpenter's shop when a voice called out to them, "Mary, come see what I have built today." Lydia turned to see a very handsome man with short, curly, blond hair waving them inside. Mary led her into Joseph's shop and introduced her to Theo. To Lydia, he was stunning. Mary didn't seem to notice.

"I was commissioned—well, Joseph was asked to do it—but I took it upon myself to complete the project. What do you think?"

FAVORED

Before them stood a lovely cradle, simply carved but well crafted. Theo seemed very proud of his work and she ran his hands over the smooth surface of wood.

"It's lovely, Theo," Mary responded.

"I think I may have found my calling after I leave the army."

Mary took note that the workmanship, however fine, was not as nice as what Joseph could do. She wanted to say so, but she held her tongue. Lydia, however, did no such thing.

"Theo, is it? I've never seen something so lovely. You are truly gifted." Mary watched as her friend lavished praise on the man. She was embarrassed for both of them.

"You really think so?" Theo asked, sounding like a child seeking his parents' approval.

"Indeed, I do. I'm sure Father would be pleased to have you build something for him. Have you met my father?" Lydia positioned herself between Theo and Mary.

"I don't believe I have."

"Oh, well. He is very busy these days. I'll have to mention your work to him."

"Thank you. You should know that everything I earn from my work goes to Joseph. So any work your father could send my way would be appreciated."

Mary smiled. Theo was helping Joseph. Her heart warmed at the thought.

"Lydia, we'd best be on our way. It's getting late, and I promised Mother."

"If you would wait a few moments, I could walk with you. I was just about to close up."

"Thank you, Theo, but that is not necessary. Mother wanted me back some time ago. I think it would be best if we go ahead and take our leave. I'll see you at home." Mary practically had to pull Lydia from the shop.

"Mary, why didn't you tell me he was handsome? He is like no man I have seen before." Lydia could hardly keep up with the pace Mary had set.

"I really hadn't noticed." Mary kept her eyes straight ahead for fear Lydia would be able to discern the truth.

The two walked in silence until they neared Mary's home. Lydia had been tossing around an idea she found very pleasing. "Mary, would you mind if I suggested to my father that we have Theo over to dine with us sometime? I'm sure Father would be interested in any insights into the Roman economy that Theo could give him. Did I tell you Father is looking to open a warehouse in Tarsus and eventually Ephesus? I don't see us being in Nazareth much longer."

"Why would I mind? I'm just surprised—that's all. Your father has always hated the Romans. Why would he want to feed one?"

Lydia was hurt that Mary had not seemed to care that her family might be moving. Perhaps she hadn't heard her. Mary did seem to live in her own world sometimes. "He may not. It was just a thought. Did you hear what I said about my father?"

"Uh-huh. Lydia, it's getting late. You'd best be getting home. Thanks again for getting me out of the house. I had a good time." Mary entered her home and closed the door before Lydia could respond.

Lydia shrugged off her friend's response and hurried home. She wanted to have her father invite Theo to dinner with them as soon as possible.

Chapter Twelve

Mary found her mother busy preparing the evening meal. She went over and kissed her cheek.

"I didn't even hear you come in. Did you have a nice time?" Anna tucked a strand of gray hair behind her ear.

"It was very nice. I enjoyed being with my friends. Thank you for allowing me to go." Mary donned an apron. "What can I do to help?"

"I just took Joseph's tray to him. He is sitting up. I'm sure he would enjoy having someone to talk to. Why don't you get yourself a cup of water and go sit with him? If he needs anything, you can get it for him."

Mary nodded and poured herself some water. As she walked to the bedroom, she wondered what she and Joseph would have to talk about. She peeked in and saw Joseph trying to pull some meat apart with one hand. The meat seemed to slide all over his plate. She stifled a laugh as she entered the room and immediately set about helping tear the meat into pieces. Joseph watched as Mary took over the task with ease. When she finished with the meat, she pulled the stool up next to the bed and sat down.

"Am I to take you're feeling better?" she asked before she took a sip of water.

"Yes." Joseph didn't know what he should say to the girl. Her mother had told him that Mary had not left his side the first night and continued to help with his care. He slowly chewed, ignoring the pain in his face and chest. "Thank you for your help." He looked at the girl sitting next to him. Her eyes were as he remembered them: deep brown. She seemed small and delicate.

FAVORED

"We are happy to be able to help with your care. Mother is very knowledgeable in the art of healing. I think you would agree."

Mary's smile, warm as the sun, heated Joseph's blood. He could only nod. For the next few moments, the two sat in awkward silence. Mary wondered what the man was thinking. Joseph had no idea what to say next, so he said nothing.

Anna broke the silence. "I brought some fresh fruit for both of you. Mary, your father is preparing himself for dinner. When you're ready, come and join us. Theo is going to take his meal on the roof. It seems he has had a very busy day."

"Do you like grapes?" Mary chided herself for the silly question. *Of course he does, you goose. Who doesn't like grapes?*

Joseph didn't seem to mind the question, however. He talked of how when he was a boy, his mother would make all sorts of pictures out of the food she prepared to try to get his two older brothers and himself to eat. He chuckled at the memory, and Mary laughed at the pictures he had painted with his words. It was still difficult for him to talk long, and he became winded easily, but Mary enjoyed the few moments she shared with him.

She excused herself to join her family for dinner and took his tray back to the kitchen. Once the family was positioned around the table, Joachim gave the blessing.

Anna had not taken a bite of food since the family sat down. She was preoccupied as she moved her food around on her plate. She wanted to address the situation concerning Theo living in their home but was unsure how to approach the subject. Joachim seemed to enjoy the Roman's company so much that the gossip in town had not bothered him. However, it had bothered Anna.

Earlier that day, Rachel had stopped by to "chat," as she put it. It had ended up being a dissertation on all the evil Anna and Joachim were allowing to enter their home by continuing to give shelter to a "dog." Rachel had gone on to say that many were concerned about the influence such a "beast" would have on their daughter. Some had even made mention that Joachim would not be allowed to enter the synagogue until he had cleansed himself and his family from the "defilement" that had come upon them.

The conversation had angered her, and once again she had lost her temper with her neighbor. It didn't matter that all the things Rachel had said, Anna had also thought. Anna felt that the whole village was turning against them. Joachim had always been respected for his wisdom and judgment in the past. She didn't like feeling that her husband might be wrong in this instance.

"Wife, are you feeling unwell tonight? You've barely touched your meal." Joachim was gentle with her. He had learned early on in their marriage that his wife responded better to a soft word or touch. The times he had lost his temper with her had turned into days of solitude for him. Anna was known for her uncanny ability to ignore completely, even if one was standing next to her, a person who had wounded or angered her. This could cause disputes that lasted for days, injuring deeply all those involved.

Anna looked up from her plate. She could feel her temples throbbing. "Rachel came by today."

"Did you have a nice visit?" Joachim saw the tension on his wife's face. The visit from Rachel had not gone well, and he didn't need to guess the reason.

"No." Before she could stop herself, she had relayed the full conversation to her husband in the presence of her daughter. By the end she was standing, spouting off all sorts of things that had been said about all of them. She wanted Joachim to send the Roman on his way and "allow life to get back to normal." In Anna's anger she had become so loud that none of them noticed Theo standing at the foot of the stairs, plate and cup in hand.

"Pardon me. I thought I would bring my utensils downstairs so you would not need to fetch them." Theo looked like a beaten pup. He calmly walked over to the sideboard and laid the items down.

FAVORED

Anna sank into her chair beside her husband. Joachim patted her hand. He understood where his wife was coming from. He had heard similar talk but had chosen to ignore it. "Theo, it seems our conversation concerns you. Join us, please."

Theo turned around to face the family that had opened its home to him. He knew the Jews considered the Romans to be filth. He didn't understand their feelings. Rome had built roads through their cities and villages, making the import and export of goods easier and enabling Hebrews to become wealthy. Only the stubborn ones refused to take part in such practices.

Rome never imposed its religion on the others, accepting each diverse view on the matter as healthy discourse that encouraged knowledge. True, Rome used the capture of weaker nations to its advantage. It took the masses to ensure the lifestyle of the rich in Rome. Romans enjoyed being pampered and entertained. So a few Jews, usually the bad apples of the bunch, had been sent to the arenas or enslaved. Rome's good outweighed the bad. *Didn't it?*

Theo took the sit Joachim offered. Anna didn't look in his direction. She had spoken her mind. The things she said had all been true as far as she was concerned; however, Anna was embarrassed that Theo had overheard her voicing her opinion. *Is it my opinion, or have I been influenced by others?* Anna thought as she nervously twirled a string dangling from her shawl.

Mary sat in disbelief. She knew her mother to be easily influenced by the thinking of others, but this was too much. Theo had been very kind to Joseph and her family. *Shouldn't kindness be repaid with kindness? That's all we are doing. Why can't people understand that and leave well enough alone?* Mary found herself feeling angry, but she wasn't sure of whom her anger was targeted. Her mother had verbally unleashed descriptions of Theo that were simply not true, as far as Mary was concerned, but she had only done so after being attacked herself by a neighbor and so-called friend. It was easier to be angry with others than one's own mother.

Joachim took a moment to formulate his thoughts before speaking. "Theo, I apologize for my wife's dialogue. It was not her intention for you to overhear what took place today. You must understand that we live in a very difficult time with difficult people. However, they are our friends and neighbors, and even after you leave our home, we will have to deal with the repercussions of our actions. My foremost concern is for the welfare of my family, both in the eyes of our friends but, more importantly, in the eyes of God."

Anna looked up at her husband. The gratitude she had begun to feel was starting to dissipate. He was not going to ask Theo to leave. Quite the contrary, he was insinuating that God might want something more, something she knew she couldn't give— wouldn't give—at the expense of their reputation.

"I believe God has a plan for each of us. You have been brought to our home for a reason. I am not going to allow the pettiness of others to dissuade my belief. True, you are not one of us, but you have been a help to Joseph and our family. I am not about to turn you out until you know where you are to go. God has protected us thus far, and I have no doubt that He will continue to do so. I am sorry, dear wife, that I cannot do as you have asked."

Anna stood and faced her husband. "I have never defied you. I may have disagreed with you, but I have always submitted to you. This time, you are making a grave mistake. You are putting a wedge between us and our neighbors allowing him to stay." Anna pointed at Theo. "I do not believe God would want this." She fled the room in tears.

Mary wanted to go to her mother but knew it would not be wise. Anna needed time to calm down. Mary's father would know how to best deal with her.

"Joachim, I appreciate your offer. I cannot turn a blind eye to the fact that I am not welcomed by your wife and neighbors.

You have done more for me in the last few days than you realize. The thought of going back to Quirinius and Dalena depressed me. You gave me a way to circumvent them but not shirk on my duties to Rome. I will be eternally in your debt. I will be gone by first light." Theo excused himself and headed up to the roof to gather his things.

"Papa, aren't you going to stop him?"

"Mary, Theo must do what he thinks is best. I am in no position to stop him."

"But you told him he could stay. Mother will calm down in a few days. Please, tell me you do not care what others think! Papa, Theo has been nothing but a help to us. Who will see to Joseph's shop? To his care? You can't let him leave like this."

Joachim stood his ground. "Theo has made up his mind. I must see to your mother."

With tears in her eyes, she fled from her father. She headed up the stairs to the roof. It wasn't so much the thought of Theo leaving that troubled her as much as the reason for it. She found Theo bending over his mat, straightening the area he had called home for the past few days. "Where will you go?"

Theo turned to the girl. The troubled look and tears on her face touched something deep within him. "There's a station not too far between here and Cana. I can be there within a few hours by foot."

"It's too dangerous, even for you, to travel at night alone."

"She's right, you know." Joseph stood at the top of the stairs. Mary immediately went to him and helped him take the next few steps toward their friend. "Won't you wait till morning?"

"Yes, that's a great idea. Maybe Mother will have calmed down by then."

"Mary, this has nothing to do with your mother." Theo saw the doubt in Mary's eyes. "Well, not everything to do with her.

Today, after you and Lydia left, the man who had requested the cradle came by the shop. He would not pay for work that I, a Roman, had done. In fact, he wouldn't even consider placing his infant in such a befouled piece of wood."

Joseph could see the hurt in the other man's eyes. "I'm sorry."

"It's for the best. I should be hearing any day now as to my new post. Being at the station will expedite the news reaching me. You must be in quite a bit of pain. Let me help you sit."

Joseph graciously accepted Theo's offer. It had taken every bit of his strength to climb the stairs. Theo helped lower him to the ground with his back resting on the outer wall of the house. Mary grabbed a blanket from Theo's mat and covered Joseph. Taking her cue from Joseph, she seated herself beside him. Theo situated himself across from the couple.

"I do feel disappointed that I won't be staying longer. It's been a nice reprieve from service. I had actually begun to consider life beyond the Roman Army—something I had not done."

"I am sorry for everything my mother said. You have been nothing but kind to each of us. I have always been taught to fear Rome and its people, but you have dispelled my fear. I just don't understand the cruelty of people." Mary hung her head in shame. She felt guilty even though it was not her fault.

"Mary, we are to be feared. Many would think nothing of taking you into slavery or even killing you. Most people only think of themselves. It has been Joseph and your family who have helped me see myself. It has not been easy these past few days to reflect on my life. I have done too many things that disgrace me. In the years to come, my service to Rome will be a reflection of things of which I am not proud. I can only hope that I will remember all of you and deal fairly with those I come in contact with as your father has done with me."

Joseph nodded in agreement. "I, too, made judgments based on what others had done. I cannot believe I am saying this, but I consider you a friend and will be proud to say so."

"I think of you no less. If there is anything you need, do not hesitate to seek me out. As soon as I know my new post, I will send word." Standing, Theo helped Joseph and, in turn, Mary to their feet. "You have taught me much, and I am forever grateful. Joseph, I hope you know what a lucky man you are."

Mary blushed at the compliment.

"I am learning," Joseph replied and smiled at Mary. "I do think it is dangerous for you to travel so far tonight. Why don't you stay at my home until dawn? If you rise early, no one will see you depart. You can take the back way to Cana and steer clear of the main roads. That way you are less likely to fall prey to any *sicarii*."

"I will do that. Thank you. Again, I am in your debt."

"No more than I to you." Joseph extended his one good arm in farewell. Theo returned the kindness and then picked up his things. He helped Joseph down the stairs into bed.

While Theo helped Joseph, Mary prepared a basket of food for Theo to take with him. She waited by the front door for him to return. "I thought you might get hungry."

"Thank you. It is time I take my leave." Theo opened the door and then paused. "Mary, don't blame your mother. She's only thinking of your reputation. The world we find ourselves living in is not of her doing."

"Yes, but I believe we are of a higher calling. Her treatment of you was wrong."

Theo quietly closed the door behind him, leaving Mary in silence. She had no idea where her parents had gone; at that moment, she didn't care. She went to the door of the bedroom to check on Joseph. The candle was still burning beside his bed. Thinking him asleep, she quietly tiptoed into blow it out.

"Are you all right?"

"I thought you were asleep, or I would not have come in."

"Mary, it is for the best."

"How can you say that? People are wrong in the way they think, lumping all Romans into one bunch of evildoers. What I have observed this week is that even some Hebrews can be evil. They cloak their unkindness in the law, but it is still unkindness. People should be accepted for who they are, and I refuse to believe otherwise."

Joseph smiled at her. She had a fire about her that he had not noticed before. He found himself strangely attracted to this side of her. "What you say is true. I know that all too well. I have withstood gossip my whole life. But, Mary, your mother is right to be concerned for your future. Our future."

Mary was stunned to hear Joseph speak of the two of them as one. It was the first time since her father had told her of their betrothal that Joseph had made mention of it. She stammered in response, "I... I don't think I will ever understand such things. And you, Joseph, son of Jacob, surprise me." She quickly blew the candle out and left the room.

Joseph lay in the quiet of the dark. He listened to see if he could tell what Mary was doing. Shortly afterward, he heard the front door open and her parents enter. He could hear them whispering to Mary, and then all went quiet. They must have retired for the night. Joseph thought on Mary's exit. He realized that he had taken for granted her acceptance of their betrothal. He smiled to himself. He may have gotten more than he bargained for. The thought intrigued him.

Chapter Thirteen

Delena stood underneath the portico, waiting for her husband. From the west blew a brisk breeze that floated over the Mediterranean Sea. The cool breeze blew at her tunic, forcing her to wrap her shawl around her shoulders. After the incident with Theo, Quirinius had decided to cut their travel short and head straight for their new home in Antioch. They had pushed hard to make it to the port city of Ptolemais. Now they awaited confirmation of the passage aboard the Ames. The ship was large enough to carry their Entourage and belongings. They would sail north to Antioch; it would be a long and possibly hazardous journey.

Quirinius had been upset with Theo's decision to seek a transfer and had taken his frustration out on Delena. He had attempted to stop the transfer but to no avail. Theo was a well-respected centurion who had many friends in the Roman military. Roman soldiers were known to stick together. Theo would receive his transfer.

Delena didn't know what awaited her in Antioch. Before they were married, Quirinius had assured her that she could decorate their new home to her heart's content. He had given her the plans of their home, and she had begun work on the dwelling before they left Rome. Artists and masons had been hired to refurbish the older dwelling to pristine condition. She wanted the latest luxuries. She would even have a private bath for herself. No more going to public bath houses unless she so desired.

Excitement over her new home had taken her mind off the man she was to marry. It had made the wedding more palatable. She had looked forward to seeing her creation and calling it home. Now she considered the place to be her permanent prison, with Quirinius as jailor.

She dreaded the long trip by ship. She had never sailed before, though the story she had told in Rome had spun around in her mind so many times, it had become truth for her. She would demurely smile at the crowds that gathered around to listen in horror to her ordeal.

"I'm originally from Ephesus, but when my parents died, I was forced to come to Rome to live with a distant aunt."

"Oh, my dear, how sorry we are for you."

"That is not the worst." Then, Dalena would bat her lashes, seeking an innocent look, before continuing her con. "The journey by sea was treacherous, and my guardian was swept overboard. All my important papers went with her. I have no idea who my aunt is and how I might find her."

"How are you living? A lovely girl like you shouldn't be out on the street. We can see that you have been raised in an *equestrian* family. Stay with us for a while. It would be an honor to help you."

Delena would be reluctant to go but would eventually give in. She used one household after another as a training ground and steppingstone to the higher echelons of the wealthy.

The truth was that she had lived in Rome all sixteen years of her life. She had never traveled until her wedding day. What seemed at first like an exciting adventure now left her feeling alone and sick. Once she boarded that ship, Quirinius would know that some of her past had been a lie.

She heard the clicking of sandals on stone. It had taken Quirinius only a short time to teach Delena not to look at other men. However, old ways were hard to break. She found herself staring at the tall, broad-shouldered man who passed her. There was nothing spectacular about him. He looked like any number of Roman guards she had seen in the past. Yet, something about the way he carried himself—not just as a guard but also as a king—made her take notice.

He noticed her as well. Her light blue *stola* with its silver belt, from which long tassels dangled, gave her an air of regality. The white shawl she had draped over her shoulders blew behind and about her in the breeze, wrapping her in purity. Her hair was wound around her head, and tucked amongst the strands were small, white, fragrant flowers. He wanted to greet her out of respect but found his throat too dry to speak. As he grew closer, the blossoms' scent lingered in his nostrils.

He nodded as he passed and kept his gaze focused on the entrance to the building. He had been called to protect the proconsul of Syria, not engage in affairs of the heart. He had heard rumors concerning the previous head of security and the wife of the proconsul, but he gave them no credence. The vision of loveliness he had just passed was nothing like the woman who had been described to him. According to close confidants, the proconsul's wife was quite brazen in her affections toward other men. This woman didn't seem to notice him.

His thoughts were interrupted by the boisterous laughter moving toward him. He stopped before he ran into the very large man from whence the laughter was coming from.

"Ah, I see our new head of security is right on time. Good. I admire promptness. Do you have your papers?"

He handed the governor all that had been given to him. Quirinius took a moment to ensure that all was in order. He looked at the man from head to toe. He was strong and capable. Quirinius had been told that the man would give him no cause for concern when it came to Dalena. He was suffering from a wounded heart. His wife had died in childbirth. Accepting the post had been a demotion for him, but he had willingly taken it in order to leave Rome and his sorrowful past behind. He had no intention of becoming involved with anyone again.

Quirinus looked out to where his wife stood. She looked

every inch the woman he desired as she looked out over the sea. It had not taken him long to bring her to submission. He was pleased to note that she refrained from joining them. This was not her custom when another man was present; typically, she made it a point to draw attention to herself. However, she remained positioned with her back to them.

"Darling, I would like to introduce you to our new head of security." Hearing his voice, Dalena turned and came to them.

"Lucas Darius, is it? I would like to introduce you to my beautiful wife, Dalena."

"The pleasure is all mine." Lucas bowed before the woman. "Sir, if it pleases you, I would like to see your accommodations and the men's before we all board."

"Yes, yes, by all means."

Quirinius waved Lucas on and turned his attention to his wife. "I am pleased to see the vision before me." He took her hand and kissed it. Dalena fought the urge to pull back. She forced herself to accept the man's affection.

"Am I to gather that all is in order for our departure?" she asked coldly.

Taking her arm in his, Quirinius walked her to the steps that led down the hill and toward the sea. "Yes. All is going according to plan. We should be able to board as soon as Lucas assures me that all is well. We will set sail for Antioch before the day's end."

Delena looked away from her husband. They walked in silence. The path was a bit rough, and Dalena found herself holding tightly to him to keep from falling. Quirinius took this to mean that her affection was favorable toward him.

"I know the last month or so has been rough. Maybe the last year, since we were wed, has been more demanding on you than I realized. It slips my mind that you are young. I trust the incident with Theo will not repeat itself." He leaned into her so no one else could hear. "By now, you know what I am capable of, should you regress to your former behavior." Dalena shivered. "My darling, are you cold?" Quirinius helped her wrap her shawl tightly around her shoulders. "Tonight, I will keep you warm. How does that sound to you?" Dalena forced herself to smile.

They neared the gangplank of the ship. Dalena could hear Lucas giving orders. He was very authoritarian in speech. Seeing the couple, Lucas motioned for them to come aboard. Dalena felt her breath leaving her. There would be no one and nothing for her in Antioch. She would be alone. She tried to focus her attention on putting one foot in front of the other, but her surroundings began to spin around her. Just as they stepped aboard the ship, she felt herself slipping into blackness.

Quirinius' hold on his lovely wife wasn't as secure as he had thought. As she fainted, she slid from his arm. If Lucas hadn't been standing so close, Dalena may have fallen backward down the gangplank, but he picked her up in his arms and carried her to a bench near the center of the ship. He gently lay her down and called out for water. Dalena's eyes fluttered open at the feeling of dampness on her face and neck. She stared up at the man who now held her. He had seen the look of fear too many times not to notice it now. Delena pulled away from him and scanned the faces around her. Quirinius was barking orders as he closed in on her.

Pushing Lucas out of the way, Quirinus knelt beside her. Every line on his face held suspicion. "Darling, what happened?" He tried to keep his voice steady, but anger was seething beneath the surface.

"I'm not sure. One minute I was walking with you, and the next I was lying here."

"Sir, here is water for your wife. It might help her recover." Lucas held the cup out for Quirinius.

He took the cup of water, nearly spilling the contents on Dalena. He didn't offer her a drink; he just handed her the cup. With trembling hands, she lifted the cup to her lips. The water

FAVORED

was soothing. Slowly, she began to feel her strength come back to her.

"Quirinius, please see me to our quarters. I feel weak." Dalena's voice was so soft that he could barely hear her.

"What did you say?"

"I'd like to go to our room."

"Of course, darling." His touch was rough as he lifted her from the bench. Dalena's knees buckled again, but Quirinius held her up.

"Would you like me to carry her, sir?" Lucas asked.

"No, I believe my darling is capable of walking on her own. Aren't you, Dalena?"

Even though she felt she might faint again, for her own good, Dalena had to muster what little strength remained. She nodded and accepted the assistance offered by her husband.

"Right this way, sir. I think you will find all is in order." Lucas led Quirinius and Dalena across the ship and down three steps into a very spacious room. Dalena was relieved to see that their room was not located in the hull of the ship. Quirinius helped her to a lovely couch covered in red velvet. Dalena was pleased that food had already been laid out for them. She felt reassured. *Maybe the trip will not be so bad.* The thought was short-lived; once Lucas left them alone, Quirinius took the opportunity to berate his wife, accusing her of fainting purposely to attract Lucas. He left her in tears.

Dalena poured herself a cup of wine and sank back into the velvet couch. Her head ached. She sipped the wine and allowed its warmth to ease the tension from her body. She went to the chest that held her wardrobe. Quirinius had sent her handmaiden below, so Dalena had to undress and don her robe herself.

Quirinius had given her strict instructions not to leave the room and to prepare for his return. She slowly unwound her hair,

138

allowing the tiny white flowers to fall to the floor. She combed through her long strands. Her hair, long and thick, was an inheritance from her mother—one of the few things her mother had given her of which Dalena was proud of.

She was startled to hear a knock at the door. She wasn't sure if she should open it. Quirinius might be testing her, but if she didn't open the door, would he think she was ignoring him? If she did open the door, would he assume she was waiting for someone other than him? Afraid of who might be waiting on the other side, she hesitantly approached the door.

She softly called out, "Who's there?"

"Lucas, my lady. I've come to see how you are feeling and if you need anything."

"I'm fine. Please go away." With fear gripping her, Dalena turned from the door. *Please, please don't let Quirinius see him here.* The prayer escaped her lips and disappeared into the air.

She heard voices outside the door. The murmurings were coming from Quirinius; she could recognize his voice anywhere. The second voice was harder to make out. It was familiar yet unfamiliar. She listened intently, trying to make out what was being said. Evidently, Quirinius had sent Lucas to check up on her. She moved away from the door as anger engulfed her. She watched the door open, and her husband filled the empty space. She wanted to disappear but instead found herself unable to move.

"I see you have done as I asked." Closing the door behind him, in a single stride, Quirinius crossed the distance between them. He drew her to him and kissed her. "I love your hair cascading around your shoulders." He lifted her into his arms and carried her to the bed.

"Quirinius, please, not now. Not tonight—I don't feel well." She felt the sting of a slap across her face.

"You will never shut me out. Do you hear me?"

Dalena allowed her mind to escape as Quirinius took pleasure

FAVORED

in her body. The will to fight had been beaten out of her. She had always considered herself to be strong, but ever so slowly, Quirinius was sucking the life from her.

Chapter Fourteen

The ship sailed toward Antioch, periodically stopping at different ports to load and unload cargo. Dalena had not realized the queasiness one could get from sailing. She spent most of her time in their cabin. On the mornings she did venture out, she found herself fascinated by the sea. To pass the time, she made up a game out of counting how many different creatures she could spot. Each day held new surprises for her.

This particular morning, Dalena could not stomach watching Quirinius nurse a severe headache and stomach convulsions—results of his overindulgence the night before.

She dressed in a simple lavender gown with violet piping around the neck, sleeves, and hem. The different shades of purple did nothing to accentuate the green of her eyes, but she liked the colors just the same. Her belt hung loosely around her waist, drawing attention to the fact that she had lost weight since her marriage. She braided her hair in one simple braid that she wound around into a bun at the nape of her neck. She fastened a piece of matching fabric to her head and wrapped the ends around her shoulders.

She quietly stepped out of their room and made her way to the *stern* of the ship. It had become her place of solitude, a place of rest and comfort. A place where no one seemed to notice her. She settled herself on a few crates she had managed to dislodge from the others. She had arranged them in such a way that she was hidden from view.

"Excuse me for intruding. Are you all right?"

The greeting brought back memories from not so long ago.

FAVORED

Dalena looked up to see Lucas standing before her. His cape flapped in the breeze made by a ship passing over open water.

"Yes, thank you." She quickly turned her attention back to the water that flowed behind the ship. She hoped this was enough of a gesture for Lucas to understand she wanted to be left alone.

"You come to the spot often. I've watched you on several occasions. You must enjoy the look of the open ocean after we have passed." Lucas leaned over the rim of the vessel, resting his elbows casually on the railing. He did not look at her but straight ahead.

"Yes, I suppose I do." Dalena looked nervously around to see if anyone was watching them.

"Don't worry. Your husband is tending to what ails him, and everyone else is busy toward the *bow* of the ship."

"Who said I was worried?" Dalena was offended by the man's assumption.

Lucas turned toward her. "I'm paid to keep my eyes and ears open to all that goes on. I can understand how you need your privacy. If others saw you here, well, let's just say you would no longer have peace."

His discernment stunned Dalena. She lifted her gaze to meet his. It was the first time that she had done so since meeting him. She saw concern and mercy in his eyes. She also saw sadness that came from somewhere deep within the man. The compassion she saw in his eyes almost caused her to break the wall of solitude that she had built for protection. However, the wall stood erect, and with a tone of skeptic cynicism, she queried, "Why did you decide to join me?"

"Fair question. I guess because you looked so alone. I know how it feels to be alone. I don't like it very much. I'm guessing you don't either. Now, tell me why you like staring out over the back of the ship." Lucas returned his gaze to the open water.

Though she had no intention of allowing this man to get close to her, Dalena was pleased by the security she felt by his presence. "It's as you said. I enjoy the look of the open ocean after we had passed."

"Why do you think that is?"

Dalena stood and went to the railing. "See what happens after we move several feet? At first, there's a wave we stir up as the ship glides through the water. Then, the ripples begin to die down until the water becomes perfectly still again. Peaceful. I like thinking that maybe life might be like that."

"What do you mean?" Lucas kept his eyes fixed on the water below them. He knew if he looked at her, his attempt to establish a relationship with the young woman would cease.

"I like to think of this ship as the good and bad that come into our lives. As the ship flows through the water, so do those circumstances. They leave in their wake waves, but hopefully, just like this water, those waves will die down and become peaceful. The ship is forgotten. I hope certain things in life will be forgotten."

"Not everything, I hope." Taking a chance, Lucas looked at the woman standing next to him. From outward appearances, she was the image of perfection. Most people only dreamed of the life she appeared to be living. What he saw was the image of a person dejected and hopeless.

Dalena sensed his eyes on her, causing her to feel vulnerable, and she didn't like it. "Enough about me. Why do you look at the water?" His gaze on her roused a familiar feeling. After what she had endured since the incident with Theo, Dalena had no desire to pursue the feelings stirring within her.

"It reminds me I'm making a fresh start…leaving the past behind and moving toward what lies ahead."

"What do you want to leave behind?"

"A life I cannot have."

FAVORED

Dalena watched as Lucas shifted his focus back to the water. "Whoever she was, she must have hurt you greatly. Was it another man?"

Lucas laughed bitterly. "If it had been, I would have known how to deal with that. No. It was not another man."

The stirrings within Dalena were slowly being replaced with compassion. "You don't have to tell me if you don't want to. I understand that some things are better kept to oneself." She, too, kept her gaze on the water below them.

"I appreciate that, but I don't mind talking about it. It actually helps. At first, the wound was too fresh to speak of it. Slowly that changed."

"What caused the change?"

"Time."

"I don't think time is the answer for me," Dalena half-heartedly said to herself.

"Oh, I don't know. A lot can happen over time. Take me, for example. A year ago I was nursing a broken heart in Rome. Now I'm on a ship bound for Antioch with a new friend standing beside me. Is it all right if I consider you a friend?"

"I don't know if that's wise. I mean…" Dalena paused. She never had another human being asked to be her friend. "I'd like to have a friend, but I don't recall ever having a friend. It's difficult to explain." Dalena could not get a handle on the thoughts that circled around in her mind. She wanted to shut herself up in the cocoon she had started to build around herself. Actually, the cocoon had existed since childhood. Isolation had always been the safest refuge for Dalena.

"I don't want to make things more difficult for you. I just hate to see someone with such vibrancy close herself off out of fear. For months, after my wife died, I did the same thing. I thought the pain would go away if I lived as a dead man. But I wasn't dead. Being alone, shutting everyone and everything out of my life, only intensified the pain. It wasn't until I joined the land of the living that the pain began to diminish."

"Your wife died? How?"

"She was to deliver our first child in a month when something went terribly wrong. We sent for the best doctor, but there was nothing he could do. After days of suffering, she left this life. Death was a blessed escape for her. It ushered in despair for me."

"I'm sorry." Dalena didn't know what else to say. It was obvious that Lucas loved his wife very much.

"Like I said, time has been my best friend."

"I think my situation is quite different from yours. Oh, look!" She pointed at a school of fish that were following the ship. "That significantly raises my totals."

"Raises your totals? What are you talking about?" The delight she had when seeing the fish reminded Lucas of something he'd see from a small child.

"It's a game I play to pass time. Nothing you would be interested in." Dalena was embarrassed that she had revealed so much to the man.

"Try me."

"I don't think it's anything that would interest you."

"Why don't you allow me to make that decision?"

Dalena shrugged. She proceeded, with some embarrassment, to describe the game she had made up. "I keep count of the different types of fish I see. I give myself more points if they are swimming together versus alone. I get no points if I have seen the fish before. It's silly; I know."

"Not at all. I think it is very ingenious of you. Can I play along? We can put a wager on who sees the most. We can settle up when we reach Antioch."

"I don't think you really want to do that. You're just being kind."

"No, I see it as an opportunity to earn some extra *quadrantes*."

Dalena laughed. "You do? I may have something to say on that subject. I don't like to lose."

"I didn't figure you did. What do you say? Tomorrow we meet back here and see who takes the lead. I'll even allow you to keep the points you've earned thus far." Lucas wanted to be a help to the woman; he had seen the way her husband treated her. It was evident there was no love between them.

"I'm not sure that's such a good idea. My husband would not look favorably on me meeting you in private. Too much has happened." Dalena glanced behind her to make sure they were not being spied upon.

Lucas took pity on her. She had the look of a trapped animal. He knew to keep his distance, but he longed to take her in a reassuring embrace. She needed to feel protected. "Dalena, I'll make sure our meeting is kept confidential. I don't want anything from you. I just want to be your friend, nothing more. Will you trust me?"

Dalena looked into the dark brown eyes of the man in front of her. She knew it was dangerous to be caught alone with him, but where fear had flourished, now hope was born. She might be trapped in an undesirable marriage, but Lucas had said that time takes care of all things. "I think it would be fun to play my little game with you. When shall we meet?"

"What is the best time for you? I'll make myself available. I'll also make sure everyone is kept busy so you have nothing to fear. Dalena, I'm paid to protect Quirinius. I'm also paid to protect you. I've seen fear and you when your husband is near. If anything happens, you can come to me. Do you understand?"

Dalena looked away. She thought about her response. The safest answer would be saying no and walking away. Instead, she heard herself say, "Yes. Morning is best. Will that be fine?"

"Perfect." Lucas turned to go.

"Lucas."

"Yes?"

"Why are you doing this? What's in it for you?" Dalena fully expected Lucas to say that he intended to be well compensated for his time and not just with money. After all, the men Dalena had known would have made her pay dearly for what Lucas was offering to do.

"I knew a girl like you. She came from a hard life. Some of her doing. Some was the hand she had been dealt. Let's just say I'm making up for a mistake." Lucas headed toward the bow of the ship, leaving Dalena to contemplate what he had said.

Chapter Fifteen

The following morning, Dalena rose with anticipation in her heart. She never had a close friend. There were girls in Rome with whom she attended parties and the *ludi*, but none of them would call Dalena a friend. Each of them had an agenda. They were willing to use everything and everyone at their disposal to achieve their desires. All the men she had known had wanted more from her than what they gave in return. Even her husband used her to sate his own lustful appetite. She was an expert at playing the same game.

At parties she had attended or at the public baths, she had overheard older women talk of having close male friends, but she herself had never experienced such a relationship. Instinctually she knew her relationship with Lucas would be different from any other relationship she had known. It had to be. Dalena was losing who she thought she was. Depression drove even the toughest of hearts to act in ways they never thought they would. If friendship was what Lucas had hinted that she needed, then friendship she would try.

She purposely wore a plain white stola so as not to draw attention to herself. Her hair was neatly done in a simple *coiffure*. She made her way to the stern of the ship and waited for Lucas to join her.

She looked out over the railing to see one lone dolphin swimming through the waves the ship churned up. She had seen several dolphins since their journey began. They always stayed together. She wondered why this dolphin was alone. She watched as the dolphin shifted course, swimming away from the vessel. "Be thankful you have the freedom to swim away," she murmured.

FAVORED

"What would you like to swim away from?"

She turned to find Lucas standing behind her. "I didn't know you were there. I was just thinking out loud. It was nothing."

"Are you going to count him?"

"No. I've seen several since we left. You can count him if you like."

"I think I will." Lucas took his place beside Dalena. "Have you been waiting long?"

"No. I was starting to wonder whether you would make it or if yesterday was just your way of handling the proconsul's wife for him."

"Nothing like getting straight to the point. You don't trust me very much, do you?" Lucas turned to Dalena. She had positioned herself so that her back was all he saw.

"Should I? You don't seem much different from countless others I've met since marrying my husband. Tell me why I should trust you." Dalena tried not to sound hostile, but she couldn't keep the skepticism from her voice. She didn't understand why she felt the need to lash out at Lucas. He had done nothing but be kind to her. Yet, something in her screen to get as far away from the soldier as possible.

"I guess you shouldn't."

Dalena swung around to face him. "Kind and honest. I've learned when something seems too good to be true, it probably is. I think I should go."

Lucas gently reached for her arm. "Do you always start new friendships off this way?"

"What do you mean?"

"Nothing." Lucas knew not to continue. He decided to diffuse the situation before it got out of hand. "How are you feeling this morning?"

150

"Why do you ask?"

"I've seen how the motion of the ship has made you feel. Never been on a boat before, have you?"

Dalena didn't know how to answer. The lies she had told to give herself legitimacy were coming back to haunt her. *Does he know my story?* Should she continue her deception or speak the truth? "I…" She fumbled for an answer. "I've never been on a ship this size—that's all."

"I didn't know the size of a ship made the difference. I thought people prone to sickness were sick no matter what vessel they happen to be on."

Dalena thought she heard a condescending undertone. "I don't have to stand here and take this from you."

Lucas laughed as he blocked her path of departure. "Pulling rank on me, are you? Look, I was just trying to have some fun. Truce?"

Dalena looked up at him. She hadn't noticed the gray in his hair before or the way his face lit up when he smiled. Tiny wrinkles appeared around his eyes when he laughed. He was older than she realized. There was a pleasantness about him that disarmed her. "I suppose so." She positioned her mouth in the pout she had come to perfect.

"Trying to show displeasure, I see. Can I make it up to you?" Lucas attempted to bow before her but lost his footing and fell forward, tangling himself in netting used to anchor the crates.

Dalena broke out into laughter. "I'm sorry. Here, let me help you. Are you hurt?"

Laughing, Lucas stood and strained his cape and sword. "Only my pride."

"Men have too much pride. If that's all that is damaged, I'm confident you will recover quickly."

"Why don't we sit?" Lucas pulled a crate over and offered it

FAVORED

to Dalena.

"Thank you."

They sat in silence for a while, enjoying the morning sun and gentle breeze that swept over them. Dalena felt so comfortable with Lucas that it made her uncomfortable. He didn't look at her the way other men did, like a delectable sweet to be devoured. Maybe he didn't find her attractive. The thought confused Dalena. She never met a man who had not thought her beautiful. If Lucas didn't think she was pretty, then what was she? Who was she?

Pulling her from her thoughts, Lucas asked, "Where is your family?"

"My what?"

"Your family? You do have family, don't you?" Lucas enjoyed teasing Dalena. He knew it kept her defenses somewhat at bay.

"Of course I do. Doesn't everybody?" Before she thought about what to say the words flowed from her mouth. "It's just, I have no living family. My mother is dead."

"What about your father?"

"I don't have a father."

"Everybody has a father."

"Well, I don't. He's dead too."

"Did you grow up in Rome?"

"No. I'm originally Ephesus. When my parents died, I was forced to go to Rome to live with an aunt on my mother's side. While traveling, my guardian was washed overboard by a terrible storm. She carried the papers with her that had my aunt's identity. When I arrived in Rome, I knew no one. Now perhaps you can understand why I am hesitant to talk about my past."

"Yes, it appears to have been very painful."

Dalena thought she heard a hint of sarcasm in his tone, but when she looked at him, his face was solemn and caring.

TERI LYN TOBEY

"How did you end up with Quirinius?"

"Why all the questions? I thought we were going to watch for fish and play my little game."

"I'm just trying to get to know you better. That's what friends do, you know."

"No, I don't know. I have found it best to keep one's life to oneself. Maybe this wasn't such a good idea." Dalena stood to leave, but just like before, Lucas stopped her.

"Dalena, I'm not trying to make this hard. I'll tell you about me if you'd like. Just stay. Quirinius is busy and doesn't want to be bothered. It's not good for you to be alone all the time. They say a person can go mad from loneliness."

"Why are you doing this?" Dalena was practically shouting. She pulled away from Lucas and looked him straight on.

Suddenly, her old defenses surfaced and her whole demeanor changed. "I get it—this is a game I am very good at." Her voice began to purr as she slithered up to Lucas, allowing her body to press against his. "You do put a different angle on things. I was beginning to think you did not find me attractive. Now I see the game you like to play." She slowly ran her hand along his face and down his chest. "I say we find a secluded, dimly lit room aboard this floating casket and enjoy our time. You do have a way about you, Lucas."

"Stop it." Lucas pulled away from her and held her at arm's length. "This is not what I want."

"I saw the way you looked at me the day we first met. I know that look. I've seen it too many times."

"I'm sure you have. I know all about you. The stories concerning the proconsul's wife have made their way to Rome."

"So you had to come and check out the merchandise?" Dalena spat the words at him.

"No. But I'm no fool. I found out all about the two people I

FAVORED

would be protecting before I ever agreed to the post. I know all about the story you told concerning your family. You're no more from Ephesus than I am. Only one scenario would make a girl fabricate such a lie—a girl out to prove her legitimacy. I am right, aren't I? The man who arranged your marriage to Quirinius had more to gain from getting rid of you than from calling you his daughter. Now you're in a loveless marriage with no way out. I agreed to protect you, to leave all I knew behind, because I wanted to do what I should have done years ago."

Dalena thought she would faint. She wondered how many other people in Rome knew the truth. She would never be able to go back. She sank down onto the crate, burying her face in her hands. "How did you find out?"

"That's not important. Don't you see? I don't care about your past. I do care about you."

"But you don't even know me."

Lucas knelt down in front of Dalena. He thought about the words he would say. He had learned early on that honesty, at least to a point, worked best. "Dalena, I had a sister. I didn't know she was my sister at first. If I had, things may have been different. She was part of a group of women they brought to us at the *statio*. I used her for my own pleasure. Only afterward did she tell me who she was. She was the daughter of my father and his *delicatae*. She had seen me with my father on several occasions. There was no mistaking my father's son. She had searched for over a year until she found me. Now she wanted me to know, to have, what my father had sired, forsaken, and sold. She could not have revenge on my father, for he had passed, but she could take it out on his son. She drew my sword. I thought she was going to kill me. Instead, she stabbed herself in front of me. She might as well have stabbed me, for the guilt sent pain through my entire being. I vowed then never to be with another woman until marriage. Now that my wife is dead, I have renewed that vow. When I got wind of Quirinius' need for a bodyguard, I asked to be considered, mostly because my wife had died and there was nothing left for me in Rome. To come here was a demotion for me. Then I learned of you. Actually, you're very much talked about in Rome."

"I can only imagine what they're saying about me."

Lucas ignored the comment. "I figured I might make up for the wrong my father and I had done to my half sister if I helped you."

"So I am the remedy for your guilt. I hate to disappoint you, Lucas, but I don't like being used. Find someone or something else to assuage your conscience. Leave me alone."

"It's more than that now. I think Quirinius could really hurt you. I've seen how he handles you in the way he speaks to you. Whether you like it or not, you need my help if you are to stay alive with that man as your husband."

"Are you planning to stay with us in Antioch?"

"Yes, if that's what it takes. That's why I thought if we became acquainted on this voyage, then maybe you would learn to trust me. Only if you trust me can I help you."

"How are you going to help me when I am alone with my husband? You can't come storming in on us. Besides, he never leaves a mark on me. The pain he causes is deeper than that." Dalena couldn't bring herself to look up. She kept her face buried in her hands. Perhaps if she didn't see him and he couldn't see her, she wouldn't feel so exposed. "This is my own doing. I can take care of myself. Don't trouble yourself."

"I can't leave it at that. I'm already committed. Whether you like it or not, I'm going to be around for a long time. Trust me, Dalena. Let me be there for you."

Finally, Dalena looked up at the man. "I don't think I can."

"We'll be in Antioch in a few days. Let's see how it goes." Lucas watched as Dalena walked away. She turned to look at him

FAVORED

before disappearing into the crowd of workers at the bow of the ship. There was a haunting look in her eyes that saddened him. He had pushed her too hard, too soon. He should have held his tongue. Lucas leaned against the railing. In his pursuit to rescue her from herself, he had not realized that she had taken a hold of his heart. He was having feelings he had not had since his wife died. It wasn't just Dalena's beauty that attracted him; it was her soul. Deep down, an innocent child cried out to be loved.

Chapter Sixteen

Theo sent word that he was stationed in Jerusalem, but only for a short time. Soon he would be departing for Egypt. Augustus wanted to maintain control of the region since conquering Antony and Cleopatra several years earlier. One way to do that was to have a strong military presence. Theo was able to maintain his rank in the army and would be commanding a large post.

Joseph slowly regained his strength and was able to return home. He resumed his work and his carpenter shop and was busier than ever. To make his betrothal to Mary official, Joseph paid *maneh* in weight equal to one hundred *shekels.*

Word spread through Nazareth concerning the bride price, for no man had ever paid that much for a woman. Some thought Joseph foolish. Others considered him to have wealth far beyond what they had assumed. Only Joseph and Joachim knew the truth. The gold had been in Joseph's family for generations. Joseph felt it only right that it be given to Joachim as thanks for all that Joachim and his family had given Joseph.

Once a week, Joseph would close his shop early. Joachim and Mary would meet him just outside the tiny town. Anna always prepared a light supper for the trio. They would sit and talk about anything that sparked the interest of the fledgling couple. All this had been Joachim's idea. It was highly unusual, but Joachim wanted Joseph to see the prize he was getting and value it above all others. He also wanted Mary to be comfortable with the man who would be her husband.

Mary had come to enjoy the weekly jaunt. She assumed it was due to the flowers, birds, and small animals she would see along the way. She also loved having time with her father. Each week,

FAVORED

as they made the trek to the countryside of Nazareth, Joachim would point out special places that were dear to Anna and him. He would educate Mary on different plants and their benefits or hazards.

Joachim often needed to stop and rest. This concerned Mary greatly, for she had never known a time when her father was slow to do anything. Mary shared her concerns with her mother, but Anna assured her that there was nothing to worry about.

On this particular afternoon, Joachim felt as if a weight was resting on his chest. He needed to rest more than normal.

"Father, do you feel all right?"

"Yes, fine."

"We can turn back and head for home if you would like."

"No. Joseph is probably waiting on us. We shall continue."

Mary waved to Joseph as soon as he came into view. A smile tickled at the corners of her mouth. Joachim was pleased to see Mary respond with warmth at the sight of Joseph. Things were going well. As soon as she reached the spot where Joseph was waiting, Mary laid the blanket Anna had sent them with on the ground. As usual, the three of them positioned themselves on the blanket. Mary took from the basket the bread, cheese, and wine Anna had prepared. After they had made the usual small talk, Joachim excused himself to stand a few feet away so Mary and Joseph would feel free to talk about whatever they chose. Joachim was not so far that he could not discern tidbits of their conversation. It amused him to hear the different things the couple chose to discuss.

Joseph watched as the breeze tugged at the tendrils that fell from under the scarf that covered Mary's head. Her dark curls framed her face. Her skin, a soft olive, made the brown of her eyes appear rich in color. Her cheeks seemed to be perpetually flushed with pink. Her lips were delicate, causing her smile to appear instantaneously. Joseph tried to memorize all the details of Mary's face.

He found himself feeling younger than his twenty-eight years when in her presence. She found joy in the smallest details. Even now, while he studied her beauty, she was laughing at a tiny lizard that had caught its leg in a thread of the blanket. Mary was attempting to set the little thing free, but to no avail. Finally, she looked up with pleading eyes for Joseph's help. He good-naturedly complied. He was not ready to admit it, but she was slowly capturing his heart.

Joachim settled himself, resting his back against the trunk of the tree that shaded him. He tried to pay attention to the discussion Mary and Joseph were having, but his body felt tired. He had not realized he had fallen asleep until Mary's shouts woke him.

"I cannot believe you would say such a thing!"

"Mary, I just want you to understand…"

"Well, I don't." Mary turned her back on Joseph and walked back toward Nazareth in a huff.

Joseph stood in stunned silence. Joachim slowly came up from his sitting position and made his way to the younger man. "What happened?"

"I honestly don't know. One minute we were talking about family, and the next… Well, you saw her. She just stomped off like a child."

Joachim laughed. "Son, you will learn that women are fickle creatures. I'm sure that by the time we return to Nazareth, Mary will have calmed down."

"I'm not so sure." Joseph picked up the blanket and basket. He knew he had said too much to Mary. Silently, he prayed that Joachim would not ask any more questions on the matter.

"So what did you say to my daughter to cause such an explosion of emotion?"

Joseph wanted to swear. He couldn't understand why Joachim

FAVORED

always probed him for answers he didn't want to give. It was not Joseph's nature to lie. Come what may, he spoke the truth. "I told her what I thought of love. That it wasn't necessary to feel love for someone as long as you provided for her needs to the best of your ability, that's law that spoke nothing of love between two people—only that they uphold their promise to each other."

"You said that, did you?"

"Yes."

"You have much to learn." Joachim shook his head at the stupidity of the young man.

"What are you saying?" Joseph looked at the elderly man. He was walking slower than usual. Joachim's face and skin appeared pale. Joseph assumed he had blown it with both father and daughter.

"Joseph, a young girl's dream is to have a life of love. She may say she wants children or a nice home, but what she really wants is to know she has your heart. Mary's greatest fear is that you will not love her. You don't have to explain your position to me, but don't try to make Mary understand it, for she won't. Just do for her as you have said. She will eventually assume your deeds speak of the unspoken love you have for her."

"Is that honest? Shouldn't she know that I believe myself incapable of loving someone again?"

"Joseph, I have not pushed you on the subject because I understand that a man such as yourself wants to keep some things to himself. I ask you, for the sake of my daughter, to tell me why you feel the need to protect yourself from loving or being loved."

Joseph realized the old man had stopped walking and was talking in slow, shallow breaths while he waited on Joseph's response. "I don't know. Perhaps I will never be free from the past that haunts my soul."

"You allow it to haunt you. You have a choice as to what road you will walk. You can either continue to dwell in the past as if it happened yesterday, or you can choose to make it a memory and move on with your future."

"You make it sound easy. I can tell you it's not. Sometimes when I look at Mary, memories of Hannah invade my mind. I've tried to memorize the features of Mary's face so that it is she I see and not Hannah. I listen to Mary's laugh and the sound of her voice so that I can escape the voice of Hannah, which still speaks in my ear. I'm not comparing Mary to Hannah, but I thought Mary might replace her. Thus far, Mary has only served to remind me of what I once had and may never have again."

"Son, Mary can never replace Hannah. You're going about this all wrong. Have you ever forgiven Hannah?"

"How can you ask me that when you don't know what happened?"

"I don't have to know the details to know that she willingly took what you freely gave and threw it back in your face. Have you forgiven her?"

"Forgiving her is not the issue. The issue is that I fell for a girl who broke my heart, and I have yet to heal from what happened over ten years ago."

"Son, the way you achieve full healing is to forgive the one who wronged you. I learned with Anna that even the smallest hurt can become a mountain of pain when left untreated. Forgiving Anna became my way of moving past the hurt and left me free to love her, faults and all. Forgiveness is a choice. You can continue to harbor resentment toward Hannah, which will inevitably destroy your relationship with Mary, or you can forgive her and begin to live anew. Forgiveness is a powerful remedy for bitterness."

"But Hannah hasn't come to me seeking forgiveness."

"No. But do you think your bitterness is hurting her or you more?"

Joseph thought on all Joachim had said. He didn't even know if Hannah was alive or dead. For the past ten years, he had been

FAVORED

holding a grudge toward a girl who, for all likely purposes, had probably not even given him a second thought. Joachim was right. He had only hurt himself, and now his bitterness was hurting Mary.

"I will do as you have said. At least, I will try. I will attempt to forgive Hannah. Will Mary forgive me? I said many things today that I know hurt her. I am such a fool."

"Mary is a remarkable girl. Seek her out and share with her your pain and your decision. She will understand. Shall we continue home?"

Joseph slowed his pace to match Joachim's. The old man did not look well. Joseph did not want to put more stress on him, but one question kept coming back to Joseph. "Joachim, sir, can I ask you just one more thing?"

"By all means."

"Do you think it possible for me to love again—truly love—someone again? Mary is special. I know that. I want to give her what she deserves and much more. Am I capable of doing that?"

"Listen to yourself. You've already begun. It is amazing what can happen between two people over time." By now, Joachim was breathless. He stopped to rest near Josiah's cart, where Josiah was busy trying to sell a bowl to an elderly woman.

Joseph stood a head taller than Joachim and had to bend down to look into the old man's eyes. "Joachim, are you all right? Do you need something?"

Joachim could barely get the words out of his mouth: "Drink, please."

Joseph hurried over to Josiah. Joachim saw the young man point in his direction. The noise and people around him began to spin as a sharp pain gripped Joachim's chest and went down his arm. He slumped down to the ground. He faintly heard Joseph yell for someone to get his wife and daughter. The coolness of the water dripped down Joachim's chin.

Joseph quickly scooped the old man up in his arms and hurried through the streets of Nazareth toward Joachim's home. Halfway, he met Mary and her mother. Joseph saw the tears that streaked down Mary's face and knew he was the cause of her pain. It broke his heart to think how insensitive he had been to his bride. Now her father might be dying.

With questioning eyes, Anna looked at her husband then at Joseph. "Joseph, what happened?"

"I'm not sure. We were making our way home when he collapsed in the street. He was out of breath and very pale."

Mary had to take two steps to Joseph's one. People following the family pushed into Mary as she kept close to Joseph's heels. As they approached the house, Joseph yelled over the crowd, "Mary, tell everyone to wait outside. Join us as soon as you can." Joseph pushed the front door open and went straight for the bedroom. He lay Joachim down and watched as Anna gently soothed her husband.

Leaving the couple alone, Joseph seated himself across from Mary at the family table. "He'll be fine."

"I don't think he will be fine. He's not been well for some time."

Joseph wanted to comfort the young woman. He wanted to embrace her and allow his body to be the strength she needed, but it wouldn't be right. Instead, he remained silent hoping his presence would speak for itself.

"Joseph, my father is going to die. Isn't he?"

"Nothing is for sure. We will wait and pray."

"I'm sorry I left you today. I shouldn't expect so much. Mother said I should be honored to be marrying a man as respected as yourself."

"Mary, I am the one who needs to ask you for forgiveness. I have much to let go of before I can start anew."

FAVORED

"Are you saying you don't want to marry me?"

"No, not at all. I'm looking forward to our union. It's me. I want to give you everything you deserve in a husband. I'm afraid I will fail you. Then again, I guess I already have." Joseph hung his head. He didn't know how to share what was in his heart.

"Joseph, I am beginning to believe there is hope for us. You will not fail me because God won't let you. Please don't give today another thought. I forgave you before you asked me."

Joseph looked up. The full understanding of all Joachim had spoken to him was reflected in the eyes of the girl sitting before him. Theo had been right. He was a lucky man.

Chapter Seventeen

Anna knelt beside her husband's bed. He was deathly white; she had seen that pallor on Miriam before she died. It would only be a matter of time before Joachim would breathe his last. Anna wiped a tear from her eye. She tried to pray but couldn't. There was no comfort to be found when facing death.

Joachim reached his trembling hand toward his wife. He enveloped her small hand in his. "My love, do not cry for me. God knows what is best. I go to rest with our fathers. There is peace in that."

"Husband, I do not cry for you. My tears, I am ashamed to say, are for myself. I am afraid."

"Now, now, you will be fine. You have Mary and Joseph to see to you."

"Yes, but I will miss you in my bed. I will miss your support and comfort when I am down. I will miss your patience with me. I will miss you." Anna broke into tearful sobs, burying her head in Joachim's chest.

Joachim held his wife close as she mourned the inevitable. He thought about the course of his life. God had been good to him. God had blessed him with a good woman, a child, and comfortable living. He had made the necessary preparations for his daughter and his wife. He stroked Anna's graying hair as he, too, wished for more time with the ones he loved. Another pain gripped his chest and arm. It was becoming more difficult to breathe. There was one more item that needed to be taken care of before he passed.

"Anna, Wife, please bring Mary and Joseph to me."

FAVORED

Anna nodded. She lightly kissed her husband on the cheek and went to do as he asked.

"Mary, Joseph, Joachim would like you both to join him."

Anna followed the two into the bedroom. Her heart broke as she watched her daughter kiss her father. Joseph stood to the other side of the bed. Joachim spent several minutes comforting his only child. Then he motioned for Anna to come to his side.

Joachim whispered something to his wife, and she responded with a nod. She left the room briefly, returning with a small box. Joseph watched as she placed the box on Joachim's chest. She drew his hands to the box and then looked at Joseph.

"Joseph, he wants you to come closer. His time is very short." Tears eased their way down Anna's cheeks.

Joseph knelt beside the bed. The memory of his own father's death flooded his mind. In the past few months, this family had replaced the whole that had been left by the loss of his own. He knew the pain that Anna and Mary would feel. He didn't want that for them, but he felt helpless to stop it. Joseph had to lean into Joachim to hear the words the man spoke lovingly to him.

Joachim placed a trembling hand on Joseph's head. "Son, I know you fear what you have lost. Give Mary a chance to help heal that place in your heart that you have sealed up. The God of our forefathers has a plan. Trust Him. Weeks ago, you gave me a high price for the hand of my daughter. It has always been my intention to return that to you. You and Mary could use the gold for your own family. I am not releasing you from your vow of marriage to my daughter. No one is to know what has transpired here today. I am bestowing a blessing to you by giving you my daughter, Mary."

Joseph looked up to find Mary standing beside her mother.

Joachim motioned for his wife to come near. "My wife, I have loved you more than myself. You have given me a happy life. I know Joseph will help take care of you. You have nothing to fear.

Mary, child." Joachim reached for his daughter's hand. "I know things are not as you want them. Give it time. Remember the teachings of your grandmother and your father." Joachim then placed Joseph's hand over Mary's. "This is what God wants. Do not stray from His desire for you." With those words, Joachim breathed his last breath.

Through her tears, Mary looked over at Joseph to see tears flowing unhindered down his face and into his beard. Before her was a man who could hurt deeply; consequently, he could love deeply.

Anna stood at the foot of the bed that had been hers and Joachim's since they were married. Her husband looked peaceful in death. They had lived happily for many years. She had hoped for more time with him. The tears that flowed from her eyes entered the well of bitterness that had built itself up in her heart. Too soon, God had taken her mother. Too soon, God had taken Miriam. Too soon, God had taken her husband.

Anna knew her feelings were wrong. She had been taught that God would do as He willed. But she didn't have to accept it. It had only been moments since Joachim passed, but the loneliness was beginning to take over the room. Anna turned and left. She opened the front door and told the crowd that Joachim had passed. Immediately, Rachel sent for mourners. The crowd dispersed as Anna closed the door. She returned to the bedroom to find Mary and Joseph just as she had left them. She touched her daughter's shoulder and silently motioned for the two to join her around the table.

She informed them that mourners had been summoned and would be arriving shortly. She and Mary needed to prepare the body for burial. Joseph would make the arrangements for Joachim's body to be buried on the outskirts of town. As Joseph took his leave, Anna asked if he had retrieved the tiny box from her husband. Joseph shook his head. Anna hurried into the bedroom. Retrieving the box, she returned to Joseph and placed it in his hands. "It was his wish." Joseph nodded and left the mother and daughter alone in their grief.

Anna went to her daughter, cocooning her in the safety of a mother's arms. Anna needed Mary now more than ever. In a matter of months, Mary would make her home with Joseph. Anna sank to her knees at the thought. She would be alone. Joseph would take care of her—Joachim had told her so—but it wouldn't be the same. The picture of a mother consoling her daughter was replaced with a daughter consoling her mother.

Mary gently stroked her mother's hair as Anna cried into her daughter's lap.

"It will be all right, Mother. You'll see. God will take care of us. He has sent us Joseph at just the right time. You'll see. All will be well."

Over her daughter's words, Anna heard the mourners approaching their home. Their cries echoed the loss that engulfed Anna's whole being. Anna raised her head. Illuminated in her daughter's eyes was a piece that Anna did not feel. Standing, Anna straightened her tunic and wiped her eyes. Mary watched as her mother busied herself with gathering the necessary items needed to prepare her father's body.

Mary followed her mother into the bedroom. The first thing Anna did was wash her husband's body. The way Anna gently stroked Joachim's body with the linen cloth made Mary feel that she was intruding on a very intimate moment between husband and wife. Mary heard the kind words Anna spoke to Joachim as she worked. Mary watched as her mother oiled his body and wrapped him in the burial cloth.

Sorrow rose, and Mary, as her mother covered her father's face, fled from the room, escaped the house, and ran. Blinded by her tears, she hurried through the streets of Nazareth, unsure where she was heading. She found herself some distance from the city, back at the spot where the afternoon had begun for her father, Joseph, and her. She hunkered down beneath the tree where her father had found shade hours earlier.

Sorrow overtook her whole body. She physically shook with each tear that streamed down her face. Grief and anger coursed through her. With each mournful sob, she would hit the ground with her balled-up fist. She wanted to throw herself on the ground kicking and screaming until she got her way. She wanted her papa alive. But no temper tantrum could bring him back.

As orange and pink rays began to replace the golden beams of sunlight, Mary heard herself praying. Caught up in her sorrow, she was unaware of her actions. It was as if she was listening to a voice, not her own, cry out to God for comfort. "God, why Papa had to die at this time I do not understand. I understand that You see the deepest part of our hearts. Papa had a very good heart. He kept all Your ways. I don't know if Mother and I can go on without him. Please, God, You must help us. I'm scared of what the future holds. I knew everything would be fine as long as Papa was there. Now, I feel abandoned. Grandmother said that You are our help and salvation. Please, God, help me now. Help mother. Do not forsake us when we need You."

I am your ever-present help in times of trouble.

The pain of losing her father was overwhelming. Her grief felt like a scratchy cloak she could not remove. It was uncomfortable and cumbersome and weighed her down as she made her way home. But, just as the dawn dispelled the darkness of night, peace returned to Mary's soul, lighting the darkest corners. In that moment she knew that no matter what happened, God was there for her. Pain and sorrow would come through the course of her life, but through such sadness, hope could flourish. She quietly thanked God for His presence with her.

She saw Joseph some distance away coming toward her. She knew he had seen her as well, for he ran to meet her. Out of breath, Joseph gasped, "Mary, your mother has been sick with worry, as have I."

"I'm sorry. Mother didn't need this now. But seeing Papa

FAVORED

wrapped up like that—I couldn't bear it, Joseph."

"I understand. Can I see you home? It's late."

"Yes. Thank you."

The two walked side by side in silence. Joseph knew Mary would need her space. He chose to stay close enough that she could sense his presence without compromising their situation.

"Joseph, may I ask you a question?"

"I suppose so."

"Is this what it was like for you when you lost your mother and then your father?"

"I haven't really thought about it much. Life and death just happen. You get used to it."

Joseph was solemn as they walked on. He had already been through one difficult conversation with Joachim. He didn't need to have another one with Mary.

"Joseph, you baffle me. While you knelt beside Papa's bed, I saw tears flowing down your face. I don't think you're used to it at all. I think you're afraid. I know I'm scared to live the rest of my life without my papa. Death may be a part of life, but we don't have to get used to it. I certainly don't want to get used to it. That thought scares me even more. I mean, if people were to get so used to death and experience no sorrow or pain, then how would they know peace or love or truly be able to experience all the good things that life has to offer? You numb yourself to one emotion; you numb yourself to all emotions. Maybe that's why you think you can't love me. You don't want to feel anything at all."

"Are you finished?" Joseph tried to keep his temper in check, but at that moment, he was sure it would be better to be caught without his clothes on than to have to endure another moment of listening to her. *Like father, like daughter.* Both left him feeling vulnerable and bare. He might as well have been naked.

"Why?"

"Because we're a few steps away from your door. I think your mother could use your words of comfort more than I."

"Oh, Joseph, I'm sorry. Sometimes my tongue gets away from me. Forgive me. I said more than I should."

"I would agree that you said quite enough. Mary, you might as well know that I had a long talk with your father before he passed. I know I have some things I need to work on. I know I'm not the kind of man you want to marry. You want to hear words that I simply cannot say right now. Your father asked you to give it time. I'm asking you to give me time. Besides, you should be thinking about your mother. She needs you to be there for her. I'll come back later and see you both to the burial site."

"Thank you." Tired and dejected, Mary entered her home. She found her mother dressed and sitting at the table.

"Joseph found you?"

"Yes."

"You'd best hurry if you intend to go to the burial grounds with the procession."

"It will only take me a moment to change."

"Joseph is planning to go with us, I trust?"

"Yes, though I am not sure I want him to go."

"Don't be too hard on him, Mary. You both have much to learn about life and love. Your father was a wise man. Do as he instructed: give Joseph time."

Mary knelt down beside her mother. "I am more concerned about you than I am Joseph."

"Death is a part of life. That is a lesson I've learned all too well."

"Now you sound like…" A soft knock at the door kept Mary from finishing her sentence.

FAVORED

As he'd promised, Joseph returned to escort Anna and Mary to the burial site. The *bier*, which Joachim's body rested on, was carried by close friends of the family. The mourners followed the bier. Anna, Mary, and Joseph followed the mourners while friends trailed behind them. The procession made its way through the streets of Nazareth and to the outskirts of town.

Mary held onto her mother's arm. Joseph held on to both of them. Only Mary and the mourners, who were paid to do so, shed any tears.

While preparing her husband's body, Anna had mourned her loss. She had cried as she wrapped his arms in cloth, knowing she would never again feel him embracing her. She had cried when she realized her husband would never see their precious daughter on her wedding day. She had grieved over grandchildren yet to be born who would never know their grandfather. It was in those final moments, alone with her husband, that Anna had mourned. She had mourned the past Joachim and she shared. She had mourned the present that would never be. She had mourned the future that had not happened yet.

Joseph stood silent beside mother and daughter as Joachim's body was placed in the ground. He was surprised that Anna had not shed one tear, whereas Mary seemed inconsolable. *Is it better to cry tears that come from deep within or to show no signs of sorrow? Was Mary right? If a person buries emotional pain, would one begin to forget how they feel altogether?* The questions simmered in Joseph's mind as he watched the mother and daughter.

Slowly the crowd dispersed, and the mourners left. Only the three of them remained at the grave. Joseph waited until, with Anna's urging, they made their way back to the house. Anna entered her home, leaving Joseph and Mary standing just outside the front door.

"Mary, I just want you to know that I think you were right about what you said earlier."

"What did I say?"

"That if people couldn't feel sorrow, then they couldn't feel joy or love, any of the other good things life has to offer. I don't want to be like that. I want to feel all that life has. I still need time to sort through some things. But, more importantly, I know I want to share and feel those things with you."

"You do?"

"Yes. Your mother needs you now. I'll give you all the time you need to mourn."

Mary watched Joseph walk up the street and turn toward his home. It amazed her how one day could hold this much sadness and yet still hold hope.

Chapter Eighteen

After a month of mourning, Anna and Mary cleansed themselves as was instructed by the law. Mary had hoped that once the mourners had gone and the normalcy of life resumed, the sadness in her heart would diminish. Such was not the case. The quiet evenings alone with her mother only intensified the loss of her father. They ate in silence. After finishing a meal, Anna would excuse herself to the privacy of her bedroom, leaving Mary the task of cleaning up and preparing the necessary items for the next day. Mary didn't mind the work. It was just that, after the evening meal, there was no mention of God or discussions concerning the teachings of the prophets as they had used to do.

With the evening tasks finished, Mary prepared for bed. She lay awake, praying her mother would find peace and comfort in God. She would think about her last conversation with Joseph. She had not seen him since her father's burial. He had told her he would give her and her mother time to mourn. Mary felt that he was staying away for different reasons. Many times she would fall asleep with the wet of tears on her cheeks.

It was difficult to understand that it was already the sixth month of the year. Time had flown by, bringing many changes. Mary's concern for her mother overwhelmed her. Anna had become virtually speechless since Joachim's death. She had always appeared younger than her years, but since the loss of her husband, Anna had begun to show her true age. The lines on her face were more pronounced. The gray hair, which had served as a frame around Anna's face, now seemed to cover her whole head like a scarf. Anna's eyes, once glowing with life, now seem to mirror the hollowness within her soul.

FAVORED

Mary was afraid it would not be long before her mother rested beside her father. For the first time, she understood the fear of loneliness that had encased itself around Anna's heart.

Rachel found ways to come over more often. She was kinder and gentler with Anna. Mary was grateful for the company; if nothing else, it forced Anna to remain a part of the living. It also served to give Mary someone to talk to.

Lydia had come over once or twice. Her family was preparing to move to Thyatira, where purple cloth and other fine silks were in abundance. The two friends would probably never see each other again.

Lydia was not overly excited about the move. Her father was Greek, but he had been converted to Judaism as a child. He had lost his family to illness and had been fortunate enough to be reared by a Jewish cloth maker and his wife, who had taken pity on the orphan boy. How they had ended up in Nazareth, Lydia was not sure, except that her father had made a fine living selling his cloth and clothing to the Roman soldiers seeking to impress the ladies.

Lydia knew the move was important to her father. She was excited to see the many new places they would pass through on their way to Thyatira. She shared all this with Mary. Still, the thought of leaving the familiar was frightening.

It scared Mary as well. Lydia was her best friend. She could share things with Lydia that she wouldn't dare tell her mother or other friends and certainly not Joseph. Mary didn't want to have to think that in a matter of weeks, Lydia would be gone. Unlike her mother, who allowed her fear to turn to bitterness, Mary took her loneliness to God.

Through the loss, fear, and loneliness, Mary's faith in the unseen God of her forefathers, grandmother Miriam, and her father grew in abundance. What started as a small kernel sown by an old woman and nurtured by a caring father was blossoming into a beautiful flower. Though she still mourned her father's passing, Mary's face held a smile that spoke of the joy and peace that permeated her soul.

One night, long after her mother had gone to sleep, Mary lay awake on her mat, watching the night sky through the tiny window above the sideboard. The stars seemed especially bright. The full moon was casting light to the earth below. Mary spoke to God of all she felt concerning all that He had created.

It was during this time that Mary became aware of a presence that was filling the room. At first, it was simply a feeling. Gradually, the room became bright with the presence of the being. The brightness blinded Mary. She felt for her blanket and wrapped herself in the safety of its warmth.

Once her eyes adjusted to the light, she was able to see the form of what appeared to be a man, shining with brilliance and regality. Yet, it was not a man at all.

"Greetings, you who are highly blessed! The Lord is with you."

Many questions went through Mary's mind, but she was too afraid to speak. Once again the being spoke to her. His voice was tender yet authoritative.

"Do not be afraid, Mary. You have found favor with God. You will be with child and give birth to a son, and you are to give Him the name Jesus. He will be great and will be called the Son of the Most High. The Lord God will give Him the throne of His father, David, and He will reign over the house of Jacob forever. His kingdom will never end."[1]

Mary heard herself ask in a voice that held reference in strength, "How can this be since I have never been with a man?"

"The *Holy Spirit* will come upon you, and the power of the Most High will overshadow you. So the Holy One to be born will be called the Son of God. Even Elizabeth, your relative, is going to have a child in her old age. She was said to have been barren

1 Luke 1:30–33 (NIV)

but is in her sixth month. Nothing is impossible with God."

Mary humbly spoke her heart, "I am the Lord's servant. May it be to me as you have said."

In a moment the room fell dark. The only light filtering through the window came from the moon. Mary felt strangely at peace. She allowed the angel's words to replay in her mind.

Elizabeth was with child. She would be with child. Mary tightly hugged herself. She giggled at the thought that excited and frightened her. *The Most High was favoring me.*

Mary nestled beneath her blanket as she relaxed on her mat. One minute she felt very special, chosen, and loved; the next she was overwhelmed and scared. One thing was certain: she had to wait upon God. She would not tell anyone about the angel's visit. She would hold dear what had been spoken until the angel's words came to pass.

Her thoughts drifted to her mother. How would she tell her mother that she was with child while being pure? *Will she believe me?* Mary was getting ahead of herself, thinking such thoughts. She had to trust God. She was in a position to do no less.

What of Joseph? She thought of her future husband. Joseph had been hurt once. What if he assumed that she had betrayed him? A tear trickled down her cheek, not for herself but for Joseph. She didn't want to hurt him. Her feelings were growing toward him. She cared about what he thought and how he felt about life—about her.

For whatever reason, God wants Joseph to be your husband. This is what God wants. Do not stray from His desire for you. The words of her father eased the tension that had been building inside her. Mary curled herself up into a ball, pulling her blanket to her chin; she folded her hands against her chest and began to pray. "I meant the words I spoke to the angel You sent. I am Your servant. I must confess I'm scared of what is to come. Grandmother said that You take care of the smallest details. There seem to be many details left unknown to me. Perhaps that is how You want it to be. Give my heart and mind peace to trust and wait on You. I've said before that I still feel like a child, even though others say I am a woman. Now, to be told that I will carry Your child—I am not sure I am ready for such an honor. Guide my steps as You did my forefathers'."

Mary felt her eyelids grow heavy with sleep. She yawned and stretched her legs. Turning over on her mat, she thought of one more request to ask God. "Please, be with Elizabeth. The angel said she is in her sixth month. What a blessing for her!" Mary then fell into a deep, restful sleep.

Chapter Nineteen

Mary did not have to wait long to know that the angel's words had come to pass. For the very month of the angel's visit, her courses did not flow. She knew that life was growing inside her. Each evening, Anna chose the solitude of her bedroom, leaving Mary alone with her thoughts and child. She secretly began to sew items the baby would need upon arrival. She would talk to the child as if He were present, sitting beside her. At times she thought herself silly for such things. The joy of knowing she was carrying the Son of God crushed whatever thought of silliness that came to her mind. However, there were two pressing decisions that needed to be made. One was how to tell her mother of this news. The second was how she would tell Joseph.

Anna and Mary sat at the table, eating their morning fruit and bread. Anna had opened the front door, allowing the warm breeze to blow carefree into the house. Mary attempted to eat a little something. She needed to keep her strength up and provide nourishment for both herself and her child, but with each morsel came a feeling of nausea that stifled her appetite.

"Mary, child, are you feeling unwell?" Anna searched her daughter's face for an answer. "You're very pale. Perhaps you should go lie down. I'll clean up and do your duties today." Anna began to clear away the table. She poured water into the basin and began to wash the dishes.

"I think a walk in the morning air is all I need. There is something I would like to talk to you about. Perhaps, after supper this evening, we could spend some time together." Mary didn't look at her mother, who was good at knowing exactly what was on Mary's mind. She was afraid if she looked into her mother's

FAVORED

eyes, Anna would discern the truth.

"By all means. I know I have kept to myself since your father's passing. A nice visit between mother and daughter would do us both good. You go on and see if the warmth of the sun can put some color back into my beautiful daughter's cheeks." Anna looked up from her task to smile at her daughter. She felt that there was no mother on earth prouder of her child than she was of Mary.

Mary smiled back at her mother. She donned her shawl and stepped out into the morning sun. She did not feel well at all. She hurried to the side of the house and lost what little she had eaten. She looked around to make sure she was alone. Feeling confident no one had seen her, she headed toward the outskirts of Nazareth. She found a shaded spot not too far from town. She was grateful for the solitude, fresh air, and warmth. She used the time to formulate what she would say to her mother. Once she told her mother, then she would tell Joseph.

Finishing her morning tasks, Anna decided to clean around the home. Having the door open had caused the dust from the road to blow into the house. She snagged her broom from the corner and began to sweep around the table and chairs, pausing for a moment as she reached Joachim's seat. Her husband had loved the evening spent around the family table. He enjoyed sharing stories of his youth with their daughter. He could repeat the words of prophets with the authority of a rabbi. "Oh, how I miss you, Husband." Speaking the words out loud stung Anna's heart. She went back to busying herself with her duties.

"It will please Mary to have her corner of this house cleaned." She took Mary's blanket outside and gave it a few good shakes. She neatly folded it and laid it on the table. Next, she rolled up Mary's mat. She took the broom and swept the floor before unrolling the mat, careful to place it back in its original position. She laid the neatly folded blanket at the foot of the mat, taking pleasure in knowing she was helping meet the needs of her family.

She caught sight of the many baskets that had accumulated in the corner beside Mary's mat. "High time we throw out the old ones, I suppose." She began to go through each basket to make sure none of them held some hidden treasure long forgotten. Anna couldn't bring herself to throw anything away. She decided to separate the baskets into two groups. One pile held the baskets she would keep, and the others she would give the poor. She was down to the last remaining few when she picked up a terribly misshapen basket that felt quite heavy. "What could possibly be in here?" Anna sat down on the floor and pulled off the lid. At first, she thought she had found old swaddling clothes of Mary's or even some of her own. But her keen eye saw the newly sewn stitching. The clothes were fairly new, not threadbare and worn. "Who would sew new swaddling clothes, and for what purpose?"

Anna turned at the sound of the door opening. She watched as her daughter froze at the sight of her sitting among the baskets. Mary couldn't move when she saw what her mother held in her hands. The tiny pieces of secret she was carrying were visible. What was once unknown was now known. Realization spread like a thick fog through the room. Mary closed the door and went over to her mother. She gently took each item from her mother's frozen hands and placed them back in the basket. Anna could not even look at Mary, let alone attempt to help her. Quickly, Mary set the basket aside and positioned herself beside her mother.

"This is what I wanted to talk to you about. There is much I need to tell you."

Anna began vehemently shaking her head. She didn't want to hear what Mary had to say. This wasn't how things were supposed to be. She had been wallowing in self-pity since losing Joachim. *Has Mary sought comfort in the arms of a man? Has she been taken advantage of? Has Joseph done this?* Anna stood and distanced herself from Mary. She couldn't look at her. She needed to think this through.

God, please help me. I don't know what to say. This isn't how

FAVORED

I wanted her to find out. Mary stood to her feet. "Mother, please. You must hear me. It is not what you think."

"How do you know what I think? Are you going to tell me you are sewing these items for a friend in need? If that is the case, why did you hide your good deed?" Anna paced the length of the tiny home. She wrung her hands to keep them from trembling. For the first time, she was grateful Joachim was not alive to see their daughter in this condition.

"No, Mother, I am not sewing the swaddling clothes for a friend. They are for my use."

Anna swung around to face her daughter. Anger, hot as coals, was burning inside her. "Aren't you getting ahead of yourself? You and Joseph are not one yet. Or have you already coupled?"

Mary began to feel weak. Her mother was thinking the worst. "No, Mother, Joseph and I have not been together."

Anna threw her hands up. "Mary, no! How could you give yourself to another? Joseph is such a good man."

Mary sank to her knees. "I did not give myself to another man."

"Oh, my child, someone has taken advantage of you! Tell me who. Joseph will deal with this matter." Anna hurried to her daughter. Kneeling beside her, she wrapped her arms around her. "I knew you were too good for such an awful deed. You've always trusted others completely. Someone was bound to take advantage of that trust."

Mary pulled away from her mother's embrace. "It is not what you think."

"Then you are not with child? But you were so sick this morning, and finding the clothes, I assumed..."

Mary lovingly looked into her mother's eyes. Peace entered her heart and, with it, courage. "Mother, I am with child, but the child I carry is from God. An angel came to me and said that I had found favor with God. I will give birth to a son. His name will be Jesus. The Lord God will give Him the throne of David. He said the Most High would overshadow me. He even said that Elizabeth is with child. Don't you see, Mother? The child I carry is from God."

Before Anna could think of what she was doing, she reached her hand up and struck Mary hard across the face. It was the first time she had ever hit her daughter. "Blasphemy! How can you say such a thing?" She took Mary by the shoulders. "Mary, speak the truth, no matter how difficult it is to say. The truth is always better than a lie."

"I have spoken the truth."

"Mary, I can't continue to listen to the lies from your mouth." Her body shook with rage as she turned away from her daughter. "I am grateful your father is dead!"

The words hurt her worse than the slap. Mary's voice rose in response to the pain her heart felt. "Oh, how I wish the opposite. He would have believed me. Miriam too."

Anna looked out the window. The brightness of the day contrasted with the darkness of her soul. In a hushed whisper Mary had to strain to hear, Anna spoke the words that reflected the whole of her life, "Don't you know I want to believe you?"

"Mother, please believe me. I speak the truth. The being was like nothing I had seen before. Miriam and Father always said God had a purpose for me. Don't you see? This is it. I am to be the mother of the Messiah."

"Don't speak of your father or Miriam." Anna used her hands to cover her ears. She couldn't bear to hear another word.

Mary gently reached out to her mother. "Please, believe me." Mary's words only served to heat an already hot fire.

Anna could not contain the whirlpool of emotions that sucked at her soul. "You think it is of my own choosing to have such little faith? Miriam taught me first, remember? I used to hang on her every word. But the realities of life step in and teach you that faith can't give you what you want. Death takes life, no matter how much faith you have. Age steals youth, no matter how much faith you have. People mistreat and abuse you, no matter how much faith you have. Children will disappoint you, no matter how much faith you have. It is not my lack of faith that keeps me from believing. It is reality. If you continue with this lie, then I will be forced to…" Anna couldn't continue.

"Mother, how can I lie about what God has done? To say that the child I carry was of another's making would truly be blasphemy. I can't do that. I won't do that."

Uncontrolled emotions began to rule Anna. Without thinking of the consequences, in disbelief, hurt, and anger, she gave her final order to her daughter: "Get what is yours and leave this house. Do not return. I never want my eyes to see you again."

It took a moment for Mary to register what her mother had said. She watched as Anna escaped to her bedroom, closing the door forever on her beloved daughter.

Mary fell prostrate to the floor. "Oh, God, God, this was not how it was supposed to be! I had peace. I trusted You. Do not forsake Your servant." Mary tearfully poured her petitions to God. "I don't want to leave my home. I want to be with my mother. But, God, she doesn't believe."

Elizabeth, your relative, is in her sixth month. Your relative…

"God, should I go to Elizabeth? Tell me what to do." The words of the angel flooded Mary's mind. *Elizabeth, your relative.* Sorrowfully, Mary acknowledged the words that entwined themselves in her heart and mind. She pulled together the items she would need for her trip. She wasn't sure how long it would take her to travel to Jerusalem. From what her father had told her, Elizabeth and her husband, Zachariah, lived just north of the city in an area known as Ain Karem. She sank into her father's chair as the task ahead overwhelmed her. "How much food should I take for the trip? Will I be safe traveling alone? What if they reject me?"

For nothing is impossible with God. Once again, the angel's words erased the thoughts that had begun to plague her.

"I am Your servant. Lead me, God."

Mary slung the satchel over her shoulder with the necessary provisions tucked inside. She balanced on her head the basket that held the treasures she had sewn with love. She knocked on her mother's bedroom door. There was no answer. Through the closed door, Mary spoke her heart. "Mother, I am leaving now. Know how much I love you. I do not hold what you have spoken against you. God will reveal the truth of what I have said to you. Perhaps when I return…" Mary left the sentence unfinished. She took one last look around the tiny house that had been her home before quietly slipping out into the unknown.

Anna heard the door to her once peaceful home open and close. She wanted to run after Mary. She wanted to take back all she had said to her daughter, but she couldn't move. She wasn't sure if it was pride, selfishness, or, as Mary had indicated, her lack of faith. Whatever the reason, Anna just sat on the edge of her bed.

Her biggest fear had come to pass. She was alone. Not another soul moved or breathed in her home. This solitude was of her doing. She had commanded Mary to leave, and she had rejected her when Mary needed her most. Now, she sat, listening to the sound of her own body inhaling and exhaling.

Where will Mary go? Lydia's family was moving, so she couldn't stay with them. Besides, Lydia's father would never allow a young pregnant girl to stay with them. He would turn Mary over for her due punishment. Anna shook at the thought. *Will Mary go to Joseph?* She said he wasn't the father, but that was when she was sticking to that ridiculous story. *What if Mary was telling the truth? Was it possible?* Anna tried to shake the thought from her mind. Mary had never lied before. *What if she was telling me the truth?*

FAVORED

Anna thought through all of Mary's options. *Would she leave Nazareth?* Fear pulsed through Anna's veins. If Mary left Nazareth, Anna would never see her daughter again.

Mary was too good to leave without talking to Joseph. Anna stood; the emotional upheaval of the day's events had taken a toll on her body. She felt cold and weak. She couldn't stop shaking. Her only hope rested in Mary's goodness. *She must be at Joseph's.* Anna reached for her shawl—she had to get to Joseph's before it was too late.

Chapter Twenty

Mary made her way through the streets of Nazareth. There was one other person who needed to know. She felt queasiness rise within her. *God, please let him understand.* If Joseph did not believe the child was from God—if he believed that Mary had broken her vow—by law, Joseph could put Mary away quietly, or he could bring her supposed indiscretion to the public forum. If Joseph chose the latter, Mary and her unborn child would die.

Mary repositioned the basket she carried on top of her head. *What should I say to Joseph? How can I make him understand and believe?* Mary prayed the entire way to Joseph's shop. He would be working when she arrived. *God, please let him be alone.* She caught sight of his home and the shop. She could hear the sound of a hammer on wood. *Maybe I should just go on to Elizabeth's. Mother could explain to Joseph why I've gone. That would give him some time to decide what to do.*

Be strong and courageous. Speak the truth boldly.

Mary knew what she had to do. She entered the shop just as Joseph was beginning to sand a piece of wood. She watched him take great care as he sanded and smoothed the roughness out of the wood. He was kind and thoughtful in his work. Her father was right. He would make a good husband.

"Mary, how long have you been there?" Joseph went to a bowl and quickly washed his hands. Mary watched as he dried them and made his way over to her. "Here, sit. This is a pleasant surprise." Joseph pulled a chair around for Mary. She sat her satchel and basket on the ground behind her and took the chair. Joseph positioned himself on top of a work table nearby.

FAVORED

"What brings you to my shop?" Joseph smiled. "Is everything all right with your mother?"

"Yes. I need to talk to you about something." Mary couldn't look into the man's eyes. She had nothing to be ashamed of; she knew she had done nothing wrong. Still, she couldn't bear to look into his eyes when she told him the news.

"You seem very serious. Nothing can be that bad."

"Joseph, you know that I am committed to my betrothal to you?"

"Yes. It brings joy to my heart. I finally feel that I'm fulfilling my duty to my family." Joseph chided himself for what he had said. "Mary, I…you know I chose you to be my wife, even before your father came to me?"

"Yes, well, no, but I understand what you're saying. It's fine, Joseph. I need to share something that has happened. I trust you will wait to speak until I have finished."

Joseph stood as his stomach began to twist in an uncomfortable knot. Whatever Mary was going to tell him would not be easy to hear. "Speak and get it over with. Do you want to break our betrothal?" Joseph couldn't keep the anger from his voice. It was as if he was being thrown back in time. *Not again, God. Not again.*

"No! I want to be your wife. It's just…you see…a month ago, I had a visit… Oh, Joseph, I don't know how to tell you. I've prayed for the right words, but no matter what words I use, I'm still afraid." Mary stood and walked around Joseph until she stood behind him.

Your refuge, your hope, your courage and strength are in Me, beloved.

"I will trust in You." Mary spoke the words aloud.

"What did you say?" Joseph turned and looked at the young woman behind him. Her deep brown eyes seem darker than

190

usual. He noticed that her face was streaked with tears that had washed away the dust on her cheeks—pale, compared to their usual flush of youth. She had the look of a frightened doe. He felt compassion for her. Whatever was troubling her did not concern her feelings for him. She was not there to break her vow.

Joseph softened and spoke reassuring me to her. "Mary, I will listen to all you have to say before I speak. You can tell me."

For the first time since she had arrived, Mary looked into the eyes of the man standing in front of her. She saw compassion and understanding.

It is time.

The words came like a rushing stream from her mouth. "About a month ago, I was praying when the whole room became lit with a strange and bright light. I couldn't make out the figure in front of me, but before I could speak, the being told me not to be afraid. He said he was from God—an angel sent to bring me great news. He said God favored me. God had chosen me to carry His Son. His name is Jesus. He will reign on the throne of David. I asked how this would happen since I have been with no man. He said the Most High would overshadow me so that the one I carry will be called the Son of God. Then the angel left." Mary had spoken quickly. She hoped Joseph had heard all she had said.

Joseph stood, stunned. The room seemed to spin around him. "What are you saying, Mary?"

"I am with child. Joseph, I swear to you that I have not been with anyone. The child I carry is of God."

"You expect me to believe this…this story! I am no fool, nor will I be made to look like a fool."

"Joseph, what I speak to you is the truth. You know of the prophecies concerning the Messiah. Can you not believe that God would choose me?"

"Mary, I am a simple man; you are a simple girl. God's Son will be born to someone not like us."

FAVORED

"Like who then?"

"I don't know! But not you. How could you lie to me? Maybe if you had just spoken the truth instead of coming up with some story to spin, I might consider other options. How could you do this to us…to me?"

"Joseph, I have done nothing wrong. I swear to you. You must believe me."

"Why did you come here? Have you told your mother?" Joseph could barely contain his hurt and anger. He wanted to lash out at someone, anyone, but the only person in the room beside him was too vulnerable and fragile. He couldn't bring himself to hurt the one person he had come to care for more than himself.

"Yes, I have spoken to my mother. She does not believe me. She is throwing me from my home. I am never to return."

"What of the one you have been with? Now that he has had his fill of you, he desires no more—is that it? So you come to me, thinking I will have another man's leftovers?"

"No, it is nothing like that. I came to you because we are betrothed. Before I leave town, I knew I must tell you the truth."

"But you have not spoken the truth! You have lied. Mary, how could you? After all I've been through. How could you? You know my past…at least some of it. You know how I gave my heart away only to have it broken. Now you do the same thing to me? Why, Mary? Why?" Joseph sank in despair.

Mary knelt beside him and reached out to console him.

"Don't touch me. I will not be defiled by a harlot."

The words cut through Mary's flesh like a knife. Fear and sorrow gripped her soul. "I am sorry, Joseph. I thought you would understand. I thought you would believe. I'm sorry." Mary stood and walked to the door where she had dropped her things.

"I don't understand, and I don't believe. I don't want to see you again. I agree with your mother; it's best for you to leave and never come back. I shall consider what course of action I will take."

"As you wish." Courage not her own overtook her. "Know that I will not choose another course concerning our betrothal until I hear what you have decided. As far as I am concerned, we are still to be wed." With that, Mary slipped from the carpenter's shop and continued on her way to Elizabeth's.

Joseph didn't even hear Mary leave the room; he was too caught up in the current of emotion that coursed its way like fire through his body. In agony, he screamed up to heaven, "How could You? Why give me another girl like Hannah? Do You enjoy seeing my pain? What sick pleasure do You derive from this?" He stood and paced the shop, knocking over whatever got his way. He felt like a caged animal seeking escape. *How could she? My hope for the future rested with her.*

Rest in Me, beloved.

"Rest in You? I think You have done enough. Wasn't it You who told me it was time? Didn't I trust You? I did all You asked of me. I believed You wanted me to pursue this girl. I am only human. I can only bear so much. Not again. Oh, God, not again." Joseph once again fell to the ground. Even his body wanted to give up. *Death would have been better than this.*

Joseph wasn't sure how long he had stayed on the floor of his shop before a soft rap came at the door.

"Go away."

"Joseph, it's Anna."

Joseph couldn't move. He heard the creaking of the door being opened.

Anna knelt beside the grieving man. "She told you?"

"Yes."

"I'm sorry. I never thought Mary…"

"Neither did I. Neither did I…"

FAVORED

"Did Mary say where she was going?"

"No."

Anna's hope shattered at the word. There was no way for her to find Mary. All she had now was time to wait. "What will you do?"

"I don't know." Joseph ran his hands through his hair. "I need time to think. I learned a long time ago not to make hasty decisions. I will not make a decision until I have had time to think."

"Joseph, Mary is all I have left. Even though I do not want to see her again, I cannot bear to have her stoned. If you find it in your heart to do so, will you please keep this between us? Please consider a mother's plea before you make a decision."

"Anna, I can make no promises to you at this time."

"I understand. I will accept your decision as God's will." Anna turned to go.

Joseph rose and faced the older woman. "Anna."

"Yes?"

"If you need anything, you can come to me. For now, we are still family. Anyway, I've come to care for you as family. Please, do not hesitate. Promise me."

"I promise. Thank you for your kindness." Anna left the man alone to ponder his loss, his thoughts, and his God.

Chapter Twenty-One

Mary took one last look at the small town that had been her home. *Someday I will return.* She chided herself for not saying goodbye to Lydia. Lydia would be angry with her. *Help her understand, God. Help her believe.* Mary turned her attention toward the long walk ahead of her. She decided it would be best to stick to the main road, finding shelter along the way that would keep her dry and hidden at night. *Protect Your servant, God.*

She had only a couple hours of daylight left; she needed to make the most of her time. Even though she was only a month into her pregnancy, she was very tired already. She couldn't imagine what it would be like to travel late during one's time. She thought about what God's plan might be for her and her unborn child. *Perhaps God wants the baby born in His holy city, Jerusalem. Maybe I am supposed to stay with Elizabeth until the child's birth.* These thoughts seemed to make sense out of the chaos that had become her life.

Mary began to look for a place to lay her head. She had walked farther from Nazareth than she had ever been in her life. There was no turning back. Fear gripped the young girl. She was truly alone. She felt tears drip from her eyes and down her cheeks. "God, why didn't my mother believe me? Why didn't Joseph believe me? I thought he was chosen by You." Through her tears and her prayer, Mary noticed a secluded area off the road.

The area was hidden by brush and rock. It would not be comfortable, but she would be hidden and, therefore, safe. She set her basket and satchel down on the ground. The basket wasn't overly heavy, but it was cumbersome. It felt good to be able to stretch. Her stomach growled.

FAVORED

"I'm sorry, little one. I know it has been a while since we ate. There won't be much tonight, I'm afraid. We must conserve our resources. I'm sure, once we get to Elizabeth's, there will be plenty to eat."

Mary silently prayed. She broke off a piece of unleavened bread. She couldn't remember when bread had ever tasted so good. She allowed herself to eat exactly five grapes. Hopefully, she would find some food along the way to supplement what little she had brought with her.

She missed her sleeping mat and blanket and watched as the moon and stars replaced the sun. The stars seemed brighter than they had appeared from the kitchen window. Mary watched as one seemed to shine brighter than the rest. It was beautiful and radiant. The sight of it brought reassurance, warming her soul. Morning would come quickly and, with it, a long day. Mary tried to close her eyes and rest to no avail.

Her thoughts, which seemed to contradict each other, drifted to her mother. *How could Mother think the worst? Why didn't she believe me? She only reacted as any mother would. She has always had trouble believing in the unbelievable. Pity her. She is the one who has lost a great joy. She is in a warm bed and has food, while you—supposedly chosen by God—lie in the open with nothing but the sky for a blanket.* As if on cue, her thoughts turned to Joseph. *He was hurt and angry. What will he do? Maybe it is best if I stay away for good. God would not want me dead. Would He? No, of course not. How can I think such a thing? I have found favor with God. Poor Joseph, I have hurt him so. He will never take me as his wife. Who will ever marry me? What is to become of me?*

Mary tossed and turned all night, fighting the thoughts that plagued her mind. The sun rose, piercing Mary's tired eyes. The queasiness started in her belly and rose unhindered to her throat and out of her mouth. Her head throbbed in rhythm, like the beating of a drum. She could not stomach food. With no time to waste, she collected her items and headed toward the road.

This would be her first full day of walking. She kept her eyes and ears open for anything that looked or sounded unusual. The warm breeze blew up dust that circled her. Mary kept her shawl wrapped around her face, but she could feel the graininess in her teeth, and her mouth tasted of dust. This did nothing but heighten the nausea in her stomach. Several times she had to stop, allowing what little contents remained in her stomach to leave her body. As the sun moved to the center of the horizon, Mary stopped to rest by a small trickle of a stream.

The water was warm but refreshing. She pulled out the bread she had brought. She ate enough to sedate her stomach. After placing the remaining piece back in her satchel, she lay down next to the stream. Between the lulling sound the stream made and her exhaustion, Mary quickly fell asleep.

"Well, well, well, what do we have here?" The voice was harsh and mocking.

"It looks like a weary maid in need of comfort."

"Yes, Philip, it does appear to be as you say."

Mary opened her eyes. The sun was bright, blinding her sight for a moment. Towering above her stood two brawny Roman soldiers. She tried to scramble to her feet, but her head was spinning, and the urge to throw up was overwhelming. It took most of her energy to squelch her stomach's desire. She would not make a fool of herself in front of these two. Determined to maintain her dignity, she slowly rose to a standing position. "Do you purposely scare every maid you come across?" Trying to act nonchalant, Mary began to pick up her satchel and basket.

"There's no need to rush off. We wouldn't mind your company, would we?"

"No, not at all. She's bound to be better at conversation than you are."

Like a scratchy blanket, fear wrapped itself around Mary.

FAVORED

God, protect me, she silently prayed. "Please don't think me rude, but I must be on my way. I'm expected back before dusk."

"Where are you headed? Perhaps we could escort you. It's not safe for a young girl to be out on the roads alone. She might run into danger of some kind."

The two men laughed. Mary sensed them closing in on her, suffocating her. Her legs felt weak and wobbly. She dropped her satchel and basket and attempted to run from the men. As if they had read her mind, one stepped to her right, blocking her path of escape, while the other grabbed her arm, causing her to stumble and fall.

"It seems the girl does need our help, for she has tripped and fallen." Jonas knelt down, his vulture-like body hovered over her, trapping her between him and the ground. He began to touch her hair and face. "We have a special one here. Her hair and skin are so soft and fragrant."

"Jonas, the commander will be joining us soon. He wouldn't approve of this behavior." Philip looked around nervously.

"I can do what I need to do before he is the wiser." Jonas began to try to lift Mary's tunic.

From somewhere deep within Mary came a blood-curdling scream. She began to scratch and claw at the man above her. Jonas tried to pin her arms to the ground, but that only unleashed her legs. She kicked him hard, causing him to double over with pain.

"What's going on here?" The stranger's voice startled the two soldiers.

Mary took the opportunity to jump to her feet. She took off running as fast as her legs would carry her. She could hear hooves pounding behind her, but she dared not look back. "Stop, I command you! I will not hurt you." The voice above the trampling of the horse's hooves sounded familiar. Mary glanced back over her shoulder. It was enough for the rider to see the girl's face.

"Mary, Mary, stop! Please! It's Theo! Mary, it's Theo!"

At the sound of his name, Mary stopped and turned around. Theo brought his horse to an abrupt stop. Jumping from his mount, he ran to Mary. Into his open arms, she collapsed in fear and exhaustion. Theo held her for as long as she needed, allowing her to cry out the fear that held her.

Mary's voice slowly returned to her as she repeated over and over, "Oh, Theo, God sent you; God sent you. Thank you. Thank you."

Theo helped Mary onto his mount and then pulled himself onto the horse. Slowly they rode back to the side of the stream. There, Jonas lay on the ground, still recovering, and Phillip stood, surrounded by a handful of men. At the sight, Mary's hands began to tremble.

Theo dismounted and then helped Mary down from the horse. He turned his attention to the two men. "I plan to ask you one time and one time only. If I am not satisfied with your answer, your punishment will be doubled. I suggest you think before you speak and speak only the truth."

"Philip, servant of Caesar, requests permission to speak."

"You may."

"Jonas and I were scouting the area as you instructed, sir, when we came across the girl sleeping by the creek. Jonas…"

Despite the pain, Jonas scrambled to his feet, interrupting Phillips' attempt at the truth. "What Philip is trying to say is that we came across the sleeping girl, and, not realizing she was asleep, thinking she was dead, I bent over her to see if she was breathing. Before I knew what was happening, she was kicking and screaming."

Someone behind Jonas hollered, "I guess you realized real quick how alive she really was!"

The roar of laughter irritated Mary. This was not a joke to her.

FAVORED

"Theo, that is not…"

"Quiet." He eyed his men before continuing. "Do you agree with what all your comrade has spoken?" He waited for a response from Philip. Theo knew the truth. Jonas had been a troublemaker before Theo had taken over as commander. Philip was a green soldier, trying to fit in.

"Well, sir…"

"Think about your future as a soldier." Theo spoke with sternness.

"The girl was asleep, but Jonas, well, he was not checking to see if she was alive," Philip answered sheepishly.

"As I thought. Jonas, you will be whipped twenty times— ten for disobeying an order by your commanding officer, and ten for lying. You'll be kept in chains until such a time that I receive your new orders. I will be requesting your removal from my command." Theo then addressed the whole garrison. "As I have already told you, we are patrolling this region in order to maintain peace and order with the Jews. We cannot bring peace and order if we conduct ourselves in such a manner. From now on, anyone disobeying the orderly rules of conduct becoming a Roman soldier will be severely disciplined and will be discharged from this command. I trust I have made myself clear."

Two men had taken hold of Jonas and stripped him of his garments. After Theo had finished his speech, someone handed him a whip. Theo gave Jonas twenty lashes. Mary couldn't stand the sound of the whip, let alone watch. She turned away, covering her ears with her hands. However, nothing she did would drown out the sound of ripping flesh. She knew that sound would stay with her for the rest of her life.

Theo finished doling out the punishment he had decreed. "We will camp here for the night." Turning his attention to Mary, he continued, "I'm sorry you had to be a witness to all of this. Most of these men have been given free rein to do as they please. I am trying to bring back discipline and honor to the Roman Army in this region."

"I thought you were in Egypt."

"I was supposed to be, but when my commander found out that I had lived with your family for a short time and I had sensitivity to the Jews, he placed me in charge of the patrols in the hillside of Judea and Samaria."

"What are you doing this far north?"

"I could ask you a similar question. What are you doing this far south?"

"Theo, I'm tired and still have far to go. Maybe that is a story for another time." Mary went off in search of her satchel and basket. She found her things, intact, where she left them.

"Mary, you know I cannot let you travel alone. It's too dangerous. Besides, it's late. The sun is going down. Stay in my tent. I'll sleep just outside where I can hear you if you need anything. You look tired and pale. You just don't look well."

"What of my journey? Can you accompany me all the way to Jerusalem?"

"Jerusalem? That's too far for you to travel alone. I can't imagine your father allowing you to do such a thing. What is so important in Jerusalem?"

"Father is gone. He died a couple months ago. I have a cousin who lives near Jerusalem. I'm going to visit her."

"I see. I was headed to Nazareth to speak to your father about some issues concerning your people, but since he has passed, there's no point in continuing my mission. With that being the case, my men and I will see you to your cousin's home. I will not take no for an answer. You will have shelter and food as long as you are in my care."

"I don't know what to say. I'm not sure it is a good idea. I mean, with all the trouble today..."

FAVORED

"Nonsense. That was one man. He does not represent all my men. Plus, you know I would not let anything happen to you. Come, my tent is up, and I smell food."

Theo led Mary to his tent. The aroma aroused a deep hunger in her. Theo pulled back the flap and allowed Mary to enter. She gasped at the sight of meat, bread, and fruit spread out on the table in front of her. Theo ordered the men serving him to bring Mary some warm water to wash with.

"I'll give you the privacy you need to wash. Then we will eat and talk. There's something you're not telling me." He left her alone in the tent.

Mary looked around to make sure she was alone before removing her tunic. She was uncomfortable exposing herself, but the water looked inviting. She allowed the water's warmth to wash over her, stripping away the dust that had caked itself to her skin. She bathed quickly and proceeded to redress, wishing that she had brought a clean tunic.

"For you. From the commander." A hand holding a folded gown reached through the opening of the tent. Mary grabbed the gown and pulled it over her head. It was soft and flowing, like nothing she had ever worn before. Mary twirled around, allowing the gown to move with the current. She was so caught up in the elegance and softness that surrounded her that she did not hear Theo reenter.

"The color suits you. I hope you don't mind. I thought you might like something clean."

Feeling embarrassed, Mary stammered, "Theo, it's too much. I will wash my tunic tonight so I can wear it tomorrow."

"As you wish. I just wanted to make you comfortable. Here, sit." He motioned to a few pillows positioned around the table.

Mary took her plate, sinking deep into the soft cushions. If her stomach hadn't been growling, she would have fallen asleep right then and there. Theo handed some fruit and roasted meat to her. Before she took a bite, Mary thanked God for blessing her so bountifully.

Theo, amused, watched Mary devour everything placed before her. He allowed her to eat before questioning her further.

"Theo, you may not believe me when I tell you this, but I believe God sent you to me. You are an answer to a Hebrew girl's prayers."

"Tell me, why would your God need to send me to you?"

Mary looked up into the gentle eyes of her friend. "I want to tell you, but not tonight, please. I am so very tired. Now that my stomach is full, I know I will just drop off to sleep."

"Very well, Mary of Nazareth. I will give you tonight. But tomorrow, you will tell me the whole of it. Even though your father is gone, I know your mother and Joseph would not have allowed you to travel this far alone. There's a mystery here, and before we walk a mile toward Jerusalem, you will tell me what I want to know." Theo blew the candles in the tent as he left.

Before falling asleep, Mary thanked God for sending Theo again. "If I questioned it before, forgive me. I know now that I am in Your hands. I am Your servant."

Chapter Twenty-Two

Mary awoke to the sounds of men's laughter, horse's name, and water splashing. When she opened her eyes it took her a moment to remember all that had happened the day before and to recognize where she was. She lay still and watched as a young boy poured fresh water into the basin, then began to set the table with food and drink. Mary noticed how quiet he was trying to be. He must have thought she was still asleep. She sat up and stretched. She could not recall the last time she had slept so soundly. However, she couldn't help but wish she had awakened from a night's rest on her own mat at home.

She must have startled the boy, for he dropped the cup he was holding, spilling its contents. As he began to dab at the liquid, he nervously spoke to Mary. "I'm sorry if I disturbed you. Master gave me strict orders not to awaken you. I was only trying to see that your needs were met when you did awaken."

"No, you didn't disturb me. I was already awake. Thank you for your kindness and hospitality."

"Thank my master." The boy quickly finished and left the tent.

Mary felt sorry for the boy. He seemed scared. She couldn't imagine Theo ever hurting him, but then again, he had given that brute of a soldier quite a heavy beating yesterday. She noticed her tunic lying on the edge of the couch, freshly washed and dried. The young boy must have done that as well. She slipped into it and decided she should try to find Theo. No doubt, he was waiting on her in order to start the journey to Jerusalem.

Mary shielded her eyes as she stepped out of the tent and into

FAVORED

the morning sun. She felt uncomfortable with the attention she seemed to draw from the soldiers camped around her. Searching for Theo, she hurriedly scanned the many faces. She finally caught sight of him near the stream. He saw her and waved; she watched as he gave orders to the men near him before heading in her direction.

"I see you decided to wake up and face the day."

"I hope I haven't been an inconvenience to you. I'm sure you want to get on the way as soon as possible."

"Mary, you could never be an inconvenience. You were extremely tired last night. I knew you would sleep late. Besides, it didn't hurt my men to have a good rest either. Have you eaten?"

"No."

"Good. Let's go in and eat. Then we will talk."

Mary had forgotten his insistence on knowing why she was leaving Nazareth to go to Jerusalem. She dreaded the conversation. She followed Theo inside the tent.

Even rest could not stop the queasiness that she felt. As good as the food looked, smelled, and tasted, Mary found she couldn't eat much. She nibbled at the bread and fruit. She couldn't even bring herself to have a sip of wine, so she settled for water. The young boy who had helped prepare the meal stood at attention by Theo's right side. He seemed eager and ready to serve his master.

Mary wanted to find out about the boy. "Is your slave someone you've had for a long time?"

"Rome can be very persuasive when it wants you to do a job in a land where you don't want to stay. He was given to me, as well as this tent with all its luxuries, on the condition that I would stay in Judea and help with the Hebrews."

"Are we that much trouble to Rome?"

"At times. Don't take offense, but the Jews are a very stiff-neck type of people. They have strange habits and beliefs. After living with your family, I have respect for your people, though I still don't understand them."

"I see. Maybe you will come to an understanding someday."

"Maybe so."

Shortly after Theo had eaten his fill, he dismissed the boy and turned his full attention to Mary. "You didn't eat much. Was it not to your liking?"

"Everything was fine."

"Did we fix something you are not supposed to eat? I tried to remember what all I ate while I was in your home. Did I not remember correctly?"

"Everything was wonderful. I'm just not very hungry right now. Maybe later I'll feel more like eating. I do thank you for your thoughtfulness."

"After all your family did for me, it is the least I can do. Seeing you safely to Jerusalem is my next task. But before we depart, you must tell me why you are leaving your mother and why Joseph is letting you go."

"I don't know where to begin. I know I can trust you, but you need to trust me. I can't tell you why I'm going to Jerusalem. I must go there, though."

"You say you trust me, but you won't tell me what is so important that it calls you away from your family?"

Mary hung her head and smiled, tears glistening in her eyes. "I can't tell you. I told Mother and Joseph, but they do not believe me. I have been called—call to something—special, but you wouldn't understand."

Theo stood. "I might. I'm not Joseph, and I'm definitely not your mother."

Mary giggled through her tears and wiped her eyes. "No, you're not Mother, and you're not Joseph." She fell quiet. Theo wasn't Joseph. More than anything, she wished she was back in

FAVORED

Nazareth. She contemplated whether she should try to tell Theo. Her heart simply didn't have peace. She stood. "I want to tell you, but I can't. I'll understand if you won't see me to Aim Karem. But I feel I have to go there, and go I will."

"Led to go there? Oh, Mary, really. Is it that simple?"

"What do you mean?"

"Are you on some mission for your god?"

"I…"

"Mary, you won't believe all the rituals I have seen performed in worship to the gods. All tribes have different gods that they worship, and they all have different ways in which they do it. Based on what I have seen, I honestly don't think anything you tell me will surprise me."

"Theo, the God I worship, the God of my forefathers…well, I believe He is the one true God. There are no other gods. So anything He asks of me, I will do."

Theo laughed at her innocence. "Let's not get bogged down with talking about religion. I know we don't agree. Why don't you just start at the beginning and tell me why you need to go to Jerusalem?"

Mary sighed. It was no use to talk to Theo about God. Her father told her that Rome tolerated the Hebrews' belief in one God as long as it didn't interfere with their rule over the land.

"I cannot tell you. Believe me, I want to, but I can't. Not yet."

Theo thought for a moment. Mary was not a deceptive girl. If she could tell him, she would. Plus he knew when he was licked.

He began to pace the length of the tent. "I can't believe Joseph would just let you leave like that. Anna as well. What were they thinking? They should know you well enough to trust you."

"Theo, Joseph and I are betrothed. He and my mother believe I have broken my vow. Joseph can either put me away quietly, or he could have me stoned for being unfaithful. I told him I would

208

consider our betrothal intact until I hear otherwise."

Theo gasped. "Unfaithful? That's out of the question. Where would they get such an idea? You haven't…?"

"No! Never!"

"I know. I'm ashamed to have thought about it." Theo continued pacing. Finally, he broke the silence that had settled on him. "If you can be a servant to a God that is unseen, then I can serve a young Hebrew girl who has come to mean much to this Roman soldier. I will see you safely to your cousin's home. You seem to think she will allow you to stay with her. If that is not the case, get word to me. I'll find a place for you to stay where you will be safe."

"Thank you. I told you last night that God had sent you to me. I was not wrong."

"I don't know about that. We need to get moving if we're going to put some distance between Nazareth and us. I wouldn't want Joseph to find you until he is at time to think things through." If Joseph did attempt to hurt Mary, Hebrew law or not, Theo knew he would be forced to stop him.

The men broke camp upon Theo's orders. It wasn't long before the small band of soldiers headed south toward Jerusalem. Mary chose to walk instead of riding Theo's horse. She had never been by herself on the back of an animal before. The thought of falling off and hurting either herself or the unborn baby was too frightening.

The day grew very long. Theo stayed close to Mary, periodically asking her if she needed to stop and rest. She always assured him she was fine. They trudged forward until Theo noticed that Mary swayed from side to side as she walked. He jumped off his horse, giving the reins to the young boy, and put his arms around the small of Mary's back to support her.

"You're exhausted. We need to stop."

"No. Really, I'm fine—just a little tired. Please don't stop on

FAVORED

account of me. I can do this."

"We have made good progress today. It's almost dusk. My men are tired as well. Now, let me help you on my horse."

Mary started to protest, but Theo wouldn't hear of it. "We have to find a place to make camp. I'm not sure how much farther we will need to walk. No arguments."

"It's just that I've never ridden a horse—or any other animal, for that matter—at least not until yesterday, with you. I'm frightened to be on the beast by myself."

"You don't seem like the type of girl to be frightened by anything. I'll stay right by your side, and I'll have Onesimus stay on the other side. You'll be fine."

"Onesimus?"

"The boy you asked me about this morning."

"Oh." Mary thought before continuing. She wasn't sure if she wanted to know the answer to her next question. "Is he Hebrew?"

"Yes. But I don't know where from. He doesn't say much to me."

"I see."

"Now, up you go." Theo gave Mary a boost, making sure she was secure on the steed before continuing on their journey.

It wasn't long before the scouts Theo had sent ahead came back with the information Theo needed. There was a flat area a few miles up the road where they could make a camp. Theo had not told Mary that he and his men had been in a number of fights with the sicarii. They had to find a safe and relatively secluded area to spend the night.

Theo was pleased to see the attention Onesimus gave to his task of keeping a steady watch over Mary. Theo had instructed him that, if anything should happen along the way, Onesimus was responsible for getting Mary to a safe place until the scrimmage had ended.

"Theo, how much farther until we stop?"

"Not too far. The scouts have informed me that they have found a nice spot for us to make camp."

"Would you be stopping if I weren't with you?"

"Probably."

"The back of a horse is a much nicer way of travel. Thank you."

"I can't believe you've never ridden on an animal before."

"I've never had the need."

"See, just up ahead? The men have already begun to set up for the night. Soon you will be able to rest."

Theo was pleased to see that his tent was already up and in order. He and Onesimus helped Mary inside. Once again, Onesimus made sure she had everything she needed for a good night of rest.

Mary couldn't believe how tired she was. She had not expected the walk to Jerusalem to take so much out of her. Before falling into a deep sleep, Mary prayed for Joseph and her mother. She thanked God for His protection of her. She prayed for Theo and Onesimus. Soon she was in a deep sleep.

Theo made sure he and Onesimus stayed close to the tent in case Mary should need anything. After he was certain she was settled and resting, Theo calculated how long it would take to reach Jerusalem at the pace they were going. At this rate, it would take them twice as long as it normally did.

Theo unrolled his mat. Stretching himself out, he looked up at the night sky. If there was only one god out there, and if he was the god Mary worshiped, then had this god orchestrated him being in just the right place at the right time to help the young girl? A god with that much power would be an awesome god, indeed—one to be feared and admired. Theo thought about the many gods and goddesses Rome worshiped. Most soldiers worship *Mars*, the

FAVORED

god of war. He had chosen that god for himself as well, more out of duty than belief.

That night, Theo had a very fitful sleep.

Chapter Twenty-Three

For two days, high winds and driving rain pelted the ship sailing north toward Antioch. Dalena had not been out of her cabin since the morning she and Lucas had met and departed—without a glance back at the man who claimed to be her friend.

She patiently waited for her maid to come and pin her hair up in a nice coiffure. Quirinius had agreed that Dalena could bring her maid into their quarters to help with her toilette. He would have agreed to anything Dalena asked for if it meant not having to spend one more minute aiding his seasick wife. Over the previous two days, Quirinius had often commented on how unattractive sick people were and remarked, "If you continue to have ill health, I might just have to divorce you."

Dalena looked at her reflection in the mirror. *I'm so very pale and gaunt. I must get off this boat soon if I am to return to my former self.*

"Your wish to get off this boat might happen sooner than you think."

At the sound of Lucas' voice, Dalena dropped the reflective metal. "What are you doing here?" She wondered how Lucas could know her thoughts.

"Quirinius sent me to tell you that your maid, Saphra, has been detained. She'll be of service to you shortly."

"No doubt she has been detained by the governor himself." Dalena could not keep the resentment from her voice. Last night, after the rain had stopped, and having endured many hours of uncontrolled stomach convulsions, Dalena went out on deck for some fresh air. She was leaning against the railing when she heard

213

laughter coming from somewhere behind her. She had peered into the darkness to see the form of her husband embracing her maid. The scene sickened her already nauseated stomach.

Not that she cared about whom Quirinius spent his time, but pride and jealousy were powerful emotions. To have such feelings surprised her, for she had wished for such a diversion for her husband. If he was using someone else to meet his physical needs, then she was free from his touch, but the idea that Quirinius would find pleasure in someone else stirred the green eye of jealousy in her. She vowed to have Saphra killed for some trumped-up charge once they reached Antioch. If anything, it might teach Quirinius a thing or two of the power she still possessed.

"Do I detect a hint of jealousy?"

"Quite the contrary. As long as he can amuse himself with whatever diversion he chooses, it means he's not bothering me. I have been waiting anxiously to have my toilette seen to so I can leave this unventilated room. By the way, I didn't hear you request permission to enter my quarters."

"That's because I didn't ask permission. The storm has kept most of us in our rooms for much too long. I might have a surprise for you."

"A surprise? From you? I don't think I will accept a surprise from you, and next time you desire entrance into my chambers, knock." Dalena picked up her mirror and returned her attention back to herself.

Lucas was not deterred in his attempt to make peace. "I will admit to saying too much to you that day on deck if you'll admit that you like my company—a little."

Keeping her gaze on herself, Dalena snapped, "I will say no such thing. I have yet to figure out how you know so much about me. I don't think even Quirinius knows as much as you claim to know. I've learned not to trust someone who knows my secrets."

Lucas drew his sword, placed it upright in front of him, and knelt on one knee, declaring, "I swear on pain of death, by my own sword, that your secrets are safe with me."

Dalena looked into Lucas' dark eyes. She figured him to be between twenty-five and thirty years of age. She couldn't fathom the reason for his concern and attention to her. He had rejected her attempt at a seduction. Since the confession he'd made a few days prior, he had made no effort to see her or apologize to her. As far as she knew, he had told no one the secret concerning her past. Dalena searched his face for any sign of treachery. With eyes that seemed to reflect his soul, Lucas gazed back at her. She saw not even a glint of dishonest character.

Cautiously, she relented, "It will be hard to avoid you if you are planning to stay on with us in Antioch. I suppose I do enjoy your attempt at chivalrous behavior."

Lucas stood and bowed before the young lady. "Then please, accept my sincere apology for being undisciplined in my dialogue on our first meeting."

"All is forgiven. I wish Saphra would get here. I really do need some fresh air. I've been sick the last few days."

"You do look a little pale."

"A little? It's going to take a lot more than a coiffure to make me presentable."

"Now, you don't look that bad. Why don't you braid your hair and let me escort you on deck? I do think the breeze and sun would perk you up. You might want to take a shawl with you, however. It's a cool breeze that blows us onward."

Childlike, Dalena questioned Lucas' attempt to compliment her, "You don't think I look too bad?"

"Not at all. You're as beautiful as ever."

Dalena thought for a moment. "Did Quirinius put you up to this in order to keep me occupied so I wouldn't wonder where he was or what he was doing?"

FAVORED

"He did send me to inform you that Saphra would not be at your beck and call for some time; the walk on deck is solely my idea."

That statement pleased Dalena. Butterflies flitted around in her stomach. The attention from a man always aroused exotic excitement in her. "Give me just a minute."

Lucas dismissed himself to wait. A moment later, Dalena stepped out of her cabin. "I'm ready for our walk. I don't know how steady on my feet I will be. I still feel weak." She was wearing a pale green stola with a beautiful, dark green palos that brought out the green in her eyes. Her hair was done in a long braid. Wisps of black hair framed her face, bringing out the paleness of her skin. There was also something different in the way she looked at him. She seemed comfortable, relaxed, almost peaceful.

Lucas gestured for her to move in from of him. "After you. We must keep up appearances, you know…I as the protector of the privileged class."

Dalena laughed. "Of course."

It seemed like forever since Dalena had been out in the sun. The brightness burned her eyes, causing them to water profusely. Even though the sailing was smooth, trying to walk proved difficult, and it took her a moment to readjust to the movement of the boat. Several times she felt Lucas' hand on her back, steadying her as they walked to the bow of the ship. His touch sent ripples of titillation through her.

Breathing in the salt air gave Dalena the feeling that she was inhaling life. The warm sun gave a blush to her cheeks. Yet, all the sensations she was feeling seemed to pull at Dalena's energy. Sensing her weariness, Lucas helped her sit on a bench anchored to the boards of the ship.

"At our last meeting, you said some things that alarmed me," Dalena began.

"Why don't we forget all about that and start over?" Lucas stood behind her, watching the horizon.

"I can't just forget about the things you said. Your words have haunted my dreams for the past two days. I know you have sworn to me your secrecy, but too many people have given me their word and then betrayed me. How did you find out such information?"

Lucas hesitated before responding. His next few words had the potential to draw her to him or push her so far away that she would never speak to him again. "Dalena, I was under the command of your father for a long time. When my service was through, my wife and I decided to live in Rome. By then, your father was a man of power and prominence. He would periodically ask for my services. He was very generous. I found myself frequently helping him deal with one situation after another. After you unwillingly revealed your identity to your father, he asked me to do some digging into your past. I located the man who had taken care of your mother's body. From there, your story began to unravel. The man I spoke with is no longer among the living. Your father gave me strict instructions to see that no one would ever find out the truth. He wanted Quirinius to believe he was marrying the orphan child Rome had come to adore. As far as I know, your father, you, and I are the only ones left alive who know your true identity. I intend to keep it that way."

Dalena was stunned. "Do you know everything?"

"I know your mother died when you were fourteen. I know what you lost in order to have her body disposed of so there would be no record of her death."

Dalena felt shame at what Lucas knew. She had lost her innocence in order to continue receiving the regular monthly sum her father would send. She needed it to survive. It wasn't the last time she made such a bargain.

With her mother's death, Dalena had changed her name and, in so doing, set about to change her destiny. She had always appeared and behaved older than she was. Her mother had often

FAVORED

spoken of her intelligence. Intelligence had served her well, but her beauty and lie concerning her family lineage were what made her acceptable in Roman high society.

She was beautiful. There was nothing the wealthy enjoyed more than to be in the presence of beauty. This gave Dalena power. She wielded her sexuality like a man wields his sword, and she had won every battle. Her husband was the spoil of her war.

Lucas' words cut into her thoughts. "I was there that night."

"What?"

"I was at the party. I was in the garden."

Dalena looked out over the water, resignation washing over her. "I thought the gods had truly blessed me when I was invited. I tried to keep my face hidden from him. Every time I look in the mirror, I see my mother staring back at me, except for my eyes. Hers were brown. Mine are green like his."

"You looked exquisite."

"I did, didn't I? Even though I kept my fan to my face, men vied for my attention. At dinner, I saw him watching me. That's when I excused myself and walked out to the garden. I didn't realize he had followed me until I heard him speak."

"He said you looked breathtaking."

Even now, the words sent a chill through Dalena. "It's not what he said; it was the way he said it. I knew with those words what he wanted. It made me want to vomit. When he turned me toward him, I saw it etched on every line of his face that he knew who I was. He stared at me for what seemed like an eternity. Did you notice what we were standing behind?"

"Yes."

"Ironic, don't you think? I can still see that statue: a loving father cradling his child."

"You stood strong. He questioned you about your mother. He

threatened to expose you. He vowed to have you killed, but you remained silent."

"When he looked in my eyes, he could not deny that his blood flowed through my veins. That alone saved me. But then, he began to plot what to do with me."

"It was during that time he sent me to find out the truth about you."

"So you work for my father." Dalena hung her head in surrender.

"I did. Not anymore. After my wife's death, a lot of things changed for me."

"So you're not here on my father's orders?"

"No. I chose to come to Syria. I've not heard from our father since my wife's death."

"In a way, I am relieved. But part of me feels truly abandoned. This means my father has indeed relinquished me to Quirinius."

"Quirinius paid a hefty sum to be proconsul of Syria. However, his position was precarious without a wife. Your father knew this. He also knew how much Quirinius desired you. Quirinius also paid a hefty sum for you."

Setting those thoughts aside, Dalena forced herself to consider her current quandary. "Now that Quirinius has found someone else to give his attention to, do you still see the need to stay on after we have reached Antioch?"

"I do. Quirinius is like many men I know. Power and wealth have made them believe they are invincible. He is the type of man who would be your friend one minute and your enemy the next. I don't trust men like him."

"What about women like him?" Dalena kept her focus straight ahead in an attempt to ignore the sensation being near a man evoked in her. The one characteristic she was sure that she and Quirinius shared was their desire for wealth and power. It

FAVORED

was a characteristic that Dalena both admired and loathed. It was obvious to her that Lucas cared little for it.

"Are you saying that you are like your husband, and I should watch my step?"

Lucas had detected the undercurrent of sarcasm in Dalena's question. He was confident that she felt she was paying an awfully high price for wealth and power. "I do not think I am different from my husband. I desire wealth and power, and I don't care what price I have to pay to get it. Now, I am on this ship headed to a foreign land. So much for wealth and power."

"I do not think you are like your husband. You dreamed of a better life and only saw one way to get it. He has had many options provided to him, and he chooses the path he walks very carefully." Lucas sat down beside her. "You need to see Antioch as a new beginning. A chance to start life anew."

"How can I start anew when I am still married to Quirinius? No, Lucas, my path was chosen for me the day I was born to a harlot. I may have adorned myself with the look of wealth, but I am still the child with whom no other children want to play."

Lucas looked into Dalena's sad green eyes. If unhappiness had a face, it would be hers. "Dalena, if you'll let me, I can be someone you trust."

She couldn't answer. Not yet. She needed time. Slowly, Lucas was earning that trust he wished for from her, but the chasm in her heart was wide and deep. Dalena believed that no one would ever close it.

Changing the subject, she asked, "You said you had a surprise for me. What is it?"

"I had forgotten all about that. I suppose it is time to tell you. By tomorrow, we will have reached the isle of Cyprus. Quirinius wants to stop for a few days. You are going to have your wish. We will disembark sometime after noon. Is that a good enough surprise for you?"

"You mean we will actually have a few days on land?"

"Yes."

"No more sickness?"

"None, at least for a few days, anyway."

"Why is he stopping? He seemed desperate to reach Antioch as soon as possible."

"I'm not sure. He claims he wants to give you time to rest and heal before sailing on to Antioch."

In truth, it had been Lucas who encouraged Quirinius to stop. He wanted Dalena to have a break from seasickness. He had made certain off-handed remarks to Quirinius concerning the isle and its many offerings. Quirinius never asked him how Lucas knew so much about the island.

Dalena thought for a moment; it wasn't like Quirinius to think of anyone but himself. Fear began to stir in the pit of Dalena's stomach. As much as she wanted to get off the Ames, she wasn't sure she should step one foot on Cyprus' soil.

Lucas watched as the look on Dalena's face changed to fear. "Dalena, I won't let Quirinius hurt you."

"I know that is what you say, and I'm sure you mean it, but Quirinius has the authority to do with me whatever he chooses. It is easier to bury the past on an island than to endure the public humiliation of a divorce or questionable death."

"Quirinius is still enamored by you. He's not ready to rid himself of you. Have no fear."

"You're sweet. Perhaps too sweet. I'm not sure you can understand the situation I am in. You loved your wife. You still do. Quirinius only married me out of political need. I only married him out of coercion and desperation. There is no love between the two of us."

Lucas sat in silence beside the young woman. There was

FAVORED

nothing to say in response to the comment he knew was true. Dalena was in a no-win situation.

Dalena reached over and gently patted Lucas' hand. "I'll be fine. Let's enjoy our time. The sky is such a beautiful pale blue. I can't see a cloud for miles and miles. Look." Dalena stood and leaned over the railing. "See, down below, I believe I can count those fish. That makes my totals significantly higher than yours. I dare say you are going to owe me quite a lot of sesterces."

Lucas smiled at Dalena's half-hearted attempt to lighten the dark mood that had overtaken them both. "I suppose you're right. I'm willing to admit defeat."

"Somehow, I can't imagine that you are used to losing, Lucas Darius. Then again, I'm not either." Dalena giggled.

"I've learned not to claim victory too soon. You never know how the tide might change."

"I'll give you that." She linked her arm through the crook of his and smiled up at him. "You know what I think?"

"What?" Lucas stood head and shoulders above Dalena. When he looked down at her, she was gazing up at him with eyes that glowed with childish delight.

"I think that as long as I have you by my side, I can endure anything. I'm proud to call you my friend."

Lucas' heart practically leaped into his throat. Then and there, he vowed to protect Dalena until breath left him. He couldn't save his half sister, but this beautiful creature was giving Lucas a second chance to make things right. Maybe the gods of his ancestors would smile down upon him once again.

"I see you two have become quite cozy with each other." Quirinius' voice seemed to echo over the whole sea.

Lucas, keeping a tight grip on Dalena's elbow, turned them to face Quirinius. "Dalena was still feeling weak from the last few days. She asked if I would help support her so she could look over the rail." He submissively bowed to the proconsul.

"Ah, yes. How are you feeling, darling?" Quirinius walked around the bench and gave Dalena a light kiss on the cheek. He offered his arm to her, and she reluctantly released Lucas and took hold of her husband's arm.

"The fresh air and sunshine have helped."

"I can see that. The color seems to be returning to your cheeks."

"I will take that as a compliment. How have you been spending your morning?" Dalena's green eyes became little slits resembling the eyes of a snake. Her question oozed with all the venom she felt.

Quirinius' eyes suddenly matched hers. The two squared off like pit vipers thrown into the same basket. "I've been busy."

Lucas watched the interchange with reluctant admiration. Dalena could not match Quirinius' brute strength, but she could outwit the man. Quirinius was prey in her hands when battling poison for poison. He smiled as the sparring continued.

"Yes, I'm sure you have." Dalena kept her eyes focused on Quirinius. She wanted him to know that she knew the truth.

Averting her gaze, and thus relinquishing his position, Quirinius looked out over the water.

Lucas inwardly laughed. Round one went to Dalena.

"Did Lucas tell you the news?" Quirinius asked.

"Yes. We are staying in Cyprus for a few days. Why, may I ask?"

"I thought you might need some time on land. You've had me worried. You've been very sick, darling."

"Since when did my health become of such a concern to you, dear husband, that you would change your plans for my well-being?" Dalena watched as the vein in Quirinius' temple began to throb. Biting the man she hated was not enough for Dalena. She desired to sink her fangs deeper.

Lucas sensed Quirinius had had enough. If the man couldn't match her wit for wit, he would use force to get her to acquiesce. Lucas forced a temporary truce. "Dalena, don't you think you've spent enough time out in the warm sun? Maybe I should escort you back to your cabin. If the proconsul agrees, of course."

"Perhaps I should be the one to escort my wife back to our cabin." Quirinius kept a firm hold on his wife.

Dalena jerked her arm away from Quirinius. "No, Husband, you stay and relax. You've had a very busy morning of business. Some time out in the sun and breeze is just what you need. Lucas, please see me to my cabin." Dalena turned from her husband and began to walk back toward the center of the ship.

Lucas waited for word from Quirinius. He knew he could not leave just on Dalena's command. He did not want the proconsul to think that he had lost control over the man sent to serve him. Such thoughts would only make things worse for Dalena.

"Go!" Quirinius barked.

Lucas was fully aware that this little tit for tat between husband and wife was not over. Dalena had only served to anger Quirinius further. If Quirinius did have ill intentions toward her, Dalena had just encouraged him to go through with them.

Lucas quickly caught up to Dalena and pulled her to the side. "What are you thinking? Those little remarks and attitude you just showed can only serve to make things worse for you. You need to learn to hold your tongue. If Quirinius wants you dead, he'll find a way to do it, and I'm afraid I'll be unable to stop him."

Dalena mirthlessly laughed in Lucas' face. "I don't care what he does to me. I'm tired of this life I'm living. All I see in my future are days of barely surviving his torture. Death would be a welcomed friend."

"You don't mean that."

"I do. I'm tired, Lucas. I have fought my whole life to survive. I don't think I can keep fighting."

"Then let me fight for you. I know you don't believe this right now, but you have much to offer the right man. When you feel like you can't make it, lean on me. I'll be there for you. You have my word."

"I know. At least, I want to believe that. But, as you said only moments ago, if Quirinius wants me dead, he will find a way to do it."

"I don't think he wants you dead. He may be spending time with that slave, but she doesn't have the regality you carry. He needs you to compliment him. A slave girl on his arm would not do that."

"I suppose you're right. I do make him look good." Dalena gave him a forced smile.

"There, that's the Dalena I've come to adore. Now, let's get you back to your cabin. I'll stay just outside the door. By the time Quirinius comes to your cabin, he will have had a little too much wine. I don't want you to be alone with him without me close by. He'll come back upset, but maybe you can use those feminine charms of yours to calm him down until he goes to sleep. Can you do that?"

Dalena reluctantly nodded. "How will you explain to Quirinius your continued presence? What if he orders you to go?"

"I'm very good at believable excuses." He laughed. "Now, let's get you back."

Dalena walked beside Lucas back to her cabin. She was hesitant to enter in fear Quirinius had hurried back. Lucas opened the door for her. Much to her relief, Quirinius was nowhere to be found.

"I'll be fine. Thank you for your thoughtfulness."

"It's not hard to be kind to someone deserving of kindness."

"If you only knew all the things I've done, you wouldn't say that."

"I know most of them. Remember?"

Dalena heard no judgment, only humor, in his voice. "How can I forget?"

"I'll be right outside the door. Try to rest."

"I will." Dalena closed the door. She leaned her back against the hardwood and thought of the man who stood on the other side. She slowly walked to the table positioned at the foot of her couch, where a small statue of *Magna Mater* stood. She lit the oil in the bowl at the foot of the statue's feet. "Magna Mater, I have entrusted my life to you. Do not turn your back on me. Set me free from Quirinius. Set me free to love someone who loves me."

She picked up the knife that lay beside the statue and made a small cut on her forearm. She allowed the blood to drip into the small flame and over the statue's feet. As soon as she was satisfied that her offering was adequate, she bandaged her arm. Then, she covered the bowl, dousing the flame.

Dalena unbraided her hair. She picked up her mirror and was pleased to see that the color had returned to her cheeks. She quickly exchanged her green stola for a soft white robe and poured two cups of wine. If Lucas thought she needed to keep Quirinius at bay by acting flirtatious, then so be it. She would do what she needed to do to ensure her freedom from the man, no matter the cost.

Dalena stretched herself out on her couch. As she waited for her husband's return, her thoughts turned to imagining herself with a man who knew all her secrets. She wondered what it would be like to give herself to a man that she could be herself with. The thought tantalized and scared her.

Chapter Twenty-Four

After sedating his anger with overindulgence, Quirinius returned to his cabin to find Lucas standing at full attention in front of the door. "Is there a problem that you are still here at my door and not resting?"

Quirinius' slurred speech and unsteadiness on his feet made it difficult for Lucas to respond to the man without laughing. "Sir, there has not been any disturbance that should concern you. I just felt it my duty to stand guard until your safe return."

"Ah, yes, yes. Quite noble of you. Now that I am here, you may depart to your own quarters." Quirinius started to open the door, but Lucas gently stopped him.

"Proconsul, your wife has been very tired and unwell as of late. I'm sure she is sound asleep by now. Your entrance will wake her. You are wise in the way of women. You know they need their rest to be fully functional. Why not sleep in another location? I'm sure I can find one that will meet your requirements."

Indeed, there was a room that would meet with Quirinius' approval. Once Lucas had assured himself that Dalena was asleep and Quirinius well attended by the indulging Saphra, he had gone about preparing alternate quarters for the governor.

Quirinius was in no state to argue with sound reasoning, nor could he think of an ulterior motive behind Lucas' suggestion. He willingly submitted, allowing Lucas to lead him to a room on the other side of the ship. Lucas attended to Quirinius' needs as any slave would do. Once Quirinius was asleep, Lucas returned to stand guard outside of Dalena's door. Soldiers were forced to learn how to rest in the roughest conditions, so it was not long

FAVORED

before Lucas found slumber, sitting on the floor with his back resting against the door.

Even before the business of the day began aboard the large vessel, Lucas was awake and seeing to the needs of his men and the crew. The ship was nearing the isle of Cyprus. The night winds had been high and in their favor. They would dock before noon.

Quirinius woke unsure of where he was. He had no recollection of the night before. The last thing he remembered was being left standing at the front of the ship, watching Dalena and Lucas walk away together. It occurred to him that, perhaps, he had overestimated the self-control the widower possessed. He lay on his bed, trying to piece together what had happened after that. Slowly, the puzzle began to take shape.

Taking great pleasure in deciding Dalena's punishment for her insubordination, he had proceeded to their cabin, only to be diverted by the tempting Saphra. The slave was not nearly as beautiful as his wife, but she was all too willing to satisfy her master wine and choice food. Evidently, he had taken too great a pleasure in the wine. He faintly recalled meeting Lucas. He looked around the room. It was small, but private, and had been furnished with his couch and personal items. There was a plate of food and a jug of wine waiting for him to partake. Quirinius poured a cup of wine and gulped it down. Wine in the morning had become his remedy for the thunderstorm that would rage in his head after a night of pleasure. He opened the door to find his slave waiting patiently to help him shave and dress. Quirinius took great care in his appearance. He could do nothing about his rotund belly. It was a product of great wealth.

Dalena, roused by the clamoring on deck, woke in disbelief that Quirinius was not in their room. At first, she was apprehensive. Then, a sense of relief flooded her soul. She knew intuitively that Lucas had diverted her husband.

She was surprised to find Saphra seated near the dressing table. The unstained piece of wood caught her attention, and for a moment she was transported back in time, recalling the Hebrew, Theo, and the whole sordid detail that had landed her aboard the Ames. She quickly brought herself back to the present. That was all in the past and she needed to focus on the present and future. Dalena fought the urge to slap the smug look off her slave's face. Saphra seemed to be laughing at her from behind those brown, beady eyes.

The thought of ending Saphra's life once they reached Antioch appeased Dalena enough for her to swallow her pride, allowing her slave to work her magic on her toilette. When Saphra had finished, Dalena looked at her image in the mirror. Her braided hair was pinned up and entwined with pearls. Her cheeks had their youthful flush fully restored. Dalena decided to wear the blue stola with the silver belt. Saphra, with a pearl comb, attached the white palos with the silver trim. She wrapped the ends around her shoulders. She admired the fetching picture she made. This was the same dress she'd worn upon first meeting Lucas. She hoped the image was not lost on him.

Dalena made her way to the bow of the ship, searching for her new friend. She ran straight into Quirinius.

"You look stunning." Quirinius lightly kissed his wife on the cheek. "I can see you are feeling much better. Lucas was right in suggesting I give you a full night of rest."

Dalena had seen the dark look of lust in Quirinius' eyes too many times not to know that he was already planning an evening alone with her. "Where did you sleep?"

"Lucas saw fit to have a room prepared for me. It was quite comfortable."

"I take it you rested well."

"Yes, yes, I did. I've been told that we will be docking very soon. Are you looking forward to our short stay in Cyprus?"

"Short stay? I was under the impression that I might be staying there for some time."

FAVORED

"What gave you that idea?" There was a wicked twinkle in Quirinius' eye.

Dalena stammered for a response. "I, well, I assumed…"

"Nonsense. Seeing you this morning only intensifies my desire for you. All of Antioch will take pleasure in having such a beautiful woman on the arm of their proconsul." Quirinius lowered his voice to a slithering whisper. "Don't you know that I intend to keep you by my side until such a time that you are no longer of service? I suggest you make yourself very serviceable to me." Quirinius smiled at his wife before turning to some men who were waiting for his attention. Dalena may have won round one, but her husband was controlling the war.

Dalena couldn't believe Quirinius had been so forthcoming in his intentions. She slowly turned and walked toward the stern of the ship. Should she be afraid or thankful? Dalena slowly came to a somewhat comforting conclusion: Quirinius thought her useful to him; she held some sort of power over him because he needed her to make him look good. This was to her advantage. With some of her confidence restored, Dalena quickened her pace. She was anxious to find Lucas.

Much to her delight, Lucas was leaning against the crates at the back of the ship, waiting for her. "I didn't know if you would show or not. I believe we have a game to play. We will have to keep it short. I have much work to do before we dock."

"I ran into Quirinius this morning."

"Did you? Did he mention if he had a good night's sleep?"

"As a matter of fact, he did. How did you manage to get him to another room? And without me being the wiser?"

"Who said I had anything to do with any of that? All I know was that he showed up slightly besotted, and rather than wake you, I suggested he sleep somewhere else. It just so happened that I knew of a wonderful little room not being used that would meet his approval."

Dalena laughed. "You never cease to amaze me. On a more serious note, Quirinius told me he would keep me around until I was of no use to him. That could be tomorrow or a year from now. My future is not as secure as I would like it to be."

"No, but at least you know nothing is going to happen when we dock in Cyprus. That should bring some peace to your mind."

"Very little. I need a plan. I need to free myself from Quirinius before he tires of me."

"I don't know how any man could tire of you. You look beautiful today. Your color is back in your cheeks. And, if I'm not mistaken, isn't that the same dress you were wearing when we first met?"

Dalena blushed. He had remembered. She wondered if Lucas knew the effect he had on her. "Yes, how astute of you to notice. Most men would not pay attention to such things."

"I guess I'm not like most men."

"No, I don't think you are. Can we not play my silly little game today? I would prefer to talk."

"Whatever you wish. Just remember my time is short."

"I understand. Did you talk to Quirinius?"

"About what?"

"How coy you are, Lucas Darius. You know very well to what I am referring. I know my husband was planning some sort of sinister plot to have me put away. Now, he is all but foaming at the mouth to keep me by his side. You must have had something to do with his sudden change of mind."

"Dalena, you give me far too much credit."

"I don't think so. Even if you won't tell me, I am eternally grateful. At least I have time to formulate a plan."

Lucas took hold of Dalena's shoulders and turned her to him. His face grew rigid with anxiety. He shook with emotion, consequently shaking her as he spoke. "Promise me you won't do anything stupid. You need to be patient and bid our time. Quirinius will be the maker of his own downfall. He won't need any help from you."

"Lucas, please, you're hurting me." Dalena pulled free from his hold on her. "What has gotten into you? What do you know?"

"Nothing." He inhaled and exhaled slowly. His pulse coming back down to a steady beat. "I just want you to be careful and on your best behavior around him." Lucas turned away from her. "I'm sorry I hurt you. It wasn't my intention."

Dalena adjusted her palos, which had fallen from around her shoulders. "You'd better go. Your men and my husband are probably waiting for their instructions. I need to think."

Lucas forced himself to face Dalena. "If you only knew..."

"If I only knew what?" Dalena looked up into the dark eyes of the man towering above her.

Lucas merely shook his head before turning to go.

The chasm in Dalena's heart widened as she watched Lucas leave. Trust didn't come easily for her; it never had. Just like a baby trying to take her first steps, Dalena tentatively had begun to trust Lucas. Now that trust was teetering, if not crumbling. *He hurt me. His hands will leave marks like others have before him.* Loneliness swept over her like a tidal wave crashing against the shore. *I thought I wanted him. I thought I could have him. I thought he was different and would save me.* Dalena walked to the railing. Her eyes scabbed the pale blue sky, then the deep blue of the sea below. "Magna Mater, mother of the earth, give me a sign. Show me what I need to do."

"Dalena."

"Lucas. You came back." She reached out for him, allowing him to take her into his arms. Burying her head into his chest, Dalena silently thanked her god for sending her a sign.

Chapter Twenty-Five

The sun beat down on Mary and the soldiers as they continued to Jerusalem. Beads of sweat trickled down Mary's face. Even the magnificent steed offered by Theo to transport her to her new home dropped from the weight of the heat. Mary looked around at the soldiers on all sides of her. Each man held his head high with pride befitting the Roman Army. However, their eyes looked weary. They had begun the journey before the sun had risen. Mary wasn't sure how long they had been walking, but it seemed forever. The ever-present slave boy, Onesimus, held the reins, guiding the stallion around every bump or hole in the road. Mary wasn't sure where Theo had gone. He had left her side shortly after the day's journey had begun, and she had not seen him since. Her back asked from sitting erect for so long, and her legs had begun to cramp.

"Onesimus. Onesimus," she called as loudly as she dared.

Onesimus brought the horse to a stop. "Yes, miss. Is anything the matter?"

"I just don't think I can sit any longer. I'd like to walk for a while if you don't mind."

"Whatever you wish. I will help you dismount." Onesimus came to the side and bent over. "Step down on my back. It will be easier for you to dismount that way."

"Oh, Onesimus, no. Your hand will suffice. I could never use you as a stool."

"It's all right, miss. That is what I am here for. Now, step down. It will be easy. Go ahead."

Onesimus waited patiently for Mary to dismount. Mary

FAVORED

felt uncomfortable using the boy as a slave. After all, he was a Hebrew like her. However, Onesimus would stay in the bent-over position until she dismounted. Realizing she had no other option, Mary stepped onto the boy's back and then down to the ground.

The boy stood, grinning from ear to ear. "I told you it would be easy."

"Indeed, you did. Thank you for your help. Would you mind if I walked beside you and we talked?"

"I suppose that would be fine with my master. He told me to do whatever you asked of me." Onesimus proceeded to take hold of the reins once again. He gave a tug, and they continued on their way.

"Do you know where Theo is?"

"No. My master stays close to the front. He has a keen eye. He sees hidden dangers the other men don't see."

"What kind of dangers?"

Onesimus heard the fear in Mary's voice. He was careful not to say something he shouldn't.

"It's fine. Don't worry. Master cares for you and your safety. You can trust Onesimus to take care of you too."

Mary knew there was no point in pursuing an answer to her question. She made a mental note to ask Theo about these "dangers" Onesimus had mentioned. "Onesimus, how old are you?"

"I'm not sure. I suppose I'm around ten. I've or take a year or two."

"I thought you might be. How long have you been with Theo?"

"A month thereabouts. I really like him. He's nice to me."

"I'm glad. Theo's nice to me too. Where were you before you came into Theo's possession?"

"Here and there."

"Where are your parents?"

"Dead, I guess. I was taken when I was very young. At least, that is what I've been told. My first master bought me to help heal the grief his mistress had at losing a child. I guess once the grief was gone, there was no need for me. I was sold to a house that had lots of children. It was my job to entertain the younger children and be of service to them. One of the children got very sick and died. The mother thought it was my fault."

"Why did she think the child's illness was your fault?"

"I'm not sure. Maybe it helped ease her grief. Anyway, she wanted me killed, but her husband took pity on me and sold me to a man sailing for Galilee. That's how I ended up here."

"What a life you have had." Mary hung her head.

"Don't feel sorry for me. I've known no other life. Someday, I will save my money and buy my freedom. Until then, I'm happy to serve my master."

"I will pray you find freedom very soon." Mary smiled at the boy.

"Do what you like."

"Don't you pray?"

"I'm not big on praying."

"But you are Hebrew."

"I've grown up around all sorts of people, who prayed to all sorts of gods. I worshiped whatever god the family I served worshiped. In most households, slaves are required to do so. My current master is not diligent in his worship, so I haven't been either. I've been in your tent. There is no statue or designated worship area for your god."

"My God is unseen. He has told us not to make any images of Him or any other god."

FAVORED

"What do you mean? I thought every god wanted an image made of him. When I was in Rome, I saw lavish temples built to honor our gods. Venders situate themselves around the temples to sell statues of the gods. No Roman domus is complete or safe without a sanctuary to the family's god of choice."

Onesimus looked blankly up at Mary. Mary realized that the boy, though he was Hebrew, had no idea of his heritage. He had no lineage to link to himself, no idea who Abraham was, or Isaac, no idea of the one true God.

"Onesimus, if you would like to hear about our people—who you come from and what we believe—I'd be willing to tell you."

Onesimus thought long and hard. "Is it important that I know? How will such knowledge benefit me?"

"Our people have a great history. We have had mighty kings and warriors who fought in battles and won victories. God gave us all this land you see before you. He watches over us and protects us. God has a plan for us. We are His chosen people."

"Then why am I a slave and you a poor girl from Nazareth? I heard Master say that is where you are from."

"I don't understand all that God has planned for us. I don't know why we are in such a place, but I know He has not forsaken us."

"How do you know this?"

"Because the prophets foretold of the Messiah who would come and rescue us. I know He will arrive soon to deliver His people."

"Who is this Messiah? How do you know He will come soon?"

Mary had gotten so caught up in her conversation with Onesimus that she had not realized how long they had been walking. The sun was high in the sky, and perspiration dripped down her forehead and into her eyes. She wiped her eyes, ignoring the burning that her salty sweat caused, and continued with their conversation. "I think we are getting ahead of ourselves. I need to tell you from whence we come so that you can understand where we are to go."

"You two must be having a very interesting conversation. Neither one of you even noticed me behind you for the last mile or so. Onesimus, you must keep your eyes and ears open at all times."

"Yes, Master." Onesimus looked sheepishly up at Theo, who now strode alongside the boy.

"Theo, don't be upset with the boy. It is my fault. I began to cramp on the horse and was bored. I just wanted to walk and talk with someone. I guess I got us both distracted."

"I'm not upset with Onesimus." Theo affectionately ruffled the boy's hair. "I'm trying to teach him to stay alert to his surroundings. A keen eye helps keep one alive. We are going to stop just up ahead. Some of the men have scouted out a nice place to rest for an hour. Then we will be on our way. We need to make it past these foothills to the east before nightfall."

"Theo, would you mind if Onesimus and I spend some time talking together? He has no idea what it means to be a Hebrew. He doesn't know where he comes from. I'd like at least to give back to him his heritage. Can I do that?"

"Is it wise for the boy to know about such things? He might stay alive longer if he doesn't."

Mary was indignant. "How can you say such a thing? Who would you be if you didn't know what it meant to be Roman? What sort of hope would you have if you didn't know who you were?" Mary was determined to convince Theo of Onesimus' need to know the history of their people. She did not realize how forceful she sounded.

"Hush. The men are going to wonder why I allow you to holler at me like that," Theo said with amused admiration. "I'll let you

FAVORED

give the boy a history lesson if you let me sit in and listen."

Mary blushed and looked around to see if anyone else had paid her any mind. Taking comfort that none seemed to have noticed, she gave her full attention to Theo. "Why do you want to listen? I heard Papa shared many things with you while you stayed in our home. What more could you possibly learn from me?"

"I don't know. Last night, I thought about all you told me. I didn't rest very well. I kept..." Theo allowed the words to trail off. He had not told a single soul about the dreams that plagued him. Now, images of a young girl screaming for help, needing him to save her or someone dear to her, invaded his demented nightmares.

Mary heard desperation and fear in Theo's voice. "Theo, God is my help and salvation. I do not fear. You shouldn't fear for me. You are welcome to listen if you think it will help you."

For a moment, Theo thought Mary had second sight into his nightmares and thoughts. "Mary...do you always put the needs of others before your own?"

Before she could answer, Theo excused himself and made his way to the front of the group. He knew deep down that he and Mary were destined to walk two different roads, but he couldn't help wondering what life would be like with a woman by his side. He tried to shake the oppressive heat that coursed through him. He was attracted to her, but she was too naïve to realize it. She was different from the Roman women he knew. She held an innocence and purity few women possessed. Mary's eyes were the deepest brown, almost black in color. Her hair was not adorned with flowers or jewels, yet it was fragrant and held a natural luster. She didn't try to be beautiful by using outside adornments. She just was. Her beauty came from somewhere deep within her soul. Theo dismissed his thoughts. Nothing but friendship, which was dangerous enough for both of them, could ever be between them. Mary was promised to Joseph. She would not break her vow. Joseph was a fool to think otherwise.

Mary didn't realize how tired she was until she sat down on the cloak Theo had placed on the ground for her. She was not only tired but hot and dusty as well. She had never imagined traveling could be this miserable. Onesimus brought over some dates, figs, and cheese for her, along with a cup of wine. It took every ounce of her willpower and a little encouragement from Onesimus to eat. The hour seemed to fly by, and before she knew it, they were walking again.

Onesimus tried to get her to mount the horse, but Mary refused. She was so tired that she knew she would fall asleep and tumble off the steed. She chose to walk alongside Onesimus. Theo had given strict instructions that all should remain as quiet as possible while they passed the foothills. From what Mary had gathered, there had been many skirmishes in this area. Theo was trying to keep them all from harm.

The young scout's heart beat in double time at the sight of the Romans entering the mouth of the foothills. He knew his older brother had sent him to do the scouting just to keep him out of his hair. The boy had never expected to see anything along the road except a lone traveler or two. Once he delivered the news concerning the Romans, his bother would have to acknowledge his importance to their small band of sicarii. He had to control the urge to run back; he didn't want to jar even one loose rock and have it roll down the rocky hillside, crying out a warning of danger awaiting the Romans. He darted behind one rock formation, then another, as he made his way to his brother.

He ignored the insults the men hurled at him as he walked through camp. They would eat their words once they heard what important news he brought.

"Othniel, it seems your baby brother couldn't take the

FAVORED

loneliness of scouting, for he has returned prematurely."

Othniel looked up in time to see Jair set from behind his second-in-command and make his way toward him. Othniel groaned. He had promised his mother that he would look after Jair, but the promise had proven to be more than he'd bargained for. Now Jair had returned to amp sooner than he should have. If the Romans didn't capture or kill Jair, Othniel knew his men would, for they had little patience for the youngest member of their band.

"Jair, I told you not to return until morning."

"I know, Othniel."

"Then why have you returned?"

"I bring important news."

"What did the boy see? A snake with two heads or perhaps a beautiful woman wants the boy to keep her company?" Then men laughed at Mikail's joke.

"Quiet," Othniel ordered. "Let the boy speak."

Jair smiled at his brother. Othniel winked at him. "Go on."

"They are coming. A hundred or more of them are coming. They will be upon us come morning."

"Who is coming?" Disgust was plainly written on Mikail's face.

Jair shot him an angry look. "The Romans. Their shields glisten like gold in the sun. Their swords are sharp and long. They appear ready for a fight."

"Are you sure of what you saw?" Othniel stared intently into his brother's eyes.

"I speak truthfully of what I saw."

Othniel turned to Mikail. "Send half the men to the other side. Put those who aim well with their slings toward the top and those better with the sword at the bottom. I will do the same. There are probably three of them to every one of us, but we have surprise on our side."

Mikail nodded and motioned for half the group to follow him. Othniel turned to Jair. "Remain here. No matter what happens, stay out of sight. If I should not return, go back to Tabor, to the house of Jedidiah. They will see that you become a man."

"But I'm already a man."

Othniel smiled at his brother. "Just do as I say so Mother will not seek me out in the afterlife and kill me again." Othniel motioned for the rest of the men to move out. Before leaving, he called back, "Jair, you did well."

Chapter Twenty-Six

It was toilsome for Mary to remain quiet for so long as she walked alongside Onesimus. The combination of worry and heat made it difficult for her to stay focused. She tried to keep her eyes on the road ahead, but she kept looking up into the foothills, unsure of what she expected to see. The thought that people who might want to hurt them were hiding amongst the beauty of God's creation chilled her.

As the afternoon wore on, exhaustion overtook her, and she stumbled several times. Realizing she couldn't walk another step, Mary leaned over and whispered in Onesimus' ear, "I must stop. I can't keep going. I'm just too tired."

"No! Miss, you must keep moving. We are almost through the pass. Just a little ways further." The young boy wrapped his arm around Mary's waist, allowing her to rest her weight on him.

Mary's mouth was dry, and she sounded hoarse when she whispered. "Onesimus, please stop calling me 'miss.' My name is Mary. You can call me Mary."

Onesimus' grin showed through his dust-caked face. "Whatever you like. You can keep talking to me if it will help. I know how much you like to talk. Just whisper. Tell me about my ancestors. Tell me about their god."

"All right. I'll try. We can trace our people back to our father Abraham. God chose Abraham to leave the land of his forefathers to settle in a land God would show him." Mary told Onesimus of the covenant God made with Abraham. She explained the birth of Isaac, the son God promised, and what that meant to Abraham and Sarah. She told of Jacob's twelve sons and how they ended up in Egypt. She spoke of Moses and how God had delivered the Israelites out of the land of Egypt and slavery. She talked in a hoarse whisper until Theo stepped in to release Onesimus of his burden.

"We are through the most dangerous part of the trip. I'll carry you, Mary. It's not much farther. Camp is already being set up." Mary made no complaint as Theo lifted her into his arms. "Onesimus, you may ride my horse the rest of the way. You did good work today."

Onesimus was grateful for Theo's kindness. The extra weight Onesimus had managed to sustain had depleted the boy of his energy. A soldier gave Onesimus a boost up. The steed stayed on Theo's heels. Onesimus marveled at the centurion's stamina.

Theo settled Mary in his tent. She had gone to sleep in his arms. There was no point in waking her. He gently laid her on the soft couch. He pushed back the damp tendrils from around her face. He fought the urge to kiss her forehead and face. Mary had said that this God of hers had sent him to protect her. He would respect this God that she believed in.

Seeing that she was comfortable and safe, Theo stepped out of the tent into the warm evening air. He felt restless. It had been a long day for everyone. Most of the men were already sound asleep; some were casting lots while others stood guard around the small encampment. Theo walked a little way out from camp and stood looking up at the night sky. He was so lost in his thoughts that he didn't hear Onesimus come up behind him.

"Master," Onesimus said softly.

Theo whirled around, pulling his short sword from its sheath.

Onesimus fell to the ground in a posture of subordination. "Master, it's me, Onesimus. I'm sorry. I didn't mean to startle you."

"Onesimus, you must loudly announce yourself before you come up behind someone. I might have killed you." Theo helped the boy to his feet.

"Might I have a word with you?"

Theo replaced his sword in the sheath. "What's on your mind?"

"It's Mary."

"It must be contagious."

"What do you mean?"

"Nothing, lad. I was just thinking about her myself."

"Where are we taking her?"

"Jerusalem. She has family there."

"So she is not to be sold into slavery?"

"No."

"I'm glad to hear it. I was afraid for her. She's nice. She treats me with respect. I like that."

"Yes. She treats everyone as equals. You did well by her today."

"You care for her?"

"You're very inquisitive tonight. Shouldn't you be resting? We have another long walk ahead of us tomorrow.

"I tried to sleep and couldn't. I've watched you. You have trouble sleeping too. How come?"

"I don't talk about that, Onesimus. Remember you are my slave, and I, your master."

Onesimus lowered his head. "Yes. I will remember." He turned to go.

"But we can still talk about why you cannot sleep."

Onesimus, obviously pleased, looked back at Theo. "Mary likes to talk. I had her talk to me to help her stay awake. She told me things."

FAVORED

"What kind of things?" Onesimus was a bright boy, a good slave. Yet, that was the point: he was a slave. Chances were that he would always be a slave. Some of the lucky ones were able to buy their freedom. Others lived and died in bondage. Onesimus didn't have a bad life. Theo wasn't sure how long he would keep the lad, but while Onesimus was under his care, Theo promised himself to teach the boy how to be a man, simply for survival's sake. Now Mary was filling the boy's head with all sorts of promises concerning the Hebrews.

"She said we are God's chosen people. Why am I a slave if I am part of this unseen God's chosen people? I've worshiped several gods. It depended on what god the family I was with worshiped, but I've never looked to a god for help. I've watched you closely, Master. You don't look to any god to help you."

"I have worshiped as the need arises, but Onesimus, I have been trained to take care of myself and to see to the needs of others dependent upon me for their survival. This god Mary speaks of is important to her and your people. Romans raised you. You know the Roman way of things. Mary can teach you about your people, your ancestors, their god. I can't. I suggest you listen to what Mary has to say, ask her your questions, and then decide for yourself."

"Do you know about this god she speaks of? Have you seen his work?"

"I know of him. I'm familiar with the stories the Hebrews tell concerning their god."

"Master, do you believe such a god exists? Do you think there is only one true god?"

"I don't know." Something stirred inside Theo, causing him to feel uncomfortable with the direction the conversation was going. "You'd better get to bed. The dawn will break before you know it. Try to rest. Ask Mary your questions tomorrow."

"Thank you, Master. I will." Onesimus somberly walked

back to camp.

Theo wondered if he had done the boy a favor or not. To take his mind off the conversation with Onesimus, Theo turned his thoughts to Mary. He decided that she could not take another day of walking, and she obviously didn't like riding. He needed to come up with a better way for her to travel. As he walked back to camp, an idea began to surface in his mind. It wouldn't take much to construct, and he could have it built before she woke. They would need to make it big enough that Onesimus could sit with her and keep her company. Theo wanted to kick himself for not having thought of it before now.

The next morning, Onesimus gently woke Mary. "I've prepared the basin for you to use if you would like. Master wants to leave soon." Just as quickly and quietly as he had entered, he left.

Mary felt her legs scream in protest as she stood up. "I don't think I can take another day of walking, little one." She rubbed her belly tenderly as she slowly moved to the basin. The water was warm. Mary wished the basin were big enough for her to sit right down in the soothing water. Still even a washing-off was better than nothing. It didn't take her long to clean the dust from her body. She ate the cheese, bread, and fruit Onesimus had prepared for her.

"Mary, it's Theo. May I enter?"

"Please, do. Sit and eat with me."

Theo entered, apprehensively, the tent. "We really need to be getting started. The men need to tear down the tent. I'm afraid it is going to be another long day."

Mary sighed. "I understand. Theo, I don't know if I can walk today like I did yesterday. Maybe we could take things a little slower?"

"I thought you might feel that way. I've prepared a surprise for you. Come and look."

FAVORED

Theo escorted Mary outside. She gasped at the sight. Before her stood four Roman soldiers holding a makeshift litter. The litter had a small canopy to protect the rider from the sun. "Theo, how did you? Is this for me?" Tears welled up in Mary's eyes.

"Yes. It's big enough for you and Onesimus to ride. I thought you might want his company. Plus, this way I can ride that beautiful horse I've been given." He laughed. "I take it you are pleased."

"I'm speechless."

"I find it hard to believe that Mary of Nazareth is without words." Theo chuckled.

Mary laughed amidst her tears of appreciation. "This is so thoughtful. Thank you."

"Here, let me help you up. It's time we were on our way." Theo lifted Mary onto the litter, then helped Onesimus up as well. "This is quite a sight. A Jewish girl and a slave riding in a Roman litter. Now, you two try not to have too much fun." Theo gave the order for the men to start the procession. He stayed close to Mary until he was sure she was comfortable riding the litter.

"Onesimus, just think: two Hebrews being carried off to Jerusalem in style and on the backs of four Roman soldiers. Lydia would be jealous." Mary laughed.

"Who's Lydia?"

"She's my best friend back home. I didn't get a chance to tell her goodbye before I left. I miss her terribly."

"I've never really had a friend. I keep to myself when I'm not busy serving my master. It's safer that way."

Mary sighed and pulled back the flap to look at the passing landscape. "I think we are becoming good friends." She closed the flap to look Onesimus in the eye. "Don't you?"

"Yes, I suppose." He didn't return her gaze. He didn't want to disappoint her. Sometimes the truth is better learned through experience. Experience had taught him to not rely on others for comfort. He was glad Mary hadn't seemed to learn that lesson yet.

Mary couldn't read on his face to know what had clouded the young boy's eyes. She decided to change the subject. "Did you get a chance to think on what we talked about yesterday?"

"Some. Would you mind telling me more?"

"Not at all. It looks like we will have all day to talk." Mary began where she had left off the day before. She told Onesimus of the laws God gave Moses in the wilderness, explaining each one in detail. She talked of Joshua and the many battles the Israelites won when they crossed the Jordan River.

Before noon, Mary had gone through the judges, telling of Sampson and his mighty rise and fall, Deborah, and many others who had led their people through victories and defeats. She had just begun to tell him about the mighty kings of Israel when the litter stopped. She pulled back the canopy and peered out. Theo was hurrying toward them. He pulled his horse to an abrupt stop beside the litter.

"Onesimus, take Mary behind those rocks and wait there till I come get you."

"Yes, Master." Onesimus scurried off the litter and assisted Mary with her descent.

"Theo, what's wrong?" Mary's face was drawn with anxiety.

"It will be fine. Stay with Onesimus. There is trouble up ahead. I'll be back as soon as I can." Theo kicked the side of his horse. The steed took a leap and headed back the way they had come at a full gallop.

Onesimus helped Mary settle herself behind the rocks to the left of the road. "You'd better kneel down and stay out of sight." Onesimus listened and watched as Mary prayed fervently for Theo and the other soldiers.

"Hush," Onesimus whispered into Mary's ear. "Someone's coming." Mary became deathly quiet as she peered out from the rocks. She felt her heart pounding inside her chest. *Oh God*, Mary silently prayed, *protect your servant. Protect this boy. Protect Theo.* She repeated the same words over and over in her mind. She watched two legs appear in her line of sight. She wished she could disappear. *Hide us, God.*

Jair listened and waited until the clashing sound of steel against steel reverberated throughout the countryside. He inched his way down the rocky slope until he was close enough to watch the battle unfolding before his eyes. He watched as men with whom he had supped and shared stories around a campfire, some from his own village, fell with the cry of death on their lips. His eyes searched for his brother amongst the men fighting, but between the dust and chaos, his brother could not be found.

One man caught Jair's eye. He wielded his sword with strength and accuracy, slaying every man that came within reach of his blade. He sat high atop the most magnificent stallion Jair had ever seen. Unwanted admiration rose up within him as he watched the Roman. Then, into his field of vision entered a familiar form. Everything from that point on seemed to move in slow motion.

His brother fought bravely and truly. Othniel, killing every man that got in his way, was moving with calculated steps toward the centurion atop the stallion. Suddenly Othniel leaped into the air as if he had sprouted wings. He flew toward the Roman, his sword aimed at the Roman's heart. Just when it looked like his sword would find its mark, the Roman turned, and in one swift jerk, his sword sliced through Othniel's body, ending his life.

Jair struggled to get to his feet to avenge his brother's death. However, a weight, heavier than the largest boulder, kept him rooted in place. He watched until the last Hebrew fell.

Mary held her breath until she heard Theo's familiar voice, "Mary, Onesimus, are you there?"

"We are here, Master." Onesimus stood first and then helped Mary to her feet.

"Oh, Theo, you're bleeding." Mary rushed to his side to see what she could do to help her friend.

"It's nothing, just a scratch. We lost several men, but we managed to kill the bandits who were waiting for us." Theo sat on the ground so Onesimus could bandage his wound. Mary watched as Onesimus took great care in his attention to Theo.

"How did you know they were there?" Mary knelt beside them.

"When the scouts I had sent on ahead didn't return, I knew there was trouble. I had a feeling." Theo shook his head in an attempt to dislodge the thoughts and feelings that swirled inside him. He grimaced as Onesimus bandaged his left side.

"Were your scouts counted among the dead?"

"Yes. One was just a boy himself." Theo sighed. "I couldn't shake the feeling we were heading into trouble. I shouldn't have sent the boy with the others." Theo hung his head.

Mary's curiosity got the best of her. "Who were these bandits? Were they Hebrew?"

Theo looked straight into his friend's eyes, which glistened with the hint of tears. He knew she knew the answer before he confirmed her suspicion. "Yes. I'm sorry. It was either them or us."

"I understand." She stood and turned her back on Theo and

FAVORED

Onesimus. She didn't want them to see the tears that trickled down her cheeks.

Theo stood and went to her side. "Mary, I'm sorry. I know how strongly you feel about your people. They would have killed you as well just because you were with us."

Mary gasped and looked into Theo's eyes. She saw his sadness and honesty. He wasn't making an excuse. He was simply speaking the truth. She nodded her understanding. She would not speak of this with anyone. She would hide it in her heart and pray for the day when they could all live in peace. She looked away staring into the blue sky that stretched before her.

"Something's bothering you. What is it?" Theo asked gently.

Mary turned to her friend, the weight of her guilt too much for her to bear. "I prayed for your safety and that of your men. Not for the safety of the men you were fighting. I didn't pray for my own people." Mary buried her head in Theo's chest.

Theo held the girl as she sobbed out her guilt. "Onesimus, let the men know that we will camp here tonight. Have them burn the dead. I'll stay with Mary until my tent is ready."

"Yes, Master." Onesimus quickly hurried off to do as Theo had instructed.

Theo felt very inadequate as he tried to console Mary. "It was not your prayer that killed those men. It was me. I cut them down with my sword. You could never hurt anyone."

"I know the words you speak are meant to comfort me, but there is no comfort for what I have done."

Theo released his hold on her. "I understand the guilt you feel. I wish I could take it from you, but I can't."

Mary read Theo's expression. "You try to justify the killing you do, but inside the guilt weighs you down. Why do you continue to kill when it haunts you so?"

"Because it is my duty to do so." He turned from Mary's

knowing gaze. He had not told anyone about his dreams. Yet, he felt that Mary knew he had nightmares. How could one Hebrew girl look past his armor and see straight into his soul? "You'll find all your needs are met inside my tent."

Mary watched as Theo slowly walked away from her. She was still crying as she entered the tent and prepared herself for rest. There was much about battle, duty, and men that she simply did not comprehend. Weariness pulled at her peace and courage.

She dropped to her knees before her heavenly Father, sobbing deep tears from her soul. She poured out her fear, anger, and grief concerning all that had transpired since the angel had appeared to her. Her mother had always said, "Crying is good for the soul." Pouring one's heart out to God was too.

Numbed by what he had just witnessed, Jair rested his body against the rock that shielded him from view. The highest calling for a man was to take up the fight against the Romans, but as the smell of burning flesh seared his nostrils, that calling appeared to be a waste—a senseless act of suicide. What was supposed to make Othniel, and perhaps himself, heroes among their people, had only served to take his brother's life. Othniel's name would never be cheered from rooftops or talked about at the gate. No one would know the man who was Jair's last link to family. He would do as his brother instructed. However, at that moment, immense sorrow caused Jair to sink into a deep sleep.

Chapter Twenty-Seven

The past few days of travel had been filled with moments of delight, but no matter the circumstances, Mary had made up her mind that traveling long distances was simply not fun. The litter Theo had been so thoughtful to have made served her well. There had not been any more skirmishes between the band of Roman soldiers and her people. Mary had found peace with the incident of a few days ago. Throughout the week of travel, her eyes had been opened to see the world from a slightly different point of view. People could be mean and cruel, whether they were Hebrew or Roman. True, oppression caused some to do things they would not normally do, but even during oppression, those who claimed to be followers of Jehovah needed to hold fast to His promise of deliverance and not take matters into their own hands. That seemed to only make things worse for everyone. This was the conclusion to which Mary had come.

A growing anxiety had taken root in the pit of her stomach. In a few hours, they would be near her cousin's home. She knew God was sending her to her relatives. She was at peace with that. However, she wondered what she would say when she arrived. She recalled meeting Elizabeth and Zechariah only once when she was very young. They seemed pleasant enough. "A childless couple" was how her mother had described them, and then she would just shake her head. It always amazed Mary how her mother could be judgmental of others who were going through the same predicament she and Mary's father had been in before Mary had been born. The angel had said that Elizabeth, in her old age, was with child. Would they accept her? She was a young girl with no husband. That was a far cry from a pregnant, married

FAVORED

woman who just happened to be older than most.

Onesimus encouraged Mary to rest and dismissed himself to give her the privacy and comfort of having the litter all to herself. However, she couldn't stop the thoughts that churned in her mind and made her stomach queasy. She thought about the young boy who had been her constant companion throughout the trip. Mary had made Theo promise three things. Mary, afraid Onesimus would be mistreated if Theo sold him, made him promise to look after the boy until Onesimus was old enough to take care of himself. The second promise was to teach the boy to read and write; the third was to allow him instruction concerning Hebrew law. Mary considered Onesimus her friend. She would miss the lad when they parted ways. She wiped away a tear that unwillingly slipped down her cheek.

She would miss Theo too. He had taken good care of her. He was like no Roman she had ever met. He listened to her stories about God and her people. He made her laugh with his keen wit, and she had come to respect his insight and knowledge. Theo had made it clear that if she ever needed anything, she should send word, and he would come to her aid.

In many ways, Mary was still a child and had the innocence of a child. She had no inkling of Theo's feelings for her. He always maintained a respectful distance from his friend. Their times together always included Onesimus. To Mary, the three of them had become the best of friends. She had found comfort with them. That was all about to change, and once again she was going to have to face the looks and questions that were sure to come when she knocked on the door of Elizabeth's home.

Mary sat up. The litter bounced along at a steady rhythm. They must have been making good time. Her ears perked up at the sound of a horse's hooves approaching. A smile broke the grim expression that had painted itself upon her face. She peered through the opening in the canvas. Much to her delight, Theo was coming toward her. He gave her a welcoming smile.

"Onesimus said you were resting. Did you rest well?"

"Not really. My mind just won't keep quiet."

Theo nodded in understanding. "I came to tell you that we only have about an hour before we reach the village where your relatives reside. Are you sure you want to walk the distance alone? I can escort you all the to the front door if you like."

Mary laughed. "Can you imagine what everyone would say to that? I can just hear it." She giggled and shook her head. "No, I think it best I travel this road alone. I do appreciate your concern and thoughtfulness. I'll be fine." Saying the words did not produce the confidence Mary was attempting to convey to Theo.

"I'm going to drop you off a few miles shy of the town. I believe you will be safe if you only have a few miles to walk."

Mary let out a sigh of relief. The shorter distance would keep her mind from wondering to all the possibilities that might await her. "Theo, I can never thank you enough for your kindness. I can't say I've loved the travel, but I have enjoyed spending time with you and Onesimus. Don't forget your promises concerning him."

The tears pooling in her eyes were not lost on Theo. "The pleasure has been all mine, I assure you. Are you sure no harm will come to you?" Theo watched as Mary hung her head, deep in thought, and chewed on her bottom lip before responding.

She looked up and smiled. "I told you last night that God is sending me there. I'm not sure what is to happen, but I know God has a plan. You know how strongly I believe God sent you to look after me this long distance. Over and over, God has proven Himself faithful to me. I trust His leading."

Theo watched as a renewed confidence filled Mary's countenance. "Your faith never ceases to amaze me, Mary of Nazareth. I'll do as you wish, but only because you ask it of me. I'm still not convinced that all things of man are ordained by this god of yours."

FAVORED

"Maybe someday you will come face to face with the knowledge that all I have said is true."

"Perhaps. Too many laws and regulations for a man to follow. Romans have a much easier lifestyle. You know how lazy a man like myself can be." He chuckled and gave his horse the lead to gallop to the front of the procession.

Mary shook her head and laughed at the idea of Theo being lazy. No one who knew him would call him lazy. She nestled back into the safety of the litter. It wouldn't be long now. She closed her eyes and began to pray. "God, I'm not sure why I am being sent to Elizabeth's. I know she, too, is with child. I am thankful that You have seen fit to bless her. Will she be sensitive to me? Will she have the faith to believe? I need just the right words to speak to her and Zachariah."

You do not have to be the one always to speak. I can speak to the hearts of those who love Me, and they will listen to My voice and heed the words I say.

For a moment Mary felt chastised. "Of course. How silly of me. Forgive my lack of faith. I do not always need to be the one to talk. I'll trust You to reveal the unknown when the time is right. But You know that is going to be really hard for me. I'm used to doing most of the talking." Mary smiled as she thought, *I must take after my mother in that way.*

The litter came to a stop. The anxiety welling up inside Mary made her stomach flutter like the beautiful butterflies she had watched dance around the many flowers in a field outside Nazareth. Oh, how she missed home.

"Mary, we're close. It's time to part if that is still your desire." Theo's voice rang with the melancholy they were all feeling.

Theo dismounted and helped Mary out of the litter. "Here is a bundle of food that Onesimus prepared and a warm blanket. Just in case something goes wrong, you know I will be stationed in Jerusalem. You can reach me there."

258

"Nothing is going to go wrong. Have a little faith, my friend."

Mary turned her attention to Onesimus, who was standing behind his master. "Onesimus."

"Yes?" Onesimus peered from around Theo.

"Onesimus, you have permission to go to Mary."

Onesimus' face lit up as he leaped from behind Theo and grasped Mary in a big hug. "I'm going to miss you, Mary. You are a true friend. Thank you for telling me all those stories."

Mary choked back tears. "Remember those stories are true. They tell of your people, our people. They tell of their struggles and their times of blessing. Most importantly, they tell of a faithful God who has made a promise to deliver His people by sending us a Messiah. Watch for Him, Onesimus. I know His arrival will be soon." Mary hugged the boy and tousled his dark hair before turning her attention to Theo. The moment she looked at him, the tears flowed willingly.

"I will never forget the first night you entered our home with Joseph. You were kind to me then and to my husband. You saved his life, and for that I am forever grateful. Now, you have bought this poor Hebrew girl, who can offer you nothing in return for your kindness, safely to the home of her relatives. I do not have the words to thank you. The sorrow at leaving you and Onesimus is almost more than I can bear. You have been a true friend." Mary choked on the words as sorrow overwhelmed her.

"Mary, don't. Your family did more for me in that short period of time than anyone has done for me in my whole life, such as it is. There is nothing I wouldn't do for you. If you only knew..." Theo didn't finish. He couldn't. It would be wrong. For the first time in his life, he put the needs of another ahead of his own wants and desires.

Mary wiped her tears. "I do not know when we shall see each other again. Know that what I have told you concerning my God is true. Remember your promise."

FAVORED

"You know I will."

"Yes. Take care of him. Take care of yourself. I couldn't stand it if anything ever happened to either one of you." Mary couldn't say another word. She turned and began to run toward the tiny village that lay within view. If she stopped and looked back, she was afraid she would run back into the safety and comfort of the friendship that had been forged. What an unlikely threesome they had become.

Theo and Onesimus watched until Mary was well out of sight. "Onesimus, we'd best continue to Jerusalem. I'd like to make it there by supper. The men deserve a much-needed rest and relaxation."

"Master, do you think we will ever see her again?"

"I don't know. Come, we have work ahead of us, and I made some promises that I intend to keep." Theo motioned for the men to begin the march toward Jerusalem. He galloped at full speed to the front of the line. He couldn't let Onesimus see the anguish that had engulfed his soul. Little did he realize that the young boy of ten, grieving the same loss as him, needed his comfort.

Chapter Twenty-Eight

As Mary drew closer to the village, she slowed her pace to catch her breath and think. She had no idea which house belonged to Zechariah and Elizabeth. If this village was anything like Nazareth, all she would have to do was ask someone where her relatives lived, and she would be shown the way. Confident that finding them would not be a problem, Mary turned her attention to the next hurdle, which would not be so easy to overcome. Would they let her stay?

I will shelter you with My wings. Move forward to your cousin's home. I am with you.

Mary continued walking. As she approached, the sounds of the village seemed to run out and greet her. Before she knew it, she was caught up in the hustle and bustle of the town. She smiled as she watched the merchants selling their wares; it reminded her of Ezra and his often-turned-over cart. Her eyes scanned the crowd, looking for a friendly face to inquire about her cousin. She spotted an elderly woman seated in the doorframe of her home. Mary watched as the woman sewed in a steady rhythm a beautiful piece of purple fabric. Her mind immediately went to Lydia. She swallowed back the tears that surfaced and began to make her way through the crowd toward the kind-looking woman. Before Mary could speak, the woman spoke to her.

"You've been watching me for quite some time. I may be old, but my eyes miss nothing. What is it you need, child?"

"I am here to visit a cousin of mine. I thought you might know her and could tell me where she lives."

"What is your cousin's name?" The woman laid down her

FAVORED

work and looked up into Mary's dust-streaked face. "By your appearance, I take it you must have come some distance."

The woman slowly rose and grabbed her crutch. Mary then noticed her misshapen foot. "Come, have a drink. The water is fresh."

"Oh, I couldn't impose."

"Now, child, I wouldn't have offered if it was an imposition. Come, have a drink, and perhaps wash your face. Then I will direct you where you need to go."

"But I haven't told you my cousin's name yet. You may not know of whom I speak."

"I grew up around here. I know most everyone in this town. Here." The woman handed Mary a cup of clear water. In one swift gulp, the cup was empty. The older woman laughed.

"I'm sorry I drank so quickly," Mary said sheepishly. "I guess I didn't realize how thirsty I was."

"Here, child, have another." The woman quickly poured Mary another cup. This time Mary took her time and enjoyed the refreshment.

"Now, you can wash here." The woman pulled out a basin and poured fresh water into it. "Wash, and then you can tell me your cousin's name. I'll wait outside."

Mary did as instructed. She quickly cleaned the dust from her face, hands, arms, and feet. Just doing that invigorated her. She opened the bag of food Onesimus had prepared for her. On the table she left the loaf of bread, along with dates, and cheese. Then she made her way back to the door and stepped out into the busy street.

"It feels good to be clean. Thank you for your kindness."

The old woman looked up from her sewing. "Now, what is your cousin's name?"

"Elizabeth. Her husband is Zechariah. He is a priest in the

temple. Perhaps you know them."

The old woman roared with laughter. "Ah, yes. God has blessed Elizabeth. Even in her old age, God has seen fit to bless Elizabeth. There might be hope yet for the rest of us."

Mary laughed. "Then you know she is with child?"

"The whole village knows. She is the talk of the town."

"Can you tell me where I can find them?"

"Yes, yes, of course I can tell you. You do know what has happened, don't you?"

"I'm not sure I know what you mean. I know Elizabeth is with child. What more is there to know?"

"Yes, God has seen fit to bless Elizabeth. But Zechariah, poor man…" The woman shook her head.

"What happened to Zechariah? He's not…?"

"Oh, no, child, he is not dead. He just cannot speak. Has not spoken a word since that day he was in the temple. No one knows what happened. He went in speaking and came out mute. Hasn't spoken a word since."

"I didn't know." Mary hung her head. She wasn't sure if she should continue to her cousin's or turn back. The tug at her heart told her to go on. "Please, tell me where I can find them. I am anxious to see if I can be of help, especially after all you have told me."

The elderly woman explained in great detail how to go to Elizabeth's, and then Mary was off. The woman's directions were very good, for Mary had no trouble navigating the streets. Soon, her cousin's home was in sight. When Mary saw the house, she was immediately filled with courage. She walked straight up to the door and gave a firm knock. She waited, but no answer came. Her heart began to pound in her chest, and doubt rose in her mind. Maybe she wasn't at the right house. Maybe they'd left and gone to Jerusalem. What would she do if no one answered?

FAVORED

She pushed the thoughts aside and knocked again. This time, she could hear movement inside. A tender voice called out, "I'm coming." In an instant Mary was staring into the gentle eyes of Elizabeth. For a moment, she thought she was staring into Miriam's eyes. The two looked so much alike, it took Mary some time before she could speak.

"Elizabeth?"

"Yes."

"I'm your cousin, Mary, Joachim and Anna's daughter, from Nazareth."

As soon as Mary had opened her mouth to speak, the baby growing inside Elizabeth leaped in her womb. A small cry escaped her mouth, not of pain but of joy! As she stepped aside to allow Mary to enter, she began to exclaim, "Blessed are you among women, and blessed is the child you will bear." She closed the door and looked at Mary. "Why am I so favored that the mother of my Lord should come to me?"[2]

Mary stared at Elizabeth in bewilderment. Elizabeth took Mary's hands in hers and began to explain, "As soon as the sound of a beautiful greeting reached my ears, the baby in my womb leaped for joy. Favored are you, Mary, for you have believed that what the Lord has said to you will be accomplished."[3]

Elizabeth took Mary in her arms and hugged her. Mary was filled with such abounding gratefulness that she began to praise God for His ever-abiding glory and mercy. The song that filled her heart sprung from her mouth in a sweet, melodious rapture of thankfulness: "My soul glorifies the Lord, and my spirit rejoices in God my savior, for He has been mindful of the humble state of His servant. From now on, all generations will call me favored, for the Mighty One has done great things for me, holy is His name."[4] Her praise continued until she could not utter another word. The two women embraced each other and together gave

2 Luke 1:42–43 (NIV)
3 Luke 1:44–45 (NIV)
4 Luke 1:46–49 (NIV)

thanks to God for blessing them both.

"Sit, sit, and let me serve you something to eat and drink."

"No, thank you. An elderly woman whom I enquired for directions gave me some water and let me wash in her home. I'm fine. Please, sit and tell me the news of Zachariah. The woman said he had gone mute after serving in the temple."

"Don't let that concern you. Zachariah is fine. He will be fine. Most do not know this, but I can share with you. Zachariah was in the temple and had gone in to burn incense before God when an angel appeared to him and told him that I would conceive a son. We are to name him John. Zachariah has always been very logical. The angel told him that, due to his unbelief, he would remain mute until all the angel told him transpires. He will be fine at the proper time." Elizabeth patted Mary's hand to reassure her.

"How do you know this?"

"His brain wasn't taken away, child, just his tongue. He wrote it all down for me. I am to name the baby John when he is born."

"It seems I learned more about God and His ways every day."

"We all do. Now, tell me about your mother and father. Are they well?"

"Father died a few months ago. Mother really hasn't been the same since. Then, with the news of…"

"You told her you were with child?"

"Yes."

"She didn't believe all you said to her."

"No."

"Is that why you have come here to us?"

"Yes. I believe God has sent me here. I don't know for how long. You see, I am betrothed to a very good man, Joseph. He is a carpenter in Nazareth. Father made the arrangements before he passed. Before I left to come here, I told Joseph about my visit from the angel and the baby. He did not believe me. I am waiting to hear what his decision is concerning our marriage." Mary sighed. "It's in his hands."

"Things are never in man's hands. God has taken care of you thus far, and I know He will continue to do so. If Joseph is a good man, as you say he is, God will reveal to him the truth when the time is right."

"It's just very hurtful when the ones you love don't believe you."

"I understand. We will wait on God's time. For now, you are welcome to stay with us as long as you like. We will make a room for you upstairs. I am in the process of preparing for new arrival. Perhaps you could help me."

"Nothing would give me more joy. If you only knew how God has taken care of me thus far, and now, the kindness you are showing to me overwhelms me."

"Mary, I must say you are as beautiful as ever. I remembered you as a little girl. Your eyes shining with the peace God has given you. Miriam spoke highly of you. She knew you were special."

"You say things that are much too nice. Is Zachariah home?"

"No, but he will be soon, and if I know my husband, he will be expecting something to eat by the time his foot hits the threshold. Come, we will prepare supper."

"Will he be willing to allow me to stay? I mean, in my condition."

"Zachariah is a righteous man. He will allow you to stay. God sent you to us. God would not have done so if He thought you would not be welcomed in our home. Besides, I kept my condition secret for six months. Your secret is safe for the time being. There will come a time when it will be made known. No question about that."

"I will continue to believe that God is my ever-present help in time of trouble."

"Good girl." Elizabeth patted Mary's knee. "Now, to dinner. Zachariah likes his meals hot and on time."

Together they began the preparations for the evening meal. Mary watched as Elizabeth glided through the motions of cooking and setting the table. Even with Elizabeth's age and her round stomach forecasting the impending delivery, she moved with grace. Mary thought her beautiful in every way. She was very much like Miriam. The thought both comforted and saddened Mary.

Right on cue, as soon as the table was ready, Zachariah entered his home. He was surprised to see the young girl standing next to his wife, but it only took an instant for him to recognize her. He immediately came to her and embraced her in his arms. She felt welcomed and accepted. Soon the three of them were all seated around the table, enjoying the bounty God had provided. Elizabeth did most of the talking; Zachariah would just nod and smile. Mary felt she had family again. She hadn't realized how much she truly had missed her father, mother, and even Joseph until she sat around that table as a participant and observer of what family represented. She hid this memory in her heart and vowed to make her home open and welcoming to all.

Chapter Twenty-Nine

It had been almost a week since Mary had walked out the front door. Each morning and evening, Anna would open the door and peer into the sun-streaked horizon. Each time, the horizon was as barren as the time before. She closed the door, the hopelessness and loneliness forging deep rifts in her soul. Today was no different.

Yesterday, Rachel brought over some lentil soup. It still sat, untouched, on the table. Rachel had been over every day since Mary had left. Anna knew her friend meant well, but part of her suspected that Rachel was just trying to find out the truth. Whoever had the latest gossip would be the center of attention at the well, and Rachel always loved being the center of attention.

Anna looked around this small home. Her gaze fell on the place Mary had slept. The emptiness of the house seemed to mock her. Mary had been right. Miriam and Joachim would have believed her. If only she had. Tormenting thoughts pushed through to the surface of Anna's bitterness. And able to deal with the inundation of ridicule and pain her thoughts caused, Anna did what she had done for the past five days. She slowly walked to her bedroom and stretched her aching body out on the bed. She didn't have the energy to face the day. Tears streamed down her face. Her eyes closed, and before she knew it, she was asleep.

This had been her regime since Mary had left. As if on cue, she would rise before dusk and peer out her door. Then she would sit, alone and still, in the dark until the rays of dawn pierced her eyes. The house had been left in the same condition since the moment Mary walked out. The baskets Anna had been going through lay scattered on the floor. The water pitcher, half full of stagnant water, was set on the sideboard. Lying unhindered in its desire to build and grow was the dust that would creep into the house. The uneaten fruit had begun to wrinkle and smell. The typical activities that would fill Anna's day, those things that gave her purpose and meaning, were not necessary anymore. Anna's whole existence had been devoted to caring for her family. Her family was gone, and with it, her existence.

Soft wrapping at the door roused her from her depressive sleep. Disheveled, haggard, and bent, Anna made her way to the front door. The brightness of the day momentarily blinded her from seeing the features of the large form standing before her. It wasn't until he spoke that she recognized him.

"Anna, I've come to check on you. May I enter?"

Anna responded in a hoarse whisper, "Joseph. Yes, by all means, come in." She stepped aside to make room for him to enter.

Joseph stood in disbelief at the sight before him and pungent orders. "Anna, when was the last time you ate?" He walked over to the water pitcher. Picking it up, he noticed that insects had already begun to make a home in the putrid water. He took note that there was no fresh food on the premises. "Anna, did you hear me? When did you eat last?" Joseph turned his full attention to the woman. He gasped. Standing before him was a wrinkled, old woman, where a lively woman had dwelt within an aged body. Eyes that once radiated with life appeared empty and hollow. Even her voice, once authoritative and strong, reeked of insecurity.

"I can't remember. I have no appetite." Anna shuffled over to her chair at the table and lowered herself. "Sit, Joseph." She motioned to Mary's empty chair. "I didn't expect to see you today."

"I told you I would come by and check on you. I always do what I say. Anna, why don't I go to the well and fill your picture with fresh water? While I'm gone, I can pick up some fresh fruit and honey. Does that sound good to you?" He sat down in the chair and offered him. He tried to focus on her face taking great care to look into her eyes. The ghostly stare she gave back to him was too painful for him. It reminded him of his mother.

"A man like you shouldn't be doing woman's work. I can take care of myself. Don't you worry about me." Anna forced a smile to her lips.

"I am worried about you. So are your friends. Rachel came by to see me yesterday."

"That busybody only wants to hear the latest news of my plight. She cares little."

"I think she cares more than you realize. You two have been friends for some time. She didn't ask me about Mary or what happened. She only said that you were not looking well and that perhaps you might listen to me. I see you have not taken one bite of the soup she lovingly made for you. You've got to keep your strength up for when Mary returns. She will need you to help deliver her baby."

"What makes you think Mary will return? We both threw her out. Remember? She won't return." Anna buried her head in her hands.

"She will want to know my decision concerning betrothal. She is an honest girl. She'll give me time to think things over, and then she will return."

"If you think her so honest, why didn't you believe her?" She spat the words at him.

Joseph knew Anna spoke from hurt and hate; still, it was difficult not to be angry with the woman. He took a deep breath. "No, I don't believe the story she told. It defies logic. But I'm trying to understand why she lied. Still, I'm confident that Mary will want to know my decision."

"What if she assumes that you will have her stoned? Do you think she will return to a man who wants her and her unborn child dead? Somehow, I don't think so. She is gone, Joseph. She will not return."

"Is that what you fear I will do, Anna?"

"Yes."

"If I told you that was not my intention, would you eat and drink something?"

"What is your intention? Have you already decided?"

"Anna, I am an honest man. I'd like to think that I am kind as well. I have no intention of making Mary's condition public. I will divorce her privately. I'll help you and Mary get settled in a different town where no one knows you. She can tell everyone that her husband was killed or taken by the Romans. Folks here will think I'm just a confirmed bachelor. I doubt Mary's reputation will be tarnished. That is, as long as she makes no mention of the baby or tells that ridiculous story of hers."

"Oh, thank you. Thank you." Anna fell to the ground and began to kiss Joseph's feet.

"Anna, get up." Joseph helped her stand. "Please, let me get you some food and water."

Anna sat back down in her chair, unable to remain standing. "Joseph, it is not that I do not eat or drink because of the decision that has washed your mind. It is because of my own guilt that I refuse sustenance."

"You have nothing to be guilty for." Joseph took the old lady's hand in his.

Anna stared down at her hand in his. She couldn't look Joseph in the eyes. She knew she would see the love a son has for his mother, but she felt unworthy of such a kindness. "I refused my daughter when she needed me most. I've looked the other way. She is flesh of my flesh, my only child, and I abandoned her."

"Any woman who feared God would have done the same thing."

"I'm not so sure. Throughout Mary's life, I have hounded

her. I never saw her for who she was. The inner beauty she has. Perhaps it was my own jealousy that colored my acceptance of her. Miriam admonished me many times to love Mary for who she is. She said that God had a plan for Mary. She told Joachim the same thing. Joachim believed Miriam. I did not. Maybe if I had, things would be different."

"Anna, you must not torture yourself like this. You are a good woman. You are a good mother. You did what you thought best. You reared a beautiful daughter, who has chosen her own way." Joseph's heart broke for Mary's mother. This woman had taken great care to nurse him back to health. She had accepted him as her son; he had accepted her as his mother.

Anna patted his knee. There was nothing left to say. She stood to go back to the safety of her bed. At least in sleep, her thoughts no longer plagued her.

Joseph grabbed her hands and knelt in front of her. "Don't you see? You have become the mother I lost ten years ago. I can't lose you too. I would rather die than go through that suffering. Some days, I wished I were dead. Then the searing pain that courses through my body would end." Joseph broke. The anguish at losing the life with Mary he had come to anticipate rose from the pit where he had buried it, escaping through wails of sorrow.

Anna gently stroked the man's head, giving Joseph the assurance of her presence as he unleashed his grief. Her own tears fell down her face. She and Joseph shared a common bond. Her demeanor changed as she wept with Joseph. The longer she held the young man, the more her senses seemed to return. Her thoughts began to change from a woman who had no one to a woman with a sense of purpose. Joseph needed her. He could be the son she'd never had. She could be the mother he missed. She would be strong for him. "Joseph, the time for weeping is over." She tenderly lifted Joseph's face up so that his eyes were looking square into hers. "Go and bring me some fresh food and water. I will make something to eat for both of us. We will talk about what

FAVORED

course of action we must take."

Joseph nodded and rose. Allowing his emotions to unleash themselves had brought him comfort. Grabbing the picture, he hurried out the door, fearing that if he took too long, Anna might change her mind. Mary would never forgive him if he let anything happen to her mother. The thought stung Joseph's heart, surprising his logical mind. Why should he still care what Mary thought of him? She was the one who'd chosen to be with another. Why did he still care? Joseph sent through the streets of Nazareth, picking up the items that would be useful to Anna.

Mary would not lie. Believe what she tells you, beloved.

Unaware he was talking out loud, Joseph yelled, "I listened to You once. I will listen no more." Instantly the still, small voice in his head was gone. It was replaced with the awareness that people were quizzically looking and pointing at him. He felt the heat of his blush rise from his neck to the top of his head. He picked up his pace and hurried to the outside of town where the well stood.

After Joseph left, Anna took the opportunity to change her tunic and to braid her hair. It was as if she had been blinded and had her sight returned. She couldn't believe the condition in which she found her home. Broom in hand, she scurried through each tiny room. She paused for only a moment in front of the disheveled baskets. She would not let her mind go there. She quickly stacked them in the corner. She poured oil over the logs and lit the fire that had burned out days ago. She began to heat the soup Rachel had graciously prepared. Joseph would be back soon, and she wanted him to feel comfortable in her presence and home. She did not want to cause the boy any more concern. He needed her to be strong for him. Once again, Anna felt needed.

The front door opened, and Joseph entered, his arms full of the scrumptious items he had purchased for her. Anna helped him set the food on the table. While she sorted the wares, Joseph placed the water pitcher, now full of fresh water, on the sideboard. "Is everything to your liking?" The question sent a flashback through

Anna's mind of her daughter earnestly seeking her approval over a meal Mary had prepared.

"Yes. It's too much. I cannot begin to repay you for your kindness."

"I can think of one way." Joseph grinned.

"What is that?" Anna smiled back as a mother smiles at a son who pleases her.

"Fix dinner for me at least once a week. I'm not too good a cook myself."

"Now, that I can do." Anna went over and stirred the boiling soup.

"That smells good." Joseph sat down in the empty chair.

Anna turned around. Seeing Joseph in Joachim's chair brought a wave of sadness that showed on her face.

"Is something wrong?"

"No. I'm just not used to seeing anyone else in Joachim's chair. It's been empty for so long."

"I'll move." Joseph started to rise, but Anna stopped him.

"No. Sit and be comfortable. It is time the chair be put to good use." She grabbed two bowls from the sideboard and spooned soup into both. Placing one bowl in front of Joseph and the other at her place, she proceeded to slice some bread and fruit.

"Everything looks and smells delicious." Joseph knew Anna was famished. He waited while she took her place at the table. She immediately picked up her spoon and began to eat. "Anna, don't you think we should seek God's blessing?" Joseph smiled at the older woman.

"Not in this house," she replied emphatically.

Joseph watched as she continued to eat. "Anna, you must not blame God. That will only bring His wrath upon you." He picked up his own spoon and began to eat.

FAVORED

"His wrath is already upon me." She took a piece of bread and dipped it into her soup. "I must confess Rachel is a pretty good cook. Don't you dare tell her I said that. Her head would grow too big for her neck." Anna laughed at her own small joke.

"Your secret is safe. Why do you say God's wrath is already upon you?" Joseph ate very slowly; he knew that Anna would stop eating, even if she wasn't full, if he finished his meal too quickly. He desired that she have her fill.

"I have been told since my birth that it was God's will that my mother died, God's will that I have only one child, God's will that my husband died. Now, my unwed daughter tells me it is God's will that she is with child. Her situation is a certain death sentence. The logical conclusion I draw from all of this is that God's will is for me to be alone." Anna dropped her bread and stared straight ahead. Her eyes blazed with resentment. Her features became stone. "I hate being alone. It's torture. I suppose my whole life has been an example of God's wrath. Well, I don't want to be alone. And now, I don't have to be. You have come." Anna's words sent chills at Joseph's spine.

"Be careful of how you speak. Joachim would not be pleased with your words. He was a very righteous man." Joseph tried to capture eye contact with Anna, but she refused to look in his direction.

"Yes, Joachim was righteous. He had great faith. So did Miriam. Mary, too, for that matter. But I have always been a doubter. Miriam knew it. Maybe that's why she focused her teaching on Mary. I know it pained her to see my doubt. I am sorry for that. But you cannot force yourself to believe in what is not real." The words, which until now had just been thoughts, surprised both of them.

"Anna, you mustn't say such things. God has taken care of His people. We are His people. You mustn't say such things. You're just hurt. You'll feel differently over time." Joseph couldn't stand to hear the bitterness booing from her mouth. He decided it was time he took his leave. "I'd best be going. Promise me you will eat and take care of yourself until I return. You can expect me next week, same day and time, if that suits you."

"I will take care of myself. You are a good boy." Anna stood.

"Do you need help in cleaning up?"

"No, I'll be fine. I'll clean up and go to bed. I feel very tired. Be safe."

"Send Rachel to me if you need anything." Joseph hesitated at the door; he wasn't comfortable leaving Anna alone.

"Go. I promise to take care of myself. I'll look forward to your next visit." Anna practically pushed Joseph out the door, closing it behind him.

Rachel quickly answered Joseph's taps at her front door.

"Joseph, good, you've been at Anna's. How is she?" Rachel searched the young man's face for the answer she desired.

"She's doing much better. I am still concerned. Check in on her for me. Let me know if there is anything she needs."

"Mary is a thoughtless girl to take off like that and not tell anyone where she was going. Didn't she know her mother would worry herself to death?" Rachel eyed Joseph, trying to discern any acknowledgment that what she had just spoken was the truth.

"Just keep me informed concerning Anna's needs. I would be most grateful to you." Joseph went on his way, feeling Rachel's gaze on his back. Anna had described her friend perfectly when she'd called her a busybody. Joseph chuckled to himself.

It was still early in the evening. He looked up at the pink sky. The breeze was warm and refreshing. Joseph decided to walk a little ways out of town before heading home. He allowed his mind to wander back over the conversation with Anna. Mary had none of Anna's bitterness. How could a daughter be so different from her mother?

Unconsciously Joseph made his way to the spot where he and

FAVORED

Mary, with her father, had spent many afternoons. He sat on the ground, reliving the moments that had brought him so much joy and peace. He was certain he could faintly hear Mary's laugh in the rustle of the trees. He caught a whiff of her scent on the breeze that ruffled his hair. He closed his eyes and envisioned her, trying to free the tiny lizard that had been trapped in the yarn of the blanket they had set upon. He'd never dreamed that anyone could replace the memory of Hannah, but Mary had. Mary was the girl who filled his thoughts. She was the girl who haunted his dreams, not Hannah. Mary was the girl who had taken his heart. Mary was the girl he loved.

Joseph stood, anger welling up inside of him. *Fool!* Joseph stormed back to his home. "I was perfectly content in my own world. I was fine with being single. I had no desire to marry. None. Not until I listened to You." He shook a fist up to the heavens.

The words that entered Joseph's mind halted him in his tracks. *A fool delights in airing his own opinions.*

"I'll give you that. I am a fool." Joseph hurried home, taking a moment to stop by his shop. He took pleasure in the fresh smell of carved wood. The shavings he had left on the floor reminded him that he had not finished all his duties. His father had always admonished him to take care in keeping the shop clean and neat. Joseph picked up a broom and began the task of sweeping up the mess.

Something clean and white beneath the shavings caught Joseph's eye. He bent down and picked up the piece of cloth. It held Mary's scent. She must have dropped it when she had last been there. His mind went back to the moment Mary told him she was with child. He really hadn't given her a chance to explain. But then, what more could have been said? She had admitted to being with child. He had not been with her. There was only one explanation: she had been with someone else. Joseph threw the cloth on the floor. He scooped the cloth up with the shavings meant for trash. Why did he feel guilty when he wasn't the one wrong?

He entered his home and poured himself a cup of wine. He stood in the dark; a sliver of moonlight cast a beam of light on the staff that stood in the corner. He picked up the staff and rubbed his hand along its etched surface. *This is the reason I let my guard down. There will be no more etchings a generations to come made upon its fine wood. This stuff is just a reminder of my failure as a man.* Joseph brought the staff down across his knee, breaking it in half. The cracking noise it made echoed through the house. The sound seemed to bounce back over and over again, slapping him. Dropping to his knees, he allowed the two halves of the staff to fall to the floor.

"I am a wretched man." He buried his face in his hands. *Maybe Anna is right. Maybe God's wrath is already upon us.*

Turn to Me, beloved.

"No." Joseph shook his head in an attempt to free the voice from his mind.

Turn to Me, beloved.

Joseph screamed and pulled out his hair. "No!"

Trust Me, beloved.

Covering his ears with his hands, Joseph ran to his bed. He flung his body onto the bed, tossing and turning as he cried over and over, "No, no, no!" Yet, no matter how loud he became or how much he tossed, the voice continued to echo in his mind. The last thing Joseph remembered before falling into a restless sleep was the voice.

Turn to Me. Trust in Me. It is time, beloved.

Chapter Thirty

Two weeks passed, that and then three, since Mary's departure. Joseph did as he had promised; once a week, sometimes twice a week, he would join Anna for supper. Rumors had spread throughout Nazareth about Mary's disappearance. Both Joseph and Anna chose to ignore the comments. It was better that no one knew the truth. Lydia had stopped by Joseph's shop before leaving with her family to try to discover news of her friend. It pained Joseph to see the hurt in Lydia's eyes when he would not reveal the truth to her. But then, Mary was the one who had made the choices that had brought pain for everyone around her. Joseph's decision to divorce Mary privately left only one option for Anna. Should Mary return, they would have to move, but where they would go remained unknown.

Anna realized that she had temporarily lost her mind after Mary left. With Joseph's visit and Rachel's companionship throughout the day, she returned to her former self. However, the bitterness that was buried within her grew up around her like a vine, choking the peace and joy that used to adorn her features. Even when she smiled, her face appeared hard like a stone that could not be broken. Her hair, which had shone like the sun, was dull. Her body slumped with the weight of the bitterness she carried.

Anna and Rachel went to the well together and stopped at several vendors on the way back. Anna bought little. Without any income, it was becoming more and more difficult to make ends meet. Joseph was all too kind to help, but Anna felt she was becoming a drain to him. If ever she had been a praying woman, now was the time to pray, but she could not bring herself

FAVORED

to do it. Miriam would have encouraged her to "trust in God and wait patiently on Him." Anna paid little attention to the voice that echoed words inside her head.

"Isn't there more produce you need for dinner tonight with Joseph?"

Oh, God, please don't let her ask about my financial condition.

"Dear, are you doing all right? I mean, money-wise? You know, Aaron and I are glad to help in any way we can. We just assumed things were fine. Joachim made a good living with his pottery, did he not?" Rachel was just a little too inquisitive for Anna's liking.

"Joachim did very well. I am fine. I just don't need as much as you think I do." Anna hurried ahead of Rachel, leaving the woman to eat the dust, and purposefully kicked up.

"How ungrateful," Rachel muttered under her breath. However, Anna's little temper tantrum also brought delight. It assured Rachel that her friend had truly returned to her former self.

As Anna neared her home, she caught sight of a figure lingering in the door frame. *Mary?* She quickened her pace. As she came nearer, she realized her old eyes had deceived her once again. The figure was that of a man. The man must have seen her, for he began to wave in a friendly greeting as she approached.

"Anna, is it really you?"

"Yes, and who might you be?" The man took some of the wares Anna carried and opened the door for her.

"It's me, Eliakim, your brother-in-law. Joachim's oldest brother." The man was beaming from ear to ear.

"Eliakim? I can't believe it. How long has it been? How is your wife? The children?" The questions poured from Anna's mouth. It had been over twenty years since she and Joachim had seen any family. Eliakim had moved himself, Anabel, his wife,

282

and their newborn baby to Jerusalem. He had tried to encourage Joachim to do the same. There was great profit to be made in Jerusalem, or so Eliakim thought. The very sensible Joachim had chosen to stay in Nazareth. Word had come that Eliakim had done well selling grain. With the money he made from selling grain, he had purchased an inn. Rumor was that he provided any man who could pay with whatever accommodations and luxuries a man might desire. He was especially good at catering to the Roman Army. Joachim was so displeased at the choices his brother had made that he broke off all ties. Now, right before her eyes, stood her last link with her husband.

"Eliakim, come and sit. You must be hungry. I'll fix you a plate."

"Thank you, Anna. You are still very thoughtful and kind." Anna set a cup of wine in front of her brother-in-law. He nodded his thanks.

"What brings you to Nazareth?" Anna took her seat opposite the man.

"I heard about Joachim. I'm sorry, Anna. I know how much you two loved each other."

"Yes, we did. I miss him greatly." Anna couldn't help the tear that trickled down her face.

"Did you know that Anabel died several years ago?"

"No. Oh, Eliakim, I'm sorry."

"I remarried a young thing and had another child. Of course, no one could replace Anabel. Joy in my life. Now, I, too, am alone, for my second wife recently passed."

"I hate to hear that. How old is the child?"

"She is five and a cute little thing. Quite a handful, though."

"I can relate. Mary was a handful at that age. I can remember her running through the streets of Nazareth, those long dark curls bouncing up and down behind her, people scurrying to get out of

FAVORED

her way. I was always yelling at the top of my lungs for her to slow down and be careful. She ran all the way home just to show Joachim the 'treasure of the day,' as the two of them called it. It was usually something as simple as a colorful rock or flower, but it was special to the both of them." Anna sighed. If only she could have those days back.

"Anna, are you all right? You look a little lost."

"I'm sorry. I've not been very good company as of late."

"Understandable. I wasn't myself for a long time after Anabel passed. It's understandable, perfectly understandable, the way you are feeling. How is Mary these days?"

The question sent a rush of anxiety through Anna's body. She had not thought of how to explain Mary's sudden disappearance. It had been easy enough to ignore the comments she heard in the street, but Eliakim was family. He would demand the truth. "Mary has…"

"Mary is such a darling girl. Did my brother find a match for her before he died? I would hope he would have at least had the good sense to do that for the child."

"Oh, yes, yes indeed. Mary is betrothed to a young carpenter here in town, a man by the name of Joseph. In fact, he is due here anytime now for supper. My, how the time flies when having such a lovely conversation. I must begin preparation for supper. You will join us, won't you?"

"I wouldn't have it any other way. I'm staying at the inn here in town. Accommodations are adequate, though small and informal. I thought it best I stay there and not here, seeing how people love to talk around here if my memory serves me."

"Indeed, your memory serves you well. How long do you plan to stay in Nazareth?" Anna rose and began setting the table for supper.

"Just until I have completed a business matter. As soon as it is settled, I will be on my way home." Eliakim rose and began to pace the tiny room. He marveled at how his younger brother could have been content in such small quarters. He had always wanted more.

"You must be famished. I have prepared stew, bread, and fruit for tonight. I hope you will find it satisfactory. I'm sure you are accustomed to much more."

"No, that sounds fine. True, I am used to larger meals, as I am sure you can see." Eliakim patted his round belly. "I remember what a fine cook you are, Anna. I am looking forward to supping with you. Shouldn't Mary be helping you? After all, it is her betrothed that is coming to dinner."

"I suppose I should tell you..." Before Anna could finish, there was a knock at the door. "That must be Joseph." Anna hurried to the door, the interruption a relief from the inevitable. "Joseph, come in."

Joseph was surprised to see the unfamiliar guest standing in the corner where Mary used to sleep. Curiosity was clearly written on his face. "I brought some fresh wine and bread for our meal."

"Thank you, Joseph. That is very kind of you. I would like you to meet my brother-in-law, Joachim's older brother, Eliakim. Eliakim, this is Joseph, Mary's betrothed." Joseph understood completely that Anna had not told this relative all the news of Mary. He respected her decision and chose to say nothing to contradict the introduction.

"It is a pleasure to meet you." Joseph extended his arm in formal greeting, which the elder man heartedly accepted.

"The pleasure is mine, young man. I am sure my brother has chosen wisely for his daughter, though I am surprised at your age. What are you? Twenty, twenty-five?"

"Twenty-five. With age comes wisdom, or so I would like to think."

Eliakim laughed at the young man's prudence. "Ah, indeed.

FAVORED

Anna, may we sit and have some of that wine our young friend has brought with him?"

"Please, do. Supper will be ready shortly." Anna busied herself as Joseph and Eliakim talked. It was nice to have men's laughter around the table. She was thankful that Joseph did not betray her. Soon Eliakim would need to know the truth, but things were so pleasant that news such as hers would only bring discomfort to their small party.

"Supper is served." Anna placed a bowl of stew in front of each man. She waited while they tasted and gave their nods of approval before she sat and began to eat.

"Where are my manners? Shouldn't we wait for Mary?" Eliakim looked up at the two of them.

Joseph looked at Anna, and Anna at Joseph. It was as though they could read each other's mind. For Anna, the silence which only lasted seconds seemed to last an eternity. To her relief, Joseph answered Eliakim's question.

"Gone to visit friends for a few months. Anna and I thought it good for her to go. You know how close she was to Joachim. His death was tragic and brought Mary much grief." Joseph lowered his head and continued to eat. He had not lied. They had thought it best she go. Her father's death did pain her. They weren't sure she was with friends.

"Very wise. It is hard enough for a young girl to wed, but to have to deal with the death of a parent and marriage—ah, that would be difficult. Mary and Joachim were very close. It must have pained her deeply." Eliakim resumed eating. "Anna, I have not tasted anything this good in a long time. You are a good cook and a good woman."

"Thank you, Eliakim." Anna smiled, but beneath her smile, sadness lurked. She was grateful to Joseph for his quick wit in answering Eliakim's question. However, talk of Mary brought a stab of despair to her soul.

Joseph's mind had taken another track altogether. He watched the way Eliakim looked at Anna. The man was smug and prayerful. No wonder Joachim had separated himself from his brother so long ago. The man had something up his sleeve. "Tell me, Eliakim, what brings you to our small town?"

"Business."

"How long do you plan to stay?" Joseph eyed the man with curiosity.

"If things go my way, a week or two at most. If not, I may have to stay longer than I planned. Of course, much of this is up to Anna." Eliakim winked and patted Anna's hand.

Anna smiled back at her brother-in-law, discerning nothing. Joseph, however, picked up on the man's intention. "I see. Are you staying here with Anna or at the inn?" he asked, looking directly into the man's eyes.

"The inn, of course. No impropriety here." Eliakim stood. "Now, if you'll excuse me, I must be going. The trip has tired these old bones. May I call on you tomorrow, Anna?"

"You do not need to ask. Family is always welcomed in my home." Anna began to clear the bowls and cups from the table.

"I'm glad to hear it. I will bring a lamb to roast tomorrow. We will have a celebration. You are welcome to join us, Joseph." Eliakim cast but a glance at Joseph's direction. His focus remained on Anna.

"Thank you. I think I just might. I am headed in your direction. Shall we walk together?"

"Wonderful. Until tomorrow, Anna." Whistling, Elaikim walked out of the house.

Joseph wasn't far behind. He gave a quick goodbye to Anna and then started at a brisk pace in order to catch up to the older man.

For a while the two walked in silence. Eliakim's whistling

FAVORED

sent pins and needles up Joseph's spine. Joseph found the man irritating. He couldn't put his finger on it, but something about Eliakim made Joseph distrust him.

Joseph couldn't stand the silence or the whistling any longer. "Eliakim, I would like to speak forthrightly with you if I may."

"By all means, son. Speak what is on your mind."

"What are your intentions concerning Anna and Mary?"

Eliakim stopped dead in his tracks. He turned to face Joseph. "How do my 'intentions' concern you?" Eliakim gave a mannerly smile, but his patronizing look made Joseph's skin crawl.

"I promised Joachim I would look after them both. I keep my promises." Joseph squared his shoulders for what he was sure would be a war of words right in the middle of Nazareth.

"Quite admirable of you. I had no intentions toward Mary if that is what concerns you. She is far too young for me. Anna, on the other hand, is just what my five-year-old daughter needs."

"You want to take Anna back to Jerusalem to be your nursemaid?"

"No, I want her to be my wife. It is my responsibility, after all, as Joachim's brother. It is my right to take Anna as my wife." Eliakim turned and continued on his way, leaving Joseph stunned.

"What if she doesn't want to be your wife?"

"She will."

"What can you offer her? I mean, she would have to leave her friends and family and go live with you in Jerusalem. Mary isn't expected back for some time. I don't think Anna would just leave without seeing Mary."

"I need a good woman like Anna to help raise my daughter. I don't want Mary around. It would just be another mouth to feed. As far as I am concerned, as soon as Anna becomes my wife, Mary is your responsibility and not mine or Anna's. Anna has nothing and no one here. She thrives on taking care of family.

Even when I'm gone, she will take good care of my little girl for me." Eliakim turned and looked at Joseph. "Look, my time is short. I am an old man. I have made a good living in Jerusalem. Be wise, son. Don't hinder her from coming with me. Encourage her. It is what Joachim would have wanted."

"I'm not sure. If he wanted you to be Anna's husband, why did he separate himself from you twenty years ago? I don't trust you, and I don't think Joachim did either. Men like you only do things to benefit themselves and nobody else."

Eliakim laughed. "You may be right. But I promise to do right by Anna. True, Joachim and I had our differences. My brother was an idealist. He couldn't see beyond Nazareth and his laws of righteousness. I, on the other hand, saw opportunity and took it. I obey the laws and offer sacrifices, but I am not blind. There is profit to be made in this world, and I intend to make it."

"I see. Anna is a wise woman. The decision, of course, is hers. I can't imagine her saying yes."

"You will be disappointed if she does?"

"Yes."

"Well, prepare yourself for disappointment. Anna longs to be needed. Raising my daughter as her own will give her purpose. Now that Mary is to be married, she is lost and alone. She'll say yes. I am confident. Until tomorrow, lad." Eliakim disappeared inside the end.

Joseph slowly walked home. Life was getting much too complicated for this simple carpenter. If Anna chose to become the wife of that man, it would be Joseph's responsibility to tell Mary if she ever returned. To whom would Mary turn with her mother gone? Eliakim had made it clear he wanted nothing to do with Mary. The responsibility would be Joseph's—all Joseph's. He had looked after Anna these past few weeks. He had cared for her as if she were his own mother. Perhaps, deep down, he wanted to maintain a connection with Mary, and Anna was the only way he could do that. Perhaps he had fooled himself all along, thinking he was doing the right thing, when the whole time he was only trying to abate his own loneliness and misery. Anger welled up inside him. He liked things simple, but for quite some time now, life had been anything but simple.

Joseph opened the door to his home. He felt old and tired, but too much plagued his mind for him to sleep. He poured a cup of wine and walked over to his shop. He was working on several pieces. One in particular, a table, was becoming very special to him. The owner had asked that intricate details of family history be carved on the legs. He wanted the table to be a gift to his family. The man was very ill and felt he had not been diligent in teaching his sons of their lineage. Joseph set to work sanding the legs so they would be smooth before he began to carve the design the man had drawn out for him. As he worked, his mind wandered over the past weeks and months. He thought about Anna and Eliakim. His thoughts naturally turned to Mary and her unborn child. He and Mary should have been preparing to wed. Why did Mary have to betray him? He didn't ask for this. All he wanted was a legacy of his own, a history his father could be proud of. He wanted Mary to bear his children, not another's. The more he thought about her, the harder he sanded. Without thinking, he grounded the wood down to a splinter. He swore as he realized he would have to replace the leg and start all over.

He should have minded his own business. He should have never allowed Joachim to encourage him. That had been his first mistake. Joseph began to pick up his tools. He grabbed the broom and tried to focus on cleaning the sawdust that carpeted the floor.

It wasn't Joachim who called you. It was I, beloved.

"No more. I am done listening to You. You sent me a girl who was unfaithful, a girl who is carrying another man's child." The heartache Joseph had been carrying spilled forth in anguish as he spoke. "I began to love her. Don't you see? I love her, and she betrayed me. How could she? I wanted the life I had only dreamed about. Deep down, I wanted a wife and family. I chose to listen. I chose to trust. Now, look at where I am. Alone. Afraid. What am I to do if Mary returns and her mother is gone? I will be all she has. I can't forgive her. I won't be able to look at her. Yet, I will feel an obligation. I am in this mess because of You."

Joseph shook the broom in the air, then threw it across the room. The weight of his anger and pain forced him to his knees. He buried his face in his hands. The wet of his tears seeped through his fingers and fell to the sawdust-covered floor. "I tried. I tried. Once again, I failed. I will never be what my father wanted."

Be what I want you to be, beloved.

Weary and weak, Joseph cried, "I can't! I don't know how."

Trust in Me, and I will show you. Walk in My ways, and I will guide you. You will be like the tree planted by rivers of water, which yields its fruit and season and whose leaf does not wither. Submit to Me, and you will prosper.

The words rushed through Joseph's mind and heart. They brought peace. Yet, no matter how much Joseph wanted to listen and believe, his heart and soul screamed something else. His feelings seemed to be flooding his senses, overwhelming his rational mind. He pounded his fist into the ground as he cried out, "I've never been afraid of anything before, not like this, but this, this blind faith You want me to have, scares me. I don't want to be made a fool of. Not again! I went through that once with Hannah. Not again!"

Joseph tried to stand, but it was as if his knees were anchored to the floor. "Don't You understand? I want to believe. I want to trust, but I am afraid. This girl has betrayed me. I can't take her back. I won't take her back."

Submit to My will for you, beloved.

Joseph cried out in agony. He tore at his hair and beard. He had become an uncontrollable madman. Suddenly, his legs found their strength. He stepped through the shop, knocking anything over that got in his way. He yelled at the top of his lungs, and when that didn't end the torture he was in, he cursed and began the whole process over again. His temper tantrum lasted until the early hours of dawn. Finally weak and exhausted, he sank to the ground and wept bitter tears.

I have a plan for you, a plan to prosper and not to harm you. Listen and wait upon Me. I will come to you.

With those words echoing in his head, Joseph made his way home. He walked in a daze of confusion and sorrow. He fell into bed.

As Joseph slept, he began to dream. At first, his dream held memories of childhood: his mother laughing, his father teaching him to carve a staff. Then the dream turned to a girl running and laughing in a field of lilies. Joseph ran after the girl, but just when he thought he could reach out and touch her, she disappeared into the mist. Joseph followed her into the mist. Fear gripped his soul, but he forged onward. Then, in an instant, the miss disappeared. A blinding light replaced it. The light took the form of a bee, and the bees spoke to him, "Joseph, son of David, do not be afraid to take Mary home as your wife because what is conceived in her is from the Holy Spirit. She will give birth to a Son, and you are to give Him the name Jesus because He will save His people from their sins."[5] As quickly as the light had appeared in the dream, it was gone. However, the mist did not return.

Immediately Joseph woke, feeling no sense of pain or loss. "Oh God, forgive this man for his unbelief. May Mary forgive me. I will do as you have said. I am Your servant."

Joseph rose from his place of submission. He quickly washed and dressed. He knew he had to find Anna and tell her all that the angel had said to him. Joy flooded his soul. The news he would share would bring peace and comfort to Mary's mother. Mary… Where was she? How could he find her?

Wait on Me, beloved.

5 Matthew 1:20–21 (NIV)

Joseph hurried to the streets of Nazareth to Anna's home. Without knocking, he burst through the front door. His intrusion startled Anna and Eliakim. "Anna, I must speak with you privately." Joseph was out of breath from the fast pace he had taken to her house.

"Too late, son. Anna has agreed to come to Jerusalem and be my wife. I plan on making the arrangements tomorrow, and we will leave in one month's time."

Joseph stood in stunned silence. "Anna, you mustn't make a hasty decision. Mary will be home soon, and everything is going to be all right. I have news for you that will delight your heart."

"Joseph, you have been most kind to this old woman. But Eliakim is right. It is my lawful duty to become his wife and help him raise his daughter. Mary is a woman now. She belongs to you. Eliakim And I have agreed that this house will be left for her, should she return. So, you see, Mary is well cared for."

"Please, may I speak to you in private? What I have to tell you is an utmost urgency. It may affect your future as well as mine."

"Whatever you have to say can be said in front of Eliakim. I told him all about Mary and her condition. He will not judge you."

Joseph was uncomfortable with Eliakim knowing too much concerning Mary and, for that matter, his own visit from the angel. Nevertheless, he had no option but to relay the details of his nightly visitor to Anna in front of Eliakim. Taking a deep breath, he dove right in. "Anna, last night, while I slept, an angel appeared to me. He confirmed all that Mary told us. The child she carries is from God. I intend on taking Mary as my wife. You do not have to marry this man. Mary and I will take good care of you."

Eliakim burst into robust laughter. "The young man is as delusional as my niece. Angels appearing in dreams. Surely you do not believe such nonsense, Anna."

FAVORED

Anna studied Joseph's face. His features, which had once been clouded with guilt and anger, were alight with peace and joy. "Is what you say really true?"

Joseph knelt in front of Anna and took her hands. "Yes, it is true. Do you have any idea where Mary has gone? I must find her and bring her into my home as my wife."

Anna searched his face. She shook her head. "I do not know where my daughter is. I can see from your countenance that you are at peace. I myself do not know what to believe. Still, I have accepted Eliakim's proposal. I will not go back on my word. Mary doesn't need me anymore, but his young daughter does. It would be good to be a mother to a child. It will give Mary the sister I could never give her."

Eliakim snickered at Anna's words. "I guess the older man is the wiser, hey, lad?" He gave Joseph a good-natured slap on the back.

Joseph stood, towering above the man. It was all he could do to restrain himself from slamming his fist into the old man's face. Something about Eliakim rubbed him the wrong way.

"Come, Anna, there is much preparation to do. Since Joseph is willing to look after Mary, I think we could sell this house for a small profit. It would be only fitting."

"Whatever you think, Eliakim."

"Anna, no, don't do this. Mary will need you to help deliver her child."

"There are midwives for that," Eliakim asserted. "Come, Anna, let us go and announce this happy news of our marriage arrangement." Turning to Joseph, he added, "I would not tell others of your dream. It would behoove you to keep that detail to yourself. You wouldn't want to damage Mary's reputation."

Eliakim hurried out the door with Anna close at his heels. She took one last look at Joseph before she left. She spoke to him in a hushed whisper, "Thank you. You are a good man, Joseph. Take care of Mary. She was just learning to love you." Anna quickly departed to do her future husband's bidding.

Joseph dropped himself into the nearest chair. Mary would be devastated when she returned to find her mother gone. How could he ever tell her all that had transpired since she'd left? She'd only blame herself.

Joseph sat quietly in what once had been Mary's home. Slowly he rose, only to drop to his knees. He had never bowed before God in prayer. Somehow, this God he had been taught to fear, whose worship required strict adherence to laws most men found intolerable, was now personal and reachable by a simple carpenter. Joseph melted out of the need to show surrender to God. It felt right and honorable.

"God, I am but a simple man. I am not wise like the elders. Nor have I been schooled in the ways of the law like our teachers. I know what I saw in my dream—the angel and the words Your message spoke to me—is from You and is to be believed. I do believe. More than I thought possible. I am struck dumb by the thought that You would choose this lowly carpenter to help raise Your Son. I know I cannot do this thing alone. I know Mary cannot do this thing alone. She has more faith and trust in You than any man or woman I know. I feel like a child coming to You like this. Maybe that is what You want. God, somehow, let Mary know that I believe her. Somehow, bring her back to me." Joseph didn't know how to end his prayer, so he just stood and nodded his head. When he turned to go, he was surprised to see Rachel standing in the doorway.

"I'm sorry, Joseph. I really didn't mean to listen in. It's just, I've never seen someone pray in that way before. It surprised me."

"Rachel, I beg you not to speak of this or what you have heard. I know I cannot stop you, but I ask you to keep my confidence in Mary's." Unbeknownst to Joseph, his face was white with a fire that brought fear to Rachel.

FAVORED

"You have my word. Where is Anna? I came for a usual weekly darning. I am surprised she is not here."

"I suppose it is all right I tell you. After all, Eliakim is trumpeting the news through all of Nazareth."

"What news?"

Joseph detected the concern in Rachel's voice. "He and Anna are going to be wed in a month's time, and he intends on taking her back with him to Jerusalem."

"Oh my. This is not good. I suspected that was the reason for his visit, but this is not good. Not good indeed." Rachel walked over to the table and sat down in one of the four empty chairs.

"Why are you distraught over this? I thought you would be happy for your friend. Anna will have the opportunity to be well taken care of, and she will become the mother to Eliakim's only daughter. It appears to be a perfect match."

"Appears is the right word for it. Joseph, I may be speaking out of line, but you are to be in a son." She posed the phrase more as a question than a statement and waited for Joseph to respond.

"Yes. As soon as Mary returns, I intend on taking her as my wife."

"Then you should know the truth about Eliakim and the reason for the estranged relationship he had with Joachim. Eliakim would like everyone to believe that the relationship deteriorated because of a difference of opinion between himself and his younger brother. But Anna told me the truth years ago. Evidently, Eliakim was betrothed to Anabel, but she was not who he wanted. He had his eye on Anna, but she had been promised to Joachim. Miriam knew what kind of man Eliakim was: greedy, dishonest. Eliakim did not always follow the ways of the law. He would pick and choose what laws he would follow. It depended on what brought him the most gain. Miriam wanted her niece, whom she had reared as her daughter, to be wed to a righteous man. Joachim, indeed, was that.

"However, Eliakim had no intention of being outdone by his younger brother. The feud finally ended when Eliakim took Anna and tried to wed her without anyone's knowledge. Of course, he was caught. The family disowned him, and he took Anabel as his wife and moved to Jerusalem. He was not kind to her. Word is that Eliakim kept several hardwoods at his inn, and not just for the soldiers who frequented his place of business. Anabel lived a very hard life with that man. She died much too young, and if you ask me, she died of heartache. Eliakim is old, but he still exudes the same evil he always has." Rachel stood and came face to face with Joseph. "You must stop this before it is too late. It will be the end of Anna to leave and wed that man."

Joseph stared into the eyes of the older woman. There was no malice or intent to speak ill of someone. What Rachel had said was out of pure concern for her friend. "If all you say is the truth, then why would Anna marry Eliakim? She is a smart woman."

"Loneliness will make even the smartest of women do strange things."

"Rachel, I tried to stop her. I told her things that should have stopped her. She just said that she would not go back on her word to Eliakim. I don't think there is anything I can do."

"We have a month." Rachel headed for the door. "Between the two of us, maybe we can talk some sense into that stubborn head of hers." She hurried out the door before Joseph could respond.

Joseph walked home with the weight of all Rachel had told him crashing down upon his shoulders. Eliakim was determined. Anna was caught up in the fantasy of being needed. *How can I stop them?*

When he opened his front door, he realized how hungry he was. He poured himself some wine and sliced some bread and fruit. The dates and nuts he had purchased earlier were to his liking. As he ate, his eyes veered to the empty corner where once had stood a staff embellished with his family's history. How could he have been so stupid?

FAVORED

After he had finished eating and cleaned up his mess, he made his way to bed. He stretched his long frame out and looked up at the ceiling. He knew the staff could not be repaired. When he cracked it over his knee, it had splintered into tiny pieces. Perhaps he could carve a new one. The old staff was lying in the scrap pile. He could use it as a model. His father had taught him every line, made him memorize every detail. Joseph set straight up as a realization struck him. The child in Mary's womb. This child who was the Son of God. Should he include Him? He was not of Joseph's flesh. Joseph lay back down as he pondered the thought. In many ways, this was all happening much too fast. There were questions with no answers.

Felt his eye was growing heavy as his mind continued to whirl. How would he raise the Son of God as his own son?

In the quiet of the moment, his heart found peace with the simple words that eased their way into his mind.

Be still and know that I am God. It is I who have made you. It is I who have called you to this task. I will lead and guide you in all things, beloved.

Joseph slept better than he had in weeks.

Chapter Thirty-One

Dalena stepped onto the dock and shielded her eyes as she took in the sights and sounds closing in around her. There were men shouting as they loaded and unloaded goods from the ship. The hustle and bustle overwhelmed her. She watched as streams of sweat poured down the backs of those working the docks.

She spoke to Lucas, who was standing beside her. "Those men, there." She pointed to one in particular who had caught her eye. "Where are they from?"

"What did you say? It's hard to hear you over all the noise. This dock is certainly a busy place." Lucas caught hold of Dalena's elbow as he began to navigate the crowd.

"That man, the one over there." She pointed again. "Where is he from?" Dalena felt as if she was shouting loud enough that everyone around her would stop and listen.

However, no one paid any attention to either her or Lucas. It struck Dalena as very strange that a man of Lucas' stature would not draw attention, let alone she herself would not be noticed.

"He probably comes from one of the eastern countries."

"Oh, I don't think I've ever seen anyone from the east before."

Lucas laughed, "Lived a sheltered life in Rome, did you?"

Dalena just gave him a playful nudge with her elbow. It was just enough to throw Lucas slightly off balance. She giggled and allowed her escort to help her from the dock and onto dry land.

"I still feel like I am on that ship. I feel like my body is continuing to sway from side to side."

"It will take some time for you to adjust to being on land. You might feel this way for a few days."

"Please, don't say that. I am looking forward to having my feet firmly planted on dry ground. I don't want to feel like I am on water the whole time we are here in Cyprus."

"Perhaps you won't. We'd better hurry. Quirinius will be waiting for us at a villa he rented for your stay."

"How did he manage to find a *domas* for our stay when we didn't even know we would be stopping in Cyprus until yesterday?"

"The moment we docked, he had me send my most trusted men to secure a place for you. Dalena, you should know your husband well enough to know that what the governor wants, the governor gets."

"Yes, I am quite aware of that fact." Dalena spoke with all the hurt and bitterness she felt.

Lucas understood the meaning behind her words. They were deeper than just domiciles or positions in government. Dalena spoke of her very soul. Quirinius wanted her, body and soul, to be all his. A girl like Dalena was not one so easily acquired as a house or a bottle of wine. She needed tenderness and trust to be had, not threats and abuse. Before he thought, the next few words just slipped out, "You remind me so much..."

"What did you say? I'm sorry. I wasn't listening. Look over there." Dalena pointed to a row of shops where a group of women, adorned in silks and jewels, were perusing the merchandise. "I wonder who they are."

"They are probably wondering the same thing about you," Lucas said, relieved that Dalena had not picked up on his slip of the tongue.

"Do you think they have noticed me?" Dalena sounded like a child entering a new playground. "Oh, I didn't think Cyprus would be this exciting. I am glad we stopped. I hope we get to stay long enough for me to enjoy myself."

TERI LYN TOBEY

"Perhaps that can be arranged."

"Do you think you can influence Quirinius to stay longer? It amazes me the way you can get my husband to do your bidding. I believe you are better at manipulation than I am."

Lucas laughed. "I don't know about that."

Dalena positioned her mouth in her infamous pout. "You will try, won't you? Between the two of us, we might have a chance."

"I'll see what I can do."

She leaned into him, wrapping his arm in a hug. "Thank you."

Lucas couldn't deny her even if he wanted to. Since they had walked off the Aimes, Dalena's whole demeanor had changed. Her smile seemed to shine brighter than the sun with all its warmth. The chaos of the deck and the energy of the city ignited an excitement in Dalena that electrified the air around them. The whole way to the villa, Dalena laughed and pointed at the wonders of the tiny island. Lucas was more willing to share his knowledge of the world or at least of Cyprus with his young student.

They wound their way through the streets and headed toward the outskirts of town.

Lucas pointed toward a hill that was just to the north. "That, my dear, is where you will be calling home for the next few days, possibly weeks."

Dalena squinted trying to block the rays of the sun. Much to her delight, she could make out a lovely villa resting peacefully at the top of the hill. Situated among palm trees, the villa appeared to belong to the isle as much as the island breeze or the sand on the beach. As she and Lucas entered the house, Dalena noticed that large, intricately carved columns circled the house on all sides. She walked up the steps and past the columns into the *atrium*. The *impluvium* in the center of the atrium was framed with a black-and-white mosaic floor. Elaborate murals depicting life in Salamis ushered her from the atrium, through the *tablinum*, and out to the *peristyle*. Extending from the peristyle was an open terrace that overlooked the beach. In the center of the terrace was a table graced with a basket of fresh fruit and a bottle of wine. Steps from the terrace led down the hillside and opened out to the beach below.

"Lucas, look!" Dalena pointed out toward the ocean. In the distance Lucas could see the fins of dolphins as they came up for air and then sank once again below the surface of the water. "It's just beautiful." She turned to Lucas and flung herself into his arms. "How did you ever find such a place?"

"I thought you might like it. I remembered it from a visit I made years ago. I sent my men to inquire about its availability. Fortunately, with your husband's status as proconsul, strings can be pulled."

"I don't know that I will ever want to leave." Laughing, she took off her sandals, grabbed Lucas' hand, and hurried down the steps toward the beach.

"Oh my, I didn't realize the sand was so hot!" Dalena took a step back.

"Hurry toward the water. The sand is cooler there."

Dalena did as Lucas instructed. Soon, she was standing on the edge where water and sand met. She stood there for some time, feeling the wet sand squish between her toes. The ocean would lap up onto the sand, surrounding her ankles in coolness. Dalena knew she had never felt anything so wonderful.

"Lucas, you must come and feel this." Dalena turned to look at her friend. The flush of excitement and happiness, along with the sun, had given her cheeks a healthy glow. Her emerald eyes shone in the afternoon sun. The breeze tugged at her hair, loosening her coiffure and allowing just enough hair to circle her face like a wreath. He wound himself caught up in her charm and beauty. It took him a moment to remember his purpose for being with her.

"Come, you can enjoy the beach tomorrow. Don't you think

it's time to prepare yourself for your husband and the evening meal? I'm sure Quirinius would not be pleased if you were not prepared appropriately for his arrival."

"Oh, why can't we just forget Quirinius for a while? He looms over us like a bad storm just waiting to unleash savage rain and thunder on all who stand in its way." Dalena turned back around to face the open ocean. The sun cast pink hues on the horizon as it began to dip low in the sky. She sighed. "I suppose you're right. It is getting late."

Reluctantly, she turned and walked back to the steps. "Lucas." She turned around to face the man who brought her this joy and happiness. "Won't you stay and eat with us? I'm sure Quirinius won't mind. He seems to like you. I know I would enjoy the pleasure of your company."

Lucas thought for a moment. "I think you'd best dine alone tonight with your husband. You'll find the ocean breeze is like a sedative. You'll be glad I didn't stay. I'll come by tomorrow. I promised Quirinius I'd take care of you and keep you from getting into trouble."

Dalena stood defiantly, blocking Lucas' way. "I am not a child. I do not need a nursemaid to look after me. If the only reason you are spending time with me is because you are obeying some order of my husband, then don't bother." Unsure of where she was going, she made her way from the terrace and into the peristyle. Realizing that the other rooms of the home were grouped around the colonnade garden, Dalena turned to her right, past the columns and fountains, and ran down the hallway and into the first open room she could find.

The room was lovely, and for a moment she forgot why she was upset. It was circular marble floors inlaid with light purple stone. In the center of the room, the ceiling vaulted, making a dome. The dome held a mural of a mother watching her children frolicking on the beach. The breeze tugged at the soft violet drapes that stood between the room and the balcony. The bed had been covered with lilacs, sending the scent of fragrant flowers throughout the room. The room even had its own private bath. In its simplicity, the room was luxurious. Knowing Quirinius would have never been so thoughtful and that the house, her room, even the beach, had been planned by Lucas caused her to fling herself onto the bed, wetting the petals beneath with her tears.

She sat up and dried her eyes as soon as she heard Quirinius' bellow. It would not serve her well if Quirinius caught her crying. She walked over to the marble dressing table. Several of her things had already been laid out for her. She picked up her mirror and made quick adjustments to her hair. She caught sight of the new gown that had been purchased for her. It was adorned in gold trim, giving richness to its deep green. Dalena held it up to herself. She would certainly look beautiful. She felt herself wanting to cry. She didn't want to look beautiful for Quirinius; she wanted to be beautiful for Lucas.

She could hear Lucas explaining the details of the house to Quirinius. The openness of the house enabled one to hear everything going on. Dalena decided that if Lucas was not going to stay for dinner, she would make him realize what he was missing. She quickly changed into the green gown. She loosened her coiffure, allowing her hair to cascade down her back. She took a jeweled comb and pinned a few strands up, entwining some of the lilac petals into her hair. Satisfied that she made a fetching picture, Dalena left her room with all the grandeur that came naturally to her.

She followed the voices and found herself back out on the terrace. The moment she walked out into the evening light, she knew she had succeeded in her plan. Both Quirinius and Lucas hushed their dialogue to stare at her. However, it was Quirinius and not Lucas who came to her side.

"My darling, how beautiful you look this evening. You have taken my breath away."

Dalena turned her cheek up for Quirinius to give her a light kiss. Reluctantly he did so, but he wanted much more.

Dalena turned to Lucas, expecting some response. All she got was a slight nod of approval. Not to be undone, Dalena turned to Quirinius and, with the ease of a cat, slid her arm around his and purred into his ear. "I thought we might want to take our meal inside this evening. The breeze blowing through the bedroom is soft and inviting."

Quirinius could barely contain his excitement. "Indeed. I must say the island air agrees with you." He turned to Lucas. "You will forgive my rudeness, but I must take back my offer of dinner this evening. It seems my wife has made plans unbeknownst to me."

Dalena looked like a cat that had just been caught. She looked at Lucas for an explanation. It was plainly written on his face. He had not accepted the offer from her, but he had from her husband. *Why?* The realization came to Dalena. *To protect me.* Dalena couldn't move. She couldn't speak. Now, she was stuck having to spend the evening entertaining her husband. "No apology necessary, sir. I completely understand. Your wife is very captivating tonight. Shall I come by tomorrow around nine o'clock?" Lucas turned away from Dalena and focused the whole of his attention on Quirinius.

"Yes, that will be fine. I'll go over some plans for our stay; then I must head into town for business. You will stay and see to the needs of Dalena for me?"

"That is my understanding of what you wish."

Lucas bowed before Quirinius and then left without even a glance Dalena's way.

The evening seemed to come and go. Lucas had seen fit to have the house prepared with two master suites, one for Quirinius and one for Dalena. As soon as Quirinius was sound asleep, Dalena slipped from underneath his arm. She wrapped her gown around her and made her way across the main room to the other side of the house, where her room was.

FAVORED

She poured water into her basin and once again tried to wash the feel of Quirinius' hands from her body. Feeling queasy, she hurried out to her balcony, and, leaning over the side, she threw up.

She watched as the moon cast shadows upon the waves. "Oh *Magna Mater*, when will I learn?"

She often wondered if the god she worshiped ever heard her. In Rome, she had gone through all the rituals of becoming a follower of the great goddess. Those secret meetings held in caves outside the city had given Dalena the feeling of power over everything in her life. She would find out if there were places of worship in Cyprus.

Dalena was turning to go back inside when her eye caught the glimpse of a figure below. A few clouds had covered the moonlight, but Dalena thought she saw someone watching her. She peered out into the darkness to try to catch a glimpse of who it was. Just at that moment, the clouds parted, and the moon's rays revealed nothing. Perhaps it was just her imagination. Dalena was just about to retreat to her room when her eyes picked up the slightest movement on the beach. It was not her imagination. Something or someone was down there. Dalena didn't know if she should scream for help or just go back inside and pretend she saw nothing. She decided the latter option was best. She went inside and stretched herself out on her bed. More for protection than warmth, she pulled the soft silk coverlet over her. She would tell Lucas about this tomorrow.

Dalena tossed and turned most of the night. Her mind kept playing tricks on her. She would have sworn the figure she saw on the beach was in her room. Her mind wandered to Lucas. She had been made the fool. He would draw her to him, then push her away.

She awoke the next morning with a severe headache. Much to her dismay, Saphra was waiting outside her door. "The proconsul wants you to be ready when Lucas Darius arrives. We'd best hurry. It is almost nine o'clock. I've noticed that man is never late."

"Saphra, please, not this morning. I don't feel well. I have a severe headache."

"I know what will fix that right up. I give it to the proconsul all the time." Saphra realized she had said too much. She looked at Dalena, who pretended not to notice. *Weasel!* She knew Saphra was sleeping with her husband. Now she was boasting about it. Dalena vowed to herself to put an end to Saphra and soon.

Saphra hurried out of her mistress' bedroom. All too soon for Dalena, she returned with some sort of concoction. However, Dalena's head hurt so badly that she would have drunk anything. Saphra's potion did help, and before she knew it, Dalena was dressed and ready to be presented to her husband.

Dalena walked down the hall with her head held high. She would not let Lucas know that her plan for making him jealous had backfired. She entered the main room and was immediately greeted by her husband. "Dalena, you left my bed last night. Did something upset you?" "No, not at all. We both had a very long day yesterday, and I was having trouble sleeping. I was afraid I might disturb you. I went to my room to try to rest."

"I see. I trust you rested well?"

"Yes. Thank you for your concern. Have you eaten?"

"Yes. A governor's job is never done. I must start early. Lucas should be arriving any moment."

"I'm already here, sir."

"Right on time, as usual. Lucas, I want your first responsibility to be Dalena. The men you have put in charge of my protection are very good, but Dalena needs someone special. Someone who will not be taken in by her charms." He reached over and pinched her cheek. "Someone like yourself."

Dalena could have sworn that Quirinius smirked at those

remarks. Quirinius took pleasure in demeaning her. Dalena smiled and pretended she hadn't noticed, but inside she seethed.

"Sir, I will give my very best to protect your wife."

"I know you will. She may go wherever she wishes as long as you are with her. I'll return for the evening meal." Quirinius turned to Dalena. "A reception like the one you gave me last night would be a pleasant surprise." He tried to give his wife a firm kiss, but Dalena turned her head ever so slightly, forcing him to kiss her cheek.

As soon as Quirinius left the house, Dalena turned on her heels, leaving Lucas standing alone. She was angry with Quirinius for treating her like a slave that needed constant guarding, and she was mad at Lucas for playing the game with Quirinius. Unfortunately for Lucas, he was the only one of the two left to be on the receiving end of her wrath.

Lucas found her on the beach, watching the waves crash against the shore. The breeze was strong, and it blew at her gown and shawl. Dalena heard Lucas call out to her, but she paid no attention. She wanted Lucas to want to be with her, not be forced to endure her company on the command of her husband.

Lucas walked up alongside and stood beside Dalena in silence. It was almost more than she could bear, and it only served to intensify her anger toward him.

"I suppose I'm stuck with your company and you with mine."

"Is that how you feel, Dalena? That you're stuck with my company?" There was nothing in Lucas' tone that gave any hint at how he was feeling. Dalena took it to mean that he felt nothing.

"I suppose I do. I do not understand how Quirinius can just bark orders at you and you heed his every word." Once the words began to flow from Dalena's mouth, there was no stopping the rush of emotion. She turned on Lucas. "I am not a child that needs tending. Nor am I a slave that needs guarding. I have a mind of my own. I intend to do whatever it is I enjoy doing and with whomever I enjoy doing it. Quirinius can't touch me. I'm finished allowing him to punish my one indiscretion. As for you. You can continue to guard me, but you will be forced to keep your mouth shut. I do not intend to allow your presence to stop my fun. I trust you understand what I mean." Dalena's eyes were flashing, and her face was flushed with anger.

"Are you finished?"

Dalena couldn't believe how calm Lucas was. Her words had not affected him one bit.

She stammered, "I…I want to go into town." She turned around and proceeded to walk toward the house.

"I don't think you want to go into town. I think you would prefer to stay right here."

Dalena whirled around. "So now you're telling me what I want! Did you know that I could tell my husband that you made advances toward me, trying to force my affection? If I told him that, he would have you killed for such insolence."

"You wouldn't do that."

"How do you know I wouldn't?"

"Because Quirinius would not believe you. I have the man's trust. I thought I had yours. Does this little temper tantrum of yours have anything to do with my not staying for dinner?"

Lucas couldn't help but chuckle.

Dalena came at him, claws out, teeth clenched. She pushed him hard enough that it knocked him off balance. Lucas stumbled backward into the water. Just then a large wave came crashing to the shore and pulled him out. Dalena stumbled on her dress in her attack, and the wave caught her and pulled her under as well. When Lucas came up for air, he couldn't see Dalena anywhere. Panicked, he called out for her, but there was no response. Lucas dove down into the water. He felt for her. Nothing. He came back up for air. Just then, he caught sight of her flailing arm just above the water. The wave had dragged her out farther. The wind was strong, pushing the waves onward toward the shore and then pulling them back out to sea. Lucas swam with all his might to reach Dalena. He dove under water near the spot where he had seen her arm. He came up for air and dove back under. He felt something brush his leg. He reached out to feel what had touched him. Grabbing the material, he pulled with all his might as he resurfaced. He reached under the water and pulled Dalena's head above the water. With her in tow, he swam back to shore.

He dragged her up on the sand. She wasn't breathing. He lifted her up into his arms.

"Don't do this. Don't you know how I feel? Dalena, I'm sorry." Lucas rocked Dalena in his arms for what seemed an eternity to him.

Dalena began to make a gagging sound as she vomited up water. Lucas looked at her face as her eyes fluttered open. She gasped for air as she tried to pull away from him. "Settle down; you're safe. Everything is all right." Lucas felt that the weight of the world had been lifted from him with the opening of Dalena's eyes.

Dalena felt exhausted. She just lay still in the comfort and protection of Lucas' arms.

After a while, she spoke, "I'm still mad at you."

Lucas smiled. "I wouldn't imagine you feeling any other way." He picked her up and carried her back inside the house. He called for Saphra but was informed that she had left for town on Quirinius' orders. One of the young girls Lucas had seen fit to purchase when he secured the house for their stay came to help Dalena. Lucas gave instructions that Dalena be given a warm bath and dressed warmly so as not to take a chill. He then went to the kitchen and gave the cook instructions as to what to fix Dalena to eat. He would personally take the tray to her.

Dalena was too weak to argue. She allowed the girl to bathe

and dress her. Once Dalena was in bed, the girl excused herself to let Lucas know she was presentable and ready to eat.

With a tray of food, Lucas entered Dalena's room. "Feeling better?" He set the tray in front of her.

"More like foolish. I guess I should thank you for saving my life."

"All in a day's work," Lucas replied. "I hope you like soup. I thought it would be good for you. You probably don't want to eat anything too heavy until you've had time to digest all of that salt water you took in."

"Soup is fine. Who is the young girl that helped me?"

"I believe her name is Dianthea. She came highly recommended. Did she do something wrong?"

"No. She was wonderful. I like her much better than Saphra. Can I keep her?"

"I don't see why not. It was your husband's money that purchased her. She's not been trained to be a personal slave. She is just a house servant."

"I'll have Saphra teach her. Then I can be rid of that little varmint for good."

Lucas laughed. "I take it you and Saphra are not getting along."

"You know very well how she is spending her time. I can't let her get by with that. It makes me look foolish."

"I see. Is that why you were upset with me? I made you look foolish?"

"Oh, Lucas, I wasn't really mad at you. I was angrier with Quirinius and, well, just a little mad at you."

"I see."

"No, I don't think you do. Quirinius treats me like his personal slave. I am to be guarded and watched over, only to be

FAVORED

turned over to him once he returns home. This isn't how I want to live. I invited you to stay last night, and you told me no, but told Quirinius yes. Why not just say yes to my invitation?"

"Because Quirinius might be suspicious if I stayed at your request. I'm here to protect you from everyone else, even yourself."

"I don't want to be protected."

"What do you want?"

"I want to be free."

"Give it time. As I said before, Quirinius will be his own undoing. Then you will have your freedom."

"I won't wait forever."

"I'm not asking you to."

"I want something else."

"What?"

With the bath, warm clothes, and food, the twinkle in Dalena's eyes had returned. "I guess that is for me to know. You'll find out soon enough."

"I'll leave you to rest." Lucas stood to go, but Dalena reached for his hand.

"Don't go. Please don't go."

"Dalena, what's the matter? You look frightened."

"I am. I didn't rest well last night because…"

"Because why?"

"After I returned to my room, I walked out on the balcony. I swear I saw someone watching me from the beach. I couldn't make out who it was or whether it was even a person, but something or someone was out there."

"It was probably just an animal of some kind."

"I don't think so. I felt the person's eyes on me. Please, Lucas, stay. I'm very tired, but I don't think I can rest unless you stay with me."

"Why didn't you tell me about this earlier?"

"I guess I was so mad at you and Quirinius that it slipped my mind. Lucas, please, believe me. This isn't some ploy to get you to stay. I really did see someone out there."

"All right. I believe you. I'll stay." Lucas patted her hand. "But I want you to rest. We both will have a lot of explaining to do about the day's events when Quirinius gets home."

"I forgot all about explaining this to him. What are we going to say? He can't know how angry I was or what I was angry about."

"I can't believe this is the same woman who only short time ago was screaming that she didn't care what her husband did or if he found out what she did, that she was going to do as she pleases."

Dalena sank back into the bed, feeling half exhausted and half defeated. "You know those things I said, I didn't really mean."

"No, I don't think I do know that. I think deep down inside, you meant most of what you said. Dalena, I know this is not the life you had planned for yourself. You have a determination and a will that have seen you through the toughest times. You are a beautiful woman, and you have learned how to use that to your advantage. Now it all feels more like a curse.

"Love and happiness can't always be found in a man's arms. Sometimes you have to learn to love yourself before you can ever be truly happy."

"Since when did you study philosophy? Is that some new requirement of the Roman Army? I was unaware that they taught that along with swordplay. I think it best you stick with what you know best, and I'll stick with what I know."

"Someday, you will learn that there is truth to my words."

FAVORED

"Right now I just want to rest. We both need to figure out how we are going to explain all this to Quirinius."

"I'll stay with you while you rest. Don't worry about Quirinius. I'll explain everything to him when he returns home."

Dalena nodded and nestled down into the softness of the bed. She fell asleep quickly.

What woke her was the sound of her boisterous husband entering her room.

"Darling, Lucas told me everything. We owe him your life." Quirinius, portraying the every-loving husband, hurried to his wife's bedside. "Lucas Darius, I intend to write your superiors. You deserve a medal of some kind for your heroic actions."

"Sir, that is unnecessary."

"Humility is an admirable quality, but one that will get you nothing in this life or the next. Take what is due you."

Quirinius turned his attention back to his wife. "You rest tonight. Lucas has agreed to stay close by in case you need anything. I have business in town, I'm afraid, that needs my attention. You're in the best of care. Lucas told me how kind Dianthea was with you. You can keep her if you like. I am moving a cot into your room for her to sleep in. She will be at your beck and call. Since you will not be in need of Saphra, I have taken the liberty of reassigning her task. She will see to my needs from here on out. Rest well, darling." As quickly as he had entered her room, he was gone.

Lucas came over to her bedside. "I stayed with you until Quirinius returned home. I trust you rested well?"

"Yes." Dalena sat up and leaned her back against the cushions of the bed. "Why does he have to insult me like that? As if I don't know what he and Saphra are up to. Oh, if I were a man, what I would do to him." Dalena balled both her hands into fists.

"He's not worth it, and neither is Saphra. Leave them to their own devices."

"Lucas, what did you tell Quirinius about today?"

"Nothing, really. Just that you waded out a little too far and that a wave caught you and swept you under—the truth, minus a few boring details."

Dalena shook her head. "Lucas, you never cease to amaze me. How you slyly get Quirinius to believe your every word is a wonder to me. Most men would have gone into some lavish detail to try and sound believable. You have such simple logic."

"I'll take that as a compliment."

"You should. That is how I meant it. Now, I would like to get up. I've been pampered enough for one day."

"I never thought I would hear those words from your mouth. However, I don't think it wise. Whether you realize it or not, you have been through a lot today."

"I do realize it. Furthermore, I have decided that all of it is your fault."

"My fault? Whatever do you mean?"

"If you had just said yes to my dinner invitation last night, all of today could have been avoided." Dalena gave Lucas a mischievous grin.

"Father taught me a long time ago not to argue with a woman. I will concede, but only because you almost drowned today."

Not realizing how weak she was, Dalena swung her legs over the side of the bed and tried to stand on her own accord. Her knees buckled under her. If Lucas hadn't been standing right there to support her, she would have fallen to the floor. "I suppose you're right. I'm weaker than I thought."

"Let me support your weight. I'll take you wherever you want to go."

"I'd like to go sit out on the terrace and watch the sunset."

"Your wish is my command."

Lucas helped Dalena out to the terrace. Dianthea brought the two some wine and fresh fruit. "I thought you might enjoy some refreshment."

Dalena smiled at the girl. There was something about Dianthea that was sweet and kind. Dalena felt very much at ease around her—unlike Saphra, who made Dalena feel as if she was constantly being stabbed with needles. "Thank you, Dianthea. Did my husband inform you of your new position to our house?"

"Yes, miss. I'm honored you would have me see to your needs." Dianthea nodded and excused herself.

"Wherever did you find her, Lucas? She is so sweet. I've never said this about another female before, but I truly like her."

Lucas laughed.

"Are you laughing at me?"

"No, not at you. You just bring me joy."

Dalena smiled. "I think that is the nicest thing anyone has ever said to me."

They sat on the terrace until the light of the moon had replaced the rays of the sun. Dalena took note of how comfortable she felt sitting in silence next to Lucas. She decided she shouldn't play silly games with him. He was not that type of man. She wouldn't make that mistake again. Then a thought pierced her mind, sending fear through every vein in her body: What type of man was he? More importantly, how would she make him love her?

"Dalena, is something wrong?"

Brought from her thoughts by Lucas' question, Dalena looked long and hard at the man sitting beside her. "Lucas, who are you?"

"What?"

"You seem to know everything about me, but I know very little about you. Who are you?"

"Now, Dalena, that's not true. I told you about my past, my

wife, and my position in the army. You know all there is to know."

"Yes, I know the details of certain events in your life, but I don't know anything about you. Where were you born? Who is your family? Are your parents still living, and if so, where? Do you have relatives? Brothers and sisters? What in your life has made you the type of man that you are?"

"So many questions. Is this what you've been contemplating as you watched the sun set? If so, you missed out on the beauty before you."

"Don't be evasive. Just tell me who you are."

"Dalena, I'm afraid there is not much to tell. Besides it would bore you. Neither one of my parents are living. I told you I had a half sister. Probably being in the army has made me who I am. Who that person is, well, I'm not sure I know. I guess you just have to take me as I am."

Dalena wasn't satisfied, but she could tell by Lucas' expression that she was not going to get anything more, at least not tonight. "You are going to stay?"

"Yes. I told Quirinius I would."

"Would you be staying if only I had asked you to?"

Lucas looked into the emerald eyes of the woman sitting next to him. Something in those eyes captivated him. Her face reminded him so much of... He shook his head to clear his thoughts, then looked straight into her eyes. "If you asked me to stay because you need me, then I would stay regardless of what Quirinius might think."

Dalena felt a warmth flood her soul. She smiled at him with a smile that reflected the joy his answer had brought her. "You've made me very happy."

Lucas took her hand to his. "Dalena, I meant what I said that day on the ship. I'm here to protect you. You're the reason I left home to come to this region. I could care less what happens to

FAVORED

Quirinius. I'm here for you. It is that simple."

At that moment, Dalena wanted more than anything to be taken into Lucas' arms. She wanted to feel the warmth of his kiss on her lips. She wanted to experience the soft caress of his hands on her skin. She desired to give herself to this man, body and soul. But that wasn't possible. I wasn't her marriage to Quirinius that stopped her. It was the vow Lucas had made with himself, the vow he'd shared with her that afternoon she had thrown herself at him. She had to respect his conviction if she wanted him to love her.

"I'm tired. I think I'd best go to bed." Dalena stood to go. The wine had served to bolster her strength.

"Should I come with you?"

"No. Dianthea can help me. Stay and enjoy the evening. I'll see you in the morning."

"If you wake in the night and see something outside your bedroom, call for me. I'll be right there."

"I know you will. Goodnight." Dalena excused herself, leaving Lucas alone on the terrace.

Lucas felt himself take a long, slow breath. Every inch of his body felt flushed with desire. He shouldn't feel this way, not about her. It wasn't right. Lucas stood, picked up his cup of wine, and took a gulp. The wine did nothing to ease his desire. If only she wouldn't look at him that way. Perhaps if she knew who he was, the desire between the two of them would end. Yet, she would never know. If she found out the truth, she would never trust him, and he would lose her forever. Lucas stared out at the open ocean. His main objective was to find a way to free her from Quirinius.

He thought over his plan—a plan already in motion, thanks to the willingness of Saphra. If Dalena only knew how cunning he really was. Knowing that no figure would be threatening Dalena tonight, Lucas made his way down the hall to the room adjacent to hers.

Chapter Thirty-Two

The weeks flew by in Cyprus. Dalena gained back some of the weight she had lost during the voyage north. She fell in love with the ocean, sand, and island life in general. She and Lucas would take long walks in the morning, return for a light meal, and play games for the better part of the afternoon. Lucas taught Dalena how to cast lots, and she took great pride every time she won a small trinket from him. The days Lucas had to spend in town with his men or with Quirinius, Dianthea would read to Dalena. It became apparent to both Dalena and Lucas that Dianthea had been taught well before becoming a slave. Dianthea picked up quickly how Dalena liked her hair done and what her favorite items of clothing were. Dianthea was one year younger than Dalena, and their relationship was evolving more into a friendship than that of a mistress and maid.

Quirinius was seldom at the villa. He preferred the busy life in the port city of Salamis.

He had rented out several rooms for himself and his entourage. Dalena was only invited to join her husband in town when an important businessman, political ally, or rival held a lavish party for which Quirinius felt Dalena's presence was a must. Dalena quickly learned how to play the political game in an arena bloodier than the Circus Maximus of the great amphitheater in Rome. She enjoyed the attention she drew from the men and relished the jealousy apparent on every woman's face in the room. Lucas warned her that some of those women she might want as friends, but Dalena ignored his wisdom, finding pleasure in the game of lust and envy in which she was the master.

It was at one such event that Quirinius informed her he

FAVORED

would be leaving Cyprus to go back to Rome. Business with Caesar was his only explanation—something to do with a census Caesar wanted throughout the whole empire. Quirinius would be in charge of making sure the census ran smoothly in Syria. Therefore, a trip to Rome was a must. Somehow, the thought of Quirinius going to Rome without her made Dalena very nervous.

She questioned Lucas about it, but he just smiled and said he would think she would be overjoyed that her husband was going to Rome. "After all, the absence of one husband might enable you to have a more pleasurable time in Cyprus."

Dalena wasn't concerned that Quirinius was leaving her, but she was anxious about where he was going without her. The thought that he might find out about her past and the truth of her identity frightened her greatly. She spent several evenings in prayer and petition to the Great Mother, Magna Mater. Dalena had chosen to worship Magna Mater because she felt a kinship with the god; as a child, Magna Mater was put out into the wilderness to die, only to end up being reared by panthers and lions. She grew up to be a beautiful, strong woman.

As a last resort, Dalena sought out a high priestess of the goddess. Fortunately, there were some on the isle who worshiped the Great Mother, thanks to the influence of the Greeks. Dalena met the priestess late one night in a cave not far from the villa. After the customary rituals were completed, the priestess asked Dalena if she had brought the necessary items for her petition. Dalena lay before the priestess the money required as well as a sacred stone. She also had a bull for the *taurobolium*. Dalena watched and prayed as the priest danced before her, the bull was sacrificed, and its blood poured over Dalena.

Dalena was required to stay in the cave the entire night, and by morning she would have an answer.

True to her work, the priestess informed Dalena that her desires would be accomplished. Dalena took this to mean that her secret was safe. However, the priestess warned her that she must maintain favor with the Great Mother for all desires to be accomplished. Dalena agreed to do all the priestess told her.

Dalena hurried back to the villa to wash and change before the household woke. She had paid a man from town quite generously to bring the bull to the cave. She didn't want anyone in the villa to know of her fears, for if she shared her fear, she would have to tell them the truth of who she was. It was best none of them knew, not even Lucas.

She quietly entered the villa and proceeded to her room. She was halfway down the hall when someone grabbed her arm. She started to scream, but the man quickly put his hand over her mouth and dragged her out the back and onto the terrace. Finally, when he had released his hold, Dalena tuned around to face Lucas, dressed as a herdsman, standing in front of her.

"What do you think you are doing? You scared me to death!"

"Keep your voice down! Do you want the whole domas to hear us?" Lucas could see that Dalena was visibly shaken. "I'm sorry. I didn't mean to frighten you. I was just trying to keep you from waking everyone. I figured you didn't want anyone to know where you had been."

"No, I don't, and that includes you. Now, if you'll excuse me, I want to wash and change." Dalena tried to leave the terrace, but Lucas blocked her exit.

"What in the world did you hope to accomplish by going through such a horrendous ritual last night? Don't you know those people only want your money?"

"That is not true! I happen to believe in the Great Mother." Dalena's eyes narrowed.

"How do you know where I went?"

Lucas' face gave away his secret.

"You…you followed me. Didn't you?"

"Yes, I followed you. That's what I am being paid to do."

FAVORED

Lucas quickly began to backpedal. "It's not what you think. I was worried about you last night. I could tell you weren't quite yourself yesterday. I came to your room to check on you. I knocked, but there was no answer. I thought you were probably asleep, but I wanted to be sure. When I opened the door and found your bed empty, I went outside to try to find you. I found your tracks and caught up to you just as you were meeting that herdsman, and I followed you both in the cave.

"I paid the man quite a hefty sum myself for his cloak. I'll dare say he made off handsomely last night. I watched the whole ceremony. Quite a little show your priestess puts on."

"Don't mock what you can't understand."

"I understand everything perfectly. It's you who have been misguided."

"What do you mean?"

"Don't you know that your high priestess and her priest are just extracting money from you? I couldn't hear everything she told you, but I bet before you left, she instructed you on how to deliver more funds to her coffer."

"You know nothing." However, the sheepish look on Dalena's face let Lucas know he had assumed correctly.

Lucas softened his tone. "Dalena, what has you this upset and fearful? Tell me. I might be able to help you."

"I can't."

"You can't or won't? Do you prefer late-night meetings in caves, having bull's blood poured over you, believing in the unreal, instead of trusting what's real? Trust what's right in front of you."

"And what's that?"

"Me, Dalena. Trust me." The pleading in Lucas' eyes softened Dalena.

"I'm fearful of…"

"What? I can't protect you unless you tell me what I need to protect you from."

"Quirinius is leaving for Rome in a few days. What if…?" Dalena turned away from Lucas.

Lucas turned her around to face him. "Dalena, help me help you. What if…what?"

Dalena didn't answer immediately. The two stood so close together that Dalena could feel Lucas' hot breath on her face and neck. She felt his strength overtake her and relinquished, giving voice to her fear. "What if he finds out about my past…who I really am?

"That I am the daughter of a harlot, whose father thought nothing more of her than to marry her off so she would not be an embarrassment to him."

Lucas laughed. "That's what this is all about? Your reputation? My dear, I told you I took care of all those who knew your little secret before I left Rome. You have nothing to fear."

Dalena felt the hairs on the back of her neck stand on end. She didn't like it when Lucas belittled her and her feelings. "How do I know that you are telling the truth? Besides, people enjoy gossip. They live for it, especially when it's about someone like me. How do I know or even you, for that matter—really know that the man who disposed of my mother's body didn't tell someone else before you took care of him?"

"I just know."

"How? You believe you know, but you don't really know. I had to make sure. I believe in the Great Mother. I believe what the priestess told me. I can rest knowing that the goddess is taking care of things for me."

"Well, if that is what it takes to give you peace, then so be it. You would rather pay twenty *denari* to someone you don't know than take the word of someone you do."

FAVORED

"Isn't there a god you believe in? There has to be. We all have to believe that there is something or someone greater than us looking out for us.

"I did. Perhaps at times I still do. I am a very good Roman soldier. I give my dues to Mars before every mission. My wife and I kept a shrine in our home to *Lares* and *Penates*. At every meal, we burned before them the two portions of food for our departed loved ones. I never thought I would have to burn good in memory of her. When we found out my wife was with child, we had a statue of Juno carved. We did everything the priest told us to do. The last thing I remember was the sound those bells made while she was in labor. Between her screams of pain, those bells would ring. To this day, I hate that sound. I guess my faith in the gods has waned from experience. I've learned to trust myself over any god." Lucas' voice held pain and betrayal.

"Lucas, I'm sorry. I didn't understand, not really, the pain the death of your wife caused you. Don't you see, for me, I have to believe in something? I guess, because I have been on my own for so long, I needed something besides myself, something bigger than me, to believe in. I need to know that someone or something greater than me is watching out for me and cares for me."

"I understand, but I think you give the gods too much credit and power. I've learned the gods care little for our day-to-day worries. Our lives mean little to them."

"Promise me you won't mention my going out to anyone."

"You know I won't. Don't give Quirinius another thought. I'm sure his stay in Rome will be short. If it helps ease your mind, I have comrades who will agree to keep an eye on the man for us. I've sent word on ahead of what they can expect."

"Lucas, I do believe you think of everything."

"You'd better wash and change. The house will be stirring before long."

Dalena hurried off to her room. The bull's blood had caked

itself on her skin. When she finished her bath, the water was red. The sight made Dalena queasy, and once again she found herself leaning over the balcony. She thought her queasiness would have subsided once she got off that horrid ship, but for the past few weeks, her stomach had felt very unsettled. She quickly dressed in her bedclothes and snuggled under the covers. Dianthea needed to find her as she always had, sleeping soundly. Dalena would need to make up an excuse about why her hair was damp, but that would come easily enough.

Dianthea quietly entered her mistress' room. Lucas had instructed to allow Dalena to sleep longer than normal. Dianthea didn't question Lucas' request. She pulled out Dalena's blue stola with the silver belt. She opened the drapes that blew softly with the breeze. Dalena stirred as the warm, late-morning air gently tickled her nose. She yawned as her eyes opened. Seeing Dianthea, she questioned, "Is it morning already?"

"Late morning, to be precise. Master Darius said to let you sleep in. I trust you have rested well."

"Yes, but I still feel tired."

"Dalena, if I may be so bold, you don't look well."

Right at that moment, Dalena felt her stomach convulse. She jumped out of bed and ran out to the balcony.

"Oh, Dalena, you are not well. My mother taught me a quick remedy for the stomach ills. I'll have cook brew up some of the liquid for you."

"No, don't bother. I've just been feeling queasy as of late. After I dress and eat a little something, I'll be fine.

"How long have you been feeling like this?"

"I don't know. Maybe a week or so."

"Well, I know you've had something on your mind. Maybe the stress has entered your stomach. Then again, it could be something else."

FAVORED

"Something else? Whatever do you mean?"

"I know it is none of my business…"

"What? Say it, Dianthea. Do you think it's something serious? Just say what you think."

Dalena knew she sounded impatient and irritable. She just assumed it was because she hadn't rested.

"Are your courses flowing regularly?"

"Well, of course they are. What kind of question is that?"

"A logical one for a married woman who happens not to be feeling well."

Dalena slumped into the chair opposite her bed. She thought over the last month. *Haven't my courses come as usual?* She pondered the question, and as the answer dawned on her, she felt sick all over again. After returning from her second trip to the balcony, Dalena crawled up on her bed and began to cry.

"Mistress, I didn't mean to upset you."

"You didn't. Oh, Dianthea, whatever am I to do? I can't be with child. I just can't."

"Why, of course you can. It is a blessed thing to carry a child. The most rewarding gift for a woman is to become a mother."

"You don't understand. How can you understand? Your mind is simple and innocent. I don't want to be a mother. I don't want to be the mother of that barbarian's child. I can't be. I won't be."

Dianthea listened in horror as her mistress wailed about her dislike of Quirinius, vowing to do whatever it took not to carry that man's child. Dianthea listened until she could hear no more. "Dalena, nothing is for sure. Calm down. Let us wait a few weeks before we say in word."

"No, I can't wait. I'm sure. What else could it be? It's been at least a month since my courses have flowed. That and the queasiness… Oh, Dianthea, what else could it be?"

"We should send for a doctor just to make sure."

"Yes. Yes, that is a good idea. I want the doctor to come today. No, not today. Quirinius is coming home today. He must not know about this. We will wait until he leaves for Rome. Then we will summon a doctor. Quickly, help me prepare myself. I mustn't look like there is anything wrong. Quirinius wanted me to wear the green gown with the gold trim, not the blue stola. Dianthea, you must fix my hair and scent it with lavender. Perhaps add some color to my cheeks as well. I must look a sight."

"First, we need to take care of that puffiness around your eyes. I will draw a bath for you. I will put some lavender oil for fragrance and sea salt to soften your skin in the water. You relax in the warmth of the bath. That should help you feel more like yourself."

Dianthea had been correct in her assessment of what would help Dalena feel more like herself. After a time of soaking, Dalena felt refreshed. Dianthea had seen fit to have some food and wine brought to her room. Dalena sat out on the balcony, enjoying the warm breeze that blew in from the ocean. She ate very little, but it was enough to invigorate her.

While Dianthea fixed her hair, Dalena gave her instructions on what was to happen as soon as Quirinius left for Rome. "Dianthea, you must go and secure a visit with the doctor in two days' time. Quirinius is to leave for Rome the day after tomorrow. The doctor should arrive midafternoon. Lucas usually goes into town to check on any orders from his superiors and to socialize with some of his men. That is when the doctor is to come. Do you understand?"

"Yes."

"I'll give you plenty of money. The doctor will receive half of his payment before he arrives and the other half after he is finished. He'll receive double what he normally gets to ensure his silence. Make sure he understands that."

"Yes. I will."

"Good. Now all we must do is wait. Oh, I hate waiting." Dalena turned around in her chair. "You must not breathe a word of this to anyone. Not a word."

"I won't."

"I believe I can trust you. I would hate for something bad to happen to you should you have a slip of the tongue."

Tears pooled in Dianthea's eyes. "Do you not trust me, Dalena?"

Immediately, Dalena felt sorry for what she had said. "Of course I do. I'm just not used to trusting someone blindly. Forgive me, Dianthea. I could never hurt you."

Dianthea nodded her consent, but Dalena knew that she had forged a rift in their relationship that only time could mend.

The next two days were a blur. Dalena was literally at Quirinius' disposal. The way he held her and touched her, one would have thought it had been some time since he had been with a woman, but Dalena knew he was continuing his relationship with Saphra. Saphra was not going to Rome with Quirinius. However, Dalena didn't want her to stay at the villa. Lucas planned to sell Saphra as soon as Quirinius left for Rome. He had softened Dalena's heart concerning physical harm of the girl by explaining that she, too, was just a pawn of Quirinius' choosing. Selling her was the logical solution, one that could be explained much easier than death once Quirinius had returned.

Lucas went to the docks with Quirinius to ensure his safe departure, and then he was going to spend time in town, as was his custom. As soon as the house had cleared, Dalena went about preparing herself for the doctor's visit. As the afternoon went on, Dalena found herself pacing nervously from one end of the house to the other. Dianthea tried to calm her to no avail.

Finally, Dalena heard sounds of a litter and a man's voice giving instructions for the men to wait around back with the litter.

Dianthea went to greet the doctor upon his arrival. Dalena went to her room to wait. Soon, Dianthea was ushering the doctor into Dalena's bedroom.

"You are the young lady who I have come to see?"

"Yes." Dalena was surprised at how old the doctor appeared. His hair was gray, and his forehead was creased with fine lines. He seemed pleasant enough. There was kindness behind his gray eyes. Dalena choked back the bile that rose in her throat at the sight of the instruments the doctor pulled from his bag.

"Have you been examined before?"

"No."

"This is what I will be using to see how far along you are if you are with child. I insert the speculum, which will widen the canal for me to be able to examine you. Uncomfortable but not painful, I assure you."

Dalena wondered how he would know whether or not it was painful. The instrument itself looked horrid. She wasn't sure how the doctor intended to use the instrument, but she did as instructed; she lay on her bed with her knees bent. Dianthea held her hand as the doctor inserted the speculum and began his examination. Tears streamed down the leanest cheeks as she endured the procedure.

When the doctor was finished and satisfied with his findings, he stepped out of the room so Dalena could wash and dress. As soon as she was ready, Dianthea showed the doctor in.

"I have wonderful news. You are indeed with child."

It was all Dalena could do to maintain composure. "How far...?"

"Early...two months perhaps, not much more. When did you notice your courses had ceased to flow?"

"Just a few days ago. I've really never paid much attention."

"A married woman should pay attention to such things. It is

FAVORED

beneficial to know such information in order to predict your time better."

"My time?"

"When the child would be delivered."

"Doctor, I trust I have your confidence. You've been paid well, have you not?"

"Yes."

"I have heard that there is a way to..." Dalena wasn't sure how to finish. She looked up at the mural that adorned her ceiling. The mother with her children appeared to be looking with scorn at her.

"Please, continue. There is no question too strange." The doctor busied himself with putting away his instruments.

"I have heard that there is a way to discontinue the pregnancy."

The doctor looked up, shock plainly written on his face. "Why would you want to do something like that? You are healthy and very capable of carrying a child to term. There is no need for such a procedure."

"I do not want to carry to term. I want the pregnancy to end. Can you do such a procedure? You would be well compensated, I can assure you."

"Money is not the issue here. I will not put an end to your pregnancy. I find such a practice unethical."

"Fine. Then tell me who would be willing to do what I ask."

"I don't know of any reputable doctor who would do what you ask. Once you give birth, it is your business what you do with the child. Put it on the rocks. Now, if you'll pay me the remainder of my fee, I will take my leave. Our business is done."

Dalena knew that the doctor was purposefully keeping the information she desired from her. She didn't want to pay the man, but she had no choice. Dalena nodded for Dianthea to give the man what was owed. Before he left, Dalena let him know that under no circumstances was he to mention his visit or the nature of his business to anyone. Once Dalena was certain the doctor understood the consequences, should he ever speak of this, she had Dianthea see him out.

Dianthea returned to find her mistress lying prostrate across her bed and sobbing uncontrollably. She sat beside Dalena until she had finished crying.

"You must think me awful not to want this child."

"No, not awful. I just don't understand."

"If I tell you something, you promise to keep my secret?"

"Yes."

"The only other person who knows the truth is Lucas." Dalena broke into sobs before sitting up to face her friend. Her eyes were wet and swollen from crying. She could barely talk, but she proceeded to explain to Dianthea why she didn't want the child.

"I was forced to marry Quirinius. I don't love him. He is often cruel. More often cruel than kind. If I bear his child, I will be tied to the man forever. I can't and won't do it." Dalena moaned and fell back on the bed.

Dianthea consoled her mistress. "I'm sorry. I didn't know. I could tell there was no love between the two of you, but I just assumed that was due to your age difference. I always wondered how someone of your beauty could be attracted to a man like him, but then I figured your father had arranged the marriage and that you were just trying to learn to love him. I didn't realize how miserable you are. Forgive me. I should have been more sensitive."

Dalena dried her eyes. "You've got to help me. We need to find a doctor who will do the procedure. No one must know about this except the two of us. Can you help me?"

Dianthea nodded. "I'm just not sure how to find the person

you need. I've never heard of such a thing."

"I only know about it because a friend of my mother's had the procedure done in Rome. I was a little girl, but things seemed to go smoothly enough. As I remember it, the woman was back to her usual routine within a month's time at most. I'm sure there is nothing to it."

"I can check around town for you. Perhaps someone may know a person that would do such a deed."

"You must be discreet. Absolutely no one must know it has anything to do with me. I hate to think what Quirinius would do to me if he were to find out. I'm not sure he wants children, but I can't imagine a man not wanting to carry on his family line."

"Are you sure this is what you want? I mean, it may be Quirinius' offspring, but you are the mother. This child is partially yours."

"I'm not ready to be a mother, and I can't bear the thought of bringing his child into this world. I'm sure."

"I will go into town tomorrow and see what I can find out. Will you be all right while I am gone?"

"Yes. Lucas has planned a picnic for us; he wants to take me out and show me more of the countryside."

"When are you thinking the procedure should be done?"

"As soon as possible. I don't want anyone in this house becoming suspicious of my condition. If you are able to find someone to do what needs to be done, set up the day and time with him immediately. I'll make sure the house is empty the day of the procedure. If all goes well, no one will be the wiser, and this whole mess will be behind us."

Dianthea consented to do all Dalena asked. However, the young slave had misgivings concerning what lay ahead. She wasn't as certain as her mistress that the procedure would be that simple. Since no reputable doctor would perform such a thing, she would have to go to the lower class to find a willing person who knew how to do what Dalena wanted.

By the time Lucas returned to the villa, Dalena was already asleep. He poured himself some wine and went out to the terrace, listening as the waves gently rolled in and out from the shore. He recalled, when he was a boy, how he had loved coming to the villa. His father would run the beach with him. They would wander out just far enough for Lucas's head to remain above the water. He had always loved the ocean. The villa held special memories for him. Lucas took another sip of wine. His father, with his one act of deception, had seen fit to ruin every childhood memory for Lucas. So much for family. Lucas threw the cup as far as he could. He went back inside and made sure that the cook had prepared the basket of food as he had instructed. He wanted tomorrow to be special for Dalena. She was free of Quirinius for a while. He wanted her to enjoy every moment of her freedom. Once he was satisfied that his request had been met, Lucas went to his room to rest.

Dalena woke with a renewed sense of energy. Quirinius was gone. Dianthea was going to find someone to take care of her problem. Today, Lucas was going to spend the entire day with her. She began to hum a tune from her childhood as she dressed for her outing; she could barely contain her excitement. By the time Dianthea entered to help with her toilette, Dalena had finished dressing. All Dianthea had to do was fix her hair. Dalena gave Dianthea a pouch full of money; she wanted to make sure Dianthea had enough to secure a date for the procedure.

As soon as Lucas and Dalena had left, Dianthea took the road that led into town. Even though she had never been to the lower side of town, she knew of someone there who might know the person she needed to speak with concerning her mistress' wishes. She left the main thoroughfare and took a side street to the houses of ill repute. She could hear the rousing laughter of men and women. Some men lay drunk in the street, while others staggered at times, bumping into the girl. Dianthea covered her face with her shawl as she picked up her pace. She had to step around the trash that littered the road. Finally she found the place she was looking for.

The moment she stepped through the door, she sensed all eyes were on her. Rallying her courage, she made her way to the counter and asked the man where she might find a girl by the name of Lilliana. After persuading him with a few sesterces, the man pointed to a back door that led outside. "Take the four stall on the left. You'll find her there." Then the man turned his attention to serving his paying customers.

Dianthea found her way and tentatively knocked on the door. A sultry voice inside called for her to come in. The voice didn't sound like Lilliana's at all, and Dianthea thought she had the wrong room until she opened the door and saw Lilliana lying in a seductive pose on a bed of strong.

The moment Lilliana saw who it was, she threw on a robe and ran to Dianthea.

"Dianthea, my dear sister, what are you doing here?"

"I've come to ask a favor of you."

"Certainly. What do you need?"

"Information. But you must not breathe a word of this to anyone. It means my life."

"Dianthea, what kind of trouble are you in?"

"I need the name of someone who knows how to do a certain procedure."

"What kind of procedure?"

"Say, if a woman was with child and didn't want to carry that child to term. That kind of a procedure."

"My poor sister." Lilliana hugged Dianthea. "I tried to protect you from this life. I thought the man who bought you was kind and would treat you with respect."

Dianthea kept the truth to herself. "Lilliana, just give me the name."

"I've heard there is such a man. He resides around the corner from here, and he's done such things on a few girls I know. Dianthea, are you sure there is no other option for you?"

"No. I have given my word to take care of this situation as soon as possible."

"Very well. Tell him Lilliana sent you, and he will do what you ask."

"Thank you. I'll come back soon. I promise."

"You don't have to do that. This is not a place I want you to come to. Just know I think of you often and wish the very best for you."

"I know." Dianthea turned to go but thought of one more thing to ask. "This man…he is gentle and knows what he's doing?"

"As far as I know. The two girls are still alive. That has to count for something."

Dianthea gave her sister one last hug before she exited the *bordello*. In tears, she made her way around the corner and to the man's door. The house was more like a shack, and Dianthea was certain her sister had made a mistake. However, she had no option but to knock. The door swung open, and a burly man towered above her.

"What do you want?" His voice was hateful, and he smelled like the garbage she had passed in the street.

"Lilliana said I should come see you."

"Lilliana, huh? What about?"

"A certain problem that needs fixing."

"I see. How long have you had the problem?"

"Two months. But it is not me. I am here on behalf of my friend."

FAVORED

"A friend, you say?" the man asked quizzically.

"Yes, her condition needs to be taken care of as soon as possible. I was told that you know how to perform such a procedure."

"What you've heard is true, but why didn't your friend come to see me herself?"

"No one must know about her condition or who she is. She is very wealthy and will pay whatever you ask, so long as you keep her secret."

"Whatever I ask?" He seemed pleased.

"Within reason. I won't let her be taken advantage of."

The burly man laughed. "Quite a little spitfire you are. I like that." He reached out and stroked Dianthea's hair and face.

"I am not in that line of work. I'm a personal servant to my mistress, and she would not allow you to treat me with less than the respect due to my position."

"High and mighty too. When does your mistress want this problem taken care of?"

"As soon as possible."

He rubbed his whiskered face. "Is the day after tomorrow soon enough?"

"That will be fine. I will meet you at the edge of town where the road veers to the north. Let's say around noon."

"This must be someone of some importance for you to keep her identity a secret like this."

"Just be there and go to the public baths to clean yourself before you come. It will scare my mistress to see someone of your appearance. I want her to be relaxed and to have the best care possible."

The man bowed. "As you wish, but I'll need to have some money to do what you have requested."

Dianthea pulled out the pouch Dalena had given her. "Here is enough for the bath, and here is half of your payment. You'll receive the other half after the job is completed."

The man closed the door behind him after he took the money. Dianthea was grateful he had not asked her what her name was and that he had not offered his name to her. It was best that all involved remained anonymous. She hurried back to the villa— she needed to be home before Lucas and Dalena so that Lucas would not question her absence.

She had not been back in the villa long when she heard Dalena and Lucas. She quickly put her shawl away and went to greet her mistress. "I take it you had a lovely afternoon."

"Oh, Dianthea, the countryside is just beautiful. We wandered through a meadow filled with beautiful, fragrant flowers. The butterflies seemed to dance around the petals." Dalena began to flit around the room as if she were gliding on air. She turned so many circles that she made herself dizzy and almost fell down. Lucas, laughing, caught her in the nick of time. Dalena just laughed and proceeded to tell Dianthea about the afternoon. "Lucas took me to a school where they train gladiators. Dianthea, it was amazing. I didn't realize so much went into the games and the training of the men. Lucas has promised to take me to the games in another week or two.

"What a glorious time we had." She snuggled up to Lucas. "How can I ever thank you?"

"Your happiness is enough. Why don't you go change and prepare yourself for the evening meal? It is such a nice night, and I thought we might partake out on the terrace."

"Splendid idea! I won't be long. Dianthea, please come help me dress for the evening."

As soon as they were out of earshot, Dalena asked, "Well, what did you find out?"

"There is a man who has done the procedure you are wanting.

FAVORED

He will be here the day after tomorrow. I will meet him at noon where the road turns north."

"The day after tomorrow. Good. Lucas will probably go into town and stay at the station awhile with his men. Did the man say how long this procedure might take?"

"No. I didn't think to ask."

"How did you find him?"

"I got the information from someone I trust."

"Good. Did you pay him?"

"I only paid him half. He'll receive the rest once the job is done."

"Perfect." Dalena hugged her maid. "You're a dear to do all of this for me. Now, we are like sisters. We have a secret only the two of us will ever know."

They spent the evening out on the terrace. Dalena and Lucas ate their meals, then cast lots until they could no longer see the dice. Dalena was unaware that Lucas allowed her to win. Every time he went into town, he picked up a gem or necklace, something he thought she might like, and used that as his lot. He enjoyed the childlike delight she took in winning. She would squeal with satisfaction each time the dice rolled in her favor.

Everything about her fascinated him. He knew his feelings for her were growing beyond mere friendship and that she felt the same about him. He knew, too, that if he allowed this infatuation to continue, it would be unfair to her. It would only serve to hurt her deeply once the truth came out. As much as it pained him to think about it, he knew he needed to find someone to divert her affection away from him. It would need to be someone with means and closer to Dalena's age. Someone who would adore her the way he did, but he had yet to come across such a person in Salamis. Perhaps when they reached Antioch such a man might be found.

"You seem lost in thought. Anything you want to share?" Dalena cocked her head to the side and gave Lucas a sly smile.

"No, just relaxing. I love sitting out here after the sun has set. I like to listen to the waves lapping up on the shore and to the sounds the different animals make when they finally leave their daytime hiding places to look for food. I have fond memories of the beach."

"You said you had been to Cyprus before. That's how you knew about the villa. When were you here?"

"A while ago. But now, I am making new memories to me dearer to me than the old ones.

"That's the important thing. Don't you think you should turn in? You've had quite the day."

"It's been a marvelous day. You won't forget your promise to take me to the games?"

"I won't forget. I trust you know what you're in for?"

"Yes. I attended games in Rome a few times. My friends and I would always pick the most handsome gladiator and throw our flowers to him. Sometimes our choice would win, and sometimes he wouldn't. Either way, I had a good time. Sometimes I miss Rome. Not so much the city itself but the familiarity of the city. Two years between my mother's death and running into my father were some of the best of my life."

"You've got a lot of life to live still, and you're claiming those two years as the best?"

"Well, they were until I met you." Dalena's voice grew soft, and Lucas felt his blood run hot. "I can't keep hiding the way I feel about you. I understand that nothing can come of my feelings, at least not yet, but I hope when my marriage to Quirinius is over and I am free, it will be you by my side still."

"Dalena, I will always be by your side."

"Don't you have more to say than that?"

FAVORED

"Don't push me to say what is not right for me to say. You are still married to Quirinius.

"Any feelings I may have for you must remain within myself."

"So you do feel something for me?"

"How can I not? But now is not the time to discuss such things."

"You're too responsible, Lucas. Don't you ever want to throw caution to the wind and just do whatever you feel like doing? Like now, I want your lips on mine. I want to feel your touch on my body. You can't tell me you don't want the same thing." She reached over and touched his arm.

Lucas stood and turned away from Dalena. "No, I can't say I don't want the same thing. But, sometimes, we must wait for our desires to be gratified. I have found after the wait, the gratification is that much sweeter."

"Ah yes. The way you waited for your wife until after you were wed. How noble of you," Dalena replied sarcastically.

Lucas felt anger rising in him. If Dalena had been a man…

Dalena continued educating him on her moral philosophy. "Still, I think pleasure can be had in the moment."

Lucas softened when he heard her voice. "Dalena, I'm not rejecting you. If you only knew how hard this is for me. If you only knew the truth…"

"The truth? About what?"

"Nothing. Just know I care about you very deeply. In fact, I would give my life for you—that is how much I care. But nothing more can come of my feelings. So please, don't push me."

"You would give your life for me?"

Lucas looked deep into her eyes. "Yes."

She stood. "I don't know what to say. I don't think there has been anyone who has felt so deeply about me. I'll wait. I'll wait a whole lifetime if that's what it takes." Dalena turned and walked into the house, leaving Lucas alone on the terrace.

She cannot wait for me. I must find someone to redirect her affections toward. He listened to the soft sounds of the night. For the first time since his wife's death, a tear fell down his cheek and onto the terrace below him.

Chapter Thirty-Three

Dalena paced the balcony that overlooked the ocean. This particular morning, she paid little attention to the breathtaking view. Lucas had left a while ago, with Dianthea at a safe distance behind. Both had headed into Salamis for entirely different reasons: Lucas to oversee necessary business in town, and Dianthea to meet at the crossroads the man who would take care of Dalena's "problem."

What caused Dalena's anxiety was not so much that the procedure was to be done today but that Dianthea was not back yet. Early morning was slowly becoming mid-morning. She did not want Lucas to return before the process had been completed. The one satisfying thought was that Quirinius was well on his way to Rome. There was no chance of him ever finding out she had been pregnant with his child—unless Lucas returned before things were finished and felt obligated to tell Quirinius.

With her patience wearing thin, Dalena left the balcony and walked out into the hall to see if there were any signs of Dianthea's return. The house seemed oppressively silent. With Dianthea's help, Dalena had seen fit to have all the other household servants busy doing tasks that required them to be away for an extended period of time. Dianthea had prepared Dalena's room with the items the two girls thought would be needed. Most linens and bowls for cleansing and wine. Neither of the two really knew what to expect, and now Dalena wished she had paid closer attention to the conversations her mother had with her prostitute friends.

As she stood in the hallway, the silence closing around her, Dalena wondered what Lucas would think of her if he knew. Would he support her decision or not? Lucas had full knowledge

FAVORED

of Dalena's predicament with Quirinius, and he seemed to understand her in ways no man had before. However, Lucas' wife died in childbirth, causing him great pain and anguish. It was obvious that family was very important to him. Maybe she should have told him about her "problem." Perhaps he would have had a better solution for her. But what other solution was there? She had heard of women in Rome who had possibly gone through with this in order to cover up an indiscretion. The procedure was not encouraged, but it wasn't frowned upon either.

She was worrying over nothing. Soon, it would all be over. Life could get back to normal.

Voices finally shattered the silence that had engulfed her. *It's time.* Dalena hurried back into the confines of her room and then back onto the balcony. When Dianthea walked in with the man close at her heels, Dalena was the picture of peace and calm.

She turned to greet the two, only to be taken aback by the size of the man. Dianthea saw her mistress' reaction and quickly hurried to her. "He has been recommended by someone I trust, and I gave him money for a bath and shave. That's what took us so long. Evidently, the baths were quite full this morning."

"I trust you, Dianthea. Let's get started; the day is waning on." Turning her attention to the man, she asked, "How long will this take? Time is of essence."

"I understand, but there is no telling how long this will take. I will stay until things get started. If it looks like everything is progressing well, I will leave. If not, I will stay and help move things along."

"What do you mean?" Concern covered Dalena's face like a veil. "I thought this was a surgical procedure that you do."

"It can be, and it might come to that, but first we will try to eliminate the situation by drinking some herbs that induce cleansing. That may be all that's required. Sometimes it takes more, though, so we shall see."

"Give me whatever it is, and I will drink it. This must be taken care of by tonight."

The man responded with a deep, mistrusting laugh. "Don't want anyone to know about your little problem, huh? Not even the man of the house?"

Dianthea responded quickly, "That's enough. No questions. Remember our arrangement? Now, get started as my mistress has requested."

"Suit yourself. I want the rest of my payment first, though." He held his hand out.

Dalena nodded at Dianthea, telling her to pay the man. Instead, Dianthea replied, "Not until the drink is in my mistress' hand."

The man looked at Dianthea, then back to Dalena. "Very well. Mix this powder in with some wine and drink it all."

Dianthea took the pouch from the man and mixed the powder in with the wine. Once it seemed mixed well, she handed the cup to Dalena, who quickly drank all of the bitter, strange mixture. She set the empty cup on the table and asked, "Now what?"

"Now, we wait. Payment, please." The man extended his hand again, and this time Dianthea reluctantly gave him the pouch with the rest of the payment inside.

"I don't feel any different," Dalena said, beginning to think this man had no idea what he was actually doing. Perhaps they had both been tricked.

"You won't right away. Soon, you should begin to experience some pain. The pain will intensify until your body is ready to expel the tissue. I could use some refreshments while we wait."

"I didn't know there would be pain involved. I assumed..." Dalena didn't finish. Fear was suddenly replacing what had previously just been mild concern.

Dianthea looked into her mistress' eyes. "Don't worry. I'll take care of you, and the man has promised to stay. I'll get him something to eat, and this will be over soon." She left the room only for a short time, returning with a platter of fruit, bread, and meat.

"Nice place, this house. It's been empty for some time. I didn't realize anyone was living here again."

Dalena halted her pacing of the room. "What do you mean? It was my understanding that the family living here was only away for a short time."

"Well, rumor has it that the family who lived here—there was some sort of tragic accident," the man replied. "Not sure of the reasons, but the man of the house was found dead. Some say his wife killed him, or it could have been his son. No one knows for sure. The family seemed to just disappear."

Dalena watched the man take a large bite out of a plum. The juice dribbled down his chin. He seemed to not mind, which made her stomach turn. Suddenly, she doubled over in pain. Grabbing her middle, she cried out.

"Now it begins. We should get your mistress to bed. She'll be more comfortable," the burly man said to Dianthea as he took another bite of food. "Well, what are you waiting for?"

Dianthea helped Dalena into bed as another gripping surge of pain took hold of her body. She reached out for Dianthea's hand. "Don't leave me! Promise me you won't leave me!"

"I won't leave you. I promise." Dianthea smiled down at her mistress in an attempt to give Dalena peace, but deep down Dianthea was terrified too. The pain Dalena was experiencing seemed to have come on much too quickly, and it seemed too intense. She knew something wasn't right. "Should she be having this much pain so soon?" Dianthea asked the man, hoping for an answer.

"It is more intense than what I've seen, but there is nothing to worry about. She said she wanted it over with quickly." The man took another greedy bite out of a piece of roasted pheasant.

Another stab of pain wrapped itself around Dalena, and she squeezed Dianthea's hand so hard that the other woman had to muffle a cry. Dalena looked up at her slave with pleading eyes.

"Please, make it stop."

"I can't, Dalena. You must remember you are strong and brave. The man said this will be over with soon. Hold onto me; we will get through this together."

Dianthea tenderly wiped the sweat from Dalena's brow as a minute lapsed into an hour, and an hour, into several agonizing hours. What should have been "over with soon" was taking much too long. Dalena floated in and out of consciousness as the pain became too much for her to bear. Finally, Dianthea had all she could take.

The man had seemed to remove himself from the room as the woman's lingering pain only intensified. Dianthea walked out onto the balcony and found the man standing down on the beach, enjoying the warm day. Watching him without a care in the world while Dalena was in so much pain only reinforced her newfound hatred for him. She had to scream down at him to get his attention. "We need you! Something is not right!" She watched as he seemed to take his own sweet time coming back to the house.

"What is all the fuss about?" The man did not seem to be bothered by the distress Dalena was in.

"This is taking way too long. She is in too much pain. Can't you do something to help her?"

"Let me check her. Take off the linens so I can see."

Dianthea didn't trust this man, but she had no choice but to do what he instructed. She removed the linens that had been covering Dalena and waited while the burly man examined her.

She could barely ask the question that plagued her mind. "What's wrong?"

FAVORED

"I don't know. I've never seen this before. There seems to be no response to the herbs except for the intense pain. I cannot tell why she is not expelling the tissue."

Dianthea could see now that the man was visibly shaken. "Think. What do we need to do?"

"I don't know."

"You have to know. She trusted you. She trusted me! Help her!" Dianthea's voice had risen to a feverish pitch.

The man took out a few grisly-looking instruments from the bag he had brought.

"What are you going to do?" Dianthea was more terrified of the instruments than what the man was going to do with them.

"I'm going to clean her out. That should get rid of the unwanted tissue." With trembling hands, the man inserted the instrument into Dalena. She could only weakly protest before falling unconscious again. When he was finished, he was covered in blood. "There is nothing more I can do," he said, standing and shaking his head at the bloody scene in front of him.

"Stop it! Stop standing there and do something! My master will kill us both if something happens to her!"

The words Dianthea yelled seemed to set off an explosion in the man's head. "This is your problem that you brought to me. As far as I'm concerned, my job is done. I can do nothing more for her." He picked up his bag and rushed out of the room.

Dianthea didn't even attempt to follow him. She knelt beside Dalena's bed and buried her head in the linens. "What have we done? Oh, Dalena." She was so caught up in her sorrow that she did not hear Lucas' return until he was upon her.

"Dianthea, dear God, what on earth?" Lucas rushed over to the bed. Dalena looked dead, lying in a pool of her own blood. "Dianthea?" Lucas picked the girl up and began to shake her violently. "Dianthea, tell me what happened!"

348

Through sobs Diantha tried to explain. "She didn't want you to know!"

"Know what? Tell me, girl! We don't have much time!"

"She was with child. She didn't want the baby. I found a man, as she requested, and she only drank a cup of his concoction. She was in so much pain, and he tried to help, but he couldn't. She began to bleed. The man left. I didn't know what else to do."

Lucas had heard all he needed. "Stay with her until I return. She mustn't die! Just mustn't die!" Lucas raced out of the house and jumped onto his horse. He flew down the road, blinded by fear. When he reached Salamis, he knew exactly where to go. He found the house of the most reputable doctor on the isle and banged on the door until an elderly woman answered. "I must speak to the physician now!" He stepped past her and made his way through the house until he found the man he was looking for.

"Physician?"

"Yes." The elderly gentleman looked up from what he had been doing. "What is this all about?" He stood slowly as Lucas, in one stride, came face to face with him.

"You must come with me. This is not a request but an order. The wife of the governor of Syria is in desperate need of your services. She may die, and if she does, I will hold you personally responsible."

"I understand. Helena, my bag."

Upon her return, the doctor took the bag from the old woman's hands, and he looked at her tenderly. "Don't worry. I'll be back as soon as I can. We have faced these situations before. Go, get some sleep, and I know I will see you in the morning." He gently kissed her goodbye and followed Lucas out the door. "My carriage is around the corner. It will only take my boy a second to hook it to the horse."

"We don't have time for that." Lucas picked the old man up and placed him onto his horse. Climbing on behind, he wrapped

FAVORED

one arm around the older man to secure him; with the other hand, he grabbed hold of the reins. With one swift kick, they were rushing back toward the beautiful home on the hill.

To Lucas, it felt like an eternity had passed before they reached the columned porch. To the old doctor, though, it was as if they had flown on a bird's wing. Without a word, they hurried into the house. The doctor had no idea what the problem was, but he knew it must be quite serious for the soldier to be in such a hurry.

When Lucas reached the door to Dalena's room, he paused with his hand on the handle. Part of him was afraid to go in and find that she had passed—the other part wanted to rush in and have the doctor heal his *inamorata*. What if the doctor couldn't help her? What if she was already gone? The questions paralyzed him at the door. It wasn't until the doctor placed his hand on Lucas' shoulder that he was freed from his comatose state. He found himself able to move again and opened the door to go inside.

The sight the men's eyes beheld was enough to make even the toughest man faint. Lucas felt his knees go weak as he began to tremble uncontrollably. Blood-soaked linens lay strewn across the marble floor. Basins filled with bloody water sat next to the bed. On the bed lay Dalena's still, seemingly lifeless body. Dianthea was mumbling incoherent words as she knelt next to her mistress. Her blood-stained, tear-streaked face looked up at the two men as they entered the room.

"Is she...?" Lucas couldn't finish the question. Fear was gripping his soul like a vice.

"I don't think so. I can hear shallow breaths."

The doctor went to Dalena. He bent over her and gently began examining her body. "She is alive. I am amazed. However, she may not be for long if I cannot stop the bleeding. Now, tell me, girl, what happened?"

Dianthea gave the doctor the gory details of the day's events.

"Do you still have the cup from which the potion was given?"

Shaking hands, Dianthea handed the doctor the cup. He sniffed the mixture, which had long since dried at the bottom of the cup.

"As I thought. Fools. This mixture is not even used by professionals anymore. I want you both to leave the room. She is strong—that is in her favor—but she has lost a lot of blood. I think I can save her. Leave so I can get started."

Lucas and Dianthea were too weak to argue. As they left the room, Lucas instructed Dianthea to go get cleaned up and then meet him on the terrace.

The moonlight seemed bright to the darkness that encompassed Lucas' soul. When he heard Dianthea's footsteps approaching, he quickly dried the tears that had escaped unwillingly.

He had shed more tears over this one woman than he had shed in a lifetime of past hurts.

"Lucas, I only did what she asked of me. However, I understand if you desire to punish me."

Lucas didn't turn to face the girl. "If I desire to punish you? My first thoughts were to kill you, but Dalena loves you, and…" Breaking, Lucas could barely finish his sentence. "I know you love her." Hoarsely he asked the only question he cared to know the answer to. "Tell me, who is this man?"

The hurt and anger in Lucas' voice only reinforced Dianthea's fear of him. "He was a man my sister told me about. I do not know his name. I didn't want to know it, and Dalena was trying to keep her identity unknown. But I can tell you how to find him." She then gave Lucas clear directions to the man's home.

Lucas turned to go, and for the first time, through the brown, Dianthea saw hatred burning as deep as red embers in his eyes. Dianthea tried to explain the thoughts that had led to such a terrible ordeal. "Dalena didn't want you to know. She didn't want anyone to know, especially Quirinius. She was afraid that if you knew, you would feel it your obligation to tell the proconsul. She didn't want to put you in that predicament. She cares for you. She would hate for you to be caught doing something foolish."

Again, without turning to face her, Lucas replied, "I won't get caught."

Dianthea listened as the clicking of the man's sandals on the marble grew faint and was replaced by the galloping of the horse's hooves. Now all Dianthea could do was wait—wait on the doctor and wait for Lucas' return. She looked out over the open ocean, thinking of how she had heard of people who took the noble way out of a complicated situation—walking out into the warmth of the water until it covered their heads like a canopy. Drowning was said to be a painless way to die. Dianthea pondered whether it was truly painless or not with each wave that lapped upon the shore.

Fury fueled not only Lucas but his horse as well. The mare seemed to sense her master's weather, taking it as her own. Her hooves pounded the cobblestone street. The clear sheen of sweat gave her coat a shimmering luster. The white lather of endurance foamed at her mouth. This was the second time today her rider pushed her fortitude, but she would do his bidding, for she knew that once the task was done, he would reward her for her service.

Lucas drove the mare forward as they entered the city. With a gentle tug on the reins, he guided his horse around the corners and turns until they reached the section of town Dianthea had described. Her directions were flawless, and he found the shack with ease.

Fortune was in his favor, for gathering clouds had diminished the moon's brightness. Behind the shack, he removed his armor, laying it on the ground beside his horse. Stealthily, he moved to the front of the shack and gave only one soft knock at the door. Someone answered the door quicker than he expected.

"You're not Gallus."

"No, Gallus sent me instead. He was detained."

The burly man tried to get a good look at Lucas, but Lucas turned slightly to the side, hindering the man's view of him. "I'll wait for Gallus." The man tried to shut the door, but not quickly enough. Lucas leaned into the man, pushing him indoors and knocking him off balance.

Lucas was the one to quickly close the door once they were both inside.

"I tried to help her. I did what she asked." The man was on the floor, pushing himself backward. Lucas spoke not a word as he closed in on the man. "Those wealthy harlots think they can do whatever with whoever and not have to pay the price."

Lucas bent over the man, his fiery eyes burning hot as he unsheathed his short sword and held it to the man's throat. "She is not a harlot. Now stand up." Even though the man was big, fear—coupled with wine—had crippled his defenses. Lucas reached for the knife that lay on the table. "Take this; go ahead." Lucas shoved the knife into the man's hands. The man had no choice but to take hold of it.

"I only did what the girl wanted. I did what I was paid to do."

In a whisper filled with hostility, Lucas replied, "Consider this the last of your payment." Lucas moved behind the man and, in the quick gesture that all good soldiers learn, broke the man's neck. He gently laid the man's body on the ground. He then took the knife that was still clutched in the man's hands and drove it deeply into his abdomen, thrusting it upward. *A noble choice for one who has done wrong.* He quietly slipped out the back window and put his armor back on before remounting his horse. His wrath had been assuaged with death. He didn't know what would await him back at the house, but he did not feel the need to hurry.

Gallus knocked on Marcellus' door. In a pouch he held money that the other man had requested. For too long Marcellus had been making some risky bets when it came to his dealings. Today,

FAVORED

he had crossed that line. He hadn't explained to Gallus what had happened, only that he needed to flee Cyrus for good. The less Gallus knew, the better off he was. Gallus knocked one more time before opening the door. The place was dark. Gallus called out for Marcellus, but there was no answer. Just then the clouds parted, and moonlight streaked through the open door, revealing the ghastly scene to Gallus. "Oh, Marcellus, you finally lost, my friend. You finally lost."

As Lucas neared the house, the early light of dawn began to break through the dark of night. The house appeared deserted. *She's dead.* As he came closer to the house, his eyes caught sight of the young stable boy standing watch near the far column. He rode his mare right up to where the boy stood.

"Good morning, sir. Just getting in I see. Dianthea thought you might be late arriving home. She asked me to wait for you until your return." Lucas dismounted from his horse and handed the reins to the boy. "My, she is quite tired. Hard ride?"

"Harder than you know. Take special care of her. She's done me a great service."

"Oh, you know I will." The boy led the horse down the path that headed toward the stables.

Dianthea was sweet to have the boy wait for me. Trying to make amends, I'm sure. Lucas stood for some time on the porch. He didn't know what awaited him inside, but he knew he wasn't ready to find out. Not yet.

He left the porch, walking around the house and down the hillside toward the beach. As he made his way to the scheduled spot that had been his place of refuge in times past, Lucas thought of the first day he had brought Dalena to the villa. He had known she would love it as much as he did, and he was right. The sand, ocean, and salty air had invigorated the girl.

He had to bend over to enter the tiny alcove that had been his hiding place, the post he had found long ago and claimed his own. Sitting on a boulder, he looked at the wall of rock behind him. He brushed the sand off that was covering the scratches he had made on the rock. The last scratch only had the date attached. It was the day he would have rather forgotten, but just like the etchings lined with the corresponding date—forever ingrained in solid rock—the memory of that particular date was deeply etched in Lucas' memory. He looked around, and sure enough, his knife lay hidden right where he had buried it. All the stains from the last time it was used were still visible. He looked at the wall with all those etchings from so long ago and raised his hand, now holding the old, stained knife. He added another scratch that matched the older ones. After completing the task, he sat back and pondered his work. There were too many scratches and notches to count. At least, to him, there were too many.

Slowly, he left the safety of the alcove and stood just outside the tiny opening. He watched as the sun rose to new heights in the sky, wondering if he had delayed the inevitable long enough. It was time he found out whether Dalena was dead or alive.

His legs felt heavy as stone pillars as he climbed up to the terrace. He did not hear a sound as he entered the house. *She's dead.* He could not shake the overwhelming sense that he had lost Dalena for good as he untied his sandals and took them off. Even the sound of his sandals clicking on the marble flooring seemed too loud for the silence that cloaked him. He made his way to the hallway that held her bedroom. The hallway was unusually dark for this time of day. Still, Lucas' keen eyesight could make out a form lying perfectly still in front of Dalena's door. He leaned over and gently touched her shoulder. "Dianthea."

She stirred and opened her dark brown eyes. When she realized who was leaning over her, she quickly rose to her feet and asked, "Lucas, did you accomplish the task you set out to do?"

"Yes." He wouldn't give her any further details. He knew she didn't desire any. "Is the physician still here?"

FAVORED

"Yes. He stayed with her all night. He wanted to wait until your return before he headed home."

"Then she is dead."

"No, she is very much alive. The physician was able to save her life."

The words sent shock waves through Lucas that overwhelmed his exhausted body. He fell back against the wall and slowly sank to the ground. Dianthea knelt beside him. "Lucas, are you okay? Do you need me to fetch you some wine?"

"Later. I was sure she was dead. Who could survive the loss of so much blood?" He searched for an answer in Dianthea's eyes, but she had no answer for him. "I want to see her.

"May I go in and see her?"

"Yes. The doctor said to knock softly when you return. After he was finished, I made sure Dalena was clean and comfortable. I had the stable boy wait for your arrival. The household servants have been told that Dalena is very sick and is not to be disturbed. The doctor says she may not wake up for several days. Once she is able to eat again, I will prepare the list of things the doctor has given me to ensure a quick recovery."

"You've thought of everything."

"Not everything, I'm afraid. Lucas, please accept my humble apology. I should have never brought that man to this house. My instincts told me he was not to be trusted, but Dalena was so set in her way. No, that is no excuse. I am so very sorry."

"You have looked after her like a sister. She loves you, Dianthea. That's saying something, for I've never known a woman like Dalena to love another woman the way she does you. She thinks of you as her sister. How could I think of you any less?" Lucas stood. "I want to see her now."

Dianthea knocked ever so softly on the heavy cedar door, which immediately opened. The first sight that caught Lucas' eye was how the very room that held so much blood and death now looked peaceful and inviting. He looked at the old physician, who, after a long night, looked even older than he had the day before.

"I'm glad you have returned, my boy. She will sleep for several days, but she's been through quite a lot. It took all my medical expertise to save her, but save her I have." The doctor stepped aside and allowed Lucas and Dianthea to enter.

Lucas walked to the bed as softly as a soldier might be capable of walking. He looked down at the woman who had captured his heart. She was lying peacefully on clean linens, and her dark hair fell loosely around her face. Her face was pale but held an angelic quality to it. Dianthea had seen fit to dress her in a lilac gown and had strewn fresh lilacs around her fragile body. She was indeed the most beautiful creature he had ever laid eyes on. The doctor whispered in Dianthea's ear, "Did you tell him?"

Dianthea just shook her head in response.

"Tell me what?"

The doctor came up and placed a comforting hand on Lucas' shoulder. "I'm afraid, son, that she may never be able to bear children. The man who 'cleaned her out,' as Dianthea told me, cut into her rather deeply. I had to fix her the best I could. I'm very sorry."

"No. Don't be sorry. You saved her life. I care for nothing else."

"Yes, I understand, but you are not her husband. He may feel quite differently once he is told."

"Then he must never be told." No one in the room misunderstood the threat behind Lucas' words.

"I sent one of our servants to fetch a horse and carriage for you," Dianthea said. "It is waiting for you just outside. I thought you may also want to eat something before you go. It has been a long night for all of us." She then led the physician out of the

FAVORED

room.

"I'm afraid I'm getting too old for this. I retired some time ago. I wonder how the centurion knew of me."

"I don't know, but I'm grateful he did. Now, eat. It will help you gain some strength back.

"I am going to get some wine and food for Lucas." Dianthea left the old man out on the terrace.

As the physician sipped his wine and ate the food the young slave girl had prepared for him, a recollection of past events slowly began to surface. With each lap of the waves upon the shore, the old man's mind brought forth a memory that he had buried so long ago. So grotesque were the images that appeared, he dropped his cup of wine. The wine flowed freely, deep red, over the floor of the terrace.

"Are you all right?" Dianthea's voice brought him back to reality.

"Yes. Just clumsy I guess. It is time I take my leave. My wife, Helena, will be worried sick about me. You have been most hospitable and kind." The physician quickly hurried through the house and out the front door.

"Wait, please!" Dianthea hurried after the old man. She caught him just as he was about to leave in the carriage she had called for him. "My master wanted to give you this. He said to tell you that you have once again proven yourself as a worthy physician and confidant. He said you would understand."

The old physician nodded as he took the large purse from the girl. The purse was, indeed, heavy. Just like before, he had been paid handsomely for his service and silence.

Dianthea didn't want to disturb Lucas, but she desired to sit with her mistress. She tiptoed into the room and Lucas nodded in approval as she pulled up a chair next to Dalena's bed. She took a long look at him. He had dark circles under his eyes, and his hair was disheveled from riding fast and hard in the night wind.

358

His brow was wrinkled with worry, and he had not bothered to remove his armor. It seemed to weigh down his tired, muscular body. Until then, she had not noticed the gray hair he had around his temples. He was older than she first thought, or perhaps it was the weariness of the previous day's events that aged him now.

The two sat in silence until the sun had set for a long time, and slivers of moonlight shone through the open curtains. Dianthea finally broke the silence, "I think we should pull the drapes closed."

"The night air is probably not healthy for her."

Lucas only nodded in response.

"Lucas, you have not touched the wine or food I brought you earlier. You must at least drink something. You won't be any good to Dalena if you get so weak, you become sick." Dianthea picked up the tray. "I will come back with some fresh wine and food." She left before he could protest.

When she returned to the room, Dianthea realized Lucas had not moved the entire time she had been gone. In fact, he had not moved all afternoon. Dianthea knelt beside him and held the cup of wine to his lips. Almost in a state of incoherence, Lucas sipped the wine. Then, she tore off a piece of bread and held it to his lips. Lucas opened his mouth, and she placed the bread on his tongue. They went through this ritual until most of the tray had been consumed. Dianthea picked up the tray and returned it to the kitchen.

Once she had cleaned the tray and had everything looking the way the cook liked it, she returned to Dalena's room. Dianthea slipped into the chair and continued the vigil she and Lucas were sharing. It was all she could do to stay awake. The events of the past thirty-six hours were finally catching up to her. She didn't know how long she had been asleep when Lucas put his hand on her shoulder.

"Dianthea, go to bed. I intend to stay here until she awakens. There is no need for both of us to lose rest."

FAVORED

Dianthea looked up into Lucas' weary face. "I don't want to leave."

"I know. But I will need you to be strong for all of us. You can't do that if you are too exhausted. Go. I'm used to going without rest these days. You are not. If she wakes, I will come to get you. You have my word."

Dianthea knew there was no arguing. She slowly rose to her feet. "I'm glad to see you up, at least. You were beginning to worry me."

"Thank you for feeding me. I think it is what I needed to jolt myself back to reality. Dalena is going to need us both to be strong for her. The worst may be over, but we are not through this thing yet."

Dianthea nodded. She slowly walked to the door, her body feeling older than its fifteen years. "I just want to say how sorry I am again, Lucas," she said, standing in the doorway.

"No need. You did what your mistress requested of you. Maybe someday Dalena will trust me."

"She trusts you more than she knows." Dianthea quietly closed the door behind her.

Lucas went over to the balcony. The night air did wonders to awaken a man's senses. He stood, looking up at the night sky. The stars were bright and too numerous to count. As a child, he had often questioned his mother as to who made the earth with its flowers and trees or the sky with the sun, moon, and stars. His mother had always responded that *Jupiter* had seen it fit to make all things and other gods and goddesses looked over his creation for him. Lucas would ask why such a powerful god would need other gods to help him. His mother never seemed to have an answer. Even this night, as Lucas looked up at the brilliance of the sky above him, he wondered what god had made the earth around him and the sky above him.

He thought of the past two days and the torrent of emotions

that had surged through his being. He realized he could never leave Dalena in the care of another. He had been sent to see that the proconsul did nothing foolish in the province of Syria. Of course, none of his superiors knew of his connection to the governor's wife. Now he had to see to his undoing for Dalena's sake. How could he have planned to find someone else for her? There was no one else for her but him. Right or wrong, Lucas loved Dalena and intended to have her for his very own.

Chapter Thirty-Four

Joseph sat in the corner of the courtyard, watching the throngs of Nazarenes laughing and enjoying themselves at what was, in the minds of many, a joyous occasion. Joseph was of a different opinion. The corner and the stool upon which he sat gave him a clear view of the blushing bride while shielding him from the gaiety around him. How could an event bring delight to so many and torment to one? Joseph pondered the question, and he downed another cup of wine.

Eliakim certainly had spared no expense. The wine was flowing, and the food was plentiful. A man could sit unnoticed for hours, enjoying the fruit of the vine, praying that with every cup his loneliness and heartache would cease. However, Joseph knew that, come morning, the loneliness and heartache would remain, and added to them would be a severe headache.

Today, though, that just didn't seem to matter.

Joseph listened to the lyre and flute as they began another redundant melody. Mary would have enjoyed herself immensely— or would she? For over a month, Joseph had agonized over how Mary would have felt about her uncle marrying her mother. He had tried to talk to Anna, but the woman would not listen to reason. Joseph sensed that Anna was using her marriage to Eliakim as a diversion from dealing with the situation concerning Mary. Over and over, Joseph had tried to convince Anna that what the angel had told him in his dream was true, but his attempts had fallen on deaf ears.

He watched as Anna smiled at Eliakim. Joseph knew her love sprung from naivety and desperation. Did Anna truly understand the type of man she was marrying? People were giving Eliakim the benefit of the doubt because it was his wedding, and everyone in town respected Joachim, but there were murmurings that Eliakim had cheated out of some payment and lied to others in order to have his way cheaply. Even though Joseph had tried to have the men who had recently dealt with Eliakim talk to Anna, none of them would. "She's old. Allow her this time of pleasure. What harm can come of the marriage?" Those were just a few of the sentiments Joseph had heard over and over again.

Mary would feel differently about the whole thing. Joseph had felt it his duty to try to persuade Anna to change her mind. With Mary gone, he was Anna's only family. Joseph still considered himself family because he and Mary were still betrothed. As far as he was concerned, that would not change. Now he felt as if he had failed Mary all over again. Eliakim and Anna were wed. Soon they would parade through the streets until they reached Anna's home, and there they would officially become husband and wife.

"Sulking over losing, I see. Not very mature for a man of your stature."

Joseph looked up at Eliakim, a man who he had grown to truly despise. "I am not sulking, and I do not feel like I have lost. Anna is the one who is defeated."

"Now, my boy, Anna will have a good life with me."

"Maybe she will have more comfort than she is used to. Perhaps helping rear your daughter will give her fulfillment. But she will not find happiness with a man like you. Anna needs a man she can respect, and she will not respect you once she sees you for who you really are."

"I should have you thrown out of our celebration for such a comment, but, seeing how everyone else seems to be having a good time, I will refrain."

Joseph stood. The combination of suppressed anger and heavy drinking was what he had needed to unleash his disdain of the man taunting him. "I fully understand why your brother and family wanted nothing to do with you. You care nothing for God and His ways. Nor do you consider the needs of your fellow man. Destroying the lives of the people around you is just a game to you. The problem is that every man or woman who comes in contact with you loses in some way." Joseph's temper had reached the boiling point, and he spat into Eliakim's face.

Eliakim could hardly keep the smile that tickled at the corners of his mouth from showing as he slowly wiped the spit from his cheek. This was what he had waited for. He wanted Joseph dead—he was a threat. He reached for the long-bladed knife he carried under his cloak and stroked it while pondering his next move. The party silenced as the crowd watched the unfolding scene.

Just as Eliakim had decided to shove the knife through Joseph's abdomen, Anna, coming from the crowd, wedged herself between the two men. With pleading eyes, she whispered to Eliakim, "For my sake, please, let this pass." She turned to Joseph and begged, "Leave, please. This is my wedding. Even if you have some misguided need to protect me, you must let me be. I have made my choice. Go."

"You have made the wrong choice." With that, Joseph left as Anna had asked him to. The sounds of music and laughter followed him out of the courtyard and into the deserted street. Joseph was beginning to think all people were alike. They used each other for their own selfish purposes, bleeding from their fellow man whatever suited their needs in that moment. The men who had felt deceived and cheated were embracing Eliakim and Anna simply because they were enjoying the wedding festivities. Tomorrow they would turn their backs on the newlyweds. Even Rachel, who had warned Joseph about Eliakim, embraced the couple. Anna had promised to give her home (which Mary no longer needed) to Rachel's son and his new bride. This was done in exchange for Rachel's support and help with the wedding.

FAVORED

He sulked all the way home. When he reached the threshold, Joseph could not bear to go in. He turned and headed to the hillside where he and Mary had spent so much time before her father passed away. Joseph stretched out on the ground, and it was there, on the hillside, where he still seemed to feel Mary's presence with him. He smelled her scent among the wildflowers and heard her laughter in the wind. It was the only place he found comfort, the only place in which his loneliness vanished, the place where he would wait and listen for the small voice within to bring peace.

Lying perfectly still, Joseph allowed the tension to leave his body. He took in deep, cleansing breaths. His ears picked up on the faint sounds of the wedding party making their way through the streets of Nazareth. He shook his head, not wanting to hear anything that could threaten his peaceful solitude.

He closed his eyes and allowed visions of a young girl with long, wavy, black hair and eyes the color of onyx to envelop him. She was running through the streets, laughing at the young boys who had just turned over Ezra's cart. She bent down to help the old man pick up his wares. Then her head turned, and her eyes, shining with kindness, briefly looked at him. Her gaze bore through his soul. Joseph smiled. It was a memory he visited often.

Your patience will be rewarded, beloved. Wait for My time.

The words reassured him. He would wait. He would wait for her forever if it came to that.

He rose to his feet, feeling refreshed, and took his time walking back into town. The effects of the wine he drank had diminished, leaving him hungry and tired. When he arrived home, he washed the dust from his body and sliced some bread and cheese. He munched on some dates while busying himself making a stew. After the meal, he went to bed but did not sleep. This was usual for him lately.

Instead of lying awake, Joseph rose and put his tunic back on. He made his way next door to his shop. He picked up the sanded piece of wood that he had been working on most recently. Only the first few carvings had been made, but Joseph was proud of his work. He was taking great care and time with this piece. He wanted each etching to be the best he could do, and he worked on it until the early morning light. Feeling weary, he went back home to eat and prepare himself for the rest of the day's work.

He had spent many nights like this, up until dawn, working on what he desired to become a family heirloom. Joseph's lower back ached from standing bent for hours. His head hurt from too much wine at the wedding, coupled with the lack of sleep. He knew he couldn't keep up the schedule he was setting for himself, but he wanted to finish the project before Mary returned.

From inside his home, he could hear the sound of Nazareth coming to life with the light of day. He would spend the day in his shop, and he vowed to spend the evening catching up on the rest his body so badly needed.

Joseph hurried next door and began to work on a few items people had brought to him for repair. He had not been working long when a group of men showed up at his door. He had known they would be coming, but he expected them to be there a few days later. Not so immediately after the wedding.

He greeted his friends warmly. "Jonas, I see you are no worse for wear. I saw you downing quite a bit of wine yesterday."

"As did you, Joseph. In fact, you drank so much, your tongue became loose."

Joseph held back a reply. "Andrew, I've just about finished the cradle you brought to me. How is Sarah feeling?"

"She's fine. This is our fourth child, you know. Sarah believes her time is short. We're grateful for your help with the cradle. But I must say that is not why we are all here."

"No, I didn't figure it was. It's seldom a group of men comes by my shop to discuss cradles and babies."

The men laughed at Joseph's remark before settling around

FAVORED

his workbench to discuss their reason for visiting.

Micah was the first to speak. "You know, we all felt bad that we didn't come to your aide yesterday with Eliakim."

"Yes, indeed," added Saul. "Forgive us."

"There is nothing to forgive. I spoke out of turn. Even if what I said was true, I shouldn't have said it then and there." Joseph looked at the group of men who sat around him. They were all Nazarenes who had grown up in this town with him. None of them had left to pursue any other life. They married girls their parents had approved of and had settled into doing whatever their fathers had done before them. Each man was trying to figure out his life based on the laws of both God and man.

"Joseph, Eliakim leaves in a few days for Jerusalem. He has yet to pay many of us for the jobs we have done for him. What is your thinking on how we should handle this situation? We do not want to distress Anna or hurt her, for Joachim's sake." Micah looked straight into Joseph's eyes. He could always count on Micah to get directly to the point of a conversation. Micah's family had sold Eliakim most of the meat that fed the guests. Word was Eliakim had accused Micah's older brother of cheating him out of the best cuts, and, therefore, he was refusing to pay. "I understand there is a quarrel between your family and Eliakim?" Joseph phrased his statement more as a question in hopes Micah would elaborate more on the situation. Joseph did not like to give out words of advice without knowing the whole story.

"Yes. He has accused us of keeping the best cuts of meat out of what we delivered to him for the wedding feast. You know us, Joseph. We would not do such a thing. If Eliakim does not pay us what he owes, we will not have enough to pay our debtors. That includes our taxes to Rome. What will they do to our families if we do not pay? I'll tell you what they will do." Micah stood as fear and anger melted into one emotion. "They will take our wives and children to sell as slaves. They might take us as well, or they might just kill us. God only knows." Micah turned away from the group, his whole body trembling.

Joseph stood and went to his friend. He placed one hand on his shoulder. "We won't let that happen." He turned to the rest of his friends. "Has Eliakim cheated all of you out of your payments as well?" He was heartsick as each man nodded in affirmation.

"Joseph, you have always been the most prudent among us. Remember when we were just boys and thought we could take on the whole Roman legion? The Roman Army was marching north to who-knows-where, but it was passing right by Nazareth." The men began to chuckle and nod as Jonas continued his story. "All we had on us were the wooden swords Joseph's father had carved for us to play with. But, like a pack of fools, we thought we could run down the hillside waving our swords at the Romans, and they would just flee out of fear. Saul was so determined; he ran straight into one of them."

"Now, that's not exactly how it was. I tripped on a rock or something and fell into the leg of one." The sheepish look on Saul's face caused the men to roar with laughter.

"Never mind the exact details. Only Joseph refused to join us, saying we should wait until nightfall and then slay as many men as we could before getting caught. He claimed we would be heroes if we waited. Instead, we were given a swift kick by the Romans and sent home in shame. We've learned to listen to you since then. So tell us what we should do, Joseph."

Joseph sat silent. Across the room was the box with a piece of gold hidden inside of it. He had hoped that he and Mary might make good use of it. Now, with his childhood friends in need, there didn't seem to be an alternative. "Eliakim will not pay any of you what he owes you. I mourn the decision Anna has made. Joachim would not be pleased with all that has transpired in Nazareth since Eliakim's return." The men around him nodded in agreement. "I have a small sum saved, but I am not sure it will be enough to cover all your debts. However, I think there is a way we can all help each other. I say we figure what is owed to each

FAVORED

man. Then we figure out what each family needs in order to pay all its debts. We pool our money together, helping each other as needed. None of you will make a profit, but hopefully, we can save each other's families from disaster and pray we will not be taken advantage of again."

"We should have listened to you, Joseph, when you admonished us not to do business with that man. We were fools." Micah reached out for his friend, and the two men hugged.

"Joseph, what are you going to tell Mary when she returns?" All eyes turned toward Benjamin, who had remained silent until that moment. The men had agreed not to mention Mary's name when they visited Joseph. There were rumors floating around town concerning Mary. Hard to believe as the rumors were, the men were sure Mary would not have left her mother and Joseph unless what was being said was true.

Joseph sighed. "I will tell her the truth. It will sadden her heart to think she missed her mother's wedding, but it will sadden her more to know who her mother married."

The others nodded in understanding.

"You have all been my friends since childhood. Do not concern yourselves with everything you hear." Joseph's speech was interrupted by the sound of galloping horses. The men waited for the horses to pass, then hurriedly left the shop and headed to the center of town.

When they arrived, they saw a group of Roman guards keeping the people at a safe distance from the centurion, who was unrolling a scroll. The guards were shoving people out of the way and ordering them to be silent. After a few tense moments, the centurion began to read the order that was on the scroll. With each word, Joseph's heart sank.

"It is ordered by Caesar that each man is to go to the town of his father in order to be counted..."

People around Joseph began to fire back questions, but the

centurion finished the proclamation, mounted his horse, and galloped with his men out of Nazareth and on to the next town.

The sound of galloping horses was replaced by loud screaming from across the way.

Joseph and his friends hurried in the direction of the sound. "Joseph, that sounds like Sarah."

They arrived just as Andrew saw the lifeless body of his youngest daughter being lifted from the ground by her brother. Andrew pushed through the crowd with Joseph close at his heels. He grabbed hold of Sarah, turning her toward him. She melted into the body of her husband as grief overtook them both.

Through tears, Sarah explained that little Hannah had run out just as the guards were riding past. They hadn't even attempted to stop. Andrew held his wife as the two mourned together. Joseph turned to go—there was nothing he could do for his friend.

As he walked, he longed for Mary to be by his side. He wanted to place his hands on her abdomen to feel the baby that was growing inside her, the child who would redeem them all from the oppression they suffered.

He returned to his shop and worked on finishing the cradle Andrew had brought to him for repair. Andrew and Sarah would mourn the loss of their youngest, but the new baby would bring joy back to the home. Joseph decided not to charge his friend for his work; it would be a gift from him and Mary. As he diligently worked, the one thought that kept going through his mind became his prayer. *Return to me soon, Mary.*

A few days later, as Joseph prepared himself for the Sabbath, he heard a soft rapping at his door. He was shocked to see Anna standing on his doorstep.

"Anna, I am pleased…"

"Shhh." Anna put her finger to his lips. After looking around, she slipped around Joseph and into the house.

FAVORED

Joseph quickly closed the door and turned to face his uninvited guest. "Anna, what is this all about? I heard that you and Eliakim were leaving for Jerusalem as soon as the Sabbath was complete."

"Yes, but I had to see you before we left. I knew there wouldn't be time for me to come after the Sabbath, so I took the chance to come now."

"I take it Eliakim is still not over our little spat."

"Joseph, you shouldn't have said anything. Eliakim is looking for any excuse to rid himself of you and, thus, Mary. He doesn't think I know his motives. I may be old, but I am no fool."

"No one thinks you a fool. I still think you made a foolish decision…"

"Let us not rehash what cannot be changed. What is done is done. I will live with my choice. I am here to simply give you this." Anna held out a large pouch that jingled with a tune only many coins could make.

"What is this?"

"It is what is owed to the men in town for the services rendered on our behalf. I am neither deaf nor blind. I heard how each man was treated by my husband. He may not care what this town thinks of him, but I care. I will not cheat those who have been my friends and neighbors for the better part of my life. Take it and see to it that each man receives what is owed to him."

"Anna, I am concerned for your safety. Should Eliakim find out what you have done…"

"He will never know. He may realize his money is missing, but not until we are long gone from here. I took care of that. I filled his money bag with rocks." Anna giggled at her cleverness. "He will assume someone along the road robbed him. He will never even consider me."

"I don't know. I'm not comfortable taking money from a man who doesn't know he's giving it."

"Joseph, you are only taking payment for services given. If I did not bring you this money, then it is I who would be stealing from the good people of Nazareth. There is no more and no less in that pouch than what is owed. Besides, I don't want you using the money Joachim gave you to pay off Eliakim's debt. The money belongs to you and Mary." When Anna mentioned Mary's name, tears welled up in her eyes. She quickly rubbed them away.

Joseph sat the pouch down and took hold of Anna, forcing her to look directly at him. "Anna, please believe me when I tell you I intend to keep my vow to Joachim and you. Mary will be my wife from now until the day I die."

Anna choked on the tears she had been trying to hide. "I am grateful. You are a good man to take my daughter."

"Mary has done nothing wrong. God is at work. He has blessed her."

"I know that is what you believe."

"It is the truth. I am not a man easily deceived by trickery. I know what I saw and heard in my dream."

"Dear Joseph." Anna reached up and stroked Joseph's cheek. "Joachim was right to choose you."

"Why is it so hard for you to believe?" He released his hold on Anna and sighed in resignation.

"You ask the same question I have asked myself countless times. I don't have an answer. Maybe, if God had done all the things I asked of Him…but alas, He did not." Anna walked to the door.

"In all the teaching from childhood stories to teachings in the temple, none spoke of God as our benefactor. They told of a God who desired His people to believe and follow His precepts. Then, only if He chooses, would He bless them. Anna, when you walk out of my door and turn your back on Mary, you are forever walking out on the greatest blessing God is giving His people. God is sending us the Messiah." Joseph didn't even fully

FAVORED

comprehend the meaning of the words he spoke.

Without turning around to look at him, Anna replied, "Tell Mary I will always love her." With that, she walked out.

Joseph stared at the empty space where Anna had stood. He couldn't understand how she could walk out on her own daughter, let alone on seeing the promise of the Messiah fulfilled. Little did he know that Anna was only the first of many who would reject God's ultimate blessing to man.

Chapter Thirty-Five

Attempting to discern the sound that had awakened her in the quiet hours before dawn, Elizabeth lay quietly next to Zachariah. Her belly grew hard as another contraction shot a mild dose of pain across her abdomen and around her back. If it hadn't been for the visit from the angel to her husband or the joy that coursed through her soul, Elizabeth would have sworn she was too old for such a feat as delivering a child. Again, the soft muffled sound of a soul in anguish reached her ears. In hopes of not rousing her husband, Elizabeth silently slipped from the bed they shared. She wrapped her mantle around her shoulders and tiptoed out of their room.

On her way up the stairs to the room where their young houseguest had taken up residence for the past three months, her belly grew hard, forcing her to stop and catch her breath. She ran a gnarled hand over her womb as she cooed to her unborn child. "Practicing for your entrance into the world, eh?" The child kicked at the sound of his mother's voice. "As anxious as I am for your arrival, we both must bide our time and be patient." Sensing her body had calmed, the older woman continued up the stairs. At the top, the sounds that had been muffled became clear and audible. Elizabeth hurried to the side of the young girl, who was wetting her bedroll with tears. Elizabeth knew it would be difficult for her to sit on the floor and even harder for her to get up, but Mary needed her comfort. She lowered herself to the floor and reached out for her young relative, who willingly accepted the comfort offered.

Mary laid her head on Elizabeth's thigh. While she continued to weep, Elizabeth stroked the girl's long black hair and marveled at its softness. Elizabeth wound one of the silky curls around her fingers as Mary's weeping diminished into mere sniffles, then slowly faded into silence. She continued to stroke the dark strands, knowing when Mary was ready, she would share the concerns that tortured her soul.

Mary lifted her head and turned to face the source of solace. She situated her body, legs crossed in front of her, head bowed. Her ebony hair fell over her shoulders, hiding her face. Her hands nervously twirled at the frayed threads that bordered her bedroll.

"Things are never as bad as they seem, child." Elizabeth gently lifted Mary's face, and she tucked the girl's hair behind her ears. She lovingly looked into the swollen doe eyes, the lashes of which still glistened with the wet of tears. "Ah, child, your heart is troubled. Share with this old woman what burdens you."

Mary averted her eyes. "The baby kicked for the first time last night."

"Oh, Mary, that is wonderful. There is no greater feeling a woman can experience than when the child growing inside her makes himself known for the first time. It is an experience that only women share. This is a special day indeed!"

"I'm starting to show. Not much, just a little. It is still disguised by my tunic, but soon it will be evident that I am with child." Mary's tone was despondent.

"So this is what troubles you?" Elizabeth nodded with understanding.

"Yes. Oh, Elizabeth, what am I to do? I am unmarried and with child. As each day passes, my situation will become harder to hide." Realizing she was complaining caused guilt to creep into Mary's soul. When she turned to face Elizabeth, there was no rebuke in her cousin's aged eyes. Mary couldn't help comparing Elizabeth to Miriam. Their hair being whiter than gray made their olive skin appear golden, giving them a youthful radiance. The brown hue of their eyes had faded over time, but that did not diminish the sparkle of peace and joy that captivated all who looked upon their weathered faces. Elizabeth, with her rounded cheekbones, more prominent nose and jaw, and a small space between her front teeth, was not as attractive a woman as Miriam had been, but both women exuded a warmth that would make even a stranger feel accepted and loved.

"You are going to unravel your bedroll if you keep pulling at those threads." Elizabeth gently took Mary's hands in hers, sending warmth through Mary's body. "Listen to me, child.

"The fears and doubts you are voicing are quite normal, but you have seen firsthand an angel of God. You have given God the credit, and rightfully so, for delivering you safely to our front door. God has not promised an easy path for any of us, but He would not choose you to carry, deliver, and rear His Son if He was going to abandon you. Why all the doubts now?"

Tears sprang to Mary's eyes.

"Mary, what is it? Why all the tears?" Elizabeth waited for Mary to regain control of her swirling emotions.

"If he were here today, living still, it would be Father's birthday." Mary pulled her hand free of Elizabeth's loving grasp and wiped at the tears that ran down her cheeks. "We would celebrate Father's birthday in the same manner year after year. Mother and I would wake up early to go first to the well and then to the market to purchase Father's favorite foods. When we would return home, Mother would shoo Father from the house with strict instructions not to return until the sun was sinking in the horizon. Father would act perturbed by Mother's demands, but nonetheless, he would comply. Mother would roast a lamb, taking special care with the spices she used for flavor. She cooked Father's favorite vegetables—asparagus covered with cheese and turnips sweetened with honey and cabbage. Of course, there would be an abundance of fruit and at least three different types of breads. Father once told me that the aroma that wafted out of the house could be savored throughout Nazareth. Father would come

FAVORED

home at precisely the right moment when the last of Mother's loving touches were added. Each year, Father would act more surprised than the previous."

Mary's tears dropped onto her lap and soaked through her sleeping gown. "Now, of all days when Mother needs me most, I am hiding here because of the shame she believes I have brought to our family." Mary sniffled. "I should have waited to tell her. I should have come up with a plausible story concerning the swaddling clothes she found. I should have..." Mary covered her face with her hands as she broke into sobs.

"There, there, child." Elizabeth's roundness and her age limited her mobility. She longed to take the girl into her arms, but the most she could do was pat Mary's knee and pray the action would convey all the love and sympathy Elizabeth had for the girl. "Mary, I understand your distress on today of all days. This may sound harsh, but I am going to speak frankly with you. You need to stop feeling sorry for yourself. It is not good for you, but more importantly, it is not good for the baby."

Mary stared blankly into her cousin's face. Deep down she knew Elizabeth spoke the truth, but still, she couldn't believe she had said it. The tiny hairs on the back of Mary's neck stood on end. She wanted to feel angry with her cousin, but how could she fault her for speaking the truth?

"My darling Mary, you are carrying our Lord. You nourish within your body our Messiah. Blessed are you among women, remember?" Mary numbly nodded in affirmation. "I love your mother. God only knows the countless hours Miriam, your dear grandmother, spent teaching her ways of faith and righteousness. Miriam had such patience. But, even as a child, your mother had a hard heart. Now, in her old age, she reaps the consequences for her unbelief.

"There is nothing you could have done or said that would have caused your mother to believe you.

"Your mother chooses to cloak her heart with bitterness. Don't get me wrong—she is a good woman. She has always given to the poor, kept the commandments and the laws given to set our people apart. She kept herself pure and married a righteous man who loved her just as she was. She is your mother, and she is to be honored. However, God has set you apart for a high calling, and you must not waver in your resolve to do His bidding, no matter the cost. Allow the truths Miriam and your father taught you to sustain you in your darkest hours. You are a young woman of great faith. When doubts surface, draw on your faith. When troubles arise, draw on your faith. When all is calm and peaceful, draw on your faith."

Mary realized the darkness that had invaded her soul was dissipating with Elizabeth's admonition. Slowly taking its place was peace, along with a resolve to heed the words of her wise cousin. "Forgive me, Cousin." Mary hung her head in shame.

"Mary, we all have moments of doubt and fear, but they need to be just that—moments."

Mary rose to her knees and wrapped her arms around Elizabeth's neck. "I love you.

"Thank you for your wise words."

Elizabeth giggled at the young woman's compliment and then moaned as another contraction gripped her. Mary released her loving hold on her cousin. "Is everything all right?"

"Oh yes, yes. There is nothing to be concerned about. The baby is just practicing for the big day, nothing more. I've had them before." Elizabeth tried to adjust her position on the floor but found movement utterly impossible. "However, I will admit, that last one nearly took my breath away."

"Should I get Zachariah?"

"No. He'll be awake shortly."

"Oh, feel." Mary sat back on her heels. She reached for Elizabeth's hand, placing it on her own slightly bulging stomach. The two waited. "There." Mary smiled. "Did you feel that?"

FAVORED

Elizabeth laughed and nodded. "Now, that is something that can turn a frown into a smile. You have a strong boy." Another contraction gripped Elizabeth. "My, I've had quite a few of these since I woke. They usually subside by now." Elizabeth rubbed her belly attempting to relax the muscles. "Mary, would you mind massaging my lower back?"

"Not at all. Elizabeth, maybe I should summon the midwife."

"Nonsense. Besides, there is one more thing I need to discuss with you."

"Anything."

As Elizabeth began, Mary recalled how her father would cup her face in his roughened, clay-stained hands, gently forcing her to pay attention to his words of admonition. As she worked her delicate fingers into the small of Elizabeth's back, she closed her eyes in an attempt to remember the sound of her father's voice.

"Mary, child, did you hear what I said?"

"Uh, no. I'm sorry."

"Mary, Zachariah and I had a long talk the other night, and we both feel that it is time for you to go back to Nazareth."

"What?" Trying to grasp all her cousin had said, she stopped her gentle massage.

"Now, hear me out. You've been here nearly three months now. You are in your fourth month of pregnancy. Your waist will continue to expand as your baby grows. It is going to become harder and harder to hide your condition. It will be difficult for Joseph to take you as his wife without lasting consequences for both of you once your condition is made known."

"I thought you came up here to cheer me up. It sounds to me as if we are backsliding just a bit." Mary bit her bottom lip to keep from crying.

"You'll understand where I'm heading in a moment. Zachariah and I both feel that it is important for you to go back to Nazareth and learn of Joseph's decision concerning your betrothal before it is too late. We have learned that Caesar requires all Roman subjects to travel to the home of their ancestors to be counted. They are taking a census so that Rome can raise our taxes. I believe you mentioned Joseph's family is of the house of David, as are you. That means he would need to go to Bethlehem to meet the requirements of Rome. It is important you learn of his plans before he leaves."

Another pain moved across Elizabeth's lower back, and she stifled the urge to cry out.

She waited for the contraction to end before continuing.

Numbed by Elizabeth's revelation, Mary was unaware that her cousin was in distress.

"But what if Joseph has decided to have me stoned?"

During Mary's question, Elizabeth took the opportunity to catch her breath. "You must trust your father's decision. Didn't you say that Joachim believed God wanted Joseph to be your husband? God has ordained your steps, Mary. Trust Him to protect you. Trust Him to reveal to Joseph the truth. Joachim was a righteous man with great faith. Rest assured that your father never would have betrothed you to Joseph unless he had heard from God." Just then, the strongest contraction Elizabeth had felt thus far grabbed hold of her worn body, and she cried out in pain.

"Elizabeth?" Mary looked at the pain-stricken face of her cousin.

"Please, go tell Zachariah where I am. Fetch the midwife. I think our son is anxious to enter this world."

"Let me help you downstairs to your own bed, where you will be more comfortable."

"I don't think that is an option for me. The contractions are strong and more frequent. If I'm not mistaken, I believe my water just broke. Help me make it to the wall so I have something to lean my back against." Mary lingered beside her relative as

FAVORED

another contraction ran its course. "Go, Mary, please."

"But I am afraid to leave you."

"Unless you plan on delivering this child yourself, I suggest you go get help. I'll be fine."

Mary nodded and darted down the stairs.

With beads of perspiration on her brown and another contraction overtaking her body, Elizabeth heard the front door open and close. She silently prayed that God would give Mary great speed and that nothing would delay her return with the midwife. As her body relaxed from the contraction, Elizabeth took a moment to relax as well. She closed her eyes and leaned back against the wall. Knowing firstborns generally took longer coming into the world gave her assurance that the midwife would arrive, in all probability, with time to spare.

At the soft touch upon her shoulder, Elizabeth's eyes opened to meet those of her husband. *Dear Zachariah.* As weeds left unattended wind themselves around wanted plants and choke the life from a beautiful garden, silence had wound itself around her husband's vocal cords, choking out the delightful sound of his voice. Over the past year, it had become harder and harder for Elizabeth to recall the sound of her husband. The soft tone he would use when teaching the youngsters in the village or the bass that would ring through the corridors of the temple when singing the psalms or the simplicity of "I love you" before he fell asleep were all memories fading over time. Together they had learned to communicate in different ways. Much of the time, Zachariah would write his thoughts for her to read, but scroll and pen were luxuries.

She had learned to see in his eyes his thoughts and desires, and Zachariah had learned to be patient rather than becoming frustrated when she didn't read him correctly.

Now, there was no mistaking the look of concern she saw on his face. "I do believe our son is anxious to enter this world," she said. Zachariah nodded in understanding. "Mary has gone for the midwife..." Before Elizabeth could finish, another contraction was upon her. Zachariah held her hand, unsure of what else he could do.

After the contraction had run its course, Zachariah used the cuff of his tunic to wipe the sweat from his wife's face. "I feel too old for this." She smiled at her own futile attempt to joke. Zachariah smiled and pointed at himself, nodding at her. "You, my dear husband, will never be too old." But as Elizabeth said the words, she knew age had slipped up on both of them. Zachariah's hair was as gray as hers was white. What she had used to call laugh lines around his eyes were wrinkles. The blue of his eyes had faded to gray, but she still saw love every time she looked into them.

Her belly grew hard. Pain surged through her lower back. She gripped Zachariah's hand as she cried out, unable to stifle the sound of pain.

Zachariah had served for years as a priest in the temple. One of his many duties included making sacrifices for the sins of Israel. He had dipped his hands in blood, and not once had his knees gone weak. Now, watching the woman he had spent the better part of his life with suffer unbearable pain to bring his child into the world caused every inch of him to feel faint.

"It's over." Elizabeth relaxed against the wall again. "I had hoped Mary would have returned now with the midwife." She looked at her husband. Zachariah walked his fingers down his forearm. "I understand she has a ways to walk. Are you trying to tell me I am being impatient? Maybe you should try telling your son to wait."

They both sat up at the sound of the door opening and closing. The hushed voices grew louder as Mary and Tishbah, the midwife, bounded up the stairs. The moment Tishbah's foot landed at the top of the stairs, she began giving orders.

"What is a man doing up here in the birthing room? Out with

FAVORED

you." She helped Zachariah to his feet and, with a slight nudge, sent his progress forward. "Mary, we will need linen, warm water, a knife, salt, and oil. Go, girl."

Mary jumped at the order. When she had reached the top of the stairs, her first instinct was to rush to her cousin's side, not fetch items for the midwife.

"I'm in good hands with Tishbah. Go ahead and bring the items she's requested."

Elizabeth's smile did nothing to hide her anguish.

"I'll be right back." Mary hesitated when Elizabeth sucked in the air around her as another contraction took over her body.

"Go. Go. I've got her. Hurry, Mary. There is no time like the present for a baby to be born." Tishbah placed herself between Elizabeth and the wall, allowing for the laboring woman to rest her full body weight against her. Whereas she had been almost harsh with Zachariah and Mary, she spoke lovingly in Elizabeth's ear. "Ah, a baby will bring the cries of joy back into this house. You may be old, Elizabeth, but you are strong, eh? We will pray it is a boy." Elizabeth caught Mary's eye just before she descended the stairs. They gave each other a knowing look.

Indeed, it is a boy. A very special boy.

Zachariah sat in one of the chairs that framed the family table. He had covered his head with the tallis to pray, but the words would not come. His mind kept wandering the room at the top of the stairs, on which his whole life labored to bring another life into the world. Many women much younger than the one who held his heart had died during the process of birthing.

Now all he could do was wait. He thought back to that day in the temple. In all his years of service, not once had the lot fallen to him to burn the incense—not until that fateful day.

He had dawned his priestly garments: the white linen coat and breeches. He recalled how carefully he had girded his belt, each blue, purple, and scarlet thread thoughtfully stitched by

Elizabeth's hands. He'd placed his cap on his head and proceeded to do the task assigned. He had made his way through the throng of people gathered to offer their sacrifices and worship unto God. The last act before he'd entered the Holy Place was to tie the cord about him. This was done so that if he defiled the sacred house of God, the punishment of which was death, he could be pulled out and buried.

Zachariah could still hear the clicking of his shoes as each step took him toward the altar of incense. He remembered the awe he had felt at seeing the golden lampstand, table of showbread, and the altar for the first time. His hands had trembled as he had extended the torch he had carried to light the altar. The small flame of the torch had become a brilliant blaze upon the altar. He had thought the light of the altar was the cause for the brightness in the holies before his mind slowly began to register what his eyes saw.

The angel had stood just to the right of the altar. He'd admonished Zachariah not to be afraid, but the entire time he was in the presence of the angel, he had shaken in his breeches. The angel had proceeded to tell him that he and Elizabeth would have a son, even in their old age. This boy, who was to be called John, would prepare the people for the Lord. He was ashamed of his unbelief, both then and now.

At the memory of the last words he spoke, Zachariah put his head in his hands. He had questioned the angel, Gabriel, on the validity of his words. At that instance, the angel struck Zachariah mute. He would speak when all that the angel said had been fulfilled. By the looks of things, that would be today.

Mary had already been up and down the stairs twice before she saw Zachariah, head in hands, sitting at the table. She gently called to him. He lifted his face from his hands to peer into her brown eyes.

"She's doing fine. The midwife has everything under control."

Zachariah nodded. She fixed him something to eat and drink

FAVORED

before she went back up the stairs with the last basin of water.

"Good, Mary. Now, come, we need your help." There was no questioning Tishbah nor refusing her. She commanded, and Mary obeyed. She imagined even Tishbah's husband did as she ordered. The thought made Mary giggle, causing both Tishbah and Elizabeth to look at her incredulously. "Mary, pay attention. I need you to get behind Elizabeth and support her back. It is time for her to push. I need to know you will keep her sitting up."

"Yes, I can do it."

"Good. Well, what are you waiting for?"

Mary grimaced at Tishbah's tone. She silently prayed that when her time came, her midwife would be gentle in speech. Mary moved into place, allowing Elizabeth to rest her full weight against her. Elizabeth cried out as another contraction sent blinding pain through her body.

"Elizabeth, I need you to use your energy to push, not cry out. Now, with the next contraction, I want you to push as hard as you can." Tishbah gave her instructions as she moved into place at Elizabeth's feet. "Bend your knees, Elizabeth, and when you push, hold onto your legs. I'll be right here to help guide this little one into the world."

Not even bringing her own children into the world brought Tishbah as much joy as helping other women deliver their babies. Tishbah's mother had been a midwife, as was her grandmother. As far back as she knew, every woman in her family had served her village as a midwife. She felt honored to be helping the oldest woman she had ever helped deliver her one and only child into the world. It was a miracle that Elizabeth was even with child, let alone one she had carried to term. Elizabeth was placing her life and the life of her unborn child into Tishbah's capable hands.

Tishbah placed her hand on Elizabeth's belly. She could feel another contraction begin to harden Elizabeth's womb. "Now, Elizabeth. Push with all your might."

TERI LYN TOBEY

Elizabeth did as commanded. She pushed as if her life depended on it, and indeed it did—hers and her unborn child's. Perspiration ran down her face, arms, and back. She had no idea where Zachariah had gone and was vaguely aware of Mary's presence. Every ounce of energy she had was going into delivering a healthy baby.

"Elizabeth, you can relax. Take some slow breaths. You're doing very well. Here comes another contraction. Push hard, Elizabeth. Push." Tishbah didn't know how much the old woman's body could take or for how long. She wanted to deliver the child as quickly as was safe and possible. "Elizabeth, I can see the baby's head. Just a little while longer. With the next contraction, I need you to push harder."

As Mary watched the process of birth unfold, she was both awed and frightened. In a matter of five months, she would be going through what Elizabeth was now. Where she would be and who would be with her were still mysteries. Hours earlier, Elizabeth had counseled her that it was time she returned to Nazareth to learn of Joseph's decision. Her father had been confident that Joseph was God's choice for her. If God could cause a woman past childbearing age to be a mother, or, for that matter, make a virgin carry His Son, could He not give Joseph the answer he needed to take her as his wife? Mary felt convicted by the thought. She began to silently pray as she supported Elizabeth. *God, I have limited You once again to what only my mind could conceive. When I thought I had no place to go, You brought me safely to my cousin's home—providing aid to see to my safe arrival. My feelings for Joseph are not hidden from You. I suppose it is time I return home and learn of his decision. I confess I am scared. Give me courage to do what I must.* She was brought from her silent prayer by the sweet sound of a babe's cry.

"Elizabeth, you have a boy—a beautiful boy. Mary, you can let Elizabeth lie back and rest. Come, I need you to wash the babe and rub him with salt and oil. Wrap him tight in the swaddling

FAVORED

cloths so his tiny limbs will grow straight."

Mary laid Elizabeth back and waited as Tishbah cut the umbilical cord, then handed the baby to her. Mary proceeded to wash, salt, oil, and wrap the baby boy. Out of the corner of her eye, she watched Tishbah give Elizabeth water. Then she began to knead on Elizabeth's stomach. Elizabeth groaned as Tishbah continued to work. She spoke gently to Elizabeth, explaining what she was doing and why. The kneading helped Elizabeth's body expel the birthing tissue.

Once the tissue had been expelled, Tishbah sponged off Elizabeth and helped her don a clean tunic. Then, Mary gently handed Elizabeth her baby boy. The weariness in her face disappeared as Elizabeth held her boy for the first time. The tiny infant's mouth searched for his mother's breast to suckle. Tishbah laughed as she watched the babe nuzzle his mother. "A babe who desires sustenance so soon after birth is sure to be a healthy babe, indeed." A nod from Tishbah sent Mary to fetch Zachariah.

From her vantage point at the top of the stairs, Mary could see Zachariah standing on the bottom step. Mary descended the stairs until she reached the second to last step. Zachariah folded his arms, moving them to and fro as if he were cradling an infant. Mary copied the motion and said, smiling, "You are a papa, Zachariah, of a healthy boy. Elizabeth is very weary but in good health and spirit. Come, see the miracle of God."

Mary stepped aside and watched as he bounded up the steps. Watching him take the stairs two at a time, no one would guess the man was older than most first-time fathers. When Mary ascended the stairs, she brought several cups of fresh water with her.

The scene she saw warmed her. There, side by side, sat mother and father. Zachariah, with his head covered by his tallis, wrapped an arm around Elizabeth's shoulder. He placed his other hand on his son's head. Elizabeth's head was bowed, but her eyes gazed lovingly upon her newborn son as he suckled.

When Zachariah finished praying, he lowered the tallis from

his head, kissed his wife on the cheek, then rose and went to Tishbah. She was staying out of the way, standing near the corner of the room. Mary poured water into cups she had brought back to the room with her. She waived for Zachariah to finish thanking and paying Tishbah. Then she gave a cup to each person in the room. Tishbah thanked Mary for her thoughtfulness, drank her water, and then took her leave.

Mary helped Zachariah support Elizabeth down the stairs and to their room, after which she carried the sleeping infant to his mother. She went back to her room at the top of the stairs and cleaned the area before sitting down to think about when she should leave. A smile cracked through her pensive expression. She wondered if he would even consider it. After all, he was probably very busy. It had been three months since their goodbye. Her heart skipped a beat at the thought of seeing Theo and Onesimus again. She would send word tomorrow with one of the shepherds who made the weekly trek to Jerusalem to sell sheep at the temple. She would request he wait for a reply before returning. In the morning, she would ask Zachariah which shepherd was brave and trustworthy. *Perhaps I will leave after the baby's circumcision in eight days.* She smiled at the thought of seeing Joseph and her mother. She was ready to go home.

Chapter Thirty-Six

Theo stood in the courtyard and listened to the madman rant. Lately it had been almost impossible to get the king to listen to reason. Theo watched as the architects, charged with lengthening the aqueduct between Bethlehem and Jerusalem, scurried—their charts flying behind them from the presence of Herod.

It was difficult for Theo to wait patiently for the client-king to summon him. After all, Herod was appointed by Rome to rule Palestine. Technically, Theo should have been summoning him. However, that was not the way things were done, especially if Theo wanted to remain in the good graces of the king and Rome. Rome was requesting that Theo try to rationalize with an irrational man. Once again, Herod the Idumean had sent the religious Jews into a fighting frenzy. For all the good Herod had accomplished throughout the region, the Jews still saw him as a foreign domination.

Theo watched as a slave girl wandered through the garden on her way to the other side of the palace. She glanced up at him, giving him a sly smile. Theo returned the acknowledgment with a simple nod. He had learned his lesson with Dalena: the women of high Roman society were too dangerous to get involved with. Slave girls and prostitutes, though, were another matter. He would bring the slave girl up to Herod. Perhaps tonight, if he played his hand right, he would have company to keep in the loneliness of the dark. It would help keep his demons at bay.

"The king will see you now." The dark-skinned slave escorted Theo into the library. Every time he entered a room, Theo was impressed. The room was a testament to Herod's loyalty to Rome—more precisely, Caesar.

FAVORED

Herod had played both ends against the middle when it came to Octavian and Mark Antony. Antony and Cleopatra had ruled most of the region of Palestine. For Herod to maintain his position as the king, he'd had to side with the couple against Octavian. In fact, Antonia Fortress, which Herod had ordered built adjacent to the temple, was named after Antony. But after Octavian defeated the royal couple and their bodies were found dead by suicide, Herod had done an about-face, declaring his undying loyalty to Octavian. Octavian, upon whom the senate conferred the title Augustus Caesar, had rewarded Herod for his loyalty by allowing him to maintain his position as client-king of Palestine.

The bust of the Roman ruler sat in the center of the room. Couches with scarlet cushions were positioned so all seated would gaze upon the sculpture. The marble floor was inlaid with mosaic tile, which accentuated the royal colors of the room. The only thing Theo did not like about the interior was Herod, who was standing in the center of the room. He was rubbing his temples while he hollered instructions to his slave.

"Those imbeciles called architects have given me a headache as well as upset my stomach. Bring me some Commiphora opobalsamum, and make it quick, or you'll find yourself in the arena sooner than you think." The slave quickly left the room, leaving Theo alone with Herod. "Make what you have to say quick, centurion. I'm in no mood for a lengthy discussion on some Jewish sect or another that I have angered."

"That is precisely why I am here." Theo thought it best, considering the mood Herod was in, to compliment the man's leadership before pointing out his deficiencies. "It amazes me to think of all the food you have done for the Jewish people. The way you paid from your own treasury to help those less fortunate during the most recent famine. Not to mention, all the families you helped after the disastrous earthquake displaced many. I wonder why some still do not look kindly to having you as their king."

"Jews are prideful, intolerant people. Keep that in mind as you run around, playing ambassador. You can't change who you are: a Roman centurion. They will tolerate you as long as you abide by their wishes. The moment you favor Rome over them, they will spew you from their mouths."

"Are you speaking from experience?" Theo liked watching the man squirm. He knew Herod had only divorced his first wife, Doris, an Idumean like himself, and married Mariamne, a Hasmonean princess, to gain Jewish support. The strategy had backfired when Herod decided to name Aristobulus III, Mariamne's younger brother, as high priest.

"Unfortunately, I am here to talk business. As a matter of fact, some of the Pharisees are upset over the new construction at the temple. Something about certain aspects of the design."

"Nonsense. I've hired only priests trained in masonry to see the project and the work. I've adhered to Jewish law. They have nothing to complain about. Tell them if they don't like it, I can replace them with men who do. I intend for the temple to be my own crowning glory. Now, leave me, Roman. However, there is one more thing before you go, I suppose. I am leaving for Callirrhoe in the morning. My stomach is causing me great pain. My physician says the hot baths at Callirrhoe will help me. Of course, he may be untrustworthy, as are so many of those who are close to me. I can always have him done away with if the remedy he recommends proves to be a failure."

"Will you be taking your slaves with you, or will you leave them here?"

"Some will come; some will stay."

"I'm in need of some slaves at the fortress. Might I pay you for the use of yours or, better, purchase one from you?"

"Choose whoever pleases you and be generous with your payment. Also, send word to Rome of my desire to please its most trusted ambassador."

FAVORED

"Might I take them tonight?"

"You need to work on your subtlety. Which one of my voluptuous girls has drawn your eye?" The dark-skinned slave returned, cutting short any further discussion on the matter, which was fine with Theo. The slave gave Herod the medication he had requested, poured him a cup of wine, and then positioned himself out of the way—yet at Herod's ready assistance.

"I will pray to the gods that you have a speedy recovery in Callirrhoe. Now, if you excuse me, I will attend to the matter we have discussed." With a wave of Herod's hand, Theo was dismissed.

He headed in the direction he had seen the slave girl go, past the colonnaded courtyard, through the garden, and to the south side of the house. It concerned Theo that Herod continued to be suspicious to the point of lunacy of those around him. He had sent a message to Rome indicating as much. Herod had put to death those closest to him: his mother-in-law, Mariamne, and two of his sons. *If I am to succeed in helping bring peace to this region, then I must convince Rome that Herod is a threat to that peace.*

Theo stopped at the door to one of the many bedrooms. Peering inside, he watched as the slave girl folded the linens in a methodical manner. Even with her simple tunic, Theo could see she was indeed curvaceous. Her hair, redder than brown, was pinned up. Strands fell loosely down her back, and due to the perspiration, tendrils clung to her forehead and face. She hummed a simple melody as she worked. Theo guessed she was somewhere between seventeen and eighteen years of age.

Katera looked up and let out a startled cry when she saw Theo standing in the archway. Her heart began pounding at the sight of the soldier. She had seen him standing in the courtyard and had smiled at him. It was only meant as a courtesy, not as an invitation to something more.

"I startled you. Forgive me. I couldn't help but listen to what you were humming. I'm not familiar with the melody, but it is quite soothing." Theo detected her nervousness. He stepped back out of the archway, giving her more space.

"I didn't expect to see anyone standing there. I shouldn't have screamed."

"You are a diligent worker. That impresses me. Your master has given me permission to choose from his slaves those whose services are needed at the fortress. It would please me to have you come to Antonia."

Katera's heart leaped into her throat. There was only one reason the centurion would want her to go to the fortress with him. Even though he had stated his intentions as a request, she knew, as a slave, she did not have a choice. "As you desire."

"Good. Gather your things. We will leave promptly." Theo, pleased that she was willing to go to the fortress with him, turned to leave. "I will wait for you on the front steps."

Katera placed the linens in the basket. She had been in this situation before. When the centurion tired of her, she would be sent back to Herod's palace. A tear trickled down her cheek.

"Katera." At the sound of her name, she turned to face the man to whom she had given her heart. "I heard. I stood in the shadows and heard everything."

"Then you know I must go. Archillius, please, just let me go. You know you have my heart. Isn't that enough?" Katera reached out for Archillius' hand.

He pulled away from her. "No. It's not enough. I want you to be my wife and I your husband. A man's wife does not go to a Roman garrison to sleep with the soldiers there."

His words slapped her. Trying to maintain her composure, Katera turned her back on Archillius. "You are not my husband, and I am not your wife. We are slaves in Herod's household. It is best if you remember that. I will understand if, when I return, you want nothing to do with me."

FAVORED

"Look at me, woman." She stubbornly kept her back turned to him. Forcing her to look at him, Archillius held onto her. "When will you stand up for yourself?"

"And end up in the arena? No. It's best to do as they wish and live another day."

"I don't want to live if it means watching you give yourself to every man who looks upon you. It's time, Katera. Herod leaves in the morning. That goon he has made overseer drinks himself to oblivion every night. If you can stall the centurion one day, we can escape tomorrow night. We'll have a whole night to get as far as we can before our absence is noticed."

Katera looked into Archillius' crystal-clear blue eyes. One strand of his thick brown hair fell over his left eye. He was strong. His strength came from the long hours of hard labor in service to Herod. Archillius' enslavement was a byproduct of battle. His father and brothers had been killed. Many times, he would talk in his sleep about battle and the days shortly after he was captured. Katera shuddered. He wasn't just strong from the work he did; his strength came from deep within his soul.

"Say you'll come, Katera. We can do this. I know we can."

Katera smiled at the handsome face that pleaded with her. "I am not as strong as you. I don't think I can. What if we're caught? It would mean certain death."

"If we're caught, we will face death together. I can be strong for both of us."

Katera shook her head. "My brave man…I cannot do as you ask. Now, let me go so I can leave with the centurion. I'll be back in a few days, and life will resume as before."

Archillius released his hold. "No, Katera. It won't. I won't be here. I am going home. I must try."

She backed away from the only man for whom she had ever had feelings. "The centurion said to hurry."

Archillius nodded. With a heaviness weighing upon him, he turned to go.

"I hope you make it home, Archillius." Katera hurried down the corridor after wishing him well. The conversation with Archillius, though, had taken too long. She wiped tears from her eyes; it did no good to cry. This was the life she had been allotted. She had been sold into slavery by a woman. From the time she was thirteen, she had served in Roman households, both as a servant and a lover. The first time she had tried to fight, but she'd quickly learned that it was best to give in. Two years ago, after her master had tired of her, she was sold to a band of merchants making its way to Palestine. Eventually she ended up in Herod's household. Going to the fortress would be another forgettable event in the life of so many other forgettable events.

Theo had just begun to pace when Katera appeared on the porch. She quickly descended the steps. He watched as she pulled her mantle over her head.

"I'm ready," she said, her voice still a little raspy from crying.

Theo was finally able to see the blueish-green tint of her eyes when she looked up at him.

"Am I the only one going with you?"

"For today." Per protocol, Theo tied her hands and then tied her to his horse. He motioned for his men to begin the march back to Antonia Fortress. Katera took a long look back at Herod's palace. Looking down from the upper balcony was Archillius. Her expression begged him to wait for her. If only he could read her mind.

The streets of Jerusalem buzzed with activity. Without provocation the crowds parted, making way for Theo and his band of soldiers. Theo was anxious to get back to his residence in the palace. At times, he felt sorry for his men and their modest accommodations in the barracks. His pity evaporated wherever his men teased him about the lavish life he was leading for a

FAVORED

centurion. Rome was going all-out to ensure he did his job, paying him handsomely for the inconvenience of dealing with the Jews in Palestine. Indeed, Rome had elevated him to the position of ambassador. Theo was not going to complain. The rooms, baths, and other amenities of the palace made up for any inconvenience.

Theo began to make plans for his evening as they entered the gate into the fortress. He dismounted his horse, handing the reins to the stable boy. As he untied Katera, he sent for Onesimus. "My servant will see to your needs. I want you to feel comfortable. Tonight, you will dine with me."

Onesimus came bounding down the steps. "Master, I'm glad you're home. Wait 'til I show you what I wrote today."

"Onesimus, lad, how was your time with the rabbi?" Theo ruffled the boy's hair. He was keeping his promise to Mary.

"Good! I learned to spell my name in Hebrew and Greek! See?" Onesimus held up a piece of parchment.

"Mighty fine. You're a quick study. Now, see to the needs of my new slave. She needs a hot bath and some new clothes."

"Right away. Come now, girl; we must do as Master requests." Onesimus took Katera's hand and led her into the palace. She was amazed at the camaraderie between Onesimus and his owner, the ambassador. The fact the centurion was having the boy educated was bizarre.

"Onesimus?"

"Yes?"

"How long have you been serving the centurion?"

"A few months now. Theo is a good master. You will like him."

She didn't believe the last statement would apply to her. The boy seemed innocent of the plans his master had for her. Onesimus led her to a bath where hot water had been poured into a marble tub, allowing the water to wash the grime of the Jerusalem streets off of her body. When she stepped out, Onesimus was there with a robe. He presented her with a silver tray. Bottles of perfumes and oils, a comb and mirror, pearls, and fresh flowers rested on the tray. Evidently, the boy did know what his master had planned for her. Katera took the tray and followed Onesimus down a long hallway. He led her to a room decorated in rich, colorful fabrics.

"You can prepare yourself here. This will be your room. I'll come take you to Master when he is ready for you. You are to dine with him tonight. There are new tunics and stolas in the trunk for you to choose from." With that, the boy left Katera alone.

Theo went straight to his office to look over papers and finish the day's business. It was the responsibility of the century at Antonia to see the civility of those visiting the temple. Every now and then, a ruckus would break out inside the temple gates, requiring Theo and his men to break it up.

"Sir, you sent for me?"

"Yes, Stephonos. How are things in our Jewish house of worship?"

"Sir, we have a situation. Apparently, a Gentile, a wealthy man from Ephesus, left the court of the Gentiles. He somehow passed through the Court of Women undetected and entered the Court of Israel before he was apprehended. He claims he did not see the signs warning of death to anyone who is not a Hebrew entering the inner courts. His story seems strange, for when he was caught, he was dressed in Hebrew garments. The Jews want him stoned for defiling the temple.

"Did he say why he entered the forbidden area?"

"Yes. He said he heard of the temple's beauty and wanted to see it up close. He said he was traveling the Roman Empire, visiting all houses of worship."

"Hm, his story does sound strange." Theo pondered the situation. "Where is this man now?"

"We have him in the barracks under guard—more for his own

FAVORED

protection than anything else."

"You say he is a wealthy man?"

"Yes."

"What work does he do?"

"Exports. He owns a fleet of ships."

"I wonder how much he thinks his life is worth."

"I'm afraid I don't see what you mean."

"Where is the high priest?"

"I believe in the temple. The Pharisees and the Sadducees have gathered to discuss the course of action they are going to pursue."

"Send for the high priest and a representative from each faction. Show them into the north court. I'll wait for you there after I speak to our unfortunate prisoner. Be sure that each representative has the authority to act on behalf of the whole."

"Do you think we should interfere? After all, the plaques are posted in plain sight. It is their law." Stephonos knew the man was lying about not seeing the signs warning of death. Stephonos was a poor soldier. As poor as many of the people who called this land home. He didn't feel the Ephesian should be above the law simply because of his wealth.

"Indeed, it is their law. We shall see what happens after I have had the chance to sort through this mess. Go now, bring me those representatives." Theo did not want to have to deal with this mess tonight, but it had to be done. He headed toward the barracks where the man was being kept.

Claudius sat on the bunk, pondering his predicament. The temple was breathtaking. He had climbed the steps leading to the Court of Gentiles. The floral designs around the entrances were colorful and exquisite in detail. He had stood in the middle of the court, marveling at the size. People surrounded him, moving to and fro. He had walked through the porticoes watching the merchants conduct the business of worship. Money changers were on hand to convert coins into shekels. Animals needed for sacrifice were being sold. Claudius watched as people dropped their money in the receptacles representing what type of animal they were purchasing and what type of sacrifice was being paid for. Unlike other temples he had visited, the only thing not for sale was an image of this god the Jew worshiped. That was his main reason for ignoring the signs: he wanted to get a glimpse of this god.

"I see my men have seen to your needs. Were you not hungry?"

"I suppose the thought of dying took away my appetite." Claudius took note of the centurion's casual attire.

"I understand." Theo eyed the man in his custody. Claudius was dressed in a white tunic trimmed in purple. He was neatly groomed, with cropped hair and a clean-shaven face. He exuded wealth. "I'll get right to the point. Why did you enter the courts forbidden to you as a Gentile?"

Claudius did not answer right away. He was aware of the history behind the Jew's god and knew his answer would sound foolish. In a barely audible tone, he replied, "I wanted to see the god of the Hebrews."

Theo broke out in laughter. "Evidently, you have not done your due diligence. The god of the Hebrews is an unseen god."

"I am aware of that fact. I wanted to see their image of this god."

"There is no image. The god of the Hebrews gave his chosen people strict instructions to not make any graven image of any god, including himself. So, you see, you have committed yourself to death for nothing."

Claudius was quiet. "In truth, I've been to several temples in the last few months. As you are aware, we have a grand temple built to honor Artemis in Ephesus. I have been to Athens, during Panathenaia—a grand festival, that is. At least a hundred cows

FAVORED

were sacrificed to Athena. I was in Rome during the festival of Mars. I'm sure you can appreciate that. I guess I am a man searching for the truth. So many gods to worship. I've heard Hebrews worship one god. I wanted to see him for myself…to see if what I am searching for might be here in Jerusalem."

"I wish you had found an answer to your search. Instead, you have brought the wrath of the Jews upon you."

"Is there nothing I can do?"

"How much is your life worth to you?"

"Why do you ask?"

"Suppose I can talk the priest into accepting some sort of sacrificial payment from you to the temple. How much are you willing to pay?"

"Whatever it takes."

"I shall see what I can do."

"But do you think a payment into their coffers will satisfy them?"

"I don't know. I would hate to see one of Rome's opulent citizens be put to death for such a stupid mistake."

"If you can arrange a satisfactory payment for my wrong, I will be forever in your debt."

"I'll return shortly with their decision."

As Theo returned to the north court, he pondered the man's explanation. Long ago, Theo had lost faith in the gods Rome worshiped. He had seen too much blood and death to believe in Mars, the god of war. The other gods simply didn't appeal to him. Listening to Mary and seeing her faith in action had caused Theo to have a deep respect for this god of the Hebrews. However, all their laws and their never-ending need to make absolution for the countless wrongs diminished any interest he might have had in becoming involved in such a strict religious order.

402

Besides, there was no way to know whether those he would meet with were men of a reasonable nature or not. Theo entered the court and was pleased to see that the men he had sent Stephonos for were all present.

"Thank you for all accommodating my request. I have learned that there was some excitement at the temple today."

"The man should be stoned for ignoring the law and defiling our house of worship." The man representing the Pharisees appeared older than the others. From his reply, Theo guessed that reasoning with him might be more difficult than he had hoped.

"Do you all feel this way?" Theo asked.

"It is our law."

"I understand that, and believe me, I will allow you to carry out the sentence of death if we cannot reach another conclusion."

"What other conclusion could there be? He ignored the posting and defiled the Court of Israel." The Sadducee's tone was less condemning than that of his counterpart.

"The man is a Roman citizen and a businessman. He is a man of great wealth. He is willing to pay—into the temple fund, of course—any amount you desire. He knows he did wrong and wants to make amends."

"Do you think our laws can so easily be purchased away?" The old Pharisee raised his gray brow and crossed his arms, emphasizing his disgust with the proposal.

"I apologize. I didn't mean to imply such things. I am only trying to come to a solution that does not involve taking this man's life."

"You mean a Roman life." The high priest's bitter tone further discouraged Theo, causing him to lose his temper.

"Fine. If you want to put the man to death, then go ahead and do so." Theo turned to leave the court, thinking the soft body of Katera was just the remedy he needed to get over these disastrous

FAVORED

negotiations.

"Wait. Did the man say how much he was willing to pay?" The young Sadducee appeared to have more business sense than the other two.

"Ziachus, you cannot be serious."

"Now, Nathanial, what harm can come from hearing the sum the man is offering?"

The old Pharisee shrugged.

Theo turned around to face the Jews again. "Whatever you require is what he is willing to pay."

The one called Nathanial responded for the rest. "We must discuss this. Give us a moment." The four Jews moved to a corner of the room. Theo could hear their murmurings, though he couldn't make out what they were saying.

"We have come to a decision." The high priest stepped out from the huddle to approach Theo. "We cannot allow a Gentile to enter our courts and go unpunished. It is our law." "I will have my men deliver him to you at first light. They will oversee his execution. You know, the only reason he entered your sacred temple was to try to get a glimpse of your god. He thought perhaps the god of the Hebrews might fulfill that which he found missing in his life."

Theo didn't give them a chance to respond. "Stephonos will see you out."

Theo once again traversed the steps that led to the barracks and to his unfortunate guest.

"Claudius, I have returned with their demands."

"Then they have accepted our offer?"

"No. They will come for you in the morning. I suggest you use tonight to send letters to your family and business associates."

Claudius' face went white.

404

"Were you traveling with anyone?"

"Yes, my secretary and a personal slave. Can they be brought to me to help prepare the necessary documents so my family will be provided for?"

"Of course. I'll see that they have a safe passage back to Ephesus."

"You've been most kind. I have a son. Did I mention him? He's a strong lad. Only five. His name is Trophimus. I named him after my brother, who died at a young age. My daughter, Claudia, is ten. A pretty girl. I guess my life has not been a total waste."

Theo didn't respond. He knew the man did not say those things in hopes of a response anyway.

"My search to find the one true god has led me to this."

"They will come for you at first light. I'll make sure you have plenty of wine to sustain your confidence. May the gods go with you."

Theo left Claudius, thankful the day was finally drawing to a close. He quickly bathed and dressed. Once finished, he sent Onesimus to fetch the beautiful slave girl and bring her to his chambers.

When Katera entered Theo's private quarters, she was met with the delicious smell of roasted lamb. Her stomach growled in anticipation. The table was laid with more food than just the two of them could eat. Her mouth watered at the sight.

Theo's mouth watered at the sight of her. Her auburn hair hung in waves down her back, with only portions of it pinned up and laced with flowers. The blue dress she had chosen was fastened at the shoulders with pearl pins and tied in the middle with a white belt. It accentuated the curves of her body. The blue of the dress brought out the lovely blue-green color of her eyes.

Her cheeks were flushed with color. Her lips were pink and full. She took his breath away. Theo couldn't think of anything

FAVORED

better to say than, "The dress is to your liking?"

"More importantly, is it to yours?" The sooner she could satisfy his needs, the sooner she could return to Herod's palace and Archillius. She hoped he would change his mind about running away.

"Yes, very much so. Sit. If you are as hungry as I am, then you must be famished. I'd like to hear all about you, starting with your name."

Katera was taken aback by his kindness. She had purposefully outdone herself in her toilette, hoping he could not resist her. Instead, he had asked her to sit and eat. Even to talk about herself. "My name is Katera."

"That's a lovely name for a lovely woman." Theo tore into the lamb, pulling a juicy piece off for Katera and handing it to her. "How long have you been in Herod's household?"

"Just over a year." Her mind was wandering back to Archillius.

"Do you like it there?"

"I suppose. It is my home." She watched him eat. He was more refined in manners than most of the soldiers with whom she had been with. His curly blond hair was cropped short. His eyes, the color of a cloudless sky, were thoughtful and soft. He had a firm jaw, a long, straight nose, and straight scars on both cheeks. His muscular body appeared strong and flawless.

"My desire is that you make this your home. You'll find that I am an easy master to please."

Katera was startled. "Do you intend to keep me?"

"I've paid handsomely for you, so of course I intend to keep you. You please me." Theo tried to read the expression on her face but to no avail. She had learned early on to hide her deepest thoughts behind a blank gaze. Theo continued, "Tell me about your life before coming to Jerusalem."

"There isn't much to tell. I was told my father died defending

Gallia, the place of my birth. Before my mother was captured, she hid me. The woman who found me took me in until I was old enough to be sold for a profit into slavery. I was shipped to Rome with hundreds of others just like me. I learned quickly how to stay alive. I'm sure this story is not new to you.

"There are thousands more like me."

Theo did not immediately respond to Katera. He knew her story was the same as countless others living throughout the Roman Empire.

"Your story touches me. I will try to make your life with me pleasant and comfortable." He finished his wine before standing and walking around to where Katera was sitting. He extended his hand, which she took, and helped her stand. He lifted her face until she met his gaze.

"I had made plans for our evening together, but I sense you need time and rest. I will not force you to do what you do not want to do. I was drawn to you the first time I saw you. Now I am captivated by your spirit."

Onesimus gently shook Theo awake. "Master, there is a man, a shepherd, waiting to speak with you. He says he's been waiting all night to talk with you. He will only speak to you.

"He comes from Aim Karem."

"Help me dress, Onesimus. Did he give you any indication as to the reason for him coming here to speak with me?"

"He did not say. Do you think this has something to do with Mary?"

"I don't know of anyone else in Aim Karem. It must be about her."

"Are you worried, Master?" Onesimus searched Theo's face. "You are worried. I wish we had heard from her to know that she was doing well."

"Onesimus, you are a bright boy. I, too, wish we had news

FAVORED

from her before now. However, we must not think the worst until I have spoken with the shepherd. See to Katera's needs. Make sure she learns the routine and is taken care of."

"Yes, I will take care of her, just like I did Mary."

"I know you will."

"I miss Mary very much."

"I do too, Onesimus." Theo finished dressing and made his way down the hall to his office.

The shepherd had a speech impediment. Theo patiently had to question the man several times to properly understand him. He was relieved to learn Mary was doing well and had actually sent the message with the shepherd. The shepherd had been instructed to wait for a reply. He was anxious to be on his way because he left his flock in the care of his oldest son, who was still just a boy. While Theo thought over what his course of action would be, he sent the shepherd to the kitchen for a good meal.

"Master?" Katera stood at the entrance of Theo's office.

"Katera, did you rest well?" Theo looked up from the charts he had been contemplating.

"Yes." She blushed. "What would you have me do?"

"I think for today you should acquaint yourself with the household staff. I have an important decision to make that requires me to pore over the events of next week. Onesimus can answer any questions you have." Theo looked back down at the papers in front of him.

"Master?"

"Yes?"

"Be frank with me now, for I'd like to know my place. This Mary I heard mentioned…is she your wife?"

Theo laughed, then stood and went to the girl. "No, Katera, she is not my wife. I am not married. She is just a dear friend."

408

"For whom you have feelings?" Katera's blue eyes bore into him.

"She is betrothed to another."

"That does not answer my question."

"I wasn't aware you asked me a question." Theo's tone was sharper than he wanted it to be.

"I understand my place. I'll leave now." Katera turned to leave, but Theo pulled her back.

"Katera, when I saw you in the courtyard yesterday, I couldn't take my eyes off you. I want you to feel like you are more than just a slave to me."

"Yet I am just your slave."

Theo saw pain in Katera's eyes. The last thing he wanted to do was hurt her. "Several months ago, Mary's family helped me survive a tricky situation. I owe her a lot. I suppose I do have feelings for her, but she doesn't know it, and nothing can come of it."

"I see. Onesimus seems attached to her as well."

"He spent quite a bit of time with her. She is Hebrew like him. It seems everyone who meets Mary adores her. If you knew Mary, you would understand."

"The shepherd brought you good news of her, then?"

"Yes and no. She needs to go back home to Nazareth. She would like me to escort her there. I want to help her, but I don't know if I can. There are many things that need my attention here. To be gone another week…and if things do not turn out for her the way she hopes…it really is nothing you need to concern yourself with. Why don't you explore the palace? Steer clear of the barracks. My men are rough around the edges."

"Do I dine with you again tonight?"

"That would be nice. I'll send Onesimus for you."

FAVORED

Theo watched Katera walk the length of the hall before he resumed his work. However, he had a difficult time concentrating. His mind kept going back to Katera. Not only was he fond of her, but he desperately wanted her to care for him. This was different than how he felt about Mary, for he knew Mary would never have feelings for him other than friendship. He had used other women for his own pleasure, and he thought he would do the same with Katera, but something about her story and the way she looked at him drew him to her.

Even before Onesimus had come to get him, he had lain awake in the early hours of dawn thinking of her. He had to remind himself that she was his slave, and he was her master. Even a few moments ago, when she had called to him, his heart had flip-flopped in his chest at the sound of her voice. Onesimus interrupted his thoughts.

"Master, is Mary all right? Does she need us?"

"She is fine, Onesimus, and yes, it seems she does need us. She is ready to go home to Nazareth and would like us to be her traveling companions."

Onesimus was so happy, he forgot his place and threw his arms around Theo's waist.

"This is grand news! When do we leave? I can have your things ready in a short time."

Katera, standing in the door, giggled at the boy's excitement. To Theo, her laugh was sweet as a lark singing in the early morning.

"Settle down, Onesimus. Mary doesn't need us until eight days from now. Seems her cousin gave birth to a healthy boy, and Mary wants to stay for the circumcision. Besides, I'm not sure we can help her. It is important I stay in Jerusalem until Herod's return. It will take at least a week there—maybe longer—and a week back."

"Not if just you and I go. We can travel by horse. Mary can

ride with one of us. We'd be to Nazareth in no time." Onesimus was not about to miss out on seeing his friend. "Katera could go with us to help." He turned to the red-haired slave. "You will just love Mary. She is the sweetest, kindest person, and she tells great stories."

"So I've heard." Katera winked at Theo.

"I don't think that is a good idea," Theo replied. "It is rough terrain between Jerusalem and Nazareth. The dangers are many. I'm not sure it is safe for you to come."

"Have you forgotten? I've traveled in much worse conditions. Besides, I'd like to meet this Mary. She seems to have stolen at least two men's hearts, and I am told she is betrothed to a third."

Onesimus looked puzzled. "She hasn't stolen anything. Mary would never do such a thing."

Theo and Katera laughed at the boy's misunderstanding. "I'm sorry, Onesimus. I didn't mean to imply that she had; I only meant…"

"No need to explain. Your apology will suffice." Onesimus sounded indignant.

Theo thoughtfully considered the time frame. It had dawned on him why Mary needed to go back to Nazareth soon. She was ready to hear Joseph's decision. Suddenly, there was no doubt in Theo's mind that he must see her safely home. If Joseph intended to divorce her, then Theo would bring her back to stay with him.

"Onesimus, you have persuaded me. We will see Mary safely home. We'll leave early in the morning, eight days from now. We will take two horses and a mule. I'll trust you and Katera to pack the necessary provisions. I think it best we travel undercover, so as not to draw attention to ourselves. Katera, you and Onesimus go to the market and purchase some simple tunics for us to wear. We'll pretend we are a nice Jewish family returning home from our pilgrimage to Jerusalem. Now, bring the shepherd to me so I can send him on his way with my reply."

FAVORED

Onesimus, excited, ran out to do as his master requested. Katera lingered behind.

"What is it, Katera?"

"Nothing. I will get busy doing what you ask."

Theo rose from his chair and crossed to where Katera stood. He pulled her into a tight embrace. "I will miss you."

Katera smiled at him. "Then she really is just a friend to you?"

"I won't lie to you, Katera. I have feelings for her, but somehow, they are different from my growing affection for you. I can't explain it because I don't understand it myself. Hasn't there been someone in your life who you cared about, but it never went beyond that?"

Katera thought about Archillius. Tonight was the night he said he would escape if he was still planning to do so. She thought she loved him, but after being in Theo's arms, she wasn't sure she knew what love was. Still, it could be dangerous for a slave to have feelings for her master.

"You don't have to answer. I can see it in your eyes. We've spent less than a day together, and yet, I am jealous of the man you thought of." Their embrace was interrupted by the shepherd's entrance.

"You sent for me?" The shepherd remained at the arched opening, embarrassed by the scene he had walked in on.

Theo released his hold on Katera. "That will be all." Katera responded with a nod and left the room. He turned his attention to the shepherd. "I expect you to deliver my message promptly when you arrive in Aim Karem."

"I will do it."

"Tell Mary I can do as she requested. There will be two of us at her door in eight days. Make sure she understands the travel will be quick and harsh." Theo gave the shepherd a few sesterces for his trouble and sent him on his way.

412

He had seven days to prepare his men for his absence. He called for Stephonos, who exhibited a natural ability to lead and make good decisions. He explained his plan to be gone, leaving Stephonos in charge and promising a bonus if things were in order when he returned. If all went well, he would send Rome a notice requesting the man be entrusted with his own century. Grateful for Theo's confidence and promising to maintain the highest degree of peace and order, Stephonos returned to his post at the temple gate.

Thinking it best he checked on what happened with Claudius, Theo left his office and descended into the lower part of the palace. He walked through the barracks and down a tunnel that led to the temple. The number of people who visited the temple on a daily basis never ceased to amaze him. Before meeting Mary and her family, Theo would have thought the worshipers were wasting their time and hard-earned money, but Mary's faith was real. Theo found himself pondering the existence of the Hebrew god.

Making his way through the mass of people, Theo found Nathanial in the throng. "Was the sentence carried out?"

"At first light, Ziachus saw fit to take it upon himself to prepare the body for burial. Too much fuss over one Gentile lawbreaker. The Gentile did ask one question before he died." "What was that?" Theo didn't like Nathanial. He was too pious, as were most Pharisees Theo had met.

"He wanted to know if any of us had found fulfillment in our service to God and His laws."

"What was your answer?"

"I don't think there was time to answer. By the way, I threw the first stone." With a smirk on his face, Nathanial walked away.

The day was getting away from Theo. He made his way back to the palace. When he arrived home, he was met by Onesimus and Katera. Onesimus tugged on Theo's arm. "Come, see what

FAVORED

we bought." He dragged Theo into Katera's room. Sprawled out on the bed were two tunics, very plain in color. The tunics had a vertical stripe that ran the length of the gowns. Two yellow mantles lay beside the tunics.

"You both have done well today. Onesimus, why don't you join us for our meal? I'd like very much to hear what the rabbi has taught you. It will be good practice for you to share with us. I am certain Mary will want to hear all about your lessons."

"Didn't I tell you he was a good master?" Onesimus asked Katera. He was smiling brightly.

"Indeed, you did. I'm beginning to see why you think so." She smiled back at the boy.

"I suggest we all get cleaned up..." Theo was interrupted by a voice calling out to him.

"Commander, commander!"

"Yes, I'm in here, Stephonos." Theo stepped out into the hall, only to have the other man run right into him.

"Sir, there is a situation at King Herod's palace." Stephonos was out of breath from running.

"Go on."

"It seems two of the slaves have run off."

Theo looked at Katera, who had gone as white as the gown she wore. "Did anyone say when this happened and which two slaves?"

"Sometime today. Can you believe it? In broad daylight. That either speaks to their courage or stupidity. It was two of the men, Nehuba and Archillius. Evidently, the overseer lost track of the men sometime late in the morning. Should we begin our search in the city or focus on the surrounding hills?"

"Gather a handful of our best men and meet me at the gate. I'll join you shortly. Half will search the city, and the other half the hillsides." Stephonos turned on his heels and left to do what he was ordered to do. "Onesimus, go to the kitchen and let them know I will not be here for our meal. You and Katera can dine together in my absence. I still expect you to share with her all that you have learned from the rabbi."

"Yes, Master." Onesimus left Theo and Katera alone in the room.

"Do you know these men?"

"Yes." She could not look into Theo's face.

"Which direction might they be headed in?"

"I don't know." Tears welled up in Katera's eyes. She tried to wipe them away, but they quietly fell down her cheeks.

"Is there more that you are not telling me?"

"Please don't ask me anything else. I can't…"

Theo reached down, grabbing hold of her arms, and pulled her to her feet. "Look at me when I am talking to you. What are you not telling me?"

"I knew. He wasn't supposed to leave until tonight. I begged him to stay. I thought he might."

Rage began to rise within Theo. "Why didn't you tell me?" He could not keep the anger and betrayal from his voice.

"No. Archillius wanted me to go with him, but I didn't. I couldn't. I came here with you. I thought you would return me to Herod once you tired of me. I thought he would wait for me. I came here as your slave—I didn't know I would feel this way."

"Shut up!" Theo threw her back to the floor. "I could have you killed for not sharing what you know! What you knew would happen!"

Katera flung herself at his feet. Grabbing hold of his legs, she begged him to listen to her. "I thought I loved him, but now, after last night with you…"

"You will address me as your master, for you are my slave."

FAVORED

Theo shook her off of him.

He left her weeping on the floor. He had never known such jealous rage could burn within him. He had seen on her face the feelings she had for the slave named Archillius. *Last night was only a night of pleasure given by a slave to her master. That is all it should be. I was foolish to think there could be more. I'll find her lover, and while she watches, I will crucify him.*

Feeling betrayed, Theo mounted his horse and set out for Jerusalem.

Chapter Thirty-Seven

Five days had passed with no sign of the runaway slaves. Theo was hot, tired, and dirty. He had not had a full night of rest. The dreams that haunted him returned each night with a vengeance. The usual images were replaced by the scene of Katera being dragged from the palace, beaten and bruised, screaming for her life. In a cold sweat, he would wake. Throughout the days, his mind was troubled by his dreams. He was irritable with his men. He pushed them beyond a soldier's standard endurance.

This particular day was no different than the past five. The sun beat down on the men, and Theo's patience was running thin. He had but two more days before Mary would expect to see him at her door. He wanted to find these slaves and make an example of them. He spent the passing hours astride his horse, trying to discern his own motives. Death was a common punishment for a runaway slave. He wasn't attempting to do anything that another commander wouldn't do. Still, he was troubled. The dreams, combined with his feelings, caused him to question his purpose.

He had bought Katera knowing what he wanted from her. He had no intention of having feelings for her. She was to be his slave and serve him willingly. Even if she knew of Archillius' plans, she had not gone along with them. She had maintained her position as a slave and done Theo's bidding. She had even admitted this much.

Theo waited while his men looked through a clump of trees. They were miles from Jerusalem. Theo questioned whether the runaways could have even made it this far. He had men combing the hillsides around Jerusalem since the moment he had heard about the slaves. While he waited, his mind drifted to Katera.

FAVORED

That day in Herod's courtyard, when she'd smiled at him, he knew there was something special about her.

Just then, from out of the trees, a body ran at full speed toward Theo. He darted to Theo's left. Theo kicked his horse, sending the steed on a full gallop after the man.

Theo could hear the sound of his men behind him. The man had nowhere to run, nowhere to hide. On horseback, Theo had no trouble catching up to the slave. As soon as he came alongside the man, he leaped from his horse and tackled him to the ground. Archillius was on his feet first. He turned on Theo and lunged at him. Theo managed to dart to his right, avoiding a head-on collision. Archillius came at him again, but Theo met his advance with a hard right, sending him sprawling. The soldiers pinned Archillius where he lay.

Surging through Theo was a jealous rage. "Let him up. He wants to fight a Roman centurion—then let us not disappoint him. He'll soon learn not to mess with a Roman." The men released Archillius and began to chant support for their commander.

"So, Roman, you want a piece of this slave?" The two men circled each other, each eyeing the other's strengths and trying to find a possible weakness. "You know, I wasn't always a slave. I was a great warrior. I fought brave and true." Archillius pounded his chest, emphasizing the description of himself.

"Then bring the best you have." Theo dodged an attempted punch from Archillius. The men cheered. Theo threw a left hook, which landed across Archillius' right cheek. Once again, he was sent sprawling to the ground. The soldiers helped the slave back to his feet, giving him a shove back into the ring they had formed around the two fighters.

Archillius and Theo knew the truth of why they were fighting. The soldiers cheering them on assumed it was a matter of oppressed versus oppressor. The fighters knew better—they were fighting over something that could send any man to war: a woman.

"You are the man who bought Katera. I saw her leave with you."

Theo understood Archillius' weakness. He couldn't keep his mouth shut and focus on the fight in front of him. He had found that to be the case with most of the men he encountered in battle. Romans were taught to focus on the fight or die. Theo had been trained well. Archillius was physically strong, yes, but it was no match for Theo's training and good sense.

While Archillius tried to bait Theo with words, Theo used the opportunity to move into a better position. In a swift circular fashion, Theo moved behind Archillius. He wrapped his right arm around the slave's throat, attempting to choke the breath from him. Archillius lifted Theo off the ground and tossed him over his head. Theo crashed to the ground while his men grabbed the slave again.

Theo gasped, "Release him. This isn't over yet."

"Brave, aren't you, Roman? You know, she willingly spent several nights with me before she was forced to enter your bed."

The words had their desired effect. Theo charged at the slave, wrapping his arms around Archillius' middle. The two went tumbling to the ground. Landing on his back, Archillius felt the air be knocked out of him. Theo began to pummel the other man's face. The soldiers, afraid Theo would kill him before they had a chance to have their fun, pulled Theo off of Archillius.

"Commander, are you all right?"

"I'm fine. Where is the other slave that was with this one?" Theo asked, pointing at Archillius as he was led away in chains.

"He was caught in the brush. He is chained and awaiting the long walk back to Jerusalem."

"Good. We'll leave as soon as I've had a chance to catch my breath. When we arrive at the fortress, lock the two in the dungeon. We'll need to wait to hear from Herod as to what he wants us to do with them." Theo brushed the dust from his face and body. He reached for his water canister and found some of the breath he had lost while he quenched his thirst. "I want to be back in Jerusalem before nightfall. Move out."

The fight had done nothing to lessen the jealous anger in Theo. He had never been one to dwell on why he felt a certain way. He had been trained to focus his mind and ability to use a sword and fist, not to discern his motives or feelings. However, since meeting Katera, feelings were all he thought about. By the time evening fell, the soldiers, with slaves in tow, entered the gate of the city.

Theo handed the care of his horse over to the stable boy. For the first time, Theo noticed the boy. He was a slave, like all those who worked at the fortress. Rome was built by the mind of her upper class and on the backs of slaves. The boy took the reins, keeping his eyes to the ground. "Sir, you need to let go so I can take care of him properly."

"I apologize. What's your name, boy?"

"Nahshon."

"A strong name. I appreciate the care you give my horse."

"Thank you, sir. May I go now?"

"Yes." Theo watched the lad walk away toward the stable. There was a sadness about him that even Theo's kind words couldn't ease. It was the same look he had seen in Katera's eyes for a moment.

He made his way through the tunnels, past the barracks, and into the palace. Without acknowledging anyone, Theo made his way to his chamber. There, he sat down to think after he closed the door behind himself. He had been with many women. Katera was different. Because he owned her, how could he know if what he felt from her were her true feelings? Archillius was right: she had gone willingly to his bed and perhaps felt forced to go to Theo's. That was the crux of what troubled him the most.

Theo felt more frustrated by the direction his thoughts were going than when he had not dwelt on them. He opened his door and called for Onesimus.

"Yes, Master?"

"See that I have hot water for my bath. Where is Katera?"

"She has not left her room these past six days. I've tried to talk to her, but she tells me to go away."

"I see. Take care of the bath. I'll be there shortly. I'm still planning on seeing Mary to Nazareth. I can't do anything about the slaves until Herod returns. Make the necessary preparations."

"Yes, Master."

"See to my bath now. I am going to talk to Katera." The dark walk down the corridor and to the slave's chambers seemed to take an eternity. His legs felt like iron. He didn't know what he was going to say, but he had to try to set things straight.

He gently knocked on her door. He could have easily forced his way in, but he wasn't going to force her to do anything she didn't want to do. "Katera, it's Theo. I thought you might want to know the status of Archillius and the other slave."

Slowly, the door opened. Even with her swollen eyes and disheveled hair, she looked beautiful. She was still in the same white tunic she had been in six days ago before he left.

"Katera, may I come in? Please. I want to make things right between us."

She opened the door wide enough for Theo to enter. "I don't know what else there is to say between us. I think you made things perfectly clear before you left. I am your slave, and you are my master. I shall not forget my place. I suppose you would like me to prepare myself and come to your bed tonight."

"Stop, Katera. I said things I didn't mean. That's why I'm here. I'm not going to force you to come to my bed. You said you had feelings for me. Whether you do or you don't, I don't know. But I think I do care for you. I guess that's all I have to say." Theo

FAVORED

started to leave, then turned. "One final thing: Archillius is in the jail below the barracks. I'll let the men know you have permission to visit him. I am still planning to leave for Aim Karem in two days." Theo then left, leaving Katera alone and speechless.

Theo sat for some time in the warm bath before making his way to the *frigidarium*. He ate his meal alone and went to bed. He hadn't been asleep long before the recurring nightmare woke him. Yawning, he climbed from his bed and made his way to the most southern tower. It stood taller than the other three towers, giving a clear view for miles around. Theo thought the moon looked especially bright—or was it that lone star that shone brighter than all the others? One the breeze, a melody he had heard before wafted up to him. He looked down in the direction of the sound. There, her silhouette visible in the moonlight, stood Katera. Her auburn hair was blowing freely in the night wind. Her voice was sweet. Thinking she was alone, she sang the tune loudly from her heart.

Theo watched her. His arms ached to hold her. She wasn't Mary. Mary had never been a slave. She was innocent to the harshness of the world, whereas Katera knew all too well how mean the world could be. Mary had her faith and Joseph. She would never understand the feelings Theo had for her. It was Mary's kindness and innocence that had attracted Theo. With Katera, he was attracted to every inch of her—her blue-green eyes and auburn hair, the fullness of her lips, the tilt of her chin, the way her body seemed to fit right into his. It was as if the two of them were made to be together. Most importantly, Theo was attracted to her suffering. Katera understood the pain. She understood being forced to do what no human should be forced to do. He knew she would understand him and his dreams, both good and bad.

Katera turned to go back to her chamber. Afraid she would see him, Theo stepped back into the shadows. He made his way back to his chamber and stretched out on his bed.

She found sleep impossible. Even after her walk around the grounds, Katera could not settle her mind. Archillius lay in the dungeon below, awaiting his sentence. She couldn't bring herself to go see him. Death was certain to be his fate; it was best they get to say their goodbyes.

Theo, along with Archillius, filled her every thought.

Katera went to her basin and splashed water on her face. For six days she had mourned Archillius and her situation. Now it appeared that Theo did have a heart. She had sensed it the night she had spent with him. Yes, she had felt a connection between the two of them, a connection she never truly had with Archillius. Still, she knew nothing about Theo. Then again, she knew nothing about Archillius except that he was a slave like herself. She had chosen to have feelings for Archillius because Katera thought he was the only choice she had. Now, like a shining coin dangling in front of her, Theo seemed to be offering a richer choice. She could not forget that she was his slave, though.

As soon as the first rays of light appeared in the sky, Katera rose from her bed. She took great care in her toilette, dressing in a simple tunic. She braided her auburn hair, rounding it and pinning it up. Curls framed her face, and her cheeks were flushed from fear.

She made her way through the barracks and below to the dungeon. The soldier on guard asked her name, then let her through. He informed her that Archillius, who had ranted and raved all night, was locked in the third cell. He couldn't come to the bars, for they had chained him to the wall to keep him from hurting someone else or himself.

It pained Katera to see Archillius in such a degrading situation. He stood against the stone wall. His arms, chained to the wall, were stretched their full length. His legs were in the same position. An iron collar was fastened to his neck, hindering him from moving his head, and his eyes were closed. The brown curls that continually fell over his eye hung there as if they were

FAVORED

also limp in defeat.

"Archillius." Katera was afraid to speak his name too loudly. There was an aura of death in the dungeon that demanded her quietness and respect.

"Katera. I knew you would come to me." Archillius opened his eyes. Circling his visible eye was a black ring. Dried blood clung to his right cheek and below his swollen nose. "The Roman may own my body, he may own yours, but he can never take away what we share in our hearts."

"Does that bring you comfort, Archillius?" Katera felt a pang of guilt for what she knew to be the truth.

"I suppose it brings satisfaction." At the top of his voice, Archillius hollered, "Did you hear that, Roman? I will always own her. Always!"

"Archillius, you do not own me."

"The moment I took you to my bed, you belonged to me."

"I see. Then you are no better than the men you fight against. I came to say goodbye. I pray your death is swift." Katera turned and walked away.

As she made her way through the tunnel, she could hear Archillius yelling, "I will die brave and true like my father and brothers! Rome will never own me!"

Katera thought to herself, *No, Archillius, they will not own you once you breathe your last, but your anger has owned you for a lifetime. It has been your murderer.*

She made her way back to the palace. Katera searched the library, courts, baths, and every room in the palace looking for Theo. She finally found Onesimus in the kitchen. "Where is Master? Have you seen him this morning?"

"Oh yes. He rose early and went to the temple. Look, the cook is preparing several meals for us to take on our journey."

"They look delicious."

"Now that I think of it, I don't think he's at the temple. He said he was going to the north tower. You will likely find him there."

"Thank you, Onesimus." She gave the young boy a hug before hurrying through the archway and toward the north tower.

Theo enjoyed watching the sun glisten off the rooftops of the city. Jerusalem wasn't Rome, but it was beautiful in its simplicity. He turned his attention toward the Mount of Olives. He could see groups of children circling the numerous rabbis who sat, teaching. Turning in another direction, he watched as the sick entered the area around the Pool of Bethesda, each of them hoping for a miracle cure. He didn't hear the quiet footsteps of Katera coming up the stone steps.

"Master, may I speak with you?" Katera spoke softly. Theo was unsure if he heard her correctly.

"Did you need something, Katera?" Theo turned to the woman. Out of all the beautiful sights his eyes had looked upon that morning, the woman standing before him outshone them all.

"Before you hear it from someone else, I want you to know that I said my goodbyes to Archillius."

Theo saw the pained look in Katera's eyes. "I'm glad you told me." He didn't feel the need to tell her that he already knew about her visit. "Are you all right? I mean, do you feel all right?" Theo didn't know how to put into words what he wanted to ask.

Katera smiled at him. "I will be."

Theo nodded. Together, the two made their way down the stairs and back to the palace.

Chapter Thirty-Eight

Mary double-checked all the food she had prepared for the celebration as she scurried about the kitchen. While Elizabeth nursed their infant son in the privacy of their room, she and Zachariah were sharing the last quiet moment of the day. In a matter of minutes, friends from the village would follow Priest Kadusah to the house for the circumcision. Mary wanted everything to be perfect for her cousins and their friends.

When the soft knock at the door sounded, Mary straightened her mantle, then opened the door to greet the priest and the countless faces smiling back at her. "Come, Zachariah and Elizabeth are expecting you." She quickly stepped to the side as Kadusah entered, followed by the mass of people. Mary found a corner to wriggle into as the tiny house bulged at the seams.

Mary thought she heard her name called over the commotion. People began to part, allowing Mary to see Elizabeth's white hair as it appeared in the frame of the bedroom door.

Then the low buzz of the crowd, whispering her name, reached Mary's ears.

People parted to allow Mary to pass through to the bedroom. "Mary, child, come stand by me. You are family, after all." Elizabeth extended her arms, embracing her young cousin. As soon as Mary and Elizabeth entered the bedroom, the opening closed and friends pressed around the doorframe.

"Now that we have everyone, what say you? Shall we begin?" Priest Kadusah looked to Zachariah, who nodded in approval.

Mary listened as the priest told of how God commanded Abraham to circumcise all males as an outward sign of God's

FAVORED

covenant with Israel. Picking up his knife, he went on to explain that the spilling of the infant's blood consecrates him to God.

Mary watched as Elizabeth unwrapped her infant son. With his arms and legs free, the infant wiggled and cooed happily. The baby's cries of joy became cries of pain as the priest cut the foreskin. In stark contrast to the baby's wails, the crowd, in unison, sent up a cry of rejoicing.

The priest motioned for quiet. He picked up the screaming boy and held him high over his head as he continued his speech, "We rejoice with Zachariah at the birth of his son. This boy will bring joy to the heart of his mother. He will establish Zachariah's seed for generations to come. I present to you Zachariah's son, who from this day forth shall be called Zachariah."

The cry of the crowd momentarily stifled Elizabeth's voice. Mary watched as Elizabeth shook her head and began firmly hollering her dissent. The priest turned to Elizabeth as she announced, "No, no! Zachariah is not the child's name!"

Kadusah lowered the child, and the crowd fell silent. "I'm sorry, Elizabeth. I don't think I heard you correctly. Did you say Zachariah was not to be the child's name?"

"Indeed, that is not the child's name."

"But, Elizabeth, this may be your only son. He should be named after his father."

"No. He is to be named John."

"Elizabeth, there is no John on either yours or Zachariah's side."

"No matter. His name is John." Elizabeth's outspokenness bridled the priest. He was not about to allow a woman, without the confirmation from her husband, to name the child.

Priest Kadusah handed the boy to his mother before turning to the father. Zachariah was smiling as he received congratulations from neighbors and friends.

"Zachariah." The new father looked up from between the faces that surrounded him.

"Zachariah, there seems to be a misunderstanding concerning what the child is to be called.

"Perhaps you could clear this up for us?" Zachariah acknowledged with a tilt of his head that he would be happy to clear things up.

"I proceeded to name the child after you, but your wife claims the child is to be called John."

Zachariah began to shake his head.

"You see, Elizabeth, Zachariah would like the child named after him, as it should be."

Kadusah had a smug look on his face that turned Elizabeth's stomach.

"No, Kadusah. The child's name is John." The house grew completely quiet again as all waited to hear how this would resolve.

A young man standing near Zachariah called out to the priest. "Priest Kadusah, come.

"Zachariah is motioning for a tablet. Come—soon we will hear what the boy's father wishes."

Elizabeth motioned for Mary to come closer to her. "Mary, fetch Zachariah's tablet and pen." Mark quickly left to do her cousin's bidding.

Her whole body shook with the anger she felt toward Kadusah. Elizabeth was visibly upset. *God, forgive me, but I just don't like that man.*

Zachariah and Elizabeth had met Kadusah when they moved to Aim Karem. Both Kadusah and Zachariah had served in the temple together several times. Elizabeth felt that if the lot to light the incense ever fell to Kadusah, he would not come out from the holies alive. Something about the man bothered Elizabeth, but he

FAVORED

and Zachariah were friends. She did, though, truly like Kadusah's wife, Ruth. Ruth had borne eight children, six of which were alive and well, with families of their own. A year ago, something had happened to Ruth. She had lost the ability to move the right side of her body. Even the right side of her face sagged. Kadusah had stopped allowing Ruth to have visitors, even from her closest friend, Elizabeth.

She came back from her thoughts when Mary entered the bedroom with Zachariah's tablet. All in the house seemed to hold their breath as they waited to read what Zachariah wrote.

Elizabeth overheard Kadusah declare this "whole thing a waste of time."

But Elizabeth knew her husband. He would uphold what the angel Gabriel had told him to name the boy. So, in one sense, this was a waste of time. She wasn't the one wasting time—Kadusah was.

Elizabeth nuzzled her infant son. *Soon, my son, the world will know what your papa and I have known since before you were conceived.*

Zachariah took the tablet from Mary, thanking her with a wink of his eye. She stepped aside and watched as his aged hand wrote the name. When he finished, he handed the tablet to Kadusah.

"Zachariah has written his decision on the tablet. Elizabeth, come to the side of your husband as we officially name your son."

Elizabeth obeyed. Zachariah smiled at his wife and patted his son's head. She knew this was his way of telling her she had nothing to fear. He had done as the angel commanded.

"I will read the tablet. It reads, 'His name is John.'" Kadusah looked as if he had swallowed a bee. The whole house was quiet, except for the voice of Zachariah praising God for the birth of a healthy son.

Kadusah dropped the tablet. Elizabeth would have dropped the baby if Zachariah hadn't stood and taken the child from

430

her arms. Most of the folks in the house stood in fear at being eyewitness to such a miracle. Not only had God given this couple, past childbearing age, a son, but God had returned Zachariah's voice. Many began to whisper that God's hand must certainly be with the child. Others questioned who the child would grow up to be.

Mary stood back, watching and listening to Zachariah, who was filled with the Spirit. As he prophesied over his son, he cradled the child in his arms. Also, hearing his words, the child within Mary did flip-flops.

Beaming with joy, Elizabeth went to Mary and clasped the girl's smooth hands in her wrinkled ones. "God is good to us. Just as the angel said, Zachariah would speak when all was accomplished. Oh, Mary, we are so blessed." Elizabeth's face appeared youthful.

Mary hugged her cousin. "We definitely have much to be thankful for and to celebrate.

"Shall I begin to serve the wine?"

"Yes, by all means. Since Zachariah is caring for John, I can help you." Elizabeth tucked Mary's arm in hers, and together the two inched their way through the crowd.

Once the wine and food began to flow, the hypnotic effect the miracle had over the crowd dissipated. Zachariah laid his sleeping son in the cradle that sat next to their bed. He mingled his way through the crowd, talking and laughing with his neighbors.

The weariness of the day was kept at bay by the joy Elizabeth felt. It wasn't until baby John began to cry that she took the time to rest. Sitting on the bed, she held her son in her arms, allowing him to suckle.

The last of the neighbors eventually left the house. Mary hurriedly cleaned up the aftermath of the celebration. Theo would arrive in the morning, and they would begin their journey back to Nazareth. She had not told Zachariah and Elizabeth of her plan

FAVORED

because she did not want any dark cloud to diminish the joy of their son's circumcision.

When Mary finished cleaning up, she knocked on the bedroom door.

"Come in."

Mary laughed with happiness at the sight of Elizabeth and Zachariah playing with John.

"I have news you might want to hear. I'm taking your advice and leaving in the morning for Nazareth. A friend is seeing me safely there. I didn't want to say anything before the circumcision."

Zachariah went to his young relative. "You are making a wise decision. Joseph will do the right thing. Trust God. I can testify that unbelief will cripple you. We are glad to hear of your decision, but you will be missed. Now, who is this friend?"

"He is a Roman soldier." Mary saw the concern on her relatives' faces. She quickly explained who Theo was in an attempt to alleviate some concern.

Elizabeth looked up from tickling her son's toes. "I don't think it's wise for you to travel with a man alone."

"We won't be alone. Onesimus will be with us. You would just love the boy. He is a slave to Theo, about ten or so. He is a Hebrew, and we had wonderful conversations concerning our heritage from God. He is a bright boy. Theo promised me he would see to the boy's education. I am anxious to see what all Onesimus has learned."

"It sounds as if all the arrangements have been made." Zachariah peered into Mary's dark brown eyes. "We trust your discernment concerning the Roman. We will pray for your safety as you travel. When you arrive home, give our blessing to your mother."

"I will. Thank you for all you've done for me these past few months. I can never repay your hospitality." Tears formed in

432

Mary's eyes.

Elizabeth joined her husband beside Mary. "No need. God sent you to us, and now God will see you home. I will pack enough provisions for you and your companions."

"That is not necessary. Theo sent word with the shepherd that he is providing all we need for our trip. We will be traveling by horseback. I should be in Nazareth in a matter of days."

"Do not fear, Mary." Elizabeth gave her cousin a reassuring hug.

"I'll remember. Theo said he will be here early in the morning. So I'd best get some rest. I think it has been a long day for all of us."

"Goodnight, cousin. We will say our goodbyes in the morning." The three hugged before Mary excused herself to go to her room.

Elizabeth and Zachariah joined their infant son on the bed. They marveled at the miracle. Neither parent knew the details of what God had in store for their boy, but they knew he had been born ahead of the Messiah in Mary's womb in order to prepare the way for the Lord. With Zachariah's tallis covering his head, the two prayed that they would do everything within their power to train their babe for his calling.

The two parents ended their day as it had begun—sitting together in the privacy of their room, with their son, John, happily nuzzling his mother's breast.

Chapter Thirty-Nine

Mary lay in the quiet dawn. It was hard for her to conceive that in a matter of days she would see her mother and Joseph. She wasn't as afraid as she'd thought she would be. Instead, she was filled with peace and excitement. God had used her visit with her cousin to teach her many things. Some lessons were practical in nature—especially childbirth and caring for an infant. Others were more like gems whose purpose was unclear, yet stored in a safe place where they could easily be treasured later.

She sighed with contentment as she nestled under her blanket. God had indeed looked upon her with favor. The child within Mary moved, and she placed her hand over her womb.

Soon, my son will be home.

Mary slipped from her bed and washed herself before dressing. She realized it might be the last time she would have the chance to do so for several days. She grimaced at the thought of the dust that would cake itself to her body. Mary didn't want Joseph to see her until after she had prepared herself, and for the first time that morning, an anxious butterfly flitted around in her stomach. *Now, we'll have none of that*, she thought to herself. *I will not fear, no matter how I may look when Joseph sees me. But, God, please let him see me at my best.*

Basket in hand, she descended the stairs and found Elizabeth already in the kitchen. "I know you said this friend of yours would take care of your needs, but I just couldn't let you leave without making sure you had enough provisions."

"Dear cousin, thank you for your hospitality and generosity. Where are Zachariah and John?"

FAVORED

"Zachariah couldn't wait to take John out to show him the sights and sounds of our village. I suspect they will be home shortly. Zachariah wouldn't miss seeing you off. Help me tie these bundles closed."

Mary did her cousin's bidding. Elizabeth had been generous with the provisions she prepared. She had even prepared three jars, filled to the brim, with wine. "Since you will be traveling by horseback, I thought the jars could be tied to the beast. I…" Elizabeth faltered. "I have something else, something just for you. Come." Mary followed Elizabeth into the bedroom.

"I've been working on this since you first arrived."

Elizabeth went to a wood chest that sat along the far wall of the bedroom. Mary noted how crowded with furniture the room had become since John's birth. Mary ran her hands along the cradle John slept in, and, briefly, doubt rose in the pit of her stomach.

"I hope you like it." Elizabeth was holding a beautiful linen tunic dyed a rich brown. The sleeves, hem, and collar were trimmed in red. "I wanted you to have something special for when you meet Joseph again." She laid the tunic on the bed and reached back into the chest, pulling out a mantle dyed red to match the trim of the tunic. "I thought the colors would bring out the deep brown of your eyes and the black of your hair."

"Elizabeth, I don't know what to say. I don't think I've ever had anything so beautiful." Mary rubbed the soft cloth between her fingers.

"Then you like it?"

"I love it. Thank you." Mary hugged her cousin.

"I said I wasn't going to cry." Elizabeth pulled away from the embrace. She used her mantle to wipe her tears. "We'd best wrap these up tight so they stay clean while you travel." Elizabeth grabbed some swaths of cloth to wrap the tunic and mantle in. "I'll trust you'll know the right time to wear these."

"When I wear them, I will think of you and the time we shared here."

"Mary, Elizabeth, we have visitors. I think it is the man you are expecting, Mary."

Zachariah's deep voice boomed through the house.

Elizabeth hurried from the room to greet her husband. "Where is he? Is the boy with him?"

Zachariah handed John to his wife. "Yes." Elizabeth placed a loving kiss on her husband's cheek as she took the baby from him.

"Zachariah, did you say Theo was here?" Mary hurried from the room and flung the front door open before he could answer.

"Mary!" Onesimus ran to Mary and threw his arms around her.

Mary returned the boy's hug. "Onesimus, how I've missed you." She looked up to see Theo grinning widely at her. "Theo, I can't believe you are really here. When we said our goodbyes, I never thought I'd see you again." Onesimus released Mary. Unashamed, she threw her arms around Theo's neck.

"Mary, I've missed you. Now, stand back and let me get a good look at you. I see your family has taken excellent care of you."

Mary blushed. "Come in, both of you, and let me introduce you to my family." Mary took Theo's hand in her and led him and Onesimus into the house.

"Zachariah, Elizabeth, this is Theo and Onesimus." Mary thought she would burst with joy at seeing her friends and being able to introduce them to her cousins.

"It is a pleasure to make your acquaintance." Theo bowed to the Hebrew couple.

"My, a Roman bowing to a Hebrew! Wait until the town hears about this."

FAVORED

"Now, Elizabeth, there will be no mentioning of this to anyone. We must consider Mary."

"Of course, Husband." Elizabeth cradled John, rocking him gently in her arms. "It seems nothing will settle this little one down except sustenance. Mary, I must go feed John. My prayers go with you as you return home. Don't forget the bundles I've prepared for your trip."

"I won't." Mary kissed her cousin, then gently kissed the cheek of the tiny infant.

"We'd best be on our way. I'd like to make it a good distance down the road before nightfall."

"Of course. I'll help you tie the bundles and jars to the mule you brought." Zachariah began to pick up the bundles of food.

"Theo, tell me about the garments you are wearing," Mary said curiously. "I don't think I've ever seen you in anything other than your uniform."

Theo picked up the jars of wine and followed Zachariah outside to where the two horses and a mule waited. "I thought it would be best to travel undercover. I'm sure we'll come across other travelers along the way. They'll be more accepting of fellow Hebrews than of a Roman, and there is safety in numbers."

Theo and Zachariah tied the provisions to the mule. "I think you were smart in your planning. It seems your mule is packed and overflowing. My wife could not allow Mary to leave without taking food for you all. You won't be hungry."

"We'll have plenty to share. Mary and I will ride my steed. Onesimus, it is time to mount up. Come, Mary. I'll help you."

Mary did as instructed. Before mounting his own horse, Theo helped Onesimus climb onto the back of the gelding. "We'd best be off."

Zachariah reached up and took Mary's hand. "Remember God is with you. Do not fear."

"I'll remember."

With a tug of the reigns, the small band of travelers began the first of many days of travel. They had ridden some time before Theo broke the silence, "Mary, what do you know about women?" He wanted to discuss his desire to have a relationship with Katera. He just didn't know where to start the conversation. There was no concern about Mary being judgmental, but he was worried about embarrassing himself when explaining the full situation.

Mary laughed. "You may not have noticed, but I am one, so I think I might know something. Why?"

"It's a slave girl I've purchased." Trying to formulate his thoughts, Theo fell silent.

Gently, Mary replied, "Tell me about her."

She listened as Theo described how he had seen Katera in the courtyard at Herod's palace. "Her hair is a rich red. When you look into her eyes, they appear blue one minute and then green the next. She sings like a bird, with a tone that pierces the heart."

He told Mary about Archillius and about Katera's feelings for him. He wanted to tell Mary about the night he and Katera spent together but couldn't bring himself to do it. Instead, he mentioned the previous night, standing on the north tower, watching Katera below, and how it stirred emotions in him.

"She is your slave? You bought her for yourself?"

Embarrassed by what Mary would ascertain from his response, he softly replied, "Yes."

Mary fell silent, deep in thought. Finally, she asked, "Theo, what is it you want from me? What help can I give you?"

"I don't know. I know my situation is complicated. Perhaps I shouldn't have purchased her, but I wanted her for my own. Perhaps the power given to me is going to my head." He chuckled. "One minute she is accepting my affection; the next she ignores me."

FAVORED

"She cares for this Archillius, the one you arrested?"

"Yes, I guess. She appears to. They were slaves together in Herod's household." Theo didn't like to think about how close the two might really be.

"This Archillius will be put to death for what he has done?"

"There is no doubt." Theo felt pleasure rising within him at the thought of the man's death. Then he thought about the Roman who had broken Hebrew law. Theo had tried to bypass the law to save him. The gratification he found in Archillius' death subsided at the double standard he realized he had harbored. *What kind of leader am I? Could I truly help restore goodwill to this region?*

"Theo, have you heard a word I said?" Mary poked his arm to get his attention.

"No, I'm sorry. I got caught up in my own thoughts. What did you say?"

"Give her time. Allow her time to get used to you and your household. She will need time to forget this other man and move on. Be kind and attentive. She might come around."

"Perhaps you are right." But Theo wanted more than for her to come around. "We'll stop soon to eat and rest before continuing."

They rode for a while longer before Theo spotted a shaded spot to stop. Other travelers had already positioned themselves to the right of the trees. Mary laid a blanket on the ground. Theo untied one of the bundles Elizabeth had packed while Onesimus poured wine into the four cups.

"Onesimus and I want to hear all about your visit with Zachariah and Elizabeth. When you mentioned your cousin giving birth and the circumcision, I expected to meet a much younger husband and wife." Onesimus joined Theo and Mary on the blanket. "God blessed Zachariah and Elizabeth in their old age with a son."

"You're saying your god did this?" Onesimus asked.

"Yes. While Zachariah was working in the temple, God told him Elizabeth would give birth to a son." Mary went on to explain, in great detail, the whole story.

Theo, feeling uncomfortable with the direction of the conversation, stood and stretched.

"We need to get going," he announced before briskly walking away.

"Let's pack up so we're ready when he returns. Do you think Master is mad?"

"No, Onesimus, not mad, just..." Mary searched for the right word. "Frustrated."

When Theo returned, he found Mary holding the reins of the gelding, standing in the middle of a group of children. She was laughing as the children timidly reached up to pet the horse.

"This family is on their way to settle in Bethsaida. This strapping young lad is Samuel; his sister, Naomi, and this little guy is Phillip."

"I want to ride the pony. Please let me ride the pony." Phillip pulled on Mary's tunic.

"I told you, Phillip; you must ask that man over there. It is his pony you want to ride." Mary watched as the toddler made his way to Theo.

Theo, pretending to be a horse, came galloping up behind them, with Phillip riding atop his shoulders. The little boy's squeals of delight echoed through the surrounding hills. "It seems this little fellow would like a ride. I think I'd like to oblige his request."

Before Mary, Onesimus, and Theo could be on their way, Theo had given all three children rides atop the gelding. Theo spoke to the children's father to see if the two bands of travelers could sojourn together. However, the family was moving at a much slower pace than them. Without any more delays, the three

FAVORED

mounted up and were on their way again.

"Theo, how many days will it take for us to get to Nazareth?"

"Just a couple. Anxious to be home?"

"I'm looking forward to seeing my mother."

"You've not said much about Joseph. Aren't you even the slightest bit afraid of what his decision will be?"

"I'm not afraid. God chose Joseph to be my husband. Father told me as much before he died. Joseph will do the right thing. Besides, my trust cannot rest in men."

"Just so you know, I intend on sticking around until I know for sure you will be safe with him. You know I like Joseph. He's a good man. I hope things work out the way you want them to."

Mary patted Theo's shoulder. "I know you are skeptical about the workings of God, but even you have to admit that what happened to Elizabeth and Zachariah was miraculous."

"There have been older couples in Rome that have given birth—granted, not quite the ages of your relatives. And the mute incident is an interesting twist but one in which there's probably a logical explanation."

"You just won't admit it, will you?"

"Admit what?"

"That you've been thinking about God and His existence. Seeing firsthand the miracle that has happened to Zachariah and Elizabeth only intensifies your uncertainties, and that frustrates you. You're used to controlling things in your life. It intimidates you to think that there is one God controlling things."

"That's enough! I wonder if Joseph knows what he's getting into."

"I think he has some idea." Mary thought back to the conversations she'd had with Joseph the day her father died. After an uncomfortable pause, she said, "I'm sorry, Theo. I said more than I should have."

"Your religion intrigues me. I'll admit to that and only that. Why don't we cease our discussion and save our energy for the next few hours of traveling we have left today?"

Mary chastised herself for her lack of sensitivity and Theo's withdrawal from the conversation. He would be all right in a couple of hours, but Mary was fully aware that she would not be able to be as forthcoming about God as she had been. She was thankful that with each step she was drawing closer to Nazareth.

Chapter Forty

Wrapped in a wool blanket, with the sun's rays shining brilliant beams of warmth upon her, Dalena was still chilled to the bone. Lucas had carried her to the balcony so she could watch the waves lap the shore. It was the first day she had been out in weeks. Dianthea had argued with Lucas about taking her out in the wind. She didn't feel Dalena was strong enough. Lucas had said she needed the warmth of the sun to help with her healing. The breeze that tugged at her hair, the sun on her face, and the salty smell of the sea rejuvenated her. Despite the chill, she felt that Lucas, indeed, knew exactly what she needed.

They had not talked about what happened. It appeared the day would remain stored in their memories but unmentioned. She had overheard Lucas and Dianthea whispering in the hall outside her door a few nights ago. From the tone of their voices, they had been arguing. She had questioned Lucas about it, but he had assured her all was well.

"Dianthea thinks you have sat out here long enough. She may be right. I'd best carry you back inside to your bed." Lucas knelt beside her chair.

"Isn't it beautiful?" In Dalena's weakened state, her voice was barely audible.

"Yes, but your beauty outshines even the most beautiful sea."

"I know you are just being kind. I am glad of it." Dalena touched the side of Lucas' cheek with the palm of her hand. "You, however, are handsome as ever."

Lucas took her hand and gently kissed it. He looked into her sunken green eyes.

FAVORED

Pronounced cheekbones, waxen lips, and a pale complexion gave Dalena a ghostly appearance. He had spent countless hours by her bedside, praying to any god who would listen, begging that her life be spared. Her appearance didn't matter to him; all that was important was that she would live. In time, she would regain her youthful beauty.

"Do carry me in now. I'm cold and need a warm bath." Dalena's words reminded Lucas that she still had much healing left. He gently picked her up in his arms and carried her back inside.

Dianthea had used the time Dalena spent on the balcony to lay fresh linens on her bed and to scatter lily petals for scent. Dianthea, too, had prayed to the gods for Dalena's life to be spared. She felt responsible for what had happened to her mistress. She vowed to serve Dalena even unto death if the gods allowed her to live. Her sacrifice of service enabled the gods to answer her prayers, or so she thought. She would not go back on her vow. Each day she was determined to make Dalena feel comfortable and beautiful.

"Dianthea has been dear to see my needs. I don't know how I shall repay her."

"She is your slave. You do not need to repay her anything. She is doing what is required."

Lucas did not hide his bitterness.

"You must not blame Dianthea. She only did what I told her to do."

"We are not going to talk about this now. You've had much activity today and are weak."

Lucas helped settle Dalena under the covers.

"Lucas, we need to talk about it. You need to know." Dalena's eyelids grew heavy as she fell against the cushions on the bed.

"Sleep for now. I'll come back after you have rested." He kissed her forehead, then left the room, only to run into Dianthea

446

outside of Dalena's door.

"You were listening."

"No, I mean, yes. I heard. Lucas, we must talk about all that happened. You are angry with me. I understand your anger, but I want to earn your trust. You need to know all that happened."

"There is nothing else you need to tell me. I understand you did what your mistress asked of you, but you were foolish. Your stupidity almost cost her life. Though she lives, she will never be able to have a child of her own. How do I tell her that? I won't. I can't. She must never know." Lucas pushed past Dianthea.

"Dalena senses the quarrel between the two of us. She cannot recover completely until she feels all is well between the people she loves. She loves us both." Dianthea saw the pain in Lucas' eyes. She sensed his resolved weakening. "It's been over a month. Isn't it time we discussed that terrible day? Isn't it time you knew the whole of it?"

"I blame you, Dianthea, for what happened to her. There is nothing you can say that will change my mind. I have spared your life because she loves you." Lucas turned from her and proceeded down the hall.

"Lucas, I blame myself. There is nothing you can say to me, no words so vile, no condemnation that I have not said to myself. I have no excuse. But please, hear me out. Hear my confession."

"Why? So you can seek absolution? Perhaps, by confessing, you think you can live with yourself? No, Dianthea, I won't let you find peace. I know you love Dalena. I know you thought you were doing what was right. I wish I could easily forgive, but I cannot. I appreciate all you did for her and me the past few weeks, but don't expect me to show you grace. I cannot. Only the gods can do that."

Lucas left the slave standing alone in the hall. He knew Dalena would sleep for some time. He had penned a letter to Caesar, who was a longtime friend. If Caesar agreed, Dalena would soon be

FAVORED

free of her marriage to Quirinius. Lucas sent the stable boy for his horse. He would ride into town, send the letter to Rome, and check on his men.

Dianthea, feeling rejected and alone, felt there was no god that would show her grace. Perhaps she deserved none. She silently slipped into Dalena's room and watched her mistress peacefully sleeping. *I would give my life for her, Lucas; you must know that.* Still, she knew Lucas would never listen to reason. He had changed since the incident that had almost cost Dalena her life. As Dianthea did every afternoon, she would wait beside Dalena's bed until she woke. She would never be able to speak to her sister again. If Lucas ever discovered her sister's identity, he would surely kill her as he had killed the man hired to "help" Dalena. Lucas had never told her he had killed the man, but she had seen the look in his eyes that night.

Dianthea busied herself sewing a lovely gown made from linen dyed green to match Dalena's eyes. Soon, Dalena would be back to her old self and would appreciate something new to wear. As she stitched the hours away, she went back through the memory of that dreadful day. *I was careful. I went to someone I trust. The man said he had been successful at such a procedure. I did all I knew to do.* Dianthea looked over at her mistress. Dalena was stubborn and, like most women of her social standing, spoiled. Dianthea couldn't fault her for either quality, for she, too, had once worn her wealth proudly. She hoped Dalena would never know what it was like to be without.

"Dianthea."

"I'm here, Dalena."

"I'm thirsty."

Dianthea lifted a cup filled with cool water to Dalena's lips. "Don't drink too quickly."

"Would you like something to eat?"

"No, I want to talk with you. Is Lucas still away?"

448

"Yes. He usually arrives close to the evening, in time to sit with you before you retire for the night."

"He won't say what is going on between the two of you. I know something is. He won't even talk about that day. I know he blames you, but that is because he won't blame me. I don't blame you, though. You did what I told you to do." Dalena reached her hand out. Dianthea took it in hers. The two held onto each other. "He'll come around. As soon as I am strong enough, I'll make him see. Just promise you won't leave."

"Dalena, I belong to you. I can't leave."

"I suppose that's true. But you want to be here, don't you, Dianthea?"

Dianthea lowered her gaze. She thought about the life she had led before the debts her father incurred, the life she'd led before he took his life. "I cannot think of another place I'd rather be." She patted Dalena's hand. "Don't concern yourself with what is going on between Lucas and I. That, too, will resolve itself in time."

"Lucas is a stubborn man. He cares about you very much." Dalena giggled girlishly.

"It is good to hear you laugh."

"I think he loves me. You know, he was sent to look after me. To make sure I behaved myself. I, well, you see, I enjoy the attention men give me. It is sustenance to me. I don't know why. But I played a little close to the flame, and I was burned. Quirinius was awfully mad—I think because I willingly went to someone for those affections he has to force me to give him. Now, the one man in whom my husband put his confidence to see that I remain chaste has fallen in love with me. It is ironic, don't you think?"

"I suppose. Do you feel the same?"

"I think so. I don't know. At first, it was just a game, like it always is with me. I know I have feelings for Lucas. He is like no man I've known. There is something strange about a man who would give up a life of luxury to go back into service to Rome. I think it is the mystery he has cloaked himself in that attracts me."

"Be careful, Dalena. I've seen a look in his eyes that I do not trust. A dark, angry look."

"You're just saying that because the two of you are not getting along. He's been nothing but kind to me. I think he arranged this villa. He hasn't come clean about it yet, but I'll get the truth from him eventually. Quirinius would never have been so thoughtful. Lucas bought you, didn't he? He knew I couldn't stand that girl Quirinius had bought to be my maid. He only brought Saphra along for himself."

"You're upsetting yourself. I think it best we end our discussion. You need to be rested before Lucas returns."

"Don't be afraid of him, Dianthea. He is a strong man, but knowing what I know about his deceased wife, he loves deeply. You'll see. In time, all will be forgiven." Dalena squeezed her maid's hand in hopes it would reassure her.

Though she had her doubts, Dianthea smiled at her mistress. Before settling back into her chair, she repositioned the coverlet over Dalena. It wasn't long before she was fast asleep and Dianthea was back to stitching the trim of the linen stola.

Lucas read and reread the letter from Quirinius. There was no disputing his request, or rather, demand. There would be no way of explaining Dalena's health without making him aware of her pregnancy. Lucas' plan was crumbling. The need to inflict bodily harm on someone, anyone, rose like a bile in his throat.

Since childhood, Lucas' need for violence had come when things in his life spun out of his control. It had a calming effect, like a sedative, for him. That was why he had joined the army— he could kill with permission.

His father, part of the equestrian class, had built an empire in hopes that his son would become part of the Roman senate. Instead, Lucas had lowered himself to the status of a foot soldier.

While stationed in Rome, he had met Minerva, fallen in love, and married her. For a time, he'd thought his attraction for violence had been satisfied while serving in the army. He and Minerva had led a quiet, peaceful life. Then, after her death, the old feelings had resurfaced. That was when he'd made a secret visit to Caesar. Octavian had been a childhood friend. The two had discussed the best way Lucas could serve his country. They had decided that certain individuals who disagreed with Caesar's plans for government could secretly be done away with. Many committed suicides, or so people assumed. Some just disappeared.

Holding the parchment in his trembling hand, Lucas knew what it would take to ease his anxiety. He made his way through the streets of Salamis. He paid an elderly man for the use of his cloak. Disguising himself as just another Cyprus resident, Lucas entered the undesirable part of town. He wound his way through the streets, past pubs and brothels. The stench took his breath away. He finally found the building he was looking for.

He walked up to the man in charge of the prostitutes. "I am looking for a certain woman." "Aren't we all?" the man answered. The men mingling around laughed. "No woman is free. No matter the reason, your visit will cost you."

Lucas gave the man his asking price to be with the girl he was looking for. He proceeded to the stalls and passed the first two. He paused only for a moment. What he was about to do would cause Dianthea great pain, consequently for hurting Dalena, but the need to regain control was greater than his concern for the two women.

He entered the stall. Some would have considered Lilliana a beauty, but the situation she had been sold into made her ugly to him.

"What will it be?" Her tone was seductive. She looked intently into his face. Lucas knew she recognized him, though she couldn't place how. She stood, allowing her robe to fall into the straw. "Have you been with me before? I think I know you from somewhere."

"No. This is my first time I've sought out your services, but you've been highly recommended."

He had not been with a woman since his wife, and seeing Lilliana's shapely form aroused him. The vow of chastity he had made had been more to keep his conscience clear. Now he second-guessed that vow. *Would it hurt to use a service I already paid for?* Lucas decided he should simply do what he had come to do and then head back to the villa. Dalena would be awake and expecting him to be there.

"Turn around while I disrobe," he commanded.

"Suit yourself." Lilliana complied. As she sat down herself, she realized who he was. "I remember how I know you. How is Dianthea?"

Before she received her answer, she fell to the ground, dead. Lucas wiped his knife clean on the cloak he had used to hide his identity. She hadn't even screamed. She'd had no idea what was happening. Dianthea could rest easy, knowing her sister had died quickly and with little to no pain. Lucas peered over the top of the stall door. No one was around. He sneaked out the back, made his way to where he had secured his horse, and rode back to the villa. His nerves were calm. His logical mind and sense of control returned to him.

When he arrived back at the villa, the stable boy was waiting for him. "Nice ride into town?"

"Yes. The weather is pleasant, and my visit with the men under my charge was productive."

"I'll see that your horse gets a good rubdown and the best grain."

"Good boy." Lucas bounded the steps, past the columns, to enter the quiet solitude of the villa. He recalled how the boy's father had taken care of Lucas' father's horse and his own pony. It was nice to know some things would never change.

He entered Dalena's room quietly, in case she was still resting. Dianthea sat next to Dalena's bed. Looking at the back of her head, he realized how closely she looked like her sister from behind. He pushed the thought from his mind.

"Is she still resting?"

"Yes, she woke up early in the afternoon. We had a nice visit before she dozed back off. I think she is getting her strength back. Before long, she'll be back to her old self." Dianthea put away the stola she was working on. She didn't want Lucas to think she was trying to win back her mistress' affection with the gift.

"Come out into the hall. I need to speak with you concerning an important matter." Dianthea followed Lucas into the hallway nervously.

"There was a letter from Quirinius waiting for me at the station. Rome has sent Quirinius to Jerusalem. He is to go from there to Damascus, then on to Antioch. It has to do with the census Augustus has ordered. Quirinius plans to meet with Herod and stay for several weeks as his guest. He wants Dalena to join him."

"But she is too weak to travel."

"Don't you think I know that?" Lucas snapped. "I've thought over all our possibilities. I can delay our travel to Jerusalem for a month, but no more. We must somehow get her well again by then. We can explain away her thinness and pallor through sailing. It made her sick before."

"That is not what concerns me. Travel, even a month or two away, could kill her. You must send word that she is unable to go."

"I can't do that. He'll want to know why. He likes to have her on his arm when he is in the presence of nobility."

"He'll take one look at her and know she is not well, and he'll want to know why. What does it matter whether we tell him now and possibly save her life or tell him after she's died?"

FAVORED

"We wouldn't be responsible for her death. You would be solely responsible." Lucas' eyes became dark and angry.

"I thought you cared for her."

With one hand, Lucas reached out and grabbed Dianthea around her throat. He pinned her against the wall. "Don't ever question my feelings for Dalena. I should have killed you instead of…" He caught himself before he said anything else.

Choking, Dianthea tried to question him. "Who…? Who did you…?"

"You'll find out soon enough. Now, do whatever it takes to speed up Dalena's healing. If Quirinius finds out all that has happened since his departure, he will torture her in unspeakable ways."

"What's going on?" Dalena, unsteadily stood, holding onto the wall. Lucas immediately released Dianthea. Coughing, she fell to her knees.

"Dianthea, are you all right?" Lucas knelt beside her. "You scared me when you grabbed my hand and placed it on your throat. I thought you might be trying to tell me you were choking."

Dianthea could see the evil in Lucas' false concern. She understood the message: if Dianthea spoke the truth to Dalena, he would kill her.

"Lucas, is she going to be all right?" Dalena attempted to get closer to the pair, but she was too weak to walk to them.

"I think she will be fine. You are fine, aren't you, Dianthea?" Dianthea nodded. "Dalena, it is not good for you to be up. Let me help you to your room." Lucas left Dianthea and went to Dalena's side.

"I'm fine. See to Dianthea. Help her to my bedchamber. She needs your help more than I." Dalena allowed the wall to support her body.

Lucas did as Dalena requested. He helped Dianthea to her

feet and into the chair next to Dalena's bed. She trembled as Lucas took hold of her, feeling as if Lucas had smashed her throat with his bare hand. Dianthea didn't understand this side of him. He was loving and kind to Dalena; she couldn't fathom him ever laying a hand on her mistress. After all, Lucas despised how Quirinius abused Dalena. After helping Dalena back into her bed, Lucas poured three cups of wine.

"Dalena, I received an important letter today."

"Is that what you two were discussing?"

"Yes."

"So your conversation did not concern my accident?"

"Not entirely. The letter was from Quirinius."

"Oh." Fear immediately clouded Dalena's pale complexion.

"He has been sent to Jerusalem on important business from Caesar. He is to meet with Herod and then go to Damascus and Antioch. He wants you to join him in Jerusalem. You know why. He enjoys parading you around at parties. You are quite impressive."

"But I can't go. How will we explain my condition? Oh, Lucas, what are we to do?"

"Before you panic, hear me out. Dianthea believes she can safely speed up your healing. I think I can delay our departure for a month. You won't be at your full strength, but we can make excuses for you when you can't attend a party, and we'll make sure you attend only the most important ones. Together, the three of us will make it work, and Quirinius will not be the wiser. Besides, by then your divorce may be approved by Caesar."

"What are you talking about?" Dalena asked.

"I should have told you, but I wanted it to be a surprise. I sent word to Caesar requesting he dissolve your marriage to Quirinius based on the man's unfaithfulness to you."

"But what of my unfaithfulness to him?"

FAVORED

"That will never be an issue."

Dianthea was slowly feeling her senses return to her. She was unable to join the conversation still.

Dalena just stared into Lucas' face. "You did this without talking to me?"

"I thought you would be pleased."

"I am. I'm just shocked."

Lucas took Dalena's hand. "It is no secret how I feel about you. Remember I promised to take care of and protect you."

"You are good to me. Is it possible Caesar would grant your request?"

"I see no reason why he shouldn't. I will tell you another secret: Caesar is a childhood friend of mine."

"Why, Lucas, you are full of surprises today."

"Dalena." It was the first time Dianthea had attempted to speak since Lucas had choked her. Her voice was scratchy. "Would you like to eat? It is important to keep your strength up through an adequate diet."

"Dianthea, are you feeling up to it?"

"Of course she is," Lucas answered for her. "Aren't you, Dianthea?"

"Yes, I feel fine. I'm not sure what came over me in the hallway."

"Let me know if you need my help," Lucas said, keeping his attention focused on Dalena.

"I can manage." Dianthea excused herself from the room. She walked down the corridor toward the kitchen. It wasn't until she was alone that she allowed herself to break down into sobs.

She worked on preparing a healthy, satisfactory meal for Dalena. The tray contained all of Dalena's favorites. She made sure there was enough for Lucas, who always had an evening

456

meal with Dalena. Dianthea was just about to carry the tray to them when an unusual character appeared on the terrace. At first, Dianthea thought she ought to call for Lucas, but something seemed familiar about the man. She finally was able to place him as the man who ran the brothel where her sister worked.

Quietly, so as to not arouse anyone else in the house, Dianthea walked out onto the terrace and motioned for the man to join her on the beach. The two made their way down the steps until they stood a few feet from the ocean.

"How did you know where to find me?" Dianthea couldn't fathom her sister had given away her location. Lilliana had never wanted her sister to have to deal with the type of men she dealt with.

"I found the information tucked away among your sister's things."

"What were you doing going through her private belongings?" Dianthea did not hide her anger.

"Now, don't get upset with me. I'm just the messenger. I'm here solely as a favor, or, I should say, out of respect for your sister."

"What do you mean?" Fear began to take root in the pit of Dianthea's stomach.

"They found your sister in the stall where she worked. Her throat was cut. I brought what meager belongings she had. Thought you might want them. They burned her body a few hours ago." The man handed her a satchel, which held the last of her sister's possessions.

Dianthea didn't need to ask the man who had done such a horrific deed. She knew who had done it. He'd almost admitted it while he had her pinned to the wall.

She barely croaked out her thanks. The man left as quietly as he had arrived. Dianthea knew Lucas and Dalena would be wondering what was taking so long. She went back to the kitchen

FAVORED

and hid the satchel in an empty barrel. It would be safe there until she could retrieve it.

She picked up the tray and headed into Dalena's room.

When she walked in, Lucas was holding Dalena's hand, and Dalena was smiling. She looked completely content. Lucas looked up and made eye contact with Dianthea. Her expression couldn't hide that she knew what he had done. He saw the truth in her eyes. He gave her a sly smile and a wink. Chills ran through her entire body.

Chapter Forty-One

"Today's the day. You are sure you want to go back home?" Theo questioned Mary before they mounted up.

"Oh yes! I can't wait to see Mother...and Joseph." Mary blushed. Her flushed complexion, radiant smile, and youthful joy announced the excitement growing inside her.

"I can see by the look on your face that you are determined. Not to mention just a little excited."

Mary laughed, "I have never been good at hiding my true feelings."

"I'm glad of it. People always know where they stand with you." Theo lifted Mary onto the stallion.

After the three of them had been riding for a while, Onesimus pulled his gelding up alongside Theo's steed. "Mary, I want to ask you something."

"What is it?"

"It's a rather personal question, but I'd like to know the answer."

"Go ahead, Onesimus. I will try to answer if I can."

"What is Joseph like? Is he handsome?"

Theo chuckled at the lad's curiosity.

"My friends and I used to sit under the trees and discuss the men of our village. If our mothers knew what we talked about..." Mary giggled, happily remembering such conversations.

"Joseph was often mentioned in our conversations."

"He must be very handsome for you all to talk about him. Is

FAVORED

he strong too?"

"He is handsome and strong, but more than anything else, he is a righteous man." Mary remembered the day the boys had turned over Ezra's cart of wares, when she had knelt down in the street to help the old man retrieve his belongings. Joseph had joined her in the act of kindness. That was the first time their eyes had locked. She recalled seeing much loneliness in his eyes. He had seemed older than he was.

"Please, go on! When did the two of you become betrothed?" Onesimus guided the gelding close to Theo's steed.

"Father initiated our betrothal. I don't think Joseph had given much thought to marriage."

"Do you love him?" Onesimus waited patiently for Mary to respond. Theo was also silently waiting for her answer.

"I want to love him. More importantly, I want him to love me. We were beginning to love, I think, before I left. Now I don't know."

Theo heard the uncertainty and longing in Mary's voice. "Mary, I don't know of a man who would not love you. Do not fear."

Theo's admonishment brought back the words the angel had spoken to Mary. She silently thanked God for what would be to some only a small encouragement. To Mary, it was something larger than Theo knew.

The trio met many travelers along the way. Most were walking to Jerusalem from villages lying north of the city. Some, like the three of them, were heading home from Jerusalem. Theo was glad he had assumed the role of a common traveler. People seemed to pay them no more attention than any of the other groups walking along the dusty road.

Sensing Mary was growing weary, Theo said, "I think we all need to stop and rest. Besides, I'm hungry, and the horses could use a drink. If I remember correctly, there is a small stream just

460

over that ridge. We'll find a nice spot to relax and enjoy some nourishment."

Theo squeezed the stallion's sides with his heels, causing the steed to set off at a quick trot. With the mule tied to his horse, Onesimus didn't dare move the gelding at such a quick pace. Eventually he came upon Theo and Mary wading in the stream. Onesimus laughed when Theo slipped, completely soaking himself.

Theo waded out of the water to help Onesimus dismount. Feeling lighthearted, Theo chased the boy around the blanket Mary was lying on. He eventually caught the boy and carried him into the stream, dunking him. Onesimus came up gasping for air while Theo laughed.

Onesimus laughed and playfully splashed Theo.

"Come! Eat and drink your wine. I know this spot. We are very close to Nazareth," Mary laughed. "I think I'll go downstream and try to wash off some of this dust."

Mary could hear bits and pieces of the conversation going on between her friends. She enjoyed hearing Onesimus' laughter. While she waded into the warm water the only thing on her mind was the fact she would be home soon. She was grateful for the opportunity to rinse the dust from her body. The day was warm enough that her tunic, mantle, and hair would be dry before they reached the outskirts of the village.

"Mary, I'd like to speak with you," Theo said from the edge of the stream. His blond hair looked almost white in the afternoon sun.

"Let me dry off first."

"I'll wait for you over there." Theo pointed to a secluded area a short distance from Onesimus.

Mary made her way to the edge of the stream. She squeezed the excess water from her hair and laid her mantle and scarf on the ground to dry. As she got closer to Theo, she could see the seriousness on his face. "Is something wrong?"

"No. I just want to make sure you know what you are doing. Also, so you know where I stand."

Mary's eyes softened with understanding. When Theo looked at Mary, he no longer felt attraction to her. His affection for her was similar to that of a brother for his sister. If someone had asked him three months ago if another woman could capture his heart away from the black-haired, brown-eyed maiden, he would have scoffed at the notion. Now, the only woman he wanted to be with was Katera.

"Theo, you know I have to go back. I need to know what Joseph's decision is. I have peace. Things will work out. They always do. God is my protector."

"Just so you understand, if Joseph has chosen a different course of action, one that would cause you harm, I will step in."

Mary linked her arm through Theo's and proceeded to lead him back to Onesimus. "I understand. But, Theo, I do believe my God has already provided a way for me."

"Where have you two been?" Onesimus stood and brushed the crumbs from his tunic.

"We were just touching base on a few last-minute details." They folded the blanket and put their provisions away.

Onesimus took Mary's hand in his. "I can't believe that in a little while we will be saying goodbye for a second time."

"I'm beginning to learn that there is never a permanent goodbye between friends. Besides, I'm sure you will be welcome to stay as long as you like. Let's enjoy our time together and not think about the goodbye." Mary hugged the boy before mounting the steed for the last time.

Mary's excitement grew the closer they came to Nazareth. She began to hum a tune. Onesimus picked up on the melody and sang along. Eventually, even Theo's voice could be heard in the breeze.

Joseph sat on the hillside overlooking Nazareth. He came to this spot often. Once again, he was imagining that Mary was there beside him. It had been just over three months since he had last seen her. At times, he feared she would never come home. When fear would rise within him, God would softly speak to his heart, reassuring him that all would be well.

He closed his eyes, picturing Mary's hair, eyes, and smile. He tried to imagine the smallness of her hand in his, the way her soft skin might feel against the roughness of his. So real were his thoughts that he thought he heard her voice in the wind. The sound moved closer and closer. Her voice was joined by others, singing a joyful tune.

Joseph opened his eyes and looked at the road below. His breath caught in his throat. For a moment, he couldn't move. He jumped to his feet, running down the hillside toward the three travelers. He began to call her name. "Mary! Mary!"

Out of the corner of his eye, Theo saw movement. He looked up toward the hill. Come at full speed toward them was a man. The man was still too far away for Theo to make out who he was. He reached for his short sword.

Mary's gaze followed Theo's. She covered her mouth. *Could it be? Was it really him?* "Theo, stop. Please."

Theo pulled the reins. Mary eased her way down from the horse and began to run up the hill. Theo watched as the man and woman reached each other. They stopped a few inches apart.

Joseph didn't need to say a word for Mary to know they would be husband and wife. The look in his eyes spoke what was unspoken. Joseph picked her up and twirled her around. He had never seen anything more beautiful in his life.

"I've waited for you. I have much to tell you." Joseph placed her back on the ground. He cupped her face in his hands. "You're more beautiful today than when I first laid eyes on you."

FAVORED

Mary's heart pounded in her chest. "I've missed you."

Theo rode up with Onesimus at his side. "Well, my friend, I see all is well," Theo said as he dismounted.

"I thought I'd never see you again," Joseph replied warmly.

"Joseph, this is Onesimus." Theo helped the boy dismount.

"I've heard much about you, Joseph. I am pleased to meet you." Onesimus bowed to the handsome Hebrew.

"There is no point in standing around here. Come to my home. I'll prepare a meal, and we'll catch up."

"I'd best go see my mother. That is…?" Mary didn't finish. She looked to Joseph for the answer she longed to hear.

Joseph gently pulled her aside. "Mary, your mother is no longer in Nazareth."

"What?"

He ached for her. Joseph knew it wouldn't matter whether he told her now or later; the heartache would be the same. "A while back, your mother married your uncle Eliakim. She has gone to Jerusalem to live with him and help bring up his youngest daughter."

"Mother's not here?" The reality was ludicrous to Mary.

"She's gone."

Feeling her legs weakening beneath her, Mary sank to the ground. Joseph knelt beside her along with Theo. Mary stared straight ahead, not speaking a word.

"Joseph, I think it best we take her to your place. This has all been quite a shock, clearly."

"I don't think I can walk," Mary said, feeling faint.

"I'm here for you, Mary. I'll always be here for you." Joseph lifted Mary into his arms.

"Place her on the gelding. Onesimus can ride with me."

"I will walk alongside her. I can support her better that way."

"Let's be off." Theo gave the stallion a gentle nudge on the reins, and they slowly made their way into town.

Every eye in Nazareth turned and watched with much curiosity as the travelers made their way through the cobbled streets to Joseph's home. Joseph could hear the whispers as they passed by. He wished he could protect Mary from the gossip that would spread like a disease through the town.

"Theo, I'll take Mary inside. We can board your horses in my barn on the outskirts of town."

"Onesimus, stay with Mary," Theo insisted. "Make sure she has some nourishment to help bring back her energy."

Joseph carried Mary inside and laid her on his bed. She had not said a word since he had told her the news about her mother. "There is some fresh bread and cheese, as well as dates and figs on the sideboard," he said to Onesimus. "You'll find water in the pitcher and wine in the wineskin. Help yourself to whatever you'd like. Try to get Mary to eat something."

"I'll take good care of her."

Joseph saw the concern and honesty in the young boy's eyes and immediately trusted him. "She is in good hands, I see. I'll be back with Theo as soon as I can."

Guarding the horses, Theo waited for Joseph to return. He, too, had noticed the stares and whispers as they made their way through town. Even now he overheard several people speculating about the strangers who had brought Anna's daughter home to her betrothed. So far, no one seemed to recognize him as the Roman who, many months ago, stayed with Joachim and Anna.

"The stable is not far from here, but I think we should hurry. Mary will have many questions once she has taken in the news." Joseph took the gelding's reins from Theo, and together they led the horses and mule to the barn. The men proceeded to brush the horses and feed them before preparing to bed them down for the night. "Tell me, friend, how did you and Mary end up traveling together?" Joseph asked.

"I met Mary along the road on her way to Aim Karem. When she needed to return, she sent word. I agreed to see her safely home."

"Did she tell you why she left?"

"No, only that she told you and Anna something you did not believe."

"If she told you what she told me, you would have had trouble believing her too!"

"I don't believe Mary is the type of girl to lie. The question is: do you believe her now?"

"Yes. I admit I didn't at first, but now I do. I intend to take Mary as my wife. I feel blessed to be her husband." Joseph's face shone with all the love he felt in his heart.

"What changed your mind?"

"I think that story is best kept for another time. I'm anxious to check on Mary."

When the men arrived back at Joseph's home, they found the table arranged with mouth-watering food. Onesimus, encouraging Mary to eat and drink, was sitting beside her on the bed. Both men were thankful to see the rosy color had returned to Mary's cheeks. The moment Mary saw Joseph, she jumped from the bed and ran to his side.

"Joseph, I must know about Mother. Tell me everything."

"I'm not sure you're strong enough." Joseph looked to Theo for support.

"I think Joseph is right, Mary. Maybe after we eat and rest... the morning would be a better time to discuss..."

"No. I understand why you men feel the need to protect me, but I don't want to be protected. I came here to learn of Joseph's decision concerning our marriage and to see my mother. Joseph, please tell me about my mother."

Joseph looked into the deep brown eyes of his beloved. In that moment he knew he could never refuse anything she asked of him.

"Mary, you should sit." Mary sat down in the chair closest to where she had been standing. "Your mother took your leave very hard. She wanted to believe you. After she heard my story and before she wed, I believe she came to believe what you told her."

"Heard your story?' Mary's eyes were filled with sadness and confusion.

"I'll explain later. After you left, your mother lost her youthful vigor. Rachel and I were very concerned for her. I visited your mother on a regular basis. It was during one of these visits that I met your uncle, Eliakim. He came to take your mother as his wife. I think the thought of being alone, in combination with helping raise Eliakim's daughter, was more than Anna could refuse."

"But Eliakim? Father had not seen his older brother in years. Mother knew the feelings Father had toward his brother. I don't understand."

"Your mother felt very guilty for turning you away. She knew I had decided to take you as my wife. I guess she figured you would be well taken care of. There was nothing left for her here."

"Do you think I will ever see her again?"

The pain in Mary's eyes was more than Joseph could bear. He stood and walked toward the door. "I don't know. Eliakim made it pretty clear that he didn't want to see either one of us at his front door."

"She married him, knowing this?"

Theo and Onesimus felt Mary's pain. There was nothing they could do to console her.

"Yes." Joseph turned to Mary and knelt down in front of her.

FAVORED

"Mary, I may not be the man you want, but I promise to do my best by you. I made a vow to your father, which I intend to keep."

Mary gently touched Joseph's cheek. "I believe you are the man God has chosen for me; therefore, you are the man I want."

The moment was so tender between the two that the others felt like intruders. "Joseph, Onesimus and I need to stretch our legs. A walk will do us good. Come, boy." Onesimus did as Theo commanded.

Waiting to share all that had happened with Mary, Joseph was grateful for their leave. He began to pace the room as he proceeded to tell his betrothed about his dream. "Mary, know that I could never have publicly humiliated you or have had you put to death. I had decided to have you put away quietly. My soul wrestled within me. I can't put words to the feelings I had. Just know I could not find peace. One night, during a fitful sleep, I dreamed an angel came to me. The angel assured me that all you had said was true."

"This is wondrous news! We both have been visited by an angel of God. My soul can barely contain the joy I feel." Mary reached her hand out to Joseph, who gladly took it in his.

Pulling Mary to her feet, Joseph held both her hands in his. "When you walked out of my shop, I...I was so angry, and..." He couldn't say it.

"I know—me too."

"You?"

"Scared to death," she laughed quietly.

"I don't know how we're going to do this. Mary, always remember and know I knew in my heart I wanted you for my wife."

"Joseph." Mary wrapped her arms around her betrothed's neck. Joseph knew he had never heard his name spoken so sweetly. He breathed in the scent of her hair. This was not a dream. This was not a memory he was trying to recall as he sat on a hilltop. Mary, all flesh and blood, was in his arms.

"Mary."

Epilogue

Taking in the fresh night air, Joseph stood at the entrance of the stable. He was thankful for the shelter. It had been a hard journey from Nazareth to Bethlehem. Mary's labor had started the day before. He yawned, and his shoulders sagged under the weight of exhaustion. Looking over at Mary resting with the infant in her arms, Joseph realized rest would not come so easily for him.

Thanks to Caesar Augustus declaring a census throughout the region of Roman occupation, throngs of sojourners made their way to their tribes' places of origin. He chided himself for not better preparing for the arduous journey. Even while walking among the crowds, it never dawned on him there would not be a single room available for them to rest.

At different times along the way he had scolded Mary for bringing so much. She would smile and nod, which seemed to frustrate him more. The small donkey was so burdened with bundles of swaddling clothes, blankets, water, food, and an assortment of items Joseph deemed useless that the beast stumbled numerous times under the weight. This made the journey harder and longer. What should have taken four days to reach their destination took them eight. He had wanted to reach Bethlehem before the Sabbath, but that did not happen.

Then Mary went into labor. She didn't mention it to him when it had started, but she began stopping at different intervals to rest.

He glanced over at Mary and the babe sleeping peacefully. Instinctively, he felt like he should be on guard as the sounds of the night echoed around him. He was no longer responsible for just one soul; he now had two other lives to protect and provide for.

He remembered the more Mary had stopped to rest, the more

FAVORED

impatient he became. "Mary, we must keep moving if we are to reach Bethlehem in the allotted time," he had said, unable to keep the anger out of his tone.

He knew her to be spirited, but when she snapped back, "I'm doing the best I can," it stopped him in his tracks. He turned to look at her and saw she was now several feet behind him.

Something was wrong.

Donkey in tow, he walked back to her. With all the kindness he could muster, he asked, "Mary, what is the matter?"

She smiled up at him before grabbing her abdomen and doubling over. She inhaled and exhaled slowly. No words were needed. He knew his wife had gone into labor, and they were still at least a day away from Bethlehem. Because it was taking them double the time to reach Bethlehem, they were alone on the road. There was no midwife to help Mary. No one anywhere as far as the eye could see.

Joseph's face went white. For a moment he thought he might faint.

Mary took hold of him. "Are you all right? You're not going to faint on me, are you?" she giggled. "Oh, Joseph. Don't look so shocked. We knew my time was nye. Maybe not so soon but nye."

He nodded at her and looked down at the donkey. What could they reasonably get rid of to lessen the beast's load? The sun was high and hot overhead. Water was a must. Joseph began to unload the food.

"What are you doing?" Mary asked. "We need food."

"We can buy food in Bethlehem. You're going to have to ride ol' Ezra," Joseph replied, giving the donkey an affectionate pat. Mary started to shake her head at him. "No arguments, Mary. We've got to make haste to Bethlehem. Perhaps we can find a midwife. Ezra can't carry you and all the things we packed. I understand you need the items you brought for the infant. We have to have water. You and I will bring enough food for today. We must reach Bethlehem by morning at the latest."

Mary nodded. It was Joseph's turn to smile. He lifted her up onto Ezra's back, grabbed the reins, and again began briskly walking toward their destination.

Joseph sat down on the ground. He couldn't sleep. He wouldn't sleep. Right now, he needed to think. He heard the roar of a lion in the distance and felt justified in standing guard. Ezra snuck up behind him and nuzzled his neck. "Ah, my friend." Joseph patted the donkey's neck. "You heard the roar, huh? A little scared, are you? No need. I'll look after all of us. I must thank you for all your help. You did well. Very well." Ezra leaned his head on Joseph's shoulder.

He had wanted to stay in the guest house of a distant relative, but they had arrived too late. Jerabum had rented it out. He said his family needed the money. He chuckled as he thought about the panic that rose up in him as they went from inn to inn seeking shelter, needing a safe place for Mary to give birth. His hope of finding shelter was dashed by the crowds of people, entire families, camped out on the narrow streets of Bethlehem. Joseph had to be careful that the donkey, carrying Mary, didn't step on or crush anyone.

Doors slammed in their faces. Both of them were irritated but for different reasons. As he went to knock on the last door, he felt like a true failure. He had not only failed Mary, but he had failed the Son of God. He lifted his hand to knock and prayed silently, *Oh, God, please let there be room.*

There was no response. Joseph considered himself a patient man, but his patience must have gotten lost somewhere between Nazareth and Bethlehem. He went to knock one last time, but before he could, the door slowly opened.

Before he could say a word, the old stranger began vehemently shaking his head. He had started to close the door, but Joseph shoved his foot into the jam and pointed to his doubled-over wife.

FAVORED

"Please," he pleaded, "she's been in labor for almost a day now. I've been everywhere.

"Please."

The man apologetically explained that their guest room was just a place on the bottom floor of their home that housed their most precious commodity: their livestock. It, too, was already occupied.

Just then, a frail voice spoke from behind the old innkeeper. "Aaron, the stable outside of town. It would give them privacy and shelter."

Aaron started to respond, but Joseph said, "Thank you. We will take it."

He waited for Aaron to grab his cloak and lantern. Aaron's wife handed Joseph a small, wrapped bundle. "She'll need food when it's all over," she said as he took the bundle from her.

"Is there a midwife available?" Joseph asked.

"No, it appears to be all strangers in Bethlehem tonight," the old woman responded.

"Come," Aaron said, closing the door behind him. "It is a little bit of a walk, but it's not too far. We rent it out to travelers in need of boarding their livestock."

Aaron whistled an unfamiliar tune as they made their way to the outskirts of Bethlehem. The narrow path was steep as they headed up the hill.

Joseph heard Mary groan several times, but he stopped himself from turning to look at her. Aaron walked quickly, and Joseph did not want to stumble or cause the donkey to misstep and lose his precious load.

The stable was dark but dry. Aaron hung the lantern on a peg and walked deeper into the cave, leaving Joseph and Mary alone. It took Joseph's eyes a minute to adjust, and he was trying to take in the sounds and smells of the stable. Joseph knew Aaron hadn't

474

gone far, for he could still hear him whistling the same tune. It wasn't long before a fire blazed and Joseph could fully take in his surroundings.

Aaron turned to Joseph. "There's more wood for the fire in the back corner. Clean water in the trough to the far right. Some buckets over there." He pointed in the direction of another room. "Clean straw for a bed. A manger there."

Mary slid off the donkey and whispered "thank you" before doubling over. Joseph rushed over to her side with Aaron. He knew Mary's contractions were happening in closer succession.

How long will this take? Joseph wondered anxiously. He hated to see Mary in so much pain.

As if he had read his thoughts, Aaron said, "Babies are born every day. Today is no different than any other day. Your first?"

"Yes," Joseph replied. Amazed at how rough and coarse his voice sounded.

Aaron helped Joseph get Mary settled. He gave the other man a reassuring nod and turned to leave. "I'll check on you all in the morning."

As Aaron left, he spoke to each of his livestock, patting each of them affectionately on the rump. Joseph could still hear that same unfamiliar tune reverberating through the cave as Aaron headed back down the hill, whistling.

"Joseph," Mary said weakly, "water, please."

He hurried to her side and brought the ladle of water to her lips. He had never delivered a baby before. He had aided his livestock in delivery, but animals instinctively knew what to do. He wasn't sure women did. *If they know, why are midwives needed?* It was not a groan but a scream that made Joseph's blood run cold.

"Help me, Joseph. It is time to push. Here, help me get my tunic off." Joseph couldn't breathe. Mary was doing the breathing for both of them.

FAVORED

"Here, get behind me and hold me up," she continued instructing. "I'll lean forward when a contraction comes, and I'll push. When it's over, I will lean back against you. Place a knife on the fire now so you can cut the cord when your son is born."

The words "your son" stunned Joseph. *Not my son,* he thought, *God's Son.*

Before he knew what had happened, Joseph cut the cord and handed the infant to Mary. She swaddled and nursed her son. Normally when a baby was born, it was the father's responsibility to name the child. But Mary named the infant. "His name is Jesus," she told Joseph. "The angel told me to name Him Jesus." Joseph only nodded as his wife closed her eyes to rest.

The baby's cry brought Joseph back to the present. He went to Mary's side and found her in a deep sleep. He picked up the babe. "Hush, hush, baby Jesus," Joseph cooed. "Your mother needs to rest." He lifted the baby to his shoulders and began to rock Him back and forth. He patted the baby's back, thinking, *I have seen my friends do this with their children many times.* He was rewarded with a belch. He laughed—even the Messiah needed to burp. Joseph cradled the boy and looked into his wide, brown eyes. *The Messiah.* His heart, bursting with love, wanted to jump from his chest.

He looked at his sleeping wife, knowing his love for her had grown and deepened. Together, they had weathered the gossip in Nazareth, choosing to ignore the rumors that circled like swirling dust around them. They worked side by side to make what was Joseph's house into a family home. He had come to respect Mary's quiet but firm way of doing things. He had not trusted another since Hannah, but now he felt secure in trusting Mary. After watching her give birth to the baby, he only respected and loved her more. He knew, deep in his heart, he would never love anyone like he loved Mary.

Mary had woken up and pulled herself to an upright position. She spoke, surprising Joseph. "He's hungry. I'm sure." She reached for their son. Joseph knelt down beside her and handed the babe to her.

Jesus began to whimper and nuzzle his mother's chest. Mary laughed and said, "Look at Him, Joseph. He is a ferocious eater. He'll grow up to be big and strong like His papa."

Joseph stood. "Are you hungry?"

Mary shook her head. "No, but I know you are. It was your stomach growling that woke me up."

He winced. "It did?"

Mary laughed, "No, but you're bound to be hungry after helping me deliver our son."

Joseph snatched some bread and cheese Aaron's wife had graciously given them. He walked back to the cave's opening. There it was again, the one thought that kept circling to the forefront of his mind. *Is He really my son?* In the distance, a wolf howled, causing the cows to bray. Even old Ezra seemed to bray a loud "hee-haw" in response. The thought, *Is He really my son?* trumpeted in his head.

"Joseph."

"Yes?"

"Will you lay Jesus in the manger, please?"

Joseph nodded and took the sleepy babe from his wife.

"He's sleepy, and so am I." Mary settled back down to rest, and Joseph stood over her, holding the babe.

He looked down into Jesus' eyes. *Could You really be my son?* He rocked the boy in his arms until His eyes closed. "That's it, little Jesus—dream all your cares away."

As he watched Jesus sleep, Joseph began to pray, "Lord, I do believe I'm holding the Messiah. If He's Your Son, how can He be mine?" A tear silently ran down Joseph's cheek. He had never thought about being a father. Now, with Jesus cradled in his arms, he longed for nothing more than to be a good, kind, and loving

FAVORED

father. He continued to pray, "If just for tonight, Lord, let me be His papa."

There was no visit from an angel, and there was no light that blinded his eyes. There was, however, a small voice that spoke to Joseph's spirit, "I chose you, Joseph, to be Jesus' earthly father. You will teach, train, and love Him as your own. You will be the one to teach Him the ways of your people. You will teach Him to walk, run, fish, and hunt. You will teach Him carpentry so He will know a skill. You will tend to Him when He is sick and mend His wounds when He is hurt. You will hurt when He hurts. Your heart will break when His heart breaks. But you will also laugh when He laughs, and you will celebrate His accomplishments. In every earthly way, Jesus will be your son."

Joseph's thoughts of uncertainty stopped nagging at him. He had been a lonely man until God gave him Mary and now Jesus. He laid Jesus in the manger. "Rest now, my son. There's no telling what tomorrow may bring."

He laid down beside Mary and wrapped a protective arm around his wife. He yawned and gave thanks to God, quietly saying, "Thank You, God, for this indescribable gift."

Glossary of Terms

Atrium: The central courtyard of a Roman dwelling.

Betrothal: A mutual promise to marry—an engagement.

Bier: A stand on which a corpse or a coffin containing a corpse is placed prior to burial.

Bow: Front of a ship.

Brassard: Armor piece that covers the upper arm.

Centurion: Equivalent of sergeant major in the Roman Army. A centurion had to be not only an excellent soldier but needed to be able to read and write. A centurion could have held a political or diplomatic role.

Cingulum: Leather belts made for members of the Roman Army that served as badges of office. The apron protected the soldiers' groin in battle.

Coiffure: A formal hairstyle. Roman women would adorn their hair with flowers of jewelry. Some would color their hair, or it was popular to cut the blonde strands of German slaves for wigs. They even had curling irons, nonelectric (of course), that could provide waves for those women who desired more curl.

Denari (Denarius): A Roman unit of money equivalent to one day's pay for a laborer.

Frigidarium: The room in the baths where the water was cold. Roman baths consisted of the *tepidaria*, or warm bath, and the *caldarium*, or steam bath. Aqueducts fed thousands of gallons of water into the system. Water was heated by a network of wood-burning furnaces connected to a network of steam pipes

FAVORED

beneath the floors. Public bathing was another form of entertainment for the Romans.

Holy Spirit: Considered to be the third member of the Trinity (God the Father, Jesus the Son, Holy Spirit). The Holy Spirit is the power (see Genesis 1:2 and Acts 10:38).

Hypocrite: An actor.

Impluvium: The pool in the atrium that would hold the rainwater before it drained into the cistern.

Jupiter: Roman god of light, sky/weather, and the state. He was the supreme god of Rome.

Lares and Penates: Bronze statuettes found in homes throughout the Roman world. At mealtime, small amounts of food were burned in a container as offerings to the departed.

Legion: Originally a legion was a levy of all eligible Roman citizens between the ages of seventeen and forty-six arranged in centuries (100 men). By 105 BC the legion went through a radical change. The chief tactical unit became the cohort—ten of which made up a legion. Each cohort had 480 men divided into six centuries of 80 men led by a centurion. Later they doubled the first cohort's strength, raising a legion's total strength to 5,280 men.

Litter: A stretcher or conveyance typically consisting of an enclosed couch mounted on shafts and carried.

Ludi: Refers to the Roman games.

Magna Mater (Cybele): The goddess of nature, the earth mother. People believed she could heal diseases, give oracles, and protect her people in war. Women favored her. The annual rites for her began on March 15 with a procession and sacrifice for the crops.

Maneh: A Hebrew weight for gold or silver being one hundred shekels of gold or sixty shekels of silver.

Mars: Roman god of war.

Palos: A four-cornered shawl draped over the left shoulder and either under or over the right.

Peristyle: A secondary section of the Roman dwelling that enclosed a courtyard. Located in the peristyle were bedrooms, dining room, kitchen, and library.

Proconsul: Governor or military commander of a Roman province.

Quadrantes (plural): A bronze Roman coin. It took four of them to equal a copper coin, sixteen to equal sesterces, and sixty-four to equal a denarius.

Sesterce: A Roman coin worth one-fourth of a denarius.

Shekels: The chief silver coin of the Hebrews equal to about a half ounce.

Sicarii: Zealots who would attack travelers on the roads in Judea.

Statio: A place where the soldiers who patrolled the roads were stationed.

Stern: Back of a ship.

Stola: A long dress with half sleeves usually worn belted.

Tablinum: Where Romans stored their scrolls. There was usually a desk and a chest for valuable documents and wealth.

Tallis: A shawl worn by Jewish men during morning and evening prayers. The shawl was made of wool or silk, rectangular

FAVORED

in shape, with fringes at the corners.

Taurobolium: The practice of sacrificing a bull by which the bull's blood is spilled over the priest or person standing in a pit below the bull. It was a substitution sacrifice so that one could identify ritualistically with the victim.

Triclinium: The dining room of a Roman dwelling. This room was often elaborately decorated with columns and statues.

Discussion Guide

ANNA

- Does Anna worry too much about what others will think of her family? Is her worry warranted? Why or why not?

- Does worry keep her from believing God's promises? Does worry keep you from believing God's promises?

- Anna blames her lack of faith on all of the losses she has faced in her life. Is her lack of faith really a byproduct of these losses, or is it ultimately her choice to not be faithful?

- Have you ever suffered a loss so great that you questioned your faith/God? Has a bitterness taken root in you, beloved, as it has in Anna?

FAVORED

JOACHIM

- How is Joachim's faith different from Anna's?

- Is his faith similar to Miriam's? If so, how?

- Do you think Joachim actually hears the voice of God? Or is he just hearing his own thoughts believing it to be God's voice?

- Does God speak to us today? Does God only Scripture to speak to us, or can we hear His still, small voice?

- When was the last time God spoke to you?

MARY

- What made Mary favored by God?

- Do you think God would have favored Mary if her faith was like Anna's? Why or why not?

- Jewish girls grew up knowing the promise of the Messiah. Do you think Jewish girls wanted to be favored by God? If yes, how so?

- Do you think Mary felt favored after her mother and Joseph's reactions?

- Do you put more importance on the thoughts of how others view you or on how God views you?

FAVORED

JOSEPH

- Did Mary trust her earthly father or her heavenly Father more when it came to who she was told her husband would be?

- Did Joseph allow his past love to grow bitterness in him? If so, how did this hinder or benefit his future and his faith?

- Did God soften Joseph's heart so he would hear what Joachim was asking of him, or did Joachim manipulate the other man's emotions? What is the difference between manipulation and the working of God in one's life?

- Did Joseph's initial response to Mary come from past hurt? How has hurt interfered in your past and present? How might it affect your future?

- Put your thinking caps on for this one—does God's omniscience overpower or supersede our free will?

- Could Joachim, Mary, or Joseph have refused God's will?

- If you answered yes, would saying no to God have stopped His plan of redemption for us all?

DALENA

- How is Dalena being favored by the gods different from how God favored Mary?

- How does being rejected by her biological father affect Dalena's other relationships, particularly with men?

- How does she try to protect herself from further rejection?

- Let's face it—we've all been rejected at some point. Who has rejected you? How did you handle this rejection? Did you look to God to ease your sorrows, or did you turn to others?

- God loves and accepts you, beloved, just as you are. Look to Him to fill the holes in your heart.

- Was there any other solution to Dalena's "problem"? Sisters, if you have solved a "problem" in this way, God loves and accepts you, as do I.

- Do we tend to solve a wrong choice with another wrong choice rather than turning to our heavenly Father?

FAVORED

- Have you done this? If you have, why do you think you tried to solve the issue on your own without turning to faith or at least seeking some sort of counsel?

THEO

- When Theo sleeps with Dalena, is it for self-gratification, or was he trying to find some sort of greater comfort in the act?

- How does staying with Mary's family change his attitude toward the Israelites?

- What are his feelings toward Mary? Is it merely friendship or something more?

- How does Theo cope with the rejection from the other Nazarenes? Does he stay to prove them wrong, or does he run?

- What is your response to rejection? Do you stay and try to make the others see your side, or do you run? Does either solution help ease the feeling of rejection?

- When Theo first sees Katera, his thoughts are initially to use her for self-gratification. Is this harmful? What causes him to change how he views Katera?

- Can Theo and Katera's relationship evolve as long as their dynamic is master and slave? Why or why not?

FAVORED

- Do you think God has a plan for Theo? Does God only have plans for His already faithful children?

KATERA

- Katera has only known a life of enslavement. How does this affect the choices she makes? Does she even have free will?

- Why doesn't she jump at the chance to escape with Archillius? Has she accepted her enslavement?

- Does Katera love Archillius? Does he love her?

- Does dining with Theo plant seeds of hope in Katera?

- What are the differences Katera sees with Theo that she has yet to see with her previous masters?

- Can Katera have a relationship with Theo beyond master and slave?

- Have you felt like you have been enslaved to negativity? Have you felt like you had no free will?

  - God can set you free. He always keeps His promises. Have hope in God, beloved!

About the Author

Teri Lyn Tobey is a writer, wife, mother, and dog lover from Indiana. Indiana has been her home since 1971. She was born to a Baptist pastor and stay-at-home mom, who, out of necessity, became a businesswoman and philanthropist. She credits her daddy with teaching her to know what she believes and why and her mother with the chutzpah to say it out loud.

She graduated from Taylor University, where she majored in psychology and met her husband, to whom she has been married for thirty-three years. They have two adult children, a beautiful daughter-in-law, three poodles, and one goldendoodle who brings her joy and plenty of "oh my" moments. While Teri has explored varied occupations and entrepreneurial adventures, running their household and keeping everyone "in line" has been her full-time job since 1991.

Teri has always gravitated toward work that involved storytelling. She has worked in the theater as an actress, artistic director, and educator. She deeply values the community that develops through shared, embodied storytelling and has cherished the opportunities she has had to work in local community theaters and schools. While these opportunities have created the necessity for writing short stories, narrations, monologues, and scripts, the call to write full time came in 2006. Like a nudge she couldn't ignore, Teri began to put down on paper the story you hold in your hands today. Her father became her editor in chief, encouraging her, challenging her, and spurring her on.

In July of 2012, when her father died, she laid her writing aside. "For ten years I put myself in the grave with my dad. God used the time to heal broken places and take me to a deeper level of surrender and understanding of Christ as my life." It has taken all these years to allow the healing of the Spirit and the love, grace, and patience of her family to make the completion of this

FAVORED

book possible, and she is forever grateful.

Learn more about Teri Lyn and future writings at terilyntobey.com.

Coming in 2025:
Fragile

Fragile takes you a step further into the lives of the characters you have come to love in *Favored*. Read how Joseph, Mary, Lucas, Dalena, Theo, and Katera come face to face in Jerusalem.

The love will grow between Mary and Joseph when the wise men warn them of Herod and their rigorous travel to Egypt. Can the two learn how to parent the Messiah as He grows into adulthood?

Will Dalena's future unravel with the discovery of Quirinius' plans for her? Will her affection for Lucas grow or be undermined and her trust shattered as she learns more about him? Can Dianthea continue to walk the tightrope between the two?

Does Theo learn that love is sacrificial? Katera is Theo's slave but desires to become more to him. Will she feel secure in his love while he still owns her and can demand anything from her?

Fragile speaks to those who have been broken by circumstances, some of our own making and others forced upon us. Hurt and betrayal can leave cracks, and gaping wounds, when left open to fester, can produce bitterness, which leaves us feeling rejected and alone. Read how God gently speaks to His beloved, guiding and healing the broken places in each of them. Each must come to a place of believing the impossible.

Printed in the USA
CPSIA information can be obtained
at www.ICGtesting.com
CBHW031935021224
18324CB00002B/2

9 798893 338157